Secret Baby

Secret Baby

Shelley V. Ashley

PIATKUS

First published in Great Britain in 1990 by
Judy Piatkus (Publishers) Ltd of
5 Windmill Street, London W1

British Library Cataloguing in Publication Data

Ashley, Shelley V.
  Secret Baby
  I. Title
  813′.54[F]

  ISBN 0−86188−940−1

Phototypeset in 11/12pt Compugraphic Times by
Action Typesetting Limited, Gloucester
Printed and bound in Great Britain by
Billing & Sons Ltd, Worcester

For Howard, who could not wait

Where did you come from, baby dear?
Out of the everywhere into here.

George MacDonald

In heaven, an angel is nobody in particular.

George Bernard Shaw

Chapter One

'Anybody out there?' asked E. Z. Jeffrey Sandlin. His voice cut through the intercom like saw grass through a summer breeze.

'Yes, sir. I was just goin' to buzz you. There's a Miss Cecil Gutman out here waitin' to see you.'

She pronounced Cecil as in B. De Mille. A man's name.

'Send her down. And tell Denise to bring her in the minute she gets here. She's a quarter of an hour late as it is.'

Sandlin slammed down the phone in irritation and started to dissect Miss Cecil Gutman sight unseen. He had the time. The corridors at McNaught, Muncheon, Sandlin and Doss were very, very long.

One: Miss. Never been married. Vulnerable and likely to do an about-face. Much too risky. Two: Cecil. Mannish. Probably as butch as hell and full of feminist prattle. No way. Three: Gutman. Sounds ethnic. Jewish maybe. They'll never go for that. Three strikes and you're out, Miss Cecil Gutman. Too bad, because you won't find many positions going at the salary we were offering.

He picked up his extra-thin gold Dupont pen and drew one angry line across her name. She was − or had been until that very instant − Candidate Number Seventeen. Sandlin felt a new surge of irritation at the thought of having to spend even a brief moment with this young woman. He shook his head in exasperation. He had been doing that periodically and uncontrollably all morning long.

Even if our client were as rich as all the Hunt Brothers put together, I wouldn't want to be involved in this. It's not really . . . not really . . . For an instant, Jeff Sandlin was at a loss for words and felt a tinge of astonishment to find himself in such an unwonted situation. Then, with a smile of triumph, he found the exact term he was looking for . . . *healthy*!

Denise O'Neil, his young and decidedly unmannish secretary, knocked once, opened the door and stood aside to let the young

1

woman she was accompanying precede her into the room. From the almost imperceptible nod of her boss's head, she understood she was to ring him in exactly twelve minutes and break off this interview by reason of a prearranged crisis.

Denise made introductions, gave the room one of her thousand - watt smiles and said, 'Y'all ring now if you need anything.' Then she bounced out in a swish of blue and white silk and long, beautifully shaped Texan legs.

Sandlin forced himself to focus his not inconsiderable powers of observation on Cecil Gutman as she made the long journey across his thick green carpet to the monolithic slab of white marble that passed for his desk. She was very tall and very thin, the kind of young woman who, if she had been a little less awkward or a little more aware of her potential, might have clawed her way up to a career in modelling for department stores. Or catalogues. She wore a cheap-looking, flowered pink skirt, a summer sweater of thin cotton and flat, thonged sandals. Her hair was pulled carelessly back and held by an elastic band; her posture was terrible. In Sandlin's orderly mind, all these things were further points in her disfavour. She had not dressed up for the interview: therefore, she was not motivated. She looked hippieish: she was not controllable. She reminded him of someone he had seen on cable TV, an English actress — Vanessa something or other. More than a hippie — a revolutionary. Associated with Middle Eastern terrorists, that sort of person.

There was very little chance that Sandlin would change his opinion of her. In no law office in Dallas was the axiom 'time is money' more readily cited and more rigorously applied than at McNaught, Muncheon, Sandlin and Doss. Moreover, whenever the penultimate founding partner's son made a snap decision, he always stood by it. Repudiating a judgement or a plan of action was an admission of time misspent and potential gain swept away forever.

None the less, Sandlin let an idle question slip through his structured, computer-efficient brain: why had she come at all? She was a shy, down-trodden creature. Perhaps she was only looking for easy money, like so many of the others he had interviewed. Raised in west Texas, Arkansas, Louisiana, or one of the wrong neighbour-hoods in Fort Worth or Dallas, they had no potential, no future anywhere.

'Please be seated, Miss Gutman,' he said in his most gracious Southern voice. 'I'm honoured to meet you. We have all the time in the world, so please make yourself comfortable.'

Exactly eleven and one-half minutes, he calculated after a swift glance at his desk clock, a little masterpiece of Peretti jade and gold.

From his manner, the girl could never have guessed that she had already been eliminated, any more than witnesses in the courtroom could anticipate that the amiable, silver-tongued lawyer in front of them was about to spring for their jugular.

Miss Gutman slipped down into the leather easy chair facing him and at last raised her head. For the first time he saw her face, perfectly lit by the sun blazing through the one window he kept without blinds precisely so he could spotlight whoever — friend or foe — was in that particular chair. The light on a twenty-first floor unobscured by any buildings of comparable height was perfect for the kind of inquisition that Sandlin liked to conduct. Even so, he broke one of his own cardinal rules and leaned forwards to take a closer look at her, an expression of total surprise on his own handsome face.

How could he have judged her plain and colourless? Was it the way she had slouched in, keeping to the shadows as though she were afraid to be seen? Or to see? Just a minute ago, the girl's hair had seemed drab, a mousy kind of brown. Now he saw it as rich as Byzantine tapestry, a shining auburn streaked throughout with threads of pale gold. And her eyes — they were, to him at least, more unbelievable than the hair. They were large and luminous, of a deep violet colour, set under thin arches of auburn eyebrows and framed by darker lashes. Altogether, she was — or had been before some deep sorrow or bitter disappointment had settled upon her and obscured her features — a strikingly beautiful young woman. Those incredible eyes seemed abnormally big in her thin, pale face, and her mouth had long ago forgotten how to smile. The bruised shadows under the eyes, her hands lying listlessly across the flowers of her cheap skirt, everything about her pointed to recent suffering.

God, he thought, *don't let it be physical. I don't care if she's crazy as a loon, just don't let her have a disease.*

'Miss Gutman, would you care to tell me a little about yourself?'

'What do you need to know?' Her voice was harsh but not uneducated. It betrayed annoyance, possibly even hostility.

'Whatever you want to tell me by way of introduction,' Sandlin said placatingly.

It all came out in a rush and just as harshly: 'I'm twenty-three years old and in perfect health. I am most anxious to take this assignment. It does not frighten me in any way. I have no ties — personal or otherwise — which would prevent me from carrying out my duties. Is that satisfactory?'

'Quite succinct,' Sandlin commented dryly, He did not want to antagonise the girl further, even though he was worried about her background. *What the hell difference does it make anyway? But the clients clearly specified* ...

'I wonder if you'd be kind enough to touch on a few personal matters, Miss ... uh, may I call you Cecil?'

He pronounced it Cecile, and she pounced on that right away.

'Call me whatever you damn please, but it's not Cecile, it's Cecil. As for my personal life, I do not want to go into it. I *will* not, in fact.'

'I appreciate your sensitivity and reserve, Miss Gutman. Cecil. They are both qualities that will raise you in the esteem of my clients. But I also feel obliged to inform you that I have spent the better part of the week interviewing candidates for this ... uh ... post. It is more difficult to fill than you might imagine, due to certain specifications set forth by the principals. I am obliged to obtain information which you might not − at first consideration − wish to give but the usefulness of which will become evident as we progress in our relationship.'

'I don't try to follow double-talk,' Cecil said. A slight curve of her upper lip showed exactly what she thought of his speech. 'I've already told you the three points about myself that are relevant to this interview − age, health, willingness. There's a fourth that, if I were you, I'd want to be reassured about right away. You don't seem to be asking, but I'll tell you anyway. I am morally trustworthy. If I set out to accomplish a task, I see it through to the end, no matter what obstacles I encounter. Once I've given my word, I keep my promises. I'm a Swede and very stubborn.'

She said all this with spirit and with a resounding ring of truth, but Sandlin heard only one word that truly interested him, and he jumped on it at once.

'Swedish. I though Gutman was more − Middle European? German, perhaps?'

'I really wouldn't know. The Gutmans have been in America for over a hundred years, and they've all been Swedes.'

'And your religious beliefs ...?'

She looked at him stonily, and he came right out with it.

'Are you Jewish, Miss Gutman?' He asked the question very softly, a kingly rabbi commiserating with his flock.

'Lutheran is what I remember as a child.'

The curve of her lips was more perceptible now. The self-effacing young woman had totally disappeared, and Sandlin felt the kind of shock that came in the courtroom when a sweet-looking young female suddenly turned on him with the viciousness of a teased rattler. He neither liked it nor understood it. Now he felt himself squirm in his well-padded executive chair.

4

'What motives prompted you to consider . . .?'

'The ad mentioned France. I need to get out of the country . . .' She stopped, appearing momentarily confused as to where this line was taking her. 'I don't mean to sound like a Mafia boss without a reliable mattress. What I'm trying to convey is that I need a change of air and scenery . . . the sooner the better.'

'My dear young lady, I'm afraid there's some mistake. Perhaps you didn't read the advertisement correctly.'

She had regained her composure, and she snapped back at him.

'I read very well, Mr Sandlin. I have a master's degree in communications. Perhaps the ad was written ambiguously to attract a greater number of applicants? Or written so as to be deliberately misleading?'

Sandlin ignored her jab.

'The legal situation in France is extremely ambiguous, to say the least. That is the precise reason why my clients are prospecting in the United States, and why they would wish you to stay here to carry out your . . . duties.'

He was startled at the rapidity with which the until now languorous young woman leapt from the comfortable depths of his leather visitor's chair. Towering over him, very straight now, she wore a curious expression that might have been relief had everything else about her not implied anger.

'That was *my* condition, Mr Sandlin. If there is no trip involved, then I won't waste your time.'

He stood up in turn, moved hurriedly around the wide piece of marble that was his desk and took hold of one of her extremely thin arms. There was no way he was going to let this woman walk out on him.

'Please, Miss Gutman, we want you to be content. I was speaking of the *preliminary* arrangements, which will take a minimum of three months. You understand surely that there is no way to calculate these things in advance. However, I believe I can intercede with my clients so that afterwards we could put you on a plane to France. If that's where you'd be happiest.' She was still trying to pull away from him, and he added hastily, 'First class. Concorde if you like.'

'How long would I be able to stay?'

'Under these circumstances, you might be obliged to remain in France until the affair was concluded. I am not in a position to make that decision myself, but − let's say you wanted to take a little trip around the French countryside for a month or so, once everything was settled. It's very possible my clients would . . .'

'Yes. That's exactly what I do want.'

'Fine. That's perfectly clear then, and I appreciate your forthrightness. Please rest assured that your wellbeing will take precedence over every other consideration if you are selected for this position. But you must answer my questions. We need some basis on which to make our final decision.'

Finally she relaxed beneath his grip. When he let her go, she sank back down into the big leather chair like a puppet whose strings had suddenly snapped.

'Now, let's get down to the facts,' Sandlin said, firmly taking charge. 'From what university did you graduate?'

She hesitated for an instant more. Then, as though preparing herself for the ordeal of disclosing even a minimal amount of information, she leaned back and took a pack of cigarettes from her linen shoulder bag.

'The University of Illinois. I received both my degrees there, a year apart. The second one in May of last year.'

'A master's in one year? Quite remarkable. And your family?'

'I have none. No one at all. If you want family references, you'll have to look for someone else.'

'Where are you presently employed?'

All this time, Sandlin was ostensibly making notes on a legal pad on his desk. In reality he was studying the young woman's reactions, cataloguing signs of emotional tension or imbalance, registering the slight tremors that shook her body from time to time. The lawyer had no need for notes. His mind recorded every single word and gesture. He never forgot a thing.

'I worked my way through school. The last two years, I was an assistant in the journalism department. Since then, I haven't done anything that would look good on a CV. I'm very poor, Mr Sandlin. When I need to eat, I waitress in a cocktail lounge. Usually the Holiday Inn.'

'With a master's degree?' he asked with a faint note of scepticism.

'You may not be aware of it ... up here.' Her hands made a wide swoop that took in the wall of glass, the art work and gold picture frames, the computer terminals, the flat ivory telephone, the carpet as thick as grass beneath their feet. 'For some people, these are hard times.'

Abruptly, she ceased speaking and sank back farther into the chair. Her head feel forwards, and she again assumed that attitude of withdrawal that seemed to overcome her from time to time.

'I had some trouble just before I left school,' she said in a very low voice, not looking at him. 'Trouble of a personal nature, I mean. Emotional. I don't want to talk about it except to say that I spent this past year trying to get over it, and I did, finally. It's finished now. Completely. Done and over with.'

Like hell it is, Sandlin said to himself, but he pushed the thought away like a troublesome fly.

'You say you are poor, Miss Gutman. The economic compensation involved in this "assignment" is perhaps not as substantial as you might have been led to believe. Besides the moral gratification of helping two fine, worthy people struck down by unkind fate, you will receive reimbursement of expenses equivalent to $30,000. We, of course, will provide you with all the necessary vouchers for these so-called expenses, but you will be paid only after you have completed the final paperwork. Do I make myself perfectly clear?'

'I don't want the thirty thousand. You can keep it yourself if you want. As a finder's fee. After all, you did find me, didn't you?'

She laughed for the first time and then shot him a shrewd look. All her diffidence had gone up in smoke, and Sandlin had the disconcerting impression that it was the young woman who was sizing him up and not the reverse. It was a feeling he disliked intensely. His irritation grew by leaps and bounds, and again he wondered why he had let himself be involved in a case with so many damned females. Jeff Sandlin was a chauvinist and proud of it; in spite of radically changing mores, his life progressed as it always had, i.e., just as he dictated. Recently he had traded in one overaged, starting-to-cause-trouble wife and had acquired in exchange several much younger women who now administered to his fun-time needs. They were, of course, duly compensated for their trouble. Sandlin knew about remuneration for work effectively accomplished but did not understand women outside the framework of their monetary value.

He did not understand Cecil Gutman at all, and that was too much to bear in a case that had been trying his patience for over a week. Wherever he turned, he found irrational and unpredictable behaviour. Even the people who had hired him were hardly better than the crazy women parading through his office.

These reflections were cut short when the door of his office was flung open. Denise O'Neil stood on the threshold, a look of consternation on her flushed, freckled face.

'Mr Sandlin, sir, I'm terribly sorry to interrupt y'all but Judge Baker just called and says he's got to have that brief in the next hour. I've got him on the line now, and he wants to know — '

'Denise,' he interrupted smoothly. 'Tell Judge Baker to go to hell.'

Denise stood for an instant in open-mouthed astonishment. Then, because she was a sharp girl, she let her eyes fall on Cecil Gutman, studying that thin figure with a glimmer of repressed excitement.

'You'd better get back to the judge if he's still on hold,' Sandlin said coolly.

'Oh. Yes, sir. I'll certainly give him your message, just the way you said it. I'll bet he hollers something awful, though!'

She giggled and skipped out of the office as Sandlin turned his attention back to the young woman, who was smoking and gazing out of the window, apparently unimpressed by a message that would have sent a federal judge into apoplexy had it actually been delivered.

'Miss Gutman, I have a questionnaire here for you to fill out in detail. On the surface, you do not fit the qualifications specified by my clients, but, because of your exceptional personality and character, I am going to stick my neck out and . . .'

He stopped, seeing Cecil Gutman's fine eyebrows rise in sceptic amusement. The sorrow had momentarily abandoned her, and she looked quite charming.

'All right, let's put our cards on the table. I think, for various reasons, that you may be of interest to my clients, although I cannot say positively until they have seen your complete file. I want you to be aware that if your candidature is accepted, even provisionally, then it will be necessary for us to initiate formalities. I will introduce you to one of my principals. If he gives me the green light after meeting you, then you will be admitted to a hospital here for a thorough check-up. You will be obliged to undergo a gruelling set of tests − not just the standard one for blood type, diabetes, lung disease, hormone irregularities, thyroid deficiency and so forth, but also for rare illnesses, hereditary problems and, above all, for sexually transmitted diseases. So if there is anything you wish to confide in me, this is the time to do it. It will spare you great deal of unnecessary discomfort and embarrassment later on.'

'I told you when I entered this room that I was in excellent health. Also that I was trustworthy. Must I go on repeating myself? I thought to do a dirty business like this one, you lawyers had to have total recall.'

She reads my mind, Sandlin thought with repressed fury. *And she doesn't like me. Not a bit. She may call herself trustworthy, but she doesn't accord a semblance of trust to the people with whom she deals. That down-trodden appearance is just a front. She's a bitch all right, but I can't afford to turn her away. If they ever found out I let a girl like that walk out of my office, a lot of shit would hit a very big fan. There's a one-in-a-million chance of finding another MA with that particular colouring. To hell with it! The faster I get this show on the road, the faster they'll take this kook off my hands.*

'Miss Gutman, I am *charmed* by you. You are obviously a young

8

woman of intelligence, ability and good breeding, and you have an engaging personality as well. I am sure we are going to have a pleasant association. Now, as I was saying, if you will just complete this form, then I can fill you in on the exact nature of this assignment.'

Chapter Two

She sat in the darkest corner of the dark bar in the underground shopping mall. The place − what she could see of it − was all Scotch plaid, polished wood and wench-style serving girls wearing lacy aprons and low-cut blouses.

From all around her came loud, gushy calls of welcome. Friends greeting friends. Lovers greeting lovers. It was Happy Hour. One drink entitled you to all you could eat from the hors d'oeuvres table in front. It was a bargain way of getting a meal, and Cecil was badly in need of a bargain. Still, she couldn't bring herself even to taste what she had already heaped on her plate − a good-sized serving of cheese nachos and refried beans. She kept shivering, and the shivering made her hand shake when she tried to pick up her fork.

It's unnaturally cold in here, almost as cold as it was in that bastard lawyer's skyscraper across the street. They claim they keep the temperature at seventy, but it feels more like sixty. The only Happy People that come to Happy Hour are Eskimos and Laplanders.

She knew it wasn't just the cold that was making her shake like this, though. One unsteady hand went out to take her margarita. Soon its icy sting would hit her right behind her eyes where a lot of other things were already throbbing.

When she had first seen the ad, she hadn't really thought she'd go. She had taken it step by tiny step, teasing herself, playing with the idea. First, she had telephoned for an appointment, then slowly walked through the subterranean shopping mall, stopping to look in the windows of boutiques selling power clothes for women, suits with big, padded football shoulders, sleek black boots, striped ties of satin or silk. She had got into the mirrored elevator and watched the numbers flash on and off in luminous green like messages from a far-off galaxy. She had walked down a hall of creamy marble and sickly yellow neon; she had sat on a metal and leather couch and coaxed a

10

receptionist into indiscretions. There were dozens of applicants, the preppy blonde in the cashmere dress had said. It seemed anybody who could read had answered the ad.

'Do you know what it's about, Miss . . . ?'

'Muffy, call me Muffy, hon'. I suppose all these ladies are comin' in hopin' to be typists or legal secretaries, though in this day and age, it could just as well be partner, couldn't it? As long as it's not my job they're after . . . Didn't they tell you when you phoned?'

Cecil knew, but she wasn't telling Muffy that $30,000 was a fortune when all the jobs going were for market analysts or computer programmers, when it was easier to get a union card to work on a construction site in New York City than it was for a liberal-arts graduate to find employment in the city of Dallas. Even the foreign service didn't want you unless you had majored in political science and gone to Georgetown. And here was a job that offered all the money and asked for what in return? Very little. Just like those idiot ads in Australia and New Zealand: send in $5.95 for a list of 1,000 highly paid jobs. No qualification needed.

Money. She hated even the word, hated to think that smug lawyer was charging $200 an hour (she was just guessing, but it sounded like a lot) to interview her, looking her over as though she were a contestant for Miss Texas Sunflower or Miss Cherry Pie. Insisting on proof of education when it would have been quicker and safer to pick a twenty-year-old moron in good physical condition. Between the masters and the mentally deficient, she would have gone for the latter every time.

So she had hung on to the idea all the time she had been sitting in Sandlin's big leather chair that her chances of being chosen were nil. But then, when she had begun to suspect that it was going to work out, that Sandlin − for some convoluted reason − was going to offer it to *her*, she had felt a wave of revulsion so strong she had hardly been able to stay in the room. It was even worse when he had explained it to her precisely and clinically, without a hint of humanity in his voice. All the time he was talking, she had forced herself to focus on the aeroplanes on their takeoff course from Love Field. They were still flying so low they seemed to scrape the roofs of nearby buildings. Clouds like scoops of frothy cream over the Mercantile Bank clock and the Flying Red Horse, and far below on the vast patchwork of expressways, overpasses and bridges, miniature cars scurried here and there like ants on vital missions. And then, between two blocks of high-rise glass and concrete, Cecil had seen something that made her gasp. It was far, far away, but she could see it perfectly: the blue ferris wheel on the grounds of the State Park. It was blinking

11

spectral gold lights at her as it turned magically in the grey, late-afternoon light.

She missed most of what Jeff Sandlin said.

Now she berated herself for being so affected by that interview. She wanted to go to France, didn't she? Wanted three of four months of freedom before her life got back on the haywire course it had always jerkily travelled − from nowhere to nowhere. And what *should* she have expected from Jeff Sandlin? He was a man incapable of empathising with anyone except his own twin brother, and even that would have put a strain on his emotional resources. No, she had to face the truth: she had gone to his office because she wanted what he was offering. Even her illness offered no real excuse.

Cecil let her mind drift back to May of last year, just before spring term ended, when she thought she had everything she ever wanted at her fingertips. There came then a black morning, a black afternoon, and afterwards black days and nights stretching out before her like sombre paths through dying Bavarian forests. Every morning when she woke, her thoughts went directly, uncontrollably to Serge. Flies swarming over sickly-sweet carrion, picking it to bare bones. Eventually she became those bones herself, a Lewis Carroll creature that grew thinner and thinner and taller and taller as though mysteriously squeezed inwards and upwards. She had not been able to work, of course, and her small savings had dwindled along with the flesh on her body. After a while, she even began to wonder if they would put her away. In Texas, a state that had accumulated nearly as many crazies as California, a place where you had to be not only psycho but actually crawling up the walls of a public building before anybody noticed you, people were starting to notice her.

The one person she could talk to was Mica, and Mica had not sympathised with her problems. Not for a minute. But she had sympathised with Cecil, and that was a beginning. '*Una sympatica atrevida*' was what she had said. Her voice was a lifeline.

Two months ago, it had stopped. The throbbing, confused urge to walk in the streets, to sit next to ponds in whose surface she could see Paris and the Parc Montsouris where Serge had played as a boy, a park of mice, a mountain of mice, mice with oversized heads and cuddly, furry bodies, mice in prams and strollers, mice coming down slides and buried in sandpiles. Mice falling.

She had put all that out of her mind.

The first week she had felt better, she had been able to sleep; the second, to eat. Then she had washed her hair, filed down her nails, which had grown long and hard the way Howard Hughes's had when he was old and crazy. And as her health returned, the slats of her mind opened up, one by one. She was able to make phone calls, ride on buses, find a job. Remember.

'Excuse me, didn't I run into you down in the vaults at the Mercantile today?'

'No. I wasn't there.'

He was tall and owlish, with thick oval glasses and silky brown hair. A serious man who had drunk too much.

'Well, some other part of the bank then? I *know* I saw you there.' He flapped his arms and fell slowly into a chair next to hers. 'I wouldn't forget a redhead like you.'

'Look, this is my table, and I don't propose to share it with you. Furthermore, I wasn't in the Mercantile today or any day. I don't even have a bank account.' She stopped short, furious for revealing even that trifling amount of information about herself.

'No bank account?' The idea was so startling that it seemed to clear his head a little.

'Please go or I'll have to call the manager.'

He leaned forwards. His eyes, magnified by thick lenses, were convex globes of disbelief.

'No cheque book? No savings account? No CDs? Not even a credit card?

'I'm alive, aren't I?'

'Listed, red, you need help.' He spoke slowly and carefully in tones of real concern. His owlish face was no more than six inches from hers. 'You need help badly. It so happens I am a professional helper. If you'd like to come round to my place and ...'

She stood up and walked as steadily as she could towards the waitress, who was waiting for refills at the bar.

'Do you have a telephone I could use?'

'Sure do, right near the front door. Hey, we just brought out some sausages for the hors d'oeuvres table. They're nice and hot. Why don't you try some on your way back?'

She was looking at Cecil with kindness. She *knew*. The owl-man knew, too. Maybe all these people did, all these young professionals who looked as though they had jogged from their offices. All those people were together, with each other. No one in the whole room was alone except Cecil. By getting up and going to the telephone, though, she showed herself to be a young woman with a real friend, a connection temporarily missed but on the point of being re-established. She didn't need a pick-up; she had someone already.

She was shaking again when the familiar voice answered.

'It's Cecil.'

'What's up?'

13

'I just got out. It was harder than I thought.'

'How harder? You knew before you went there, didn't you?'

'Don't give me a lecture. I can't take it right now.'

'OK. Tell me.'

'I have to check into a hospital for a complete physical. Quite soon. The idea of being shut up in a hospital room ... it's affecting me pretty badly. Maybe I'd better ...'

'*Better* is right, *querida*. Better make up your mind. This is a crazy stunt you're trying to pull. Shilly-shallying won't do much good.'

'You're right. You're always right, damn it! Only I didn't expect them to choose me. And I think they have, provided I pass the physical. At least, that's the impression I got from the bullshitting lawyer who interviewed me.'

'Well, that's terrific, isn't it? Isn't that what you were hoping for?'

'I don't use the verb "hope" any more, Mica. I tore that page right out of my dictionary.'

'Quit stalling me with the college talk. I got a lot riding on your decision, too. You going to take it or not?'

'How the hell do I know? Yes ... I suppose so. I think I'm going to do it.'

'At least for once you made a goddamn decision.' Her gruff Latin voice seemed to fade as she said the words.

'Oh, Mica, please don't! Please! You're the strong one. You've got to understand.'

'What is there to understand?'

'How scared I am. You're the only person in the whole world that I can tell that to. Mica, I'm ... I'm absolutely terrified by what I've just done.'

Chapter Three

Jeff Sandlin removed the file from his office safe. Its codename 'Saint-Germain' came from the boulevard in Paris where his clients lived when they were not in New York or Rio de Janeiro or Cap d'Antibes or Gstaad or on one of their plantations in the Caribbean. The file was so secret that no one − except a partner with whom Sandlin had felt obliged to discuss the ethics of the matter − knew their names or even the exact nature of the services the firm was rendering for them.

The advertisement had run simultaneously in four big-city Texas papers and instructed interested parties to call an unlisted number that rang on Denise O'Neil's desk. Denise's job was to discourage − in as few words as possible − crackpots, psychos, transvestites, religious fanatics, sex maniacs, drunks, drug addicts and people selling insurance, lottery tickets, cosmetics and/or low-cost fringes. It took a little more tact to get the Chicanos and wives of Vietnamese fishermen from Corpus Christi off the phone. Blacks were the hardest of all. It was illegal to come right out and ask, Are you or aren't you? Consequently, a few young women slipped through Denise's tight net and came in for an interview. They all got the 'Judge Baker on the line' treatment, but Jeff Sandlin watched them leave with regret; one or two he would have liked to interview outside office hours.

Age, too, was important. Anyone over thirty was politely but firmly refused. One woman who sounded seventy but said she was thirty-five refused to accept her disqualification; she tied up the unlisted number for nearly an hour trying to find out what fee was being offered. Denise had clear instructions not to antagonise anyone.

Two callers were reporters hoping for a human-interest story, but the tale Denise told − that she herself was the woman looking for help, that her minister had authorised her to place the ad, that she was doing it to please her aged mother who was dying of cancer in a

15

nursing home — sounded so improbably dreary that both reporters hung up without pursuing the matter.

The twenty or so young women who got through the preliminary screening were given the firm's name and address, together with the day and hour of their appointment. Sandlin wanted to interview them in a hotel room or some other neutral place, but Denise, with a surprising show of spunk, vetoed that, saying the episode was traumatic enough for a woman without the added fear of being lured into a trap.

Everything went according to schedule except for one bothersome hitch: Denise O'Neil knew the identities of all the principals. Somebody had to second Jeff Sandlin. He wasn't about to start making his own phone calls or typing his own telexes or operating fax. In any case, he had already told Denise the whole story on Sunday afternoon while they were lying on her water bed sipping kir royales and watching a porno movie. He had felt a sudden need to impress her, and it had all spilled out. He had never before betrayed a trust, and he wondered if it had happened because he was growing old. The episode troubled him, so much so that, the very next morning, he signed up for an intensive exercise, massage and weight-loss programme at the health club on the top floor of his building.

Sandlin knew exactly what procedure he was due to follow now that he had ferreted out the exotic Miss Gutman, but he read through the instructions again anyway. It gave him a little thrill to see the client's name in black and white. It was a name that figured on the plaques of several expensive objects scattered about his own home.

The first call he made was to Sam Sweeney. He knew the doctor by sight because they often lunched at the same restaurants and clubs and, one spring, their wives were co-chairpersons on a Turtle Creek azalea show. Sandlin didn't particularly like the doctor, who was not only a good six inches taller than he, but also harder and leaner. Sweeney was, in fact, so hale, hearty and hell-gone with Irish charm that Sandlin liked to fantasise that he was an impostor, one of those men with no degree or medical training who suddenly put out a brass plate and start, often with remarkable success, to treat people. Of course, doctors like that always tripped up on some technicality and finished in jail. The thought of Sam Sweeney behind bars was so pleasing that Sandlin allowed himself a tight little smile before he remembered that the doctor, only too real, was on his way to becoming a world-class celebrity. As the file open on his desk testified, he also tended to the medical needs of one of the richest families in the world.

Sandlin pressed the intercom.

'Denise? Get me Dr Samuel Sweeney. Try the Medical Center first. If he's not there, they can probably reach him on his beeper. Otherwise I've got half a dozen other numbers you can try, including his home.'

'OK, hon'.'

'Denise,' he repeated testily. 'I've told you several times. There's an office vocabulary and an after-hours vocabulary. Under no circumstances are the two to mix.'

'Sorry, sweetie.'

He released the button and started to tap on his desk with his gilt-edged ruler. He was irritated again. He couldn't handle her; he should never have taken up with a girl half his age. He had known that from the very beginning, and yet . . .

The intercom light blinked once.

'The doctor's on the line, *sir*.'

He smiled and put down the ruler. She was a girl who knew *exactly* how to humour him. In the office and out.

'Dr Sweeney? This is Jeff Sandlin over at McNaught, Muncheon – '

'Jeff, why are you giving me that crap? I know who you are. Didn't we have a squash match about a year ago during the course of which I – pardon the pun – squashed your ass?'

'Your memory beats mine, Sam, and that's no mean compliment.' Sandlin smiled to himself; he never, of course, forgot anything, but it was politic to give the doctor a little edge. 'I must have repressed the whole sorry episode.'

'Hate to lose, huh?'

'You're damn right I do! I'm waiting for a return so I can have a whack at yours. Ass, I mean. But that's not why I'm calling you, Sam. I have your name in a file here – '

'Jeez! Another malpractice suit? Call Tony, will you, Jeff? He handles all that stuff for me. I don't have time to bother with it.'

'No, no, my friend, no one's suing you that I know of, but a certain party in France gave me your name as the person to contact – '

'France? You don't mean Christine, do you?'

'I was instructed not to mention names during the preliminary stages,' Sandlin replied primly. 'This concerns – '

'I *know* what it concerns, for Christ's sake. I'm the guy who put this whole thing together, and the one who recommended she use a Dallas law firm, which, I presume, is you. So . . . did you find anybody?'

'A young woman just walked out of here – twenty-three years old, born in Waco, baptised a Lutheran, an authentic Texas Wasp except for some long-dead Swedes who – '

'What's she look like?' the doctor cut him off.

17

Sandlin frowned in annoyance. He hadn't been able to finish a single sentence since he got Sweeney on the line. He decided that the doctor was as crazy as the Parisians. Looks had nothing to do with the matter, unless Sweeney just wanted to fantasise about the gynaecological examination he would soon be conducting on Cecil Gutman. He wondered if a doctor could really remain indifferent when he put on his rubber gloves and started to touch all that pretty . . .

'You still on the line, Jeff? Can't you hear me? I asked you what the woman looks like?'

'Tall and skinny. Kind of beautiful, I guess, in a pinched way, but certainly not much there to get your wick in — '

'Her hair? Eyes?' The impatience in Sweeney's voice was on the rise.

'Well, that's exactly why I called you. I can deliver according to instructions, but there are problems I must discuss with you. She's a redhead, and she's got the colour of eyes Elizabeth Taylor's supposed to have but probably doesn't.'

'Yeah. Hmmm. She educated?'

'Smart but smart-assed, too. Master's. U of I. Personally, I wouldn't recommend her at all except for — '

'What's the trouble? You're not giving this to me straight.'

'Well, this is as straight as I can shoot: she may be a nutcase.'

'How bad is it?'

'She's very high-strung, obviously tripped up by something in her past. Maybe she got dumped by some jock in school and can't — '

'OK. I'll look into the health angle. I'm taking this whole thing off your hands as of right now, Jeff, so don't give it another thought. When's she coming over here?'

'I told her your secretary would give her an appointment. She'll be calling in.'

'Fine. I'll arrange to see her first thing tomorrow morning. What else?'

'That's it for the moment. I'll keep the interviews going until you give me the cut-off signal. Oh yes, I've got to call Paris.'

'Great! Tell Christine you spoke to me. Tell her . . . tell her it's going to work out and not to worry. Do that for me, will you, Jeff?'

'Be glad to, old buddy. When will I hear back from you?'

'The preliminaries will take about a week, but in two to three days, *I'll* know. I always do. Take care of yourself, Jeff. Never forget you're God's gift to orphans, widows and traffic-accident victims. Especially the ones in ambulances.'

He slammed down the phone, and Jeff Sandlin was left listening to a dead line. A look of absolute rage settled upon his handsome, portly face.

Chapter Four

If Cecil had disliked Jeff Sandlin on sight, she *hated* Dr Samuel Sweeney. By the time she had been in the Medical Center for three days, her favourite pastime was thinking up ways to avenge herself on the doctor: setting fire to his pride-and-joy Mercedes, getting his medical licence revoked on malpractice charges, or — best of all — seeing him wind up as a patient in this very hospital.

In rare moments of lucidity, Cecil had to admit that it was not the doctor personally that she hated but rather the pain and indignity to which she had been submitted since she arrived here. Grudgingly, she admitted that Sweeney might have a certain charm, that against a background different from the sewer-green walls of this torture chamber of a hospital, she might even have liked him.

Still, her grievances against the doctor were numerous. Right at the top of her list was the fact that he had insisted she check into the hospital when it was obvious that all the tests he wanted to perform on her could just as easily have been done on an outpatient basis. He simply wanted to have her under his thumb the better to torment her. Then, before she had even had a finger pricked, Dr Sweeney announced point-blank that she would have to quit smoking if she cared to maintain her candidacy. Cold turkey. Not only that, but every sort of alcohol was out, too.

'Wine, beer, sherry, you name it, babe. The strongest thing you'll be drinking from now on is Diet Coke. As for drugs, nix, nil, naught. No tranquillisers, no flu pills, not even a vitamin or an aspirin without my prior OK. Got it?'

He'd get his, if Cecil had anything to say about it. In the meantime, it was the absence of tobacco that affected her the most.

'You ought to thank me,' Sweeney said crisply. 'It's your life, but since I've got a vested interest in it now, too, and since I don't have time to follow you around to see if you're being naughty or nice, I'll

19

start by confiscating that carton of cigarettes I saw in your bureau drawer.' A positively sadistic smile crossed his devil-may-care Irish face. 'There aren't any for sale in the lobby downstairs, either, so don't bother trying.'

Cecil was infuriated. The fact that he treated her like a half-witted child was more than enough to get him on her hate list. Taking away her cigarettes put him in the category of a Nazi torture expert.

Fortunately, she was rushed about so much that she had little time to dwell on her misfortunes. Wednesday morning, she had scarcely got out of her clothes and into a hospital gown that made her look like a hung-over Halloween prankster when a male nurse appeared with a new questionnaire for her to fill out, this one twenty-five pages long. It covered every detail of her life from birth weight to the kind of sports she played in college. There were four whole pages devoted to the medical history of her immediate family. Most of this she left blank since both of her parents had died in an automobile accident when she was eight years old; she had no brothers or sisters and, except for the grandmother who had raised her, she knew nothing about any other family members. The whole questionnaire ended up being really about her and her grandmother, which was fitting, she supposed, and brought back memories of Nana that were surprisingly tender.

Just as she had got started on that, the Great Doctor breezed in with his no-smoking ban and then breezed out again. After that, a whole series of nurses, orderlies and young residents wandered in to distract her from the questionnaire by taking her blood pressure and temperature, extracting what seemed life-threatening amounts of blood from her right arm, and sending her down the corridor to give urine and stool samples.

A photographer came in to do face shots from three different angles. 'Like a jailbird,' he told her cheerfully. By then, that was exactly how she felt.

At twelve, she had been given a light, rather pleasant lunch on a tray and then had gone downstairs for a battery of tests which had left her, by six o'clock, exhausted, famished and raging against Sweeney again. Half the afternoon she had passed in the hands of a midget dentist, who, after a complete X-ray of her mouth to measure, explained gleefully about her skeletal condition and decalcification. He decided to clean her teeth and refill an old cavity. The rest of Wednesday had been spent lying on the hard block of an X-ray table in the basement while she and a bespeckled, middle-aged technician exchanged old Woody Allen jokes. All this time he sat behind his protective wall, playing at being a movie director. The swishing movements of his machine told her each time one of her organs was immortalised on film.

None of this was really bad, but neither was it her favourite way of passing time, especially after a morning of being jabbed, pricked and poked. By the time she got back to the relative safety of her room, she thought she probably had anaemia from the blood-letting and cancer from the radioactive exposure. Not that Dr Sweeney and his cronies would care. Any part of her future after the next year was of complete indifference to them: once she had fulfilled her contract, they would discard her like an empty bean pod, of no further use to anyone.

If Wednesday was annoying, Thursday was a nightmare. It started in Sweeney's office on the twelfth floor where he had another questionnaire for her, this one devoted entirely to matters of sex and reproduction. Then Sweeney and his nurse Estelle put her on another hard slab – a gynaecological table – and poked some more. It seemed to go on for hours. When she got back to her room, she was astonished to find it was only ten-thirty.

She barely had time for a sip of water, though, before an orderly was taking her to the elevator and still another examination room, this one filled with machines of every sort, a true chamber of Dr Frankenstein.

'Here,' said a little man with a German accent and tinted glasses that made him look like an ageing rock star, 'you have electro-cardiogram, biometric, spirometric, tonometric, audiometric tests.'

Cecil soon gathered that she was being tested to see if her heart beat, if her reflexes worked more or less normally, if she could hear, smell and see. She was blindfolded and asked to identify tactually a whole series of ridiculous objects, asked to differentiate between wet and dry, soft and hard, round and square. Her dexterity was tested, as was her ability to respond to light signals, to repeat sound patterns. It was a battery of tests appropriate for a child trying to get into kindergarten, and some half-witted theoretician had probably correlated it with emotional balance or intelligence or – who knows? – fertility. Having no choice, she went along with it. By eight o'clock, she was in bed and fell into a troubled, anxious sleep.

Friday was not hard physically, but it was the most trying to her. The first thing in the morning, before breakfast even, she was given an ultrasonic examination of the pelvic region and was then escorted to the psychiatric department, where she was interviewed by two residents and, finally, by Sam Sweeney himself. By this time, she knew she wasn't going to get breakfast and no longer cared. She couldn't have eaten anyway.

Sweeney wanted to know everything about her breakdown. To her surprise, she found herself telling him most of it. She kept back only one thing − the one part that had been the worst and about which she had lied on every questionnaire. Finally Sweeney shook his head.

'You can't hide a thing like that from your own doctor,' he said sympathetically. 'I knew yesterday.'

'Oh, go rot in hell!' she lashed out. She wanted to slap him but burst into tears instead. She cried for a long time and then, feeling better, despised herself for having done it.

Dr Sweeney watched her wipe away her tears, his usual sardonic smile back in place. 'I know you hate me, forcing you to quit smoking and subjecting you to all those tests. And then I pry out your last little secret.'

'Hate is the wrong verb, Dr Sweeney. In your case, I passed beyond hate two days ago.'

'Good. It confirms how basically sound your judgements are.'

'You mean after all you've found out about me, you still have something of which you can approve?'

'Oh, come on, Cecil, don't play the modest young girl with me. It doesn't wash. One thing that comes out in all these tests is that you're obstinate and proud. You have a very high opinion of yourself, most of which, I might add, is justified.'

'Yes, I suppose it takes a certain amount of talent to have a nervous breakdown. It's not within the reach of your ordinary patient, is it?'

'You had a love affair that went sour. It happens all the time. The only unusual aspect about yours is that you cared. Most people don't.'

'Really, doctor? You're telling me I got sick because I slipped on the last drop of love left in the world?'

'I'm telling you what I see all around me. There are a lot of emotions going by that grandiose word, but very few of them stand up to serious investigation.'

'I can see you're one of the cynics that make our happy world go round.'

'I may be, and then again, I may not. Let's talk about you, Cecil. You hate me, and I like you. I'm not sure why.'

'Maybe some little thing you discovered in the twenty-six hours of tests you had done on me. Something you found in my blood or my pancreas or my thymus? Certainly not in my heart. I don't think you'd like what you saw there.'

Sweeney threw back his head and laughed. He had, she noticed, quite beautiful teeth.

'Probably this is how people should get married. Test each other for every possible disease, genetic flaw and mental defect, and then try to match up whatever positive elements are left.'

'Are you proposing marriage?'

'Unfortunately, I already have a wife.'

'Unfortunately?'

'An all too Freudian slip of the tongue.'

He laughed again, a little less happily, but still she had caught a glimpse of the way people fell under his charm.

'So what *are* you proposing, then?'

'A job. You still want it, don't you? I'd hate to think you went through all that misery for nothing.'

'I told your lawyer friend that once I gave my word, I didn't go back on it.'

'Sandlin's not necessarily my friend, but he is a lawyer, and he's drawn up a lot of papers for you to sign. Shall I tell him to come on over with them?'

'Can't I go home now?' Her voice suddenly took on the intonation of a tired child. 'I have a roommate. I'm sure she's worried. I never expected to stay here so long.'

'No, I want you in the hospital until the paperwork's done. Once that's out of the way, I'll be giving you some pills that will help to get this little show on the road. Then there are one or two manipulations to do, painless but necessary. I'm going to go ahead and schedule the first one for Monday morning.'

'You mean you're okaying me? Definitively?'

'Isn't that obvious?'

'And you want to start now? Today?'

'The sooner the better. Jeff was supposed to have explained all that to you.'

'I got the impression it might be a rather long drawn-out affair.'

'It is in most hands. Not in mine.'

'Of course. How silly of me. I forgot I wasn't dealing with a run-of-the-mill doctor but a bona fide genius.' She could not keep the sarcasm out of her voice, but Sweeney didn't seem to mind. His ego was probably impervious to any kind of attack. 'How long then?'

'Sweetheart, I'll have you pregnant within six weeks!'

Chapter Five

Samuel Sweeney had had the Midas touch since that early June morning when all nine and a half pounds of him had come sliding out of his mother and been deposited upon her soft, welcoming bosom. He grew up in Highland Park in the very heart of Dallas, a community so exclusive that it maintained its own police and fire departments, its own park and swimming pool (labelled 'public' but open only to residents of Highland Park, a regulation which effectively excluded every minority in the state of Texas).

Not only had Sam Sweeney grown up in this rarefied atmosphere, but he had lived on Highland Park's very best street, Beverley Drive. When he was fifteen and passed his driving test on his first try, he found a white Cadillac convertible waiting for him in the driveway, and when he was seventeen and received his acceptance letter from Harvard, Sam Sr left in the entrance hall the receipt for a $10,000 deposit which he had just made into his son's savings account.

In spite of such a background, Sam Jr developed into a nice person. At Harvard he fell in naturally with boys and girls who would be leaders in their chosen fields. Two months after graduation, Sam married the prettiest and brightest of those girls, Judith McKinney-West, known as Jude, a Smith College theatre-arts major and a Phi Beta Kappa. After an island-hopping honeymoon in the Caribbean, the newlyweds moved back to Texas. Right through his years at Harvard, Sam had played the cello, and by the time he started to look for a good medical school, he was an excellent amateur musician. This, more than anything else, got him into Baylor, where a famous group of researchers needed a cellist for their weekend string quartet.

So brilliant was Sam Sweeney at Baylor that one of his mentors predicted he might become the Christiaan Barnard of his generation. Sam was pleased by the compliment, but he had already decided against specialising in cardiology in general and heart transplants in

24

particular. That field was overploughed, and he guessed rightly that it was going to become even harder in the next fifteen or twenty years for an ambitious young surgeon to make a name for himself shuffling hearts around chest cavities. A brand-new speciality was opening, however, and Sam, faster than any of his fellow students, saw the potential and decided this was the direction he would take.

Dr Samuel Sweeney became famous, just as his professors had predicted, but in the field of human fertility. Before long, a procession of women arrived in his blue-and-gold-striped waiting room. They came from all over the world, movie stars who had one abortion too many or had let the biological clock tick all the way up to midnight; a veiled lady from Dubai with a shameful infection; a member of the Japanese imperial family; even a president's daughter, accompanied by two Secret Service men who waited patiently in the hall during her battery of long, complicated tests.

With so much going on, Sam had little free time. Still, he was growing restless. His operations left him charged up, and when he got home at night, he could not sleep. He knew much too much about drugs to prescribe any for himself, and he felt a little silly playing the cello at three o'clock in the morning in the music room of his vast, stately home. Jude, wisely enough, never nagged Sam for being around so little. Instead she became an active club-woman, socialite and political groupie. When Sam did happen to be home, Jude usually was not, so they failed to communicate in either of the two ways available to married couples. If they still loved each other, it was from across an ever-widening chasm.

At some point Sam found that going to poker games with his old cronies from Harvard and Baylor was a relaxing thing to do. There was always a game going on somewhere in town. He could drop in for an hour or two at eleven o'clock or even later if he felt like it. The male championship, the cigars and the watered-down scotch they drank to keep themselves going all pleased some secret part of himself. More than anything, though, he went for the thrill of winning. At the very beginning − when he first started playing − Sam was very lucky. He won often. He didn't need the money, of course − he already had more than he knew what to do with − but he thrived on the excitement, on the possibility that he might lose a month's income in one single streak of cold dice. And after a while, he started to do just that. By then he had graduated to sessions with the high rollers, the big boys who thought nothing of flying him out to Vegas for a weekend, all expenses paid. After that, he seemed to be climbing all the time, from Vegas to Curaçao to London. The names got bigger, the places more exotic. There was no limit to the generosity of his new-found friends.

25

Somewhere along the road, Sam Sweeney quit playing the cello. He also quit making love to his wife, and he quit noticing his two children altogether. It was the classic tale of a forty-year-old, emotionally deprived American male, but there was nothing classic about the men who began to follow Sam. They waited in dark corners of the parking area of his office building or near the hospitals where he operated, always in pairs, always with short, clipped messages that sounded like made-for-TV movie dialogue. 'Hey doc, hi'y'a doin'? Mackie says, bring him the dough for Monday. He says he can't wait this time. He says he won't postpone again. He knows a good doc like you won't want to disappoint a good friend like Mackie.'

That was about the extent of it. They didn't actually threaten to break his fingers so he couldn't operate, or anything so blatantly crude. He was too important, too well known, his own friends too highly placed. Or so Sam liked to think. Maybe it was just that he still brought them a steady income, rolling the dice three or four times a week as though he didn't have a care in the world.

His work never suffered. He was still King Midas at the hospitals, the golden boy, as great an innovator as they had ever seen around these parts. In fact he was on the verge of a breakthrough in embryo transplants so revolutionary that everyone expected him to make *Time* or *Newsweek*, not to mention the wire services and evening network news. The pressure, though, was becoming a little more than he could cope with; he was working now just to pay the boys. About this time, he found he could no longer bear the sight of his frail, lovely wife, surrounded as she was by a wasteland of designer clothes, designer furniture and designer *linge de maison*. He begrudged her and the children every penny they spent; he grew positively allergic to both their house in Dallas with its gigantic, tax-write-off mortgage and their deficit-ridden, tax-write-off cattle ranch in Brownsville. He couldn't afford any of that any more. Worse, he didn't even want it.

Sam Sweeney did not know *what* he wanted until, after a consultation with the wife of a Scandinavian tennis champion in Zürich, he continued on to a poker game in Gstaad and, the next day on a downhill slope, ran into Christine Schomberg. Literally. She was flying down the mountainside wearing cut-off jeans and a man's white, ribbed undershirt, and when they collided, Sam thought, for a few stunned minutes, that he was dead. That this slinky, gorgeous woman had killed him. Later, when he came to know what emotion that stunned, breath-knocked-out-of-him moment had foretold, he also came to know that she was always that reckless. That she drove her Porsche at breakneck speeds, that she was a *passionnée* of underwater photography at imprudent depths, that she liked to hang-glide and sky-dive, that her idea of an escapist weekend was exploring a volcano or fact-finding on the West Bank in Israel. Christine was anything but a proper, decorous woman.

She simply didn't give a damn.

In the indoor pool at Gstaad, the snow cold and bright all around them, he watched as she executed a perfect dive from the high board and then lost her suit of green jersey as she continued down into the water's clear depths. Without a backward glance for her lost piece of clothing, she climbed out of the pool and stood absolutely still on the white tiles, acknowledging admiring glances that were only her due. Sam, too, watched as though he had never before seen female flesh. Clinically, he admired her perfect sense of balance and movement and her fine bone structure; artistically, he enjoyed her control of dramatic effect; personally, he wanted her. Violently.

A few minutes later, Christine was beside him on the blue module sunning couch, stretching out to profit from the maximum of noonday rays. Sam did not have to take his eyes off her to know that all the men and most of the women were still staring.

'Are you going to stay like that?' he asked laughingly, but with a tinge of uneasiness all the same.

'Why not? I'll borrow your shirt when I go back to the changing room.'

'Aren't you afraid ... they might ask you to leave?'

'Me? Ask me to leave? You must be joking, Sam. No one ever asks *me* to do anything I don't want to do.'

Later that day, with her wild red hair whipping back and forth across her tanned face, she looked like an actress in a high-budget porn film, but she was real and it was he, Dr Samuel Sweeney, riding with her. Yes, he, who, even in Las Vegas with all the girls Mackie and his other new friends had offered him, had never experienced anyone even remotely like Christine Schomberg, née de la Rouvay, one of the world's richest women through her marriage to Frederick Schomberg, noble through her own family's claim to be 'wrong side of the blanket' descendants of Louis XV.

'It started when Madame de Pompadour was mourning her dead child,' Christine told him later when they were soaking together in a hot tub with a spectacular view of the surrounding, snow-covered peaks. 'Old Louis had this little girl from the Parc des Cerfs − do you know about that?'

'No, but I'm sure you're going to tell me.'

'It was a neighbourhood in Versailles across from the palace. Louis kept a whole collection of young peasants there, some of them hardly

27

more than children. One of these little girls pleased him so much he bought her a house in Saint-Cloud. He used to go there and play at being her husband, a common fellow. He would put on a coachman's habit and take her on picnics to the Bois de Boulogne and then asked the strollers, "Tell me, my friend, what do you think of our king?" Eventually, Louis and the girl had a child together, and the little boy accompanied them on the picnics and rides through the woods in the carriage. It was all very pretty until Louis grew tired of his mistress. As a parting present, he bestowed a *titre de noblesse* on the son.'

'And that's how you got yours?'

'Yes, isn't that nicer than being a cardinal's ugly sister?'

It was charming tale whether true or not, and it had great appeal to a boy from Texas, even one who had seen more of the world and met more royalty than Louis XV had ever dreamt of in his provincial palace. But then, everything about Christine Schomberg captivated Sam Sweeney.

The doctor was tired. He was just past forty and should have been in the prime of life, but it had been a long time now since anyone had taken care of *him*. Almost, it seemed, since he had gone from his mother's warm breasts to the starched white uniform of his first governess. Perhaps it was the Midas touch again, his own godliness that made him already sensually dulled, bored beyond description by all those worldly goods he was on the point of losing, goods, he now clearly saw, that were plated with fool's gold. Even those harbourers of doom, the little men who, each week, brough him increasingly menacing messages in their tired Peter Lorre voices, bored him. The very idea that his own godly reputation would soon be tarnished left him cynically unmoved.

And then on a Swiss mountain, a woman knocked him for a loop. She was a woman who wanted to give and not take − to give him back every single thing he had lost.

She was starting by returning his *joie de vivre*.

Later, Christine made him a proposition, one so carefully thought out and so impeccably presented that Sam wondered if their violent crash on the ski slopes had really been the accident it seemed or only another proof of her extraordinary athletic ability. What did it matter, though? What Christine was suggesting to him was, after all, simple. Simple for him, although hardly so for anyone else in the world. Her proposition also appealed to his gambler's spirit, and it was this, above all else, that finally decided him.

On their last night in Gstaad, over several wonderfully chilled *grandes dames* and plates of *homard à la nage*, with snow falling fast and furious outside and light from candles playing across her tangled hair and tanned, angular face, with her strange eyes as bright as purple marbles, they talked it out. What Christine so desperately wanted was not legal, nor was it ethical. On the other hand, it could help three people immensely, one of the three being himself. It could harm no one ... no one, that is, except one anonymous girl somewhere in the wide world, a girl who, to be perfect, would have red hair, violet eyes, a pliable nature and a good degree of intelligence. Yes, if he faced the facts squarely, what Christine was proposing would be against the best interests of this hypothetical girl. With luck, however, with *his* Midas touch, she would never know what had been done to her, what had been taken away, how she had been tricked.

So Sam looked into Christine's fierce, lovely eyes and said, 'I wouldn't do this for anyone else in the world, even myself. I want you to believe that, even though I am going to profit by it. I will do it for two reasons: number one, because it's risky, and number two, because you want it so much.'

'You're sure, Sam darling? Absolutely sure? Please tell me you won't back out when you return to your own little world? Your safe world?'

'There's nothing safe about it, I thought I explained that to you.'

'All right, but things may look different to you back in Texas. You're all so religious over there, always searching your souls to see if you've had unclean thoughts. Maybe we should do it here − in England or Holland, some place closer.'

'Stop it, Christine! It's in my hands now, and I'll set it up the way *I* want, with the least possible risk to both of us.'

'I'm sorry, *mon amour*. After all, you're the doctor, aren't you? Let's drink to that, and to something equally important. To you and me. Our future.'

As they raised their glasses, smiling at each other like conspirators in a small war, Sam knew he had never, in his whole life, set off on a course that gave him a greater feeling of danger, a greater sense of being at the razor's fine edge.

Chapter Six

The marriage of Christine Teresa Lilianne Isabel Luisa Quadros de la Rouvay, daughter of the penniless and minor French marquis, and Frederick Felix Schomberg, heir to one of Europe's biggest corporate empires, was not exactly a love match. It was more like two already highly volatile gases mingling by accident and then going on to provoke an earth-shaking explosion. Or, as Frederick's cousin-in-law Edith-Anne Schomberg phrased it, 'He was a roiling sea of oil on which somebody carelessly threw a lit match. What I'd pay money to know is, who threw the goddamn match?' Christine de la Rouvay was not liked by Edith-Anne Schomberg.

Like many other wealthy French families, the Schombergs were of Alsatian origin. Until the most recent times, they were also work-oriented, thrifty and puritanical Protestants. The origin of their staggering fortune went back to the first half of the nineteenth century when four industrious brothers in Colmar foresaw the expansion of the railway in Europe and proceeded to transform their modest ironworks into the fastest-growing metallurgical concern in France. As clever at seizing business opportunities as they were at sailing unscathed through the tumultuous French politics of the period, the founding brothers quickly built up an enormous empire. Each took control of one specific area. Hubert stayed in Colmar turning out steel components, while Gustave emigrated to Pennsylvania to open an American subsidiary. Gustave's son, Le Second Gustave, as he was known in the family, expanded the US interests to coal mining and investment banking.

Felix, after a long association with Hubert in Colmar, eventually moved to a small town outside Nancy where he set up facilities for manufacturing scales, stoves and other articles in metal. By the mid-twentieth century, this branch of the business, which married the Schomberg name to radios, television sets, washing machines and other popular appliances, was by far the best known.

The fourth and youngest brother, Thomas, was something of an oddity. He took the family genius for innovative technology and applied it to the manufacture of glass, opening still another factory bearing the Schomberg emblem in eastern France. The glass-making business was never profitable, but because Thomas was imaginative, and his son Cyril a genius, it did serve the useful purpose of casting an artistic aura over the Schomberg empire.

A cultural alibi was more than welcome at a time when Zola was using the Schomberg in Colmar as the setting for one of his most famous novels illustrating worker exploitation. The year after Zola's work appeared, many of the exquisite glass pieces created by the shy and dreamy Cyril began to find their way not only into the national museums but also into the homes of influential politicians.

Because it had grown large enough to be self-perpetuating, several generations of plodding Schombergs failed to reduce the family fortune. On the contrary, like some bloated parasite mercilessly feeding on the French economy, it expanded in every possible direction. Another industrial revolution was underway in the Western world, however, this one so discreet in arriving only one member of the house of Schomberg was capable of reading the warning signs and understanding their significance.

This Schomberg was a very young man, barely out of business school and with little or no track record. No matter; he saw, long before anyone else, that heavy industry in general and steel in particular were dying concerns in Europe. Facing eighteen months of military service, he obtained a deferment from the head of medical services for the French army itself. Once all threat of those lost months was behind him, Frederick Schomberg set out to make a name for himself and, in the process, save the dynasty.

Five years later, the shining jewel in the Schomberg crown — the Colmar plant — was gone. It had been a brutal closing, but its loss was hardly a tragedy for the conglomerate. Already Frederick was creating nearly as many jobs as those he had curtailed in Alsace, expanding the company into new technologies like industrial robots, artificial intelligence and electronic components. The European press heralded him as a giant, the first true descendant of the four founders. He was not yet thirty years old.

On a gusty autumn day on a drive back to Paris from Colmar, Frederick Schomberg asked his chauffeur to stop at the glass factory outside Luneville. It was purely a whim. Luneville was a picturesque town known for its pottery, embroidery and Cyril's unique but now

31

rather *démodé* style of glass-making. Even though it had never brought in any money, some crazy thing or other was always going on in the factory, and Frederick Schomberg felt bored and in need of distraction.

On that particular day, a young designer was on the premises arguing about what she perceived to be a particularly hideous sample for a gold-embellished line of glassware destined for a sheik in Qatar. When she heard that the dashing young Frederick Schomberg, the darling of investment counsellors, bankers and gossip columnists, had dropped into the factory for a visit, she went straight into the office to take a look at him.

Frederick glanced up from some sketches and saw a young woman dressed all in russet colours of suede with a man's shirt and string tie; her long, wavy hair matched the suede and danced about her face as she prowled restlessly about the room.

She only needs a stetson, Frederick thought whimsically, *and she'd be an absolutely perfect cowgirl.*

She was of medium height but seemed much taller with her high-heeled snake-skin boots and her arrogant way of walking. He knew she was studying him. She made not the slightest pretence of hiding it.

Christine saw a thin young man, almost a boy in appearance, with dark straight hair and warm chestnut eyes. He did not look in any way capable of closing down factories, revitalising a dying industrial town, taming leftist labour unions and, from what she had heard recently, taking over all the family business interests after pushing aside several would-be manager relatives, both in France and in the United States. He did not look any of that, but, instinctively, she knew he was. Whether because of the surprise of his vulnerable, boyish looks or the magic of his story – she herself never knew for sure – Christine de la Rouvay loved Frederick Schomberg instantly, from the moment of that first glance.

When she returned to Paris that evening, she rode in the back of the Schomberg limousine.

The family was aghast at the news of their engagement. It wasn't that Christine was a nobody, a fortune hunter, a little parvenu. In fact, by the standards of her own family, the Schombergs were much farther down the ladder of social rank. After all, the de la Rouvays claimed to be descendants of Louis XV, and Christine herself had a way, completely unconscious, of course, of looking at members of the Schomberg family as though old Louis's blood was pounding hard and fast in her veins, and they were among her most humble subjects.

Since Frederick apparently loved her beyond reason, there was little the family could do but sulk and gather secretly to discuss the situation. As far as they were concerned, Christine had two incorrigible faults: she had no money to speak of (meaning no figure with six zeros or more behind it) and, more important, she was a Catholic. For three centuries, the Schombergs had been adept at preserving their Protestant identity in a predominantly Catholic country, resorting to emigration and even fake conversions when circumstances dictated. Maintaining this faith had caused much worthy Schomberg blood to flow. Now, for the first time, a Roman Catholic was being thrust into the very heart of the family. Something had to be done, but what?

If Frederick knew of these conclaves, he chose to ignore them. They were all afraid of him, even his older brother, Hubert Bayard, who would have been running the Schomberg empire himself if he had not involved himself in several unpleasant incidents which had been permanently inscribed on his record. His mother, Marguerite, known as Rita, had spent a small fortune in fees and bribes to clear Bayard's record, but no board of directors would ever appoint him − even nominally − to head a Schomberg corporation.

Bayard had never married. After his father, Hubert, died, he moved back to the family estate in Saint-Cloud to live with Rita. He owned a dozen race horses to which he devoted an inordinate amount of his time, money and affection, driving back and forth between Paris and Deauville during the season and letting himself be photographed for *Jour de France* and other modish publications at his stables. He attended every opening to which he was invited − night clubs, trendy new restaurants in Les Halles, presentations of jewels and furniture, even flower shows. He was one of the dependable regulars of Parisian society: he loved to escort dowager ladies to *haute couture* collections, ooing and ahing with them over chic hats, furs and evening ensembles. He also maintained one of France's finest collections of locks and keys, some of his pieces going back as far as Roman times. The speciality that had made his name in the collecting world was Alsatian locks with visible mechanisms. He liked to approach guests admiring his pieces in Rita's study and say, 'Allow me to give you the key to key collecting,' or, if he was a little tipsy, 'I *know* they're phallic, darling. Why else would I spend all my time handling the rusty things?'

Bayard was very happy with his life and wanted it to continue just as it was. Of course, it *would* be nice to throw off Rita's financial yoke and have some money of his own. And it *would* be better still to escape the one thing that disturbed the apparently calm surface of his life and caused him to fly into uncontrollable rages − his brother's mockery. Frederick made fun of him at the drop of a hat − because he was lazy, because he sponged off Rita, because he looked fat and drunk in a photo in *Figaro-Madame*, because he received phone calls from women over seventy and boys under seventeen, because he got mad at something Rita said and slit all her Nina Ricci bath towels down the middle with his straight razor. Frederick's mockery was cold and dispassionate, but Bayard perceived it as the hot, spitting venom of a censorious father-ogre. He would do almost anything never to experience it again.

Much less satisfied with his life was Frederick and Bayard's first cousin, Xavier Schomberg. By various twists and the fate of France in general and the Schombergs in particular, Xavier had come to be in charge of the steel mills in Colmar. He was a proud, aloof man who had never quite got over the fact that the family had no title and never would after squabbling with Napoleon III and thereby missing their last chance for aristocracy. None the less, Xavier was a serious businessman, and he identified completely with the mills whose founding had coincided with the beginning of the family's immense wealth.

Xavier was also Hubert Schomberg's man of confidence, and it was generally accepted that he was being groomed to take charge when Hubert retired. The old man had, at one time, put all his hopes in his elder son Bayard, but when it became obvious to everyone — and to the father most of all — that Bayard would never be anything but an indolent, possibly pathological playboy, Hubert tried to assuage his pain and disappointment by turning to another branch of the family. If Bayard had failed him so utterly, then so might his younger son, Frederick, then a shy and seemingly withdrawn teenager. He wanted different and fresher genes for the company.

His nepher, Xavier, had all the trappings of a successful business-man; his wife, the former Edith-Anne Grumman, was from a wealthy Alsatian family that had many useful connections in the world of business and finance. Xavier was hard-working, self-righteous and humourless, and if he had weaknesses or passions, no one ever learned of them, least of all Hubert. Xavier was the perfect second-in-command; he even had a certain charm based on a refusal to commit himself on any question whatsoever if it could be referred back to Hubert.

Because he had been hand-picked by his uncle to succeed him, Xavier's fall from grace was doubly painful and humiliating. A week after her husband's death, Rita called a general meeting of the stockholders. This was a legal necessity but for all practical purposes a waste of time, for Rita herself controlled the majority of shares in the company. In any case — and to everyone's amazement — she completely dominated the meeting, persuading two of the American second cousins, Thomas and Gustave Schomberg-Smith, to vote with her on every important issue. The main result of that meeting was that Frederick became titular head of the company. It was a daring coup d'état for Frederick was ten years younger than Xavier and, until then, the most important job he had ever held was that of computer repairman to an American TV network during a summer vacation from HEC. When that same 'boy' two years later announced his intention to liquidate the family holdings in steel, Xavier declared all-out war on his cousin.

The ensuing feud lasted for three years and ended by Xavier's seeing the mills closed and sold off, and himself relegated to a small subsidiary business turning out garden machinery in a village just at that point where the suburbs of Paris fade into the wet, green, seemingly endless fields of Normandy. Xavier could not have been farther from the world of high finance and big business had he been banished all the way to the island of Elba.

Neither he nor his tense, coldly attractive wife Edith-Anne ever forgave Frederick. They went to Rita to voice their complaints, but this was foolish in the extreme: they were attacking the person she loved most in the world. That confrontation only served to make Rita extremely suspicious of her nephew and his wife and ended by burying them deeper still in their mountain of garden tools.

Rita had many qualities, including good sense, astute economic judgement and great personal charm, all of which she had passed on to Frederick, for whom she was willing to do almost anything, including condoning a marriage of which she did not approve. For years the tiny, fierce Rita had been a moderating influence in all the family feuds and back-stabbings. Because she controlled so much stock, everyone listened when she spoke.

For the past year, however, Rita Schomberg had begun to get forgetful in peculiar ways. She went into her maid's bathroom for a shower instead of using her own; she tried to unlock the front door of her house with a nail file; she could no longer recall Edith-Anne's name (to which Bayard replied, 'It's her face I've been trying to forget').

One afternoon, when a limousine brought her home from a shopping expedition to the Faubourg Saint-Honoré, Rita gave the chauffeur a diamond and ruby bracelet worth over a million francs in lieu of a tip. That kindly man, who had been driving for her for ten years whenever her own chauffeur was off duty, returned the same evening with the bracelet. He explained to her son what had happened.

Bayard lost no time in calling Frederick.

'Mother's flipped, brother dear. We'll have to put her away. I think she's senile.'

'Don't talk like a fool, Bayard. Both of us are farther down the road to senility than Rita is or ever will be.'

'You just don't want to admit that our *chère maman* is getting on.'

'When I'm over there, all five feet two of Rita is getting on with what she has to, and you, dear brother, are trailing far behind. No doubt it's your taxing social schedule that slows you down so much?'

They were approaching dangerous ground, and already Bayard felt his blood pressure rising. He could not hold his tongue, however. For once, he even had an important point to make.

'But Frederick, she's been doing some very odd things around here lately. I'm almost afraid to go on living with her.'

'Then by all means move out!' came the instant reply. Without a word of farewell, Frederick slammed down the receiver, leaving Bayard fuming as usual.

Two weeks later, Frederick brought a balance sheet to Saint-Cloud for Rita's perusal and signature. She went over it carefully and then made several astute comments, surprising her son, as she often did, by her grasp of the complexities of the Schomberg business. When they finished, Rita invited Frederick to her private sitting room for Grand Marnier in front of the fire. She sat quietly for a while, and Frederick sensed there was something on her mind. He waited patiently, knowing that however difficult a subject it might be, she would broach it sooner or later. At last she straightened and turned to face him, a questioning look on her still-unlined face.

'Darling, is there any good news? From Christine ...?'

'Meaning?'

'Meaning I don't want to pry, but I'd be so happy to hear that we were to be blessed ... with a child.'

Frederick saw that her immense eyes were suspiciously bright, and he was surprised to find himself moved by her words.

'Take my word for it, Rita, we're giving it our very best efforts. Can you bear with us just a little longer?'

She did not take up his easy tone. 'Frederick, I may not have all the time in the world. I wouldn't want anything to happen to me without first knowing that the family succession had been assured.'

'You make us sound like the British royal family! First, nothing is going to happen to you, because I won't permit it. I need somebody to find those omissions and errors on the balance sheets.'

'Please, darling, don't keep moving away from the subject.'

'I'm not. I'm getting to it in my own clumsy way. Christine and I

36

have had a few − let's say − manufacturing snags, but those are being straightened out now. I think I can safely promise you that our production line will be moving along before the end of the year, maybe even sooner?'

'Does that mean Christine's seeing a specialist?'

'*We're* seeing one together. A top man in his field.'

'Just tell me in plain words, darling. Is there going to be a baby?'

'Yes, delivered with full guarantee, too. Is that plain enough for you?'

'It is. If you tell me it's going to happen, then I know I don't have to worry any more.'

All hint of tears had vanished now. Rita gave her son a beautiful smile that lit up her tiny face and made her look, for an instant, like a fresh young schoolgirl. As she leaned forwards to kiss him on both cheeks, she put all of her immense love and devotion into the embrace. Then she excused herself, went into the adjoining bedroom and shaved off a sizable patch of her lovely, still blond, curly hair.

Doctors were called in, nurses hired and Bayard had the unique satisfaction of telling his brother, 'I told you so.' Even though her doctors did not immediately come up with a label for her illness, Frederick could no longer pretend that his mother was in perfect health.

Thus, some one hundred and forty years after its success story began, the great Schomberg family was reduced to wars, deaths, mergers and a general weakening of the bloodline, to one increasingly bewildered matriarch, several distant cousins more American than French, and three heirs in Europe: Frederick, and his beautiful but wilful descendant of Louis XV; Bayard, the effete dandy who would never marry, never procreate; and Xavier, the cousin who began to make every visible effort to bury old quarrels and regain lost prestige before Rita died.

Xavier and Edith-Anne Schomberg had one supreme advantage over their cousins: they were the parents of two strapping boys. Schomberg heirs.

She waits. Only four-thousandths of an inch across, she is nevertheless monstrous in comparison to her suitors, 80,000 times bigger than the weakest of the million who covet her. Moving not at all, she does nothing to attract her sperm-lovers, yet they scramble towards her as if she were Salome removing the veil in some incredibly erotic dance.

The infinitesimal creatures swimming towards her are engaged in a mortal race. Like water snakes in a primal sea, they cut through the milky solution, whipping their tails from side to side to project themselves forwards. Already, some of them have reached her. They form a melee, fighting like wild dogs for a place as close as possible to her seemingly adamantine wall. One of these frenzied creatures finds a tiny niche and wriggles his head once, a second time, a third. Desperate, he tries again. Suddenly, against all hope, a gap opens. Without a second's hesitation, he bores inward to enter an unknown place from which he will never exit.

Then, as in a tale of magic, the newly forged fairy circle closes, and the thwarted suitors are left without. To wither and die.

The conqueror's moment of triumph is short-lived. He is locked inside the gigantic ovum now. Once all escape routes are blocked, the matriarch starts to devour her captive with total impunity. Already she has consumed his tail and midsection. With more than half his body gone, he makes a last-ditch attempt to save himself, ballooning up inside her until she herself is invaded and put in danger. She can no longer reject him: he is the male pronucleus.

After winning his beloved against such overwhelming odds, the sperm had come close to being cannibalised. Instead, he has forced the ovum to recognise him, and now the two of them assume a common identity. They are the zygote.

Struggles continue. The cell splits and then splits again. The thing that results is ignominiously forced into a syringe, and from this launching pad is shot out into the dark universe. Like a space ship lost in a far galaxy, it spins round and round, searching for a haven or port of call in a hostile world. The skies themselves grow angry and contract, trying to eject the lonely traveller who had dared penetrate them with such brazen and foolish audacity.

Time passes — eternity, perhaps, for this infinitely small and lost bit of matter. At some moment in this interminability, rootlike hairs form on the walls. With these it is able to implant itself in the very flesh of the host. It clings there, precariously at first, then with greater assurance, for the haven it has found suddenly seems secure and inviolable.

The suitor and his beloved are joined now for better and worse. They throw into their common pot all the ingredients they possess, minute matter that will determine their whole future. They become an entity, an embryo, a creature that is still so pitifully weak that it can do only thing really well, and that is to grow.

Chapter Seven

Mica stood in the doorway holding a package wrapped in silver paper, red streamers cascading from a big bow on the top. A look of complete surprise covered her face.

'*This* is a hospital room in your country?' She started hesitantly towards Cecil, her eyes darting from one side of the huge room to the other as though anticipating an ambush.

Cecil laughed. 'No, it's not a usual room, if that's what you were asking me. They just moved me in here – a promotion of sorts. Oh, Mica, this smells good! Thank you so much.'

She kissed her friend and started to tear off the streams of ribbon and the pretty silver paper.

'A lot of mixed herbs! Just what was needed to bring a little life into this sterile place. I think it should go on the window ledge, don't you? Right in the sun?' Noticing Mica's silence, she turned back and threw her arms out to embrace the whole room. 'Well, what do you think? You're in the best suite in the Medical Center. The *Presidential* Suite, or at least that's what the nurses call it. Only right now, it's been assigned to your roommate!'

Mica shook her head incredulously. 'Be thankful you're here and not in some of the places I've been sick in. They must think a lot of you to spend this kind of money.'

Cecil pinched off a sprig of mint and started to chew on one of the leaves. 'Me!' she exclaimed with disdain. 'They don't give a damn about me personally, but they want *it* to take. That's why I have to have soft music, soft food, lots of light, fresh air, calm. What you see here is really just a glorified breeding stable.'

Mica went on shaking her head. She, who was strength personified, seemed for once to have lost her aplomb. 'We don't have these problems where I come from. At home, a woman sleeps once with a man, *y por supuesto*, she's right away embarrassed.'

39

Cecil smiled. 'What is there to be embarrassed about?'

'*Embarasada*. Pregnant. The first or second time they do it. After that, they have to get married, and then they have six, seven kids, maybe even more until the husband runs away and starts over again with somebody else. The women in my country, they're not waiting in hospitals, they are all in church lighting candles and praying *Dios* not to send more babies.'

'Well, I must have some Latin blood because it seems the first try worked for me, too. Everyone here is very excited about it.'

'You mean . . . ?'

'Yes, I'm nearly a month pregnant. They're absolutely sure now. Dr Sweeney's as puffed up as a balloon fish. He told everybody he'd do it in six weeks, and nobody believed him, but he had a magnificent panoply of new techniques to try out, and I was the guinea pig.'

'What's so great? You see on TV every week somebody having a baby for somebody else.'

'There have been thousands of IVF births and plenty of surrogate mothers, but nobody's actually done what Sweeney's trying on me. There's a terrific race on.'

'I don't understand all those technical terms.'

'It's easy when you hear them from morning to night like I do. IVF is *in vitro* fertilisation, which means they start the baby in a lab using the mother's own egg and the father's sperm. When and if they get an embryo, they put it back inside the mother. Then, if it takes, she has a more or less routine pregnancy afterwards. A surrogate, up until now, up until me, actually, has been a woman hired by a couple to be inseminated artificially by the husband. The baby she carries for them is hers, too, but Super Sweeney says I may be the first woman in the world to give birth to a child to whom she isn't biologically related. There are some other similar *in vitros* scheduled for next spring, but Sweeney's hoping we'll beat them to it. And that, Mica darling, is why I'm at the centre of so much attention here.'

'You're pretty casual about all this.'

'I'm told you can get used to anything.' Cecil's voice took on a sombre note, and Mica was instantly sorry she had let the criticism slip out. More than anything in the world, she wanted to see her friend as light-hearted as she had been only a moment ago. Cecil Gutman was the centre of Micaela Quesad Martinez's life.

Having arrived in the United States almost five years ago, on foot, no amount of coaxing, even from Cecil, had ever persuaded Mica to talk about the unidentified Central American country from which she had fled.

'If nobody knows where I come from, how can they send me back?'

was Mica's patent reply to each fresh bout of questioning about her homeland.

At first glance, the life she made for herself in the United States was austere: because she was an illegal alien, she had no status in her adopted country. Furthermore, she had neither friends nor family nor lover, and very few material possessions. Mica, though, loved her house and her little car and her job as a shampoo girl in a Cedar Springs hair salon. She loved the food she bought at the supermarket and the clothes she made for herself. She was thrilled to have a television set with so many channels. She was amazed to see people walk past armed policemen in the street without flinching. Mica thought her life was perfect. She had not even known she was lonely until the afternoon she caught a glimpse of Cecil Gutman sitting on a park bench. Never had Mica seen anyone at once so lovely and so desolate-looking as this tall, red-haired, pale-skinned girl. Without a moment's hesitation, Mica had taken Cecil back to her little house in Oak Cliff and started to take care of her. She had been there ever since. Cecil was Mica's only friend, her only emotional link to her new country.

'How long they keeping you here?' she asked Cecil, letting her gaze travel across the luxuriously appointed room to the window. On the roof of the next building, something huge and grey hovered like a menacing bird ready to crash through the glass and into the room where they were.

Seeing Mica's startled look, Cecil said, 'It's just a helicopter. The things land and take off all day. A nurse told me that that building belongs to one of the Hunts. Thank God the thick glass keeps out the noise.'

'How long they keeping you here?' Mica repeated harshly.

'Can you believe it? The sadist of a doctor wants me in here for another two months. Now that things are going so well for him, he's not taking any chances on a miscarriage. It seems these kinds of babies have a tendency to slip out at the beginning, so Sweeney says I'm to be a great sloth and just lie here until the danger's past. Then and only then will the Great Man let me get on a plane.'

'You going to have the baby here or over there?'

Cecil had asked that very question of Dr Sweeney the week before, and he had come up with one of his usual bantering replies. 'Our French friends were surprised when they heard you wanted to spend time in their lovely country. After I broke them in to the idea, though, they rather liked it. If there aren't any complications – and with me around, there cannot be, of course – we'll go ahead and schedule our show for the American Hospital in Paris. It's tops in France, and our friends over there like it. Also, since I went to school with the head of obstetrics, there won't be any problem about me "unofficially" supervising the delivery. Well, what do you say to more fun-time in Paris?'

'Actually, I'd like to be as far away from here as possible when it ... it ... happens.'

'Keep it like a dream, huh?'

Cecil looked at him in surprise.

'How did you know?'

He shrugged. 'I spend a lot of time with women, listening to them express their hopes and fears, things they don't dare tell anyone else. You may think me superficial and callous, but I *do* know women. I even emphathise with you lovely creatures.'

Too much so, Cecil though at the time. And you know too much about Cecil Gutman, too.

'Well, where?' Mica's voice broke into her reverie. 'I got to repeat everything twice today?'

'They've made arrangements for me to deliver in Paris.' Seeing her friend's crestfallen look, Cecil seized her hand and pulled her close. They stood for a moment like that. Mica seemed hardly to breathe. Then Cecil pulled away and guided her through the door into the adjoining room. 'Take a look at this, Mica – my very own salon complete with stereo, TV, VCR. All I have to do is pick up the phone and an hour later, a messenger walks in with whatever cassette or book or record I ordered.'

'Yeah, this is pretty nice,' Mica said. 'A lot better than my house, I guess.'

'Oh, come on, Mica, that doesn't sound like you at all. You know perfectly well that if you got tired of washing rich people's heads, you could always start decorating their houses. You can turn a perfectly ordinary room into a movie set with stuff you pick up at garage sales.'

'I don't want to talk about me,' Mica said, trying to suppress a smile of pleasure. 'Tell me how it feels to be pregnant. You like it?'

'I refuse to think about it,' Cecil said harshly. 'This is not my baby, and I don't want any more to do with it than I can help. In any case, I've got two months to go before I can leave for France, and I've decided to follow the doctor's orders and do nothing. Think of nothing.'

'Have you told *him* you're coming?'

'Him?' Cecil pretended not to understand.

'In Bordeaux.'

'Oh. I haven't, actually. If I write, his mother will get hold of the letter and tear it up. That's what she did once before, you know.

When I get to France, I'll probably go straight to Bordeaux and . . . and . . . just walk in on him, I guess.'

'What if he's not so glad to see you? You gonna crack up again?'

Cecil laughed. It was shaky, but it was a real laugh none the less.

'I can't. I've got a job to do, don't I? In a strange way, I think all of this is good for me. The attention, I mean. The people here, apart from the doctor, are very considerate. You should see the look on some of their faces when they come in and see this suite. They take me for an oil heiress.'

'Who's paying for it?'

'That's what's so funny. I don't even know. Sandlin's always popping in and out with things for me to sign, but he won't answer my questions. He's as close-mouthed as you are. He says the family prefers to remain anonymous and that even when I get to Paris, I probably won't have any direct contact with them. Sweeney will be there, of course. He's set everything up for the first week in June.'

'You sure talk about the doctor a lot. You in love with him or something?'

'Oh, I wish he were here to hear that! It would add more fuel to his already powerful ego, and he'd simply adore you for asking the question.'

'So just you and the doctor will be there?'

'I wish you could come.'

'Me, too, I wish.'

'Listen, I have an idea. Since they're giving me all that money, why don't I send you a ticket once I'm over there?'

'*Querida*, I have no papers, no passport. I cannot go anywhere. Already, it is a miracle I got this far. And that I stay.'

'Oh, Mica, I'm sorry. I wasn't thinking. It's just that I'll be so lonely in Paris . . .'

'Maybe not. Maybe you'll be with *him*.'

'Do you think so? I keep rehearsing our meeting, but when I come to the part where I have to explain that I'm pregnant . . . and under what circumstances . . .'

'If you need me then, remember, I cannot come,' Mica said in a sombre voice. 'No matter what happens!'

A look of fierce grief appeared on her round face.

'Let's don't talk about it any more. Look! I want to show you something.'

Cecil pulled a hundred-dollar bill out of the pocket of a brand-new velvet robe which Denise O'Neil had delivered to her that morning, along with half a dozen nightdresses. 'They thought I needed some spending money to keep me from getting bored and disturbing the child's emotional balance.'

'Spending on what? What do you need?'

'I don't *need* anything. I just thought it might be fun to splurge for once in my life.'

'You like money now? You never cared before.'

'Mica, for once stop being so serious! There's a perfume store in the lobby. You and I going down to buy a bottle of our favourite perfumes. We're going to blow this hundred dollars right now.'

Her large violet eyes were flashing, luminously alive. Mica had never seen Cecil look so beautiful as she did now with her long red hair falling over the deep plush of the blue robe.

She's happy. That is what I wanted, isn't it? 'OK,' she said aloud. 'Let's go then. Do we get a big bottle for fifty dollars?

'Probably not,' Cecil sighed. 'But it will be fun, all the same.'

Chapter Eight

'I don't want to overwhelm you with a lot of complex medical terms.'

'Don't. Just tell me.'

'She's passed the critical stages. You can plan to break open the champagne for June the first or thereabouts.'

'Oh, Sam! That's the most wonderful gift I ever received.'

'Good. Let's go back to my hotel so you can fully express your appreciation.'

'Oh, shut up! Can't you see this is a special moment?'

To his amazement, she began to cry.

It was one of the last fine days of the year, and Dr Samuel Sweeney and Christine Schomberg were sitting outside on the terrace of one of the nicest restaurants in the Bois de Boulogne, drinking Pernods. Christine had just taken Sam for a rambling visit to the woods to see the 'Brazilians', the long-legged, scantily dressed transvestites who had abandoned the beaches of Copacabana and Ipanema for the alleys of this immense park, a territory bigger than all of Monaco. Because of the beautiful weather, the Brazilians were out in full force, leaning suggestively against trees or the backs of camping cars with conveniently curtained windows. Sam had gaped and panted, pretending to be overcome with lust, and Christine had egged him on with her taunts. It had been a happy time, and now here she was, her head down on the table and her body shaking with sobs.

'For God's sake, Christine, you know you should never pay attention to what a man says. Just watch what he does. One act is worth a thousand words, as some hack or another said so rightly.'

'So?' She asked between sobs. 'What are you trying to tell me?'

'I'm reminding you − ever so gently and only because you seem to have forgotten − that I did this for you because I care for you a great deal.'

'I know. And you should remember something, too. When women cry, it's not always because they're sad.'

'Then, contrary to all appearances, this is a joyful moment?'

'Very joyful. One of the happiest moments of my entire life.'

'I'll drink to that. *Garçon, encore deux pastis, s'il vous plaît*!'

'We should be doing this in Saint-Tropez,' Christine said, raising her tear-streaked face. 'No one drinks Pernod in Paris.'

'We'll drink it in Saint-Tropez, too. We'll have plenty of other things to celebrate together.'

Christine produced one last sobbing hiccup, blew her nose with Sam's handkerchief and attacked the Pernod with gusto. 'You're right. Maybe you'll give me another baby next year.'

'So now you want two, do you? I suppose you plan on keeping that poor girl working for you year in and year out?'

'Why not? If we pay her enough?'

'I'm sorry to say I think this is a one-shot affair. In any case, you mustn't tempt the anger of the gods. You don't want them pursuing you through the sky with fiery bolts, do you?'

Her eyelashes were still thick with the recent tears, but she managed a wan smile. 'I can't really answer that. Not until I hold her in my arms.'

'*Her*? I thought it was a Schomberg you wanted.'

'I want a *baby*, Sam. Neither the surname nor the sex matters to me. I know I'm wild and a little crazy, but I do love children. Right now, I'm as happy as though you'd just announced I was pregnant myself. *Please*. Tell me all about it.'

'Well, there's this embryo who cost one hell of a lot of money and who will cost a lot more before it turns into a baby and goes to nest in your chalet or castle or mansion or wherever you Schombergs spend your time. I did a sonogram last week, and guess what?'

'There's nothing wrong, is there?' Christine looked totally stricken, and Sam regretted his little joke.

'Not really. It's just that he or she's got a silver spoon in his or her mouth. First thing I noticed, as a matter of fact.'

'Oh, and I thought you Americans believed we are all created equal.'

'Rot!'

'Why so vehement, darling?'

'Because this child of yours is about as far as one can get from the concept of equality. Any fertilisation is, but yours is worse than most. If you consider a sperm potentially as one-half of a human being, then every time you make a try at conception − or just make love without trying at all − there are 250 million bits of life left to dehydrate on the sheets. Do you know what right-to-lifers are?'

'Something very American, I'm sure.'

'They're anti-abortionists, people who march in the streets in favour of embryos, 25 per cent of which would abort spontaneously anyway, not to mention all those that perish at birth or immediately afterwards.'

'We have these people over here, too. So what? Are you trying to convince me that nature is wasteful? That she's the sort who buys two dozen scarves at Hermès and leaves food on her plate at Maxim's?'

'Always the little snob, aren't you? No, I see nature more like a car factory with a broken assembly line, turning out billions of products that nobody wants.'

'And yet you, of all people, fight for the sanctity of human life.'

'Me? You've never understood me, sweetheart. All these cultural barriers keep us from communicating except between the satin sheets. That's why we're so compatible. In my opinion, a fetus that doesn't make it just sinks back into some great secretarial pool of life and waits to be called back into service at a more propitious moment.'

'Tell me then, why do you do it? For the money? To get that Kennedy-looking Irish face into the newspapers? Or is it because you want power over all of us desperate women? Tell me.'

Sam leaned back in his chair and smiled at her, teasing her with his silence. The afternoon sun had formed a glorious halo around her thick auburn hair, and her eyes shone like brilliantly cut but angry stones.

'You don't know yourself? Am I right?' Christine asked after a minute. She was annoyed. Sam reached for her hand, and when he touched it, he felt a faint shock. He could have sworn that a spark flew up into the air just above their joined hands.

'Did you see that?'

'What?' She was still pretending to be angry with him.

'That flash of electricity. That's what I do — ignite the spark that brings a particular individual into being. And every time I do it, it inspires in me both awe and wonderment.'

'There you go being cynical again. Making fun of me.'

'I am not. I'm telling you the truth. For once.'

Christine studied his Irish-handsome face to see what she could read in it. 'That's very grandiose, but I feel it as well, Sam, that what is happening is awe-inspiring.' She looked off towards the distant trees, and her strong features seemed to grow harder as though she was casting off a façade of superficiality that was necessary for her everyday life.

'I can never thank you enough for what you're doing for me, Sam, what you're giving me. Don't laugh at me because I want to say this. You *are* a god-figure to me. You have both magical knowledge and

47

the ability to use it. But you don't understand us over here; you don't know what it's like to live in a certain stratum of stociety where people are too idle and too rich. I'd feel much more secure if it were I carrying my baby instead of this girl you've conjured up in Texas.'

'Why, for Christ's sake?' It was Sam's turn to be astonished. 'I okayed the girl. She'll do a good job for us. Anyway, what choice did you have?'

'None,' Christine replied grily. 'Sam, listen, I've never talked about this before, but ... this ... family, the Schombergs. I don't know how to make you understand the kind of people they are. You can't even imagine, coming from a different place, your cowboy country ...'

'Cowboys have been known to go berserk and shoot a dozen people before breakfast,' Sam said dryly. 'What's going through that beautiful red head of yours, anyway? You're just playing at being the anxious mother-to-be, imagining some terrifying and totally improbably destiny for your baby.'

'Stop being so condescending!' Christine snapped. 'Oh, Sam, I'm sorry, but I can't control this fear. I feel — all the time — that something could happen.'

'Happen to whom?'

'To me. To you. To this girl, Cecil Gutman. Or worse ...' This time, her voice faltered altogether. 'To ... my ... child.'

Christine Schomberg, the most fun-loving rich girl in Europe, was not laughing now.

No longer a thing but not yet a fetus, the embryo is floating in its dark, sealed pouch. With a snout as wide as a piglet's and hairless skin a shiny porcine pink, it is anything but human.

From the lumpy head, ears as big as dust specks start to form. Inside its mouth, a tonguelet sprouts.

Little buds like thickening tumours appear on its nearly formless stalk. Feeding voraciously on their host, they will grow to be arms, legs, a thyroid, a liver, a pair of lungs. For the moment, though, they are nothing at all.

Between the budding legs, a ridge has formed. There are no sensations of pleasure there, no sensations of any kind. The embryo cannot feel; it reacts to nothing within or without its body.

The head is moving aimlessly now. It almost touches a bent, reptilian tail.

No bigger than a pinpoint, the heart beats.

As tiny and mindless as the embryo of a boar or a cat or a mouse, the thing floats and grows. And grows.

Chapter Nine

As different as they seemed, Frederick and Bayard Schomberg were really two sides of the same coin. Both were enterprising, extremely intelligent and successful in whatever they undertook. Frederick channelled his energies into bringing the family business back from near ruin to the ranks of top international conglomerates where it belonged, and Bayard devoted himself to the seeking of intense and often perverse pleasures. Neither of the brothers could tolerate frustration.

Because his father had never shown the slightest interest in him, Frederick had learned early in life to repress whatever personal desires and frustrations he experienced, along with a possibly darker side of his personality. For this reason, he retained that air of boyish innocence which had so charmed Christine de la Rouvay the day she met him. With Christine, Frederick let down his guard as far as he was capable; he revealed to her some of his hidden needs, and she, in turn, soothed and comforted him. Christine, too, received a great deal from their relationship, much, that is, beyond the financial security and social standing which came automatically with the marriage. Christine knew she was and would be the only important woman in Frederick's life, and this feeling of uniqueness, of having been chosen from among many contenders, gave her great personal satisfaction. It made her feel what her family had always told her she should be — a queen.

The trouble came because Frederick was rarely there. He spent his days in factories and company boardrooms, and his nights in limousines, the cabins of aeroplanes and hotel suites. The amazing thing to Christine was that her husband, who was a genius at organising an empire of over one hundred and twenty different companies, was not able better to manage his personal life. She thought it easy to move through different worlds, to juggle husband, lovers and career.

Christine had received the Luneville glass factory as a wedding present from Frederick. Her first initiative after she took over the business was to hire a commercial director, a tense young man whom she sent abroad to prospect new markets. When he returned from New York with a briefcase full of orders, Christine enlarged and modernised the plant and took on nearly a hundred new workers. Maintaining Cyril's traditional line of *pâté de verre* lamps and vases, she also introduced sculptures, perfume bottles for the *haute couture* houses and modern glass fixtures for bathrooms, kitchens, patios and executive suites. During the second year of her reign in Luneville, the Christine Schomberg Collection was launched internationally with a massive publicity campaign. In the course of the third year, the glassworks turned a profit for the first time in its history. By the fourth, Christine had started to accumulate independent wealth. Now she spent no more than two days a week in eastern France; the rest of the time, she worked in Paris on design and marketing problems. She also kept up a busy social life, gave her husband, with whom she was still in love, as much of her time as he desired, and amused herself with lovers of varying nationalities.

Even though they came from amazingly different backgrounds, all the men in Christine's life were endowed with those same qualities that had originally attracted her to Frederick Schomberg − juvenile, almost naive charm which camouflaged a diamond hardness at their core and ruthless obsession with their own profession and interests. With Christine, these basically cold men awoke to hitherto unknown and singular passions. They always fell in love. She never did. Christine had a happy marriage, the kind that had worked well in France for centuries. She enjoyed her career and her social position and saw nothing immoral or hypocritical in being unfaithful to her husband as long as she made him a good wife. The only thing missing in Christine Schomberg's life was a child.

In her quest to conceive, Christine had gone from expensive private specialists to the great, shabby public hospitals of Paris and, finally, to a series of last-chance clinics in Switzerland. It was in one of these that she first heard Samuel Sweeney's name.

'You know, JR, one of those terrible Texans crazy with wine, women and gambling. Too risqué for us, *chérie*, but *so* charming. You could never trust yourself alone with him. Still, if you really want to have a child, then he's the one you have to see.'

Christine told Frederick all this in a considerably more diplomatic way. First of all, his male ego was already badly bruised by what he considered to be a serious lack in himself, and, second, he could very well have lived without a child. He wanted to please his wife and mother, though, so eventually he agreed not only to finance the very complicated procedure outlined by Christine but also stoically to submit his own body to the many physical indignities involved.

Bayard, who made a habit of listening behind closed doors, heard these plans and was secretly gleeful. So brother dear was practically impotent, and his wife shoddy goods as well. Probably the bitch had had one abortion too many, and now she was paying the price. The next day, Bayard went to a public library and read up on IVF. He concluded that Frederick and Christine — in view of their physical problems — had no chance of success. And if their scheme did not work, as he was now sure that it would not, then Rita would make Frederick get rid of that little Catholic upstart. In the meantime, and as an extra precaution, he himself would take a hand in their affairs. He parted with some of his own cash and hired a private detective to follow Christine.

A month later, Bayard was at once thrilled and nauseated by what he had learned. The slut certainly didn't waste her time. In addition to all the painters, writers and musicians she had stashed away in various European capitals, Christine turned up at charity balls, private poker games and scrubby Arab bars with her own fertility specialist. She made no effort to hide the nature of their relationship, either. It was outrageous! Christine was a she-devil, a woman on winged feet who rushed into places where even he might fear to tread. What was the point in worrying, though, or bothering poor, sick little Rita with such stories? Soon enough he would have the bitch turned out of her house and into the streets where she belonged.

Bayard had a fantasy that occupied an increasingly great place in his mind. If anything happened to Frederick (he usually skipped over this beginning part because it was so unlikely that anything *could* happen to his healthy young brother), then he, the surviving heir, would take over the Schomberg affairs. Now, as he sipped a cocktail in the bar of a great Parisian hotel on the Avenue George V, Bayard suddenly *saw* Rita give him power of attorney for all her stock; he *saw* Rita and himself putting his fool of a cousin Xavier to work running the company for *him*. However badly Xavier managed the company, there would be enough money to keep Bayard in champagne, race horses, and locks and keys for the rest of his days. He could take little Rita on long, luxurious cruises while she was still able to travel. He would have all her attention, because the son she loved more than the elder, rightful one would be gone, gone off the face of the earth in a . . .

Here Bayard began to tremble. He spilled nearly half his cocktail down the front of his yellow silk shirt. He had already forgotten exactly how and why Frederick was gone. No matter. It was done, wasn't it? He, Bayard, was master of the family and keeper of Rita's fate. He was a multi-millionaire with no one to tell him how or how not to squander the Schomberg money.

He signalled the waiter to bring him a fresh drink and waved at several acquaintances across the room just to show how happy he was, to prove that he was a man *sans ennuis.*

His pleasant fantasy would be harder to turn into reality, of course, if the little red-headed fortune-hunter somehow produced a child. But she never would. Of this, Bayard was certain. She and her fool of a Texan doctor would never pull it off, and if by some incredible miracle they did, then he, Bayard Schomberg, one of the most influential and clever men in the world, would see that the monstrous thing never saw the light of day. He could do that. It was easy. An embryo, a fetus, what chance did it have against a grown man? A strong, brilliant, inventive man, the toast of Paris and Deauville?

Bayard thought about this for some time and then began to laugh. Tears rolled down his cheeks. He held his sides from the sheer joy of it all. It was too delightful for words.

Getting up from his table, still clutching his sides, he went out into the brilliantly lit hall to find a telephone. He could and would take one tiny step towards the realisation of his dream.

Bayard asked for the number of the garden-tools factory in Normandy, the place to which his cousin had been unjustly exiled by his brother.

'Xavier? This is Bayard. I was wondering, could you possibly come into town on Friday?'

'Whatever for? I'm up to my ears in spring orders here. Is Rita worse?'

'No, the little pet is holding up bravely. She's her usual sweet self, no cause for concern there. Actually, I'm calling because I wanted to invite you to lunch. At the Boeuf sur le Toit.'

'Save your francs, Bayard. I won't come up with a loan no matter what story you invent this time.'

'Cousin dear, you do pain me with your eternally suspicious mind. I won't be needing any more loans. Ever. I have something to discuss with you, but I don't want you to breathe a word of it to Edith-Anne.'

'Suppose you start by telling me what it is?'

'I'll explain the whole thing to you on Thursday. Shall we say one o'clock? I have a business proposition to make to you, *mon cher,* one that I think you'll find too good to refuse. For the moment, though, it must stay strictly between the two of us.'

'All right,' Xavier replied glumly. 'Thursday at one. But if this turns out to be another loan scam, Bayard, I guarantee you you won't get any dessert.'

'Why ever not?'

'Because I'll have wrung your fat neck long before we get to the last course.'

For some time, it has been an inchoate thing, almost teratical in appearance. Its face is still anamorphous, with eyes that, if they could only see, would stare out from either side of its overlarge head. Two unjoined nostrils flat on a snout. Unfunctional, buttonlike ears lie low on its neck while an outsized heart is − almost literally − in its mouth. Fine, eerily translucent skin covers its body.

Suddenly, dramatic things happen. The eyes move forward to take up a permanent position on either side of the nose. On the stubby arms, ten infinitesimal bumps flare up, proemial fingers. The cloaco loses its birdlike form. The yolk sac, until then the source of the embryo's nourishment, shrinks and hangs uselessly under the amnion.

Growth become prodigious: from head to rump, the embryo already measures over a centimetre! Its appearance has gone from fish to monkey. Its gills have almost closed, but the upper jaw protrudes grotesquely. Its mouth is a slit. With its simian face and lumpy body, this might be a tiny ape. There is no way to tell.

Only one thing differentiates the embryo now from those of other primates, and that is potentiality. This still negligible bit of matter has the potential to become a human being.

Chapter Ten

The flight got into Charles de Gaulle very early in the morning. Half-asleep, Cecil went through passport control and then stepped on to what looked like a moving bridge encased in a tube of clear plastic. She was carried noiselessly across an enormous, glassed-in hall criss-crossed in every direction by other bridges carrying other weary passengers.

Laboratory mice, Cecil thought. We're only mice engaged in some useless experiment, one group travelling upwards all day and the other downwards so some dry scientist can cut us open.

Cecil started running on the rubber mat then, desperate to get out. She emerged at ground level in another hall filled with Africans in brightly printed robes and headscarves; convoys of Japanese bus-inessmen; ascetic-looking Hindu families; French women snuggled into pre-Christmas furs; English girls in rag-chic; all of them with the vaguely confused expressions of people who have landed on an unknown planet and are worrying about the oxygen level outside the building.

Cecil collected her luggage, which was one medium-sized canvas bag. Neither the suitcase nor Cecil stirred the slightest interest in the Antillais customs official leaning sleepily across his counter. Outside the gate, she found herself face to face with a tall, very alert young man in a neat navy-blue uniform and a visored cap.

'Mademoiselle Gutman?'

'Yes?'

'I'm René. Let me take your bag. I'm to drive you to your hotel.'

'Oh, I didn't expect ... No one said anything.'

Cecil felt almost like an actress arriving in Paris for a film premiere. Imagine being met by a chauffeur! It was silly to be impressed, but she could not quite suppress a feeling of elation.

'Things are often done at the last minute around here,' René replied, offering a friendly, open smile. Already he was guiding her towards the lifts. 'You'll get used to it.'

The metal doors opened directly on to a dimly lit parking area. René walked slightly ahead of her, carrying the canvas bag and leading the way. There was a gassy, asphyxiating odour that was making her dizzy. She took half a dozen more steps and then stopped to lean against a cement pillar.

'Is something wrong, Mademoiselle?'

'I'll be fine in just a second. It must be jet lag. The flight from Dallas was quite long. Really, I feel all right.'

She did, normally. Dr Sweeney's staff had expressed boundless admiration for the way she was carrying this baby. Even Jeff Sandlin was trying to take some of the credit, congratulating himself (when nobody else did) for having chosen her from among so many other candidates.

'Don't fret, honey, you're bouncin' round just the way Dr Sam likes to see 'em,' Sweeney's chief nurse Estelle told her during her second month of pregnancy when Cecil was frantic to get out of the hospital. 'You'll be playin' football before long. Just wait it out. You'll see.'

Cecil had not even had morning sickness, except for a few queasy sensations which were easily set to rest with a cup of tea and crackers. Better still, her feelings of anguish, the storms of bitter unhappiness and despair, all disappeared as if by magic, leaving her optimistic and full of energy. Her good health, of course, made it even harder for her to stay in the hospital. She passed the days reading, watching movies, taking sun baths downstairs in the garden, chatting to Mica and the nurses, even starting the research for her doctoral thesis.

'It happens all the time,' Sam told her cheerfully. 'A patient comes to me suffering from severe depression, and then, once she's pregnant, she feels great. I know, I know, I see your feminist hackles rising, so let me set you straight right away – it's mostly physical. Hormones that have been out of whack for years suddenly begin running smoothly again, and the woman receives a strong, totally unexpected whiff of euphoria.'

Cecil had to admit that she had not felt better since before her grandmother died. Certainly not since the day Serge had told her he was returning to Bordeaux because his mother was threatening suicide if he brought home an unknown American bride. Leaving that very afternoon, he assured her he would be back, he'd write, he'd send for her, he'd keep in touch, he'd call ... All that shit.

Even though Sam had put her on a strict diet, she and Mica had sneaked down to the hospital drugstore nearly every evening and bought boxes of English chocolates, which they consumed while watching video cassettes in her lounge. Amazingly, she had not gained much weight − five or six pounds. Mica had put on eight. Cecil had been so thin that this extra weight did nothing more than fill out her face and figure, making her look healthier and prettier. No one could see that she was pregnant. All the way across the Atlantic, a Yalie had valiantly tried to convince her that the most exciting way to see Paris was from the window of his hotel room. Or at least from the bed next to that window.

Maybe I should make a career of this, Cecil thought with irony. A baby a year, all expenses paid and thirty thousand on top. It beats teaching.

René was holding open the door of a black Mercedes limousine, and Cecil settled into the soft leather of the back seat with a sigh of relief. She must have slept for a while, for the next thing she knew, they were on the *autoroute* and already she could see the first bleak blocks of flats outlined against a grimy December sky.

As they moved into the heart of Paris, nothing Cecil saw changed that first impression of moroseness and grisaille: the City of Light was considerably dimmer than it had been in her dreams. She knew, of course, that she had so glorified Paris that it could never measure up to her expectations. She had endowed every pavement café and every flowering chestnut tree with the incandescence of her love for Serge. Now, when she saw the wrought-iron chairs and tables of the cafés stacked to one side for the winter and the trees pruned and painfully bare, they seemed almost perfect symbols for her wasted love.

Even when René, trying to please her, made a detour to show her the Arch of Triumph with the Concorde obelisk faintly visible at the far end of the magisterial Champs-Elysées, Cecil felt not a flight of excitement but only a sense of *déjà vu*, as though these mythical landmarks were only sets from a Hollywood musical or slick photos in a travel magazine. Chains of holiday lights were strung across the Avenue George V in front of her hotel. Glowing softly through the sleety morning greyness, they too only served to remind her that − barring a miracle − she would be spending Christmas in Paris alone.

After saying goodbye to René, who declined a tip and politely refused to identify his employers, Cecil checked into the hotel and was shown upstairs to a large and beautifully appointed room. She had two things to do in Paris, and as she unpacked, she tried to decide which to do first. Fatigue won over either. She stretched out on the bed and let herself drift into deep, uneasy sleep.

She awoke with the distinct impression that someone was in the room, although what that room was or where it was located, she had not the faintest idea. It had grown dark, and she could just make out a vague shape moving stealthily towards her.

'Who's there?' she asked sharply, sitting up and swinging her legs over the side of the bed, ready to run.

'Oh! I'm sorry, Mademoiselle. I thought the room was empty. I came in to turn back the bed.'

Cecil shook her head, trying to wake herself. 'Why — why is it so dark in here?'

'It's these winter days, Mademoiselle. And the sleet. It seems as though we haven't seen the sun here in months.'

'What time is it?'

'It's five o'clock, Mademoiselle. Shall I come back later?'

'Five o'clock! Then I've been asleep for nearly seven hours.'

'Can I get you something?'

'No, that's all right.'

The shadowy figure slipped out through the entrance hall, and it was only after she was gone that Cecil realised they had been speaking all that time in the dark. She had never seen the woman's face. Had she been the maid at all or perhaps a sneak thief, a *rat d'hotel*? Cecil remembered now how quietly she had been moving towards her when she first awoke, and that her voice had been soft and educated, not a maid's voice at all. Cecil shrugged off the feeling that something out of the ordinary had happened. She was in a foreign country and could not be expected to grasp the local customs. She switched on her bedside lamp. It was amazing that she had slept so long. Another day lost from her life. There had been so many others.

Briefly considering going out for a hamburger, Cecil suddenly realised that she could order anything she liked from room service and charge it to her bill. Anything! It was her first night in Paris, wasn't it? Why should she spend it walking through cold and sleet to a cheap restaurant?

Cecil studied the hotel menu and then rang for caviar, blinis, Norwegian smoked salmon, profiteroles and a half-bottle of Dom Perignon. If only Sam knew! While she was waiting, she idly added up the price of the items she had ordered and then converted the total into dollars. She gasped when she saw the figure. She wondered what would happen when the bill came in. Would Jeff Sandlin call her to complain? Or would a meal at that price seem perfectly normal to those people? Perhaps they would never even see or hear of the bill; it would be paid by an indifferent employee who would not know who had eaten it or care if he did. What a strange world she had entered! She who despised money and had told Jeff Sandlin to keep his fee just for the pleasure of putting him in his place, now found she liked being in a room decorated with satins and tapestries, she liked staying in a luxury hotel. It was fun to lie in bed and wait for caviar and champagne while an icy storm raged outside.

Why should she feel guilty? It was their child she was carrying, wasn't it? Enjoy the fun while it lasts, she reminded herself. She was a scholar; she would observe the heretofore unknown life style of the super-rich.

Once she had finished the last of the almost sinfully delicious profiteroles, Cecil picked up the telephone. She was still hesitating about which call to make, and she saw with annoyance that her hand was trembling. Finally, she took the easy way out and called Dimitri.

'Cecil! Cecil Gutman? I can't believe you're in Paris. Is Serge with you?'

'No ... no, he isn't. I'll tell you all about Serge when I see you, Dim.'

'How long are you staying?'

'That's just it. I'm not sure. I'll probably leave in a day or two for Bordeaux.'

'You *are* on your way to see him, then?'

'Yes ... Look, can we get together?'

'*Mais oui, mais oui*! The sooner the better. Do you want me to come into Paris and show you the sights − the Lido, the Moulin Rouge, the Opéra? I'm not very rich, but we'll find something we can afford.'

'Don't worry. I've got plenty of money with me, and I don't want to go to any of those places anyway.'

Dimitri laughed explosively. 'What happened? You must have got a terrific job after graduation.'

'I did. An unbelievable one.'

'Well − tell me! I'm dying to hear about it.'

'Let me ask you something first, Dim. Have you seen Serge at all lately?'

'*Naturellement*. The only two Russians from the University of Illinois have to keep up with each other, don't they? Serge isn't a real *Russki*, of course − not like me. Let's see. Serge and I had dinner together in Paris − it must have been in October. Didn't he mention it to you in one of his letters?'

'That's what I wanted to tell you, Dim. Serge and I are ... estranged. He hasn't written or called me in over a year.'

'*What?* You can't be serious! Only two months ago, Serge told me you were wrapping up a few matters in Texas and then you were coming here to get married. I thought you were calling to invite me to your wedding.'

58

Cecil smiled thinly. She found she was gripping the receiver so hard her arm was hurting. 'So he let you believe we were still engaged?'

'I tell you, Serge talked about you constantly. The two of you are my very best friends, and I love to hear about your sterling qualities, Cici, but Serge was so insistent that even I got a little bored. This must be a misunderstanding between the two or you. A lovers' quarrel.'

'Dim ... one reason I called, I wanted to ask you ... Could you possibly come with me? To see Serge, I mean? I'm very nervous about meeting him again. If you were there, it would be like old times − the three of us joking around together.'

'There's nothing in the world I'd like better, Cici, and I'd have jumped at the chance if you'd come even a week earlier, but I just got drafted. Can you believe it? I'm packed and waiting for my travel orders right now.'

'Oh no!' Cecil cried out in dismany. 'You mean into the French army?'

'Well, it's certainly not the Soviet one. It so happens that it's not the French one either. My dear mother called the Foreign Office and chatted up some old friends, and now I'm off to Moscow. I've been assigned to the Cultural Office there. They can whisk me away at any time, but it probably won't be for another week or two.'

Cecil felt her spirits drop. She had been counting on Dimitri for support during the trip to Bordeaux, and now he was off to some distant, thoroughly inaccessible place. She would be truly alone. Just as Mica had predicted.

'Listen, Cici,' Dimitri went on chatting, 'why not come out here and see where I live? It's a marvellous old place, once a castle and now a ruin. Full of dissidents and eccentrics like me. And only a short walk from the Russian cemetery in Sainte-Geneviève du Bois.'

'That sounds nice, Dim. Not tomorrow, but maybe the next day?'

'Great! Let me explain how to get here on the train. I'll be waiting for you at the station, of course.'

'I'd rather come in a taxi.'

'A taxi? Cecil, I can't believe this is *you* talking. It's a thirty or forty-dollar ride out here.'

'I'm only in Paris for a few days. Let me blow my money without an argument, OK?'

'*Mon dieu*! What *is* this job of yours, anyway?'

Cecil made a stab at explaining. 'I'm doing some confidential research for a ... wealthy French family.'

'What are you researching? Perhaps I can give you some leads before I go.'

'That's the snag. I'm not allowed to reveal anything about it until the job's completed.'

'It's not the DST you're working for, is it?'

'What's that?'

'Our very own CIA.'

Cecil burst out laughing. 'I wish it were. It would probably be easier than what I'm really doing. Shall I bring some champagne when I come out?'

'What! This is a religious community. An ex-monastery.'

'Ex being the dominant word, right?'

'You're clairvoyant!'

'Then what do you want?'

'I told you our ruin is as Russian as yours truly. Bring a bottle of vodka! Bring two bottles! Or just bring yourself. I can't wait to see you!'

Cecil put down the receiver. She felt excited and happy, no longer alone. Thank God she hadn't called Bordeaux first!

She might well have ruined her very first evening in Paris.

It is lying comfortably at the bottom of its fluid-filled sac when a brusque movement by the woman as she turns in her sleep projects it upwards. Very slowly, it floats down again, coming to rest as still as a submarine on an ocean floor.

The thing that anchors there is no longer an embryo but a fetus. It has cast off its aura of a bird within a yolk; of a gill-bearing fish; of a monkey with protruding jaw and prehensile tail. It has become instead a tiny, ancient man. It floats in its dark world like a contemplative sage, one hand poised to hold up a bent, heavy head. Its skull is bald and shiny, its limbs tiny and frail. The weight of the world seems balanced on this enormous head and puny body.

Stiff whiskers have grown on its upper lip, its palms, even the soles of its feet, and then fallen away to make ready for a fine, wheat-coloured down, wisps of delicate hair that cover the body. Its very own hair-shirt.

Nails have already formed on tiny hands and clench and then open, searching ... what?

The mouth sucks in minuscule gulps of amniotic fluid. Digestive muscles contract as though expecting food, but the stomach remains empty. As always.

This is a dangerous moment for the fetus. An array of vessels criss-cross the surface of its large head like blood-filled creeks. Its nerve cells are still immature, its cerebral lobes small. It is vulnerable.

Shimmering like a strange planet under skin as fine as rice paper, the brain starts to send out faint signals. Something like a mind glimmers on the far horizon of being.

The fetus, so close to the woman's heartbeat, feels a stirring with no name; almost love.

Chapter Eleven

Frederick tiptoed into the darkened room, thinking his mother was asleep. When he saw that her large brass bed was empty, he crossed to the door leading to her private sitting room and knocked.

'Come in!' came Rita's voice, wide awake, chirpy even.

He opened the door and was surprised to see that this room was almost as dark as the bedroom. There was nothing to illuminate it except a flickering, silvery glow coming from one corner. He felt a sudden, irrational fear as he stood on the threshold: the idea flashed through his mind that something terrible was happening here, something about which he did not want to know. Then he realised that nothing at all sinister was going on; his mother was simply watching television with the lights off.

'Rita?' he called out tentatively. 'It's Frederick.'

Lately, his mother's condition had deteriorated faster than even the most pessimistic of her doctors had predicted. In desperation, Frederick had called in a young specialist, who had immediately started her on a new and highly experimental drug which might regenerate some of the non-functioning nerve connections in her brain. The young neurologist had warned Frederick and Bayard to wait before passing judgement. He could not guarantee permanent improvement. No one knew what effect the drug might have in the long run.

'Darling!' Rita called. 'Come over and sit next to me on the couch. I'm having a simply lovely time watching *Champs-Elysées*. There's a procession of stupendously bad singers tonight. It's great fun!'

Frederick crossed the immense stretch of darkness to his mother and bent down to kiss her on each cheek. Her good spirits were a tonic to his own, and he thought with relief that he was going to be able to talk to her tonight. The sound on the set was turned very low and, mercifully, the voice of the punk rocker could scarcely be heard.

'I have some good news for you, Rita,' he said, groping his way to a place on the brown velvet couch next to her. 'I've waited a couple of months to tell you because we wanted to be absolutely sure ...'

'It's not Christine?' she asked in a rush of breathless excitement. 'She's not expecting, is she?'

Frederick was speechless. His mother, who for weeks had not known where she was and sometimes not even who she was, had suddenly come back into the dark room as her old, superbly intuitive self. She was reading his mind as she had done since his very earliest memories.

'Not exactly,' he was forced to reply. Then, as she leaned into the light of the flickering screen, he saw her happy look crumple into one of extreme disappointment, and he decided to tell her the truth. 'Christine's not pregnant, but we are having a baby, Rita dearest.'

'You mean adoption?' The crestfallen look was still on her face.

'No, nothing like that. Christine and I had physical problems, as I told you some time ago. There was actually nothing insurmountable that prevented us from conceiving, but Christine could never carry a child to term even if she did become pregnant. Every doctor we saw confirmed that. Our situation seemed hopeless until we consulted an American doctor named Samuel Sweeney. You've probably seen him on TV talk shows. He speaks fluent French.'

'I *have* seen him,' Rita said. 'A handsome devil, rather like one of the Kennedy boys. And a good accent for a Yank. So what has this man done for you and Christine?'

'He's been the guiding force behind a modern-day immaculate conception. The child is Christine's and mine, but it was conceived in vitro, in a laboratory dish if you wish. Another woman is carrying it for us, a surrogate, *une mère porteuse*. Rita, I know this all sounds peculiar, but the technology in this field is quite complex, the more so because the most basic human functions are involved. Can you follow what I'm saying?'

'Stop talking as though I were an idiot child!' Rita snapped. 'I know all about the procedure. There is an article explaining it in every newspaper and magazine I pick up. Who is this woman carrying your child?'

'An American. Someone very reliable that Dr Sweeney found for us.'

'I want to meet her.'

'I'm sorry, Rita, but that's impossible. Sweeney believes that it's best for all concerned to keep a distance from – '

She cut him off. 'If I understand correctly, this American doctor is working for us and not the contrary. You are paying him, aren't you? And handsomely, I would imagine.'

63

'Of course we are, but you must give Sam Sweeney credit for having more experience in these matters than —'

'I *said* I want to meet her, Frederick. The woman is carrying my grandchild. Possibly the only one I'll ever have. How old is she?'

'Twenty-three, I believe.'

Twenty-three! A child herself. I must see and talk to her. As soon as possible.'

Frederick sighed. 'If that's what it takes to make you happy, then I'll try to arrange it.'

'Just knowing your child is on its way has already made me happy. More than you can imagine. When is it due?'

'The first week of June. Dr Sweeney will deliver the baby himself. At the American Hospital in Paris.'

'June! And already it's nearly Christmas. That's right, isn't it?' She looked at her son in momentary confusion, then regained her composure. 'You should have told me sooner. You know I haven't been well lately. Old age, I suppose, a terrible thing to happen to anyone. Some days, I find I'm ... quite forgetful.'

'You're always the same to me.'

'I'm not, and there's no point in lying about it. We have to face facts, Frederick. This baby changes a number of things. I'll want to modify my will. See if Monique can come out to the house next week. Tell her to be prepared to draw up a codicil for my signature.'

Frederick gave her hand a reassuring squeeze. He had dreaded telling his mother such a complicated story, but it had gone wonderfully well, and now he felt an uncharacteristic lump in his throat, a mixture of pride at the thought of having given her so much pleasure and grief at the idea that she might not live to see his child. Thank God he had waited until she was better to give her the news.

As he sat companionably next to her, he watched as the punk rocker disappeared from the screen to be replaced by the handsome MC of the show.

'Darling, please tell Christine how pleased I am. She mustn't feel ashamed or diminished in any way because it's happening this way. In the end, we'll have the very same, wonderful baby, won't we?'

'Of course we will. And Christine's in great shape. It was I who felt a little foolish about the whole thing — a blow to my masculine pride, I suppose.'

'Don't be silly. We're lucky to live in an ago of advanced technology where such things are possible. Otherwise, this might have stayed a family tragedy, a catastrophe for the Schomberg dynasty. Listen, darling, I just thought — isn't there something we can pick up out of this?'

'Pick up?' Again he felt that uneasy fear, the apprehension that his mother might say or do anything at all.

'For the company? Shouldn't we be looking into genetic engineering?'

'You don't miss a thing, do you?' He laughed. 'I asked Gradwohl last week to start researching the field for us. So our minds are, as usual, on the same track.'

'Well, let's keep things that way. Get that girl over here as soon as you can.'

'You never let up!' Frederick kissed her again on each cheek and stood up. 'I'd better go. I promised Christine I'd take her to a new place in Les Halles tonight. She'll be glad to know you were in such fine spirits.'

'Darling, I've been in *ecstasy* ever since I turned on this programme. It's changed my whole view of life. Haven't you seen who's on the screen? I thought you'd say something about it, especially since I saw you glancing at him when you first came in.'

'I'm afraid I haven't seen anybody worth mentioning tonight, but then I'm hardly a pop fan.' He smiled down at his mother. 'Don't tell me you've fallen for one of those rockers?'

'Don't be ridiculous! I mean right now. Look! Look! Can't you see – there, right there, holding the microphone!' Rita was becoming dangerously excited. She rose from the couch and took hold of her son's shoulders, turning him around so he faced the set. 'Look, darling! It's Hubert! Your father! I could cry, I'm so happy to see him. I can't imagine what he's doing with that snake, can you? But look how handsome he is! Oh, I simply can't wait 'til he gets home tonight after the show!'

Frederick stood frozen in the dark room watching France's most popular master of ceremonies tell still another joke and then stand aside as he introduced his guest, a pretty West Indian snake charmer.

Rita was leaning forwards, her thin, tiny hands outstretched to the TV screen. She appeared to have forgotten her son's presence altogether. On her face, lit by the silver glow of the set, was a look of total joy, of rapturous gratitude. She was about to be reunited with her husband, the love of her life, a man who had been dead now for nearly ten years.

In the shadow-filled bathroom that gave off Rita's sitting room, Bayard, too, stood rooted to the ground by shock. He had listened assiduously to every word uttered by his mother and brother. Not one of them had pleased him.

It seemed only yesterday that Bayard had formulated his plan, a grandiose one in which he himself captured both the Schomberg empire and his mother's love in one fell swoop. And there, in the very next room, was his troublesome little brother, a person Bayard had blocked so successfully from his mind that he seemed no longer to exist. Bayard felt his head spin, and something foul rose from his entrails to settle in his throat, choking him. For a moment he feared he would vomit into the toilet bowl, and then both Rita and Frederick would discover him here crouching ignominiously in his lair. His brother's appearance had stunned Bayard, just as his father's ghostly visitation had rendered Frederick dumbstruck. Not only was the unwanted brother alive and well, he was full of news about a child. A child that had been conceived in some devilish way, a witch's whelp he was proposing to deliver to Rita.

Bayard had told himself over and over again that this could never happen. What dark forces had let it come about? What power was stronger than his own? He would find out and, once he knew, he would act before such a miscreation came into being. He would not let a child of the devil and the devil's whore live.

He, Bayard Schomberg, would save the world from its evil presence, and, at the same time, he would save himself.

Chapter Twelve

The name was painted with a flourish in great but fading letters on the wooden panel at the entrance gate: Tatyana Muyshkin. Underneath was a date: 1928.

When her persistent ringing of the rusted bell brought no response, Cecil pushed open the gate and found herself in the courtyard of what once might have been a great country house. On one side, a small chapel was well on its way to becoming a pile of ivy-covered rubble, and on the other, a stone tower had been ruthlessly guillotined by wind and rain. Everything Cecil saw, in fact, was in a state of alarming disrepair and abandon. The main building, whose steps she was now climbing, seemed to Cecil like a peculiar cross between a medieval castle and a manor house that had undergone trans-formations over the centuries and then been left to get by as best it could. Shutters hung at crazy angles and no longer bore any trace or paint, and an impressive number of tiles were missing from a section of roof that overhung the front door.

As Cecil raised one gloved hand to knock, she caught a whiff of an unlikely mixture: mildew, manure and something absolutely wonderful cooking inside. More minutes passed before a fat and incredibly old woman pulled open the door and peered out with such a look of astonishment that Cecil felt she must have entered a time warp.

'Mr Tartakovsky?'

As the old woman shook her head, Cecil tried again. 'He was — I mean *is* — expecting me for lunch today. Cecil Gutman?'

Abruptly, a sunburst of a smile appeared on the woman's wide, Slavonic face. 'Oh, you Dimitri's friend, *da*? He so happy to see you, and now he gone and that's a shame, why they send for him today, I don't know, no notice, nothing, and just when you coming from so far away.' The woman spoke French with an atrocious Russian accent, and Cecil had the additional trial of trying to follow her run-together thoughts.

'You don't mean Dimitri's left!' she exclaimed, hoping against hope that she had misunderstood. 'Not on his assignment to the Soviet Union!'

'*Da, da*, that's it, he want to call you, but nobody know where you are, you don't give name of hotel or nothing, so he can't find you. This morning, big black car come for him, he go to catch plane and maybe he's in Moscow now.'

'Moscow,' Cecil repeated stupidly, trying to hold back the floor of tears she felt close to erupting. 'Did he − did he leave a message for me?'

'*Da, tri*!' The old woman began to count on the fingers of one pudgy hand. 'One, you invited visit him there, when you want. Two, you go see Russian cemetery while you out here. Three ...' She stopped counting, and the radiant, wrinkle-producing smile appeared once more. 'After cemetery, you come back here eat borscht with me. I show you orphans.'

'Orphans? I'm sorry, I really don't understand.'

'Before he go, Dimitri tell me show you pictures my little orphans. They all gone now, every single one, and me, I last of old nurses who took care of them in Madame Tatyana's house.'

'You mean this was once an orphanage?'

'Sure, everybody know that. Even Grand Duke, he come here, take picture of me and my orphans. I show you.'

'Of course.' Cecil shook her head. 'I should have guessed. Where else could Dimitri Tartakovsky possibly have lived in Paris except in an orphanage for White Russians? Oh, if only he'd waited for me, what fun we could have had joking about this!'

Nothing moved anywhere. Frost lay lightly on the dead brown grass, and the branches of the trees were stark against a sky of dulled pewter.

Cecil was surprised that such absolute stillness could exist only a few miles from the centre of Paris. As she followed the narrow lane towards the cemetery, she tried to shake off the feeling of abandonment that had settled upon her when she heard that Dimitri was gone. She knew no one in France now except Serge, and she still had no idea how he would react when she called him. It had been a long time since she had felt so thoroughly alone. In Dallas, there had been Mica and ... Sam. Like it or not, Sam *had* been a friend.

A limousine turned into the lane ahead of her. It was almost as wide as the road itself, and something about the car seemed quite familiar to her. It was gathering speed now, implacably bearing down on the very spot where she stood. Brought out of her reverie by a sensation of imminent danger, Cecil jumped off the road just as the car pulled to a stop. It was not more than three feet from her, and the man opening the door on the driver's side was René, the young chauffeur who had met her at Roissy airport. Cecil stifled a cry.

'Excuse me if I startled you, Mademoiselle Gutman. I'm sorry to interrupt your outing.'

Hoping René would not notice how her knees were knocking in fright, Cecil tried to be casual. 'Why, hello, René. Are you just out here visiting the Russian cemetery? What a remarkable coincidence that we should meet up like this again.'

René did not smile. He touched the brim of his cap and said, 'I've been asked to bring you back into town, Mademoiselle. My employers wish to meet with you urgently.'

Cecil switched to a cold and decidedly unfriendly tone. 'How did you find me?'

René smiled reassuringly. He looked just as he had at the airport – charming and inoffensive – and Cecil felt foolish for being so harsh with him.

'I went to your hotel. You'd gone out, so I asked around. The doorman remembered giving this address to a taxi driver. It wasn't a normal place for an American tourist to go, so it stuck in his mind.'

'Is your following me around like this normal?'

René looked unhappy. 'I'm not following you, Mademoiselle. I was given instructions to bring you back to the house as quickly as I could. If I drive you into town, it will save you searching for a taxi.'

Cecil shook her head. 'It's quite hopeless, isn't it? I'm not allowed even one day of privacy in Paris. I suppose you have to expect this sort of thing when you take a job working for rude and impossible people.'

René looked thoroughly shocked. Obviously, no one had dared insult his august employers in such a way before. Cecil did not give him a chance to recover.

'I'll come back with you, René, provided you leave me alone after this. I don't give a damn what your bosses think or say. There's absolutely nothing in my contract that says I have to be at their beck and call every single day I'm in France. They may have bought my services for next June, but they certainly don't own me for the entire nine months.'

'I'm sorry, Mademoiselle,' René replied, a look of deep embarrassment on his young face. 'I'll try not to bother you again.'

He held the door open for her as she climbed into the back of the limousine. A few seconds later, they were moving at breakneck speed towards Paris.

69

Chapter Thirteen

'I want to see her alone.'

'That isn't very nice of you, my pet. After all, it was I who found her for you.'

'Why in the world would you want to be here to chat with an unknown American girl? She can't possibly hold any interest for you.'

'You're wrong, dearest one. I'm *very* interested in her. I'm practically *dying* to see what our little Christine picked out to do the job she couldn't do herself.'

'You know I don't like your criticising Christine. It's unfair, and it's wrong. That's another reason I don't want you with me when I interview the girl. You'll make all kinds of sarcastic remarks and scare the poor thing to death.'

'You're always ready to judge me harshly, Mother mine, and in this case you're being dreadfully unfair. You know you have to have your little rest at four o'clock. Doctor's orders. While you nap, I thought I'd show the girl around the house. She might even like to swim or play a game of tennis. That is, if you're planning to ask her to stay over for supper.'

'Yes, perhaps I will. That is considerate of you, Bayard. All right, remain if you wish, but don't say a word against Christine or your brother, and don't upset the girl. Her trip is supposed to be an enjoyable one. We don't want her taking a dislike to France and rushing back to America. Disappearing with our child.'

'No, Rita dear, we won't let this happen. We'll keep her here with us. One way or another. Leave it to me.'

Bayard sat back in the chintz-covered armchair next to his mother's bed. On his plump, rosy face settled a contented expression, the look of a large cat with the canary already hanging half out of its mouth.

The limousine pulled up to a high gate of wrought iron surrounded by

70

stone walls with jagged pieces of broken glass embedded in the top. René turned back towards Cecil. 'I'll just get out and open the gates. I won't be a minute.'

'Oh, do take your time.' Sarcasm dripped from her voice. 'Really, there's no place I'd rather be than in this draughty car.' Instantly she regretted it. René was not to blame for her ruined day. She was on the point of finding out who was, though, and even the idea of meeting that person made her angry again. All the way here, on the Autoroute du Sud and then on the circular *periphérique* to the Porte Saint-Cloud exit, she had wondered about the identity of the woman who had sent for her in such an imperious manner. She knew it was a woman because the only thing René would say in response to her persistent questioning was 'Madame will explain everything when you meet her'.

Cecil had tried to empathise with the woman, had tried to picture her standing distraught in her bedroom awaiting news of her unborn child. Her imagination failed her completely, though. Everything about the mystery woman spelled power, fortune, security; she, Cecil, had none of that. She had, in effect, nothing at all.

René was back in the car, guiding it up a gravel path bordered on both sides by ancient chestnuts, firs and cedars. Only a few minutes ago, at the Saint-Cloud hill, they had been in view of the Eiffel Tower and the curling river, and now they were in a park as thickly wooded as a forest. Cecil had thought estates like this had vanished with the war. She moved the mystery woman up a notch in terms of wealth.

The limousine made a sharp right and pulled up in front of a massive, three-storey house of dark stone. A bony, red-faced woman of about fifty wearing a flowered dress opened the door at the exact moment René turned off the motor. She was wringing her hands and looked upset.

'I found Miss Gutman,' René called up to her. 'She was out in the Essone.'

'Thank goodness. Madame was so worried when you didn't get back with her by lunchtime.'

Cecil climbed the steps to a veranda sheltered by a *marquise* of glass and iron scrollwork. It looked like a Guimard and was by far the prettiest thing about the gloomy old house.

'Should I take her straight up?' René asked the woman.

'Oh no! You can't!' She turned to Cecil with a startled look. 'Madame is taking her nap. I'm not to wake her before five.'

Cecil was shivering in the late-afternoon chill; surrounded by so many trees and high bushes, the house was completely obscured from the already weak December sun. 'Can we go inside?' she asked René in a plaintive voice.

The woman murmured an embarrassed excuse and ushered Cecil into a vast entrance hall holding a few pieces of heavy, utilitarian furniture, the kind that lasted for generations. It was almost as dark in the hall as it had been outside on the veranda.

'Rene, did I understand correctly? Is the woman who plucked me away from a pleasant day in the country now taking a nap? Is it true that she won't be able to see me for almost an hour?'

'Please, Mademoiselle,' the housekeeper said anxiously, 'I'll make you a nice cup of tea. Or would you like something to eat?'

'I would *not*. The only thing I want to do now is leave. I'm tired, and I want to go back to my hotel.' She looked at René insistently. He fidgeted with his cap, not knowing how to reply.

'That's all right, René, Henriette. You may go now. I believe I have just time to offer Miss Gutman a drink and show her the house before Madame comes down.'

The far end of the corridor was in total darkness, and out of this emerged a man. He was very tall and plump, and he wore a calf-length robe of navy terry cloth with a large gold S and a crown interwoven over the heart. As he came closer, Cecil saw the wisps of blond strands that had been worked carefully over his balding scalp to give an impression of luxuriant growth. His eyes, an intense and rather attractive blue, looked straight at her. They fairly danced with amusement.

'Allow me to introduce myself — Bayard Schomberg. And I insist on offering my excuses for our prodigiously negligent family. We were hoping to give you an absolutely splendid welcome to Paris, but from the look on your face, I'm prepared to wager that we've achieved exactly the opposite effect.'

It was obviously intended as a speech of appeasement, but only one tiny drop of curiosity came to dilute Cecil's boiling rage. 'Schomberg? I have a TV set at home that never works, plus a dryer that's always on the blink as well. I recall a Schomberg label on both of them. Would you by chance be responsible?'

'My dear, I simply wouldn't *know*. You must ask my dear brother or some other working member of this family. All I do is *spend* the money. I haven't the slightest idea where it comes from.'

'I suppose, then, that you're the ... the ...' Her voice faltered, and for a few seconds she feared she wouldn't be able to get it out at all. '... the ... father?'

'Father? Father of whom, or perhaps, in my case, should I say of what?' Then, as understanding dawned, Bayard Schomberg burst into peals of delighted laughter. 'No, no! Oh, but it is sweet of you to think so. I would *never* foist my genes on a poor unborn creature.

Again, it's my dear brother who must take the responsibility for your predicament – Frederick Schomberg. I do *so* hope you've never heard of him.'

The man was quite bizarre, and Cecil had always had a weakness for oddballs. She found herself rather liking him. He certainly was not what she had expected when she saw the forbidding walls of the estate topped with spikes of broken glass.

'I hate to disappoint you, but I think I saw his picture in the business section of the *International Trib* on the plane coming over.'

'God forbid you should read such rot. If you'd got hold of some really interesting magazines like *Realités, Country Gentleman, Vanity Fair, Maison et Jardin*, then you might have seen *my* picture. I race at Deauville, you know, and I always attend the polo matches and the garden parties when Prince Charles comes over. So exciting.'

'I'll be sure to look for you, but concerning this moment, it's very disconcerting to be summoned here as though as it were a matter of life and death and then, when I arrive, to find Madame asleep and you in your bath.'

'Oh, how witty! How perfectly delightful! Rita will simply adore you, take my word for it. But I wasn't bathing, dear child, I was having a relaxing swim in our greenhouse gymnasium while awaiting your much anticipated arrival. Please, let's take ourselves out of this draught-filled hall and into a warm place where we can fix ourselves a drink. I promise to fill you in on every little detail of our remarkable family while the two of us get tipsy together.'

Bayard Schomberg already had a firm grip on Cecil's arm. Before she could utter a word of protest, he was guiding her towards a door on the right side of the hall. For such a flabby-looking man, Cecil noticed, he had fingers of steel.

'Now, shall I mix you a cocktail, or do you take it neat like I do?'

'I'm afraid I don't drink. Doctor's orders,' Cecil replied sweetly, putting her recent dinner at the hotel out of her mind. 'A Perrier, if you have one.'

'Of course, the little mother-to-be. Charming! Charming! You don't mind if I have a nip, do you?'

They had come into a medium-sized room which Cecil took to be the family den. There were several leather couches and armchairs, two games tables and a high, mirror-lined bar against one wall.

'Have you been to Paris before? Would you like me to give you a tour of a typical French house? It's terribly bourgeois, you know, not at all chic, but we've made it quite comfortable, and we don't lack for space. Twenty-six rooms plus the pool, spa sauna and indoor tennis court. Do you play, by the way?'

'No, but I do swim.'

'Oh, I *knew* you would. You Americans are so athletic. I promised Rita I'd take you down to the greenhouse for a swim and a sauna before supper.'

'Supper?'

'Oh, didn't that silly chauffeur tell you? Of course we want you to stay and take a meal with us. Rita is dying to have a chat with you, girl talk, you know. I thought you could relax a little downstairs, and afterwards we'd dine and perhaps go out to a club. Or have René drive us around Paris to see the Christmas lights. So clever of you to come at this time of the year.'

'I didn't exactly pick my dates, Mr Schomberg. And much as I appreciate your offer, all that activity rather overwhelms me. I'm still suffering from jet lag.'

'I know exactly how you feel. That's why I suggested the sauna, the one thing that will get you back on schedule after a long, arduous flight. That and a swim.'

'Bayard, this child doesn't want to swim. Why, it's wintertime, and there's sleet and ice on the ground. She'd freeze if she went into our pond!'

Taken by surprise for the second time since she entered the house, Cecil turned just in time to see a tiny woman appear in the doorway. She was wearing a gown and negligee set of pale-blue silk trimmed in darker, extremely fine lace. A sleeping mask was pushed up high into her blond curls, and she looked dazed. The woman was very pretty, but even in the subdued light of the den, Cecil could see that she was over fifty.

No wonder she hired me to have her baby: she's not young at all. Probably her husband wants a child, and she's at the limit to carry it herself. From the picture I saw in the Trib, Frederick Schomberg is a lot younger than his wife.

'Bring her over her, Bayard, I can't see in this bad light. Please indulge me, my dear, I haven't been well.'

Cecil walked reluctantly towards the woman. The anxiety she had first felt when she saw the limousine turn into the lane at the Russian cemetery returned and exploded into something stronger. She was out-and-out afraid of this tiny, birdlike woman with the vacant look in her eyes; afraid of her obsequious housekeeper and her too polite chauffeur; afraid of the massive, ugly, dark house and everything in it except possibly Bayard Schomberg. He alone seemed pleasant and even charming in an old-fashioned, slightly ridiculous way.

The woman lifted her hands and took hold of Cecil's face, pulling

74

it down forcefully so she could embrace it. The kiss was hard and wet and quite unpleasant.

'Rita, my pet, this is Miss Gutman. You've been dying to meet her. You do remember, don't you?'

'What are you saying, Bayard?' Her voice betrayed annoyed impatience. One clawlike hand moved from Cecil's cheek up to her cap of knitted yellow wool. With a sudden movement, she snatched it off and ran her fingers through the long auburn strands of hair that she had released.

'So it's Christine, after all. It's Christine who's having the baby. Why didn't someone tell me? Bayard, you should have − I'm sure you knew all along. Christine, darling, I'm so glad it's you and not this American girl everyone keeps talking about. Why did Frederick hide it from me? Was it to be a wonderful surprise? A Christmas present?'

Tears of joy welled up in the intensely blue, absent eyes. Bayard Schomberg was trying to move her back into the hallway when, with one angry gesture, she threw him off and grabbed at Cecil's hair again. The woman obviously was quite ill. Cecil knew now why she had felt that swelling of anxiety when she had first laid eyes upon her. She could always recognise mental derangement; it was like a faint, foul odour that only she could smell. An odour of rot.

'Mother's not herself this evening, Miss Gutman. You will excuse her, won't you?'

'Mother?' Up close, the woman did look older, but hardly old enough to be the mother of the middle-aged man beside her.

'Oh, I didn't get around to introducing you, did I? Yes, you'd never guess it by looking at her, but this little beauty is my own dear mother, Marguerite Schomberg.' Then he added, as though in afterthought, 'And the mother of Frederick Schomberg, who is soon to be the proud father of your baby. It's all so complicated, isn't it? I mean, these kinds of situations are simply not covered in etiquette books. Such a lapse when you come up against them in real life, don't you agree, Miss Gutman?'

Marguerite Schomberg was still resisting her son with all the force of her five-foot-two-inch frame; she turned back to Cecil once again and said, 'Christine, tell this fool to stop calling you other names. He doesn't like you, you know. He never has. He wishes you harm. Beware of anything he says or does tonight.'

'All right, Rita my pet. Miss Sanchez is waiting upstairs to give you a nice, soothing massage. You will wait for me to come back, won't you, Miss Gutman? I know you will because I can see you're just bursting with questions about our uniquely loving and united family.'

*

75

When Bayard Schomberg returned to the den some ten minutes later, Cecil was curled up on one of the leather couches leafing through a French decorating magazine and trying not to cry. All the tensions of the day seemed to be on the verge of erupting within her; in spite of herself, she couldn't help feeling pity and commiseration for the tiny, obviously mad little woman who had, finally, been carried upstairs by force. Bayard went to the bar and poured Cecil a stiff whisky. She took a few sips and waited to see if it would make her feel the way it did heroines in mystery novels – instantly better.

'I can see you are confused and upset, and I dont blame you in the least,' Bayard said cheerfully. 'The two lovebirds Frederick and Christine – who is my dear brother's wife, as you have surely guessed by now – should have been here to welcome you. Instead they're somewhere in Switzerland on a Christmas skiing holiday. You'll have to put up with me until they return in January.'

'Are there just the four of you?' Cecil asked as she took another sip of the whisky. She put down the glass and pressed her fingers to her temples in a weary gesture. She felt more tired than she could remember since her illness – and already just a little tipsy. It had been hours since she had had anything to eat.

'Yes, the Schomberg succession is reduced to me and my dear brother. That's why we're all so eager to see your baby born. There are some American relatives, but they hardly count because their business was separated from ours after the war. Oh, did I forget my cousin Xavier and his wife Edith-Anne? And their two sons? So silly of me. Of course, they're French, too, but the main family line was passed from my father Hubert to me. Frederick is my younger brother.'

'And you're not married, Mr Schomberg?'

'I'm afraid I'm another of life's cripples, my dear, a sensualist born to experience, and an aesthete born to appreciate and observe but neither to create nor to procreate. Miss Gutman, you will see our poor family in a way few outsiders ever do. I simply know you are going to help us immensely, Cecil. I can call you Cecil, can't I? I feel we are destined to become great friends. You see, you are needed most desperately to bring health and sanity into our midst.'

Sanity! Cecil almost laughed out loud. *Well, perhaps compared to the Schombergs, I am at the high-water mark in terms of good health.*

'What shall I tell Cook to prepare for you? Your very favourite dish? No, don't look like that. We want you to be happy here. Put yourself in my hands, and I promise I'll give you an evening you'll never forget.'

This time she did laugh. He was preposterous but amusing. It was easy to see how he had achieved his success on the social circuit. Old ladies must adore him. He had an engaging, almost childish enthusiasm, and, despite his sarcasms, he seemed truly anxious to please.

'Come along now. While you're dictating tonight's menu, I'll show you the pool. We have bathing suits of every size and shape, but of course you can swim without one here. You'll have the place all to yourself. You and baby!'

Cecil stood up wearily. She no longer had the strength to resist. *What the hell*, she told herself emphatically. *You decided to embrace the life style of the rich and famous. Go ahead and do it*!

The heat was wonderfully soothing, and Cecil awoke to find all the tensions of the day oozing out of her pores. How long had she been asleep? There was a small hour-glass on a wooden ledge over her head, but she hadn't bothered to set it when she first came in. She must have been in here at least fifteen or twenty minutes because she could tell that the temperature had risen significantly. She swung her legs over the side of the wooden bench and sat up. She was in a large sauna, easily big enough for half a dozen people to stretch out in. There was a stove box piled high with flat stones that looked as though they had come from a riverbed, and all kinds of accessories — a round thermometer set into the wall about six inches from the ceiling, curved wooden headrests at each end of the benches, several whisks made of birch twigs tied together in bunches, a water-filled bucket and a long-handled ladle to asperse the stones, as Bayard had suggested, should she want some moisture in the air. She didn't feel the need: the sauna was pleasantly hot and dry, even, perhaps, a little warmer than she would have liked.

She wondered lazily if Sam Sweeney would approve of her taking a sauna. Oh, enough of Sweeney! Lately, she had found that the doctor imposed himself on her will so persistently that she could not make a single move without seeing his handsome Irish face alternately reprehending and teasing her. He certainly wouldn't like what she had been doing so far in Paris, drinking champagne and whisky and letting herself be badly upset, once when the maid sneaked into her room at the Prince de Galles and again this afternoon when she saw the limousine bearing down on her on the cemetery road. It was downright silly to be afraid of René. She tried to conjure up his kindly face, but already Sweeney was back again, superimposing himself over René, over every single person she tried to think about. Was she falling in love with him? How utterly stupid! Sweeney was not only married, he had hundreds of rich, beautiful women at his feet. Or

77

rather at the tip of his own magic wand – the scalpel.

Cecil thought about the afternoon in the hospital in Dallas when she had been sitting in the sun wearing the new blue robe. She had not even known Sweeney was in the room until she felt his fingers in her hair and heard his voice, uncharacteristically low and filled with emotion, telling her how much he liked the colour. He had gone on twisting the strands between his fingers, just as Marguerite Schomberg had done today. Except that Bayard's mother had thought she was Christine, had mixed the two of them up completely. Cecil straightened up with a jolt. Was that what Sweeney had been thinking, too, that her long red hair resembled that of Christine Schomberg? Was he infatuated with Christine then, and not . . . ?

What did it matter, anyway? She loved Serge. It was because of Serge that she had got herself into this crazy situation in the first place. Except that ever since she had become pregnant, she had felt . . . *amoureuse*. For the first time since her break-up with Serge, she had started to notice other men, find them attractive. It was just too perverse! She decided not to waste another minute thinking about it.

The sauna was definitely heating up, but it was still agreeable, and Cecil felt too lazy to move after all the whisky Bayard had poured into her. She stretched out luxuriously on the bench and let herself imagine – just for a second – how it would be if Sam Sweeney took her in his arms, how it would feel to have those strong fingers race through her hair again, travel across her lips, down her body . . .

No, she hated him! Hated everything about him! She must not weaken like this, let her defences down with another man. God, it *was* hot! She looked up at the wall thermometer and was astonished to see that it had moved up to 80 degrees. Was that normal? Hadn't it read 70 degrees when she first came in, before she drifted off to sleep? Bayard had told her the sauna was 'good and ripe', whatever that meant. She should have enquired about the proper temperature while he was still around.

Cecil stood up and found that the floor planks were burning her feet. She threw her towel down and trod on its thick surface to reach the thermometer. She expected to find a thermostat next to it but there didn't seem to be one. Of course, there couldn't be electric switches in such intense heat. The controls must be outside the room. She had been in other saunas, but she had only the vaguest notion of how they worked. There had always been an attendant to get her out in time, some grumpy woman who stuck her head in every five minutes with dire warnings of diabetes, insolation and heart attacks.

Cecil sat back down on the bench and then shot up again. The thing felt as though it had caught fire. She spread the beach towel Bayard had given her across it and lay back, but it was still too hot. She could see the thermometer from where she was lying; the needle had moved to 85 degrees. Was that Fahrenheit or Centigrade? She thought they only had centigrade in Europe, but it couldn't be that high, could it? Wasn't normal body temperature 37 degrees centigrade? Could a human support temperature twice that of its own body? She had no idea.

Oh, why am I so ignorant? Cecil berated herself. *This is the sort of information both Serge and Dimitri would have at their fingertips. I'd better get out of here before I roast and the Schombergs decide to serve me for supper. Probably Madame wouldn't even notice. If she took me for her daughter-in-law, she might just as easily mix me up with a plate of well-done beef.*

Sacrificing one foot, Cecil hopped to the door. She tried to push it open, but it wouldn't budge.

This could only happen to me, she thought bitterly. *I'm the one person in the world who could get trapped in a scorching hot sauna.*

Cecil dropped the towel back on the floor and stepped on it, but the heat was unbearable. The needle had moved up again, this time to 87 degrees. Who had set the thermostat, anyway? Bayard or one of the servants, probably. Whoever it was might have asked her first if she was used to such intense heat. Had the door stuck somehow when Bayard closed it? He knew she was pregnant. Why hadn't he checked that it was functioning before he went off and left her a prisoner? Such terrible heat couldn't be good for the Schomberg heir.

Cecil pushed harder against the door, but still nothing happened. The palms of her hands were blistering, and sweat poured down her face, obscuring her vision. For the first time, she realised there were no windows in the room. She had never liked closed places, and now she felt a claustrophobic hysteria rise up out of her stomach, out of that very spot where the fetus was trapped in its own closed cage.

There were two small panes of glass set high in the door; they were made of frosted glass, and she could not see through them, but probably she could break them. Even a tiny opening would let in some cool air. What could she use, though? Certainly not her hands; already there were ugly red patches on the palms of both where they had touched the burning door. The ladle? She picked that up and rammed it into the centre of one of the panes; the handle splintered and then snapped in two. Cecil stifled a sob. There was nothing else in the room with which to try breaking the glass.

Cecil realised she was having all the symptoms of a panic attack; her heart was racing, her breath stilled. The walls seemed to be moving inward. Yes, they *were* closing in on her. It was like an Edgar

Allan Poe story: she was in a grave; there was no air; no one knew she was here.

If I don't get out now, I'll faint and fall straight on that burning floor and die!

She stepped back as far as she could against the bench and then lunged at the door with one shoulder, colliding in a sickening thump with its fiery surface. The door did not move an inch.

Cecil jerked around to look at the thermometer, at the same time telling herself that she shouldn't. Oh, God! Ninety-two degrees! Could it possibly have gone up five degrees in only a couple of minutes? Or had she lost all track of time? Had she been in this hellish place for hours or minutes?

She turned back to the door and noticed for the first time that it had a square handle set halfway down in the wood.

The stupid thing opens in! I've been standing here trying to push on a door that needs pulling! With a feeling of absolute relief, Cecil grabbed the burning handle and pulled in towards her with all the strength she could muster. Nothing happened.

It came to Cecil then that she was truly trapped. She might burn to death or suffocate or die of a heart attack or a blood clot of simply out of fright. No one would come. She began to pound on the door with both fists, screaming out the names of both Bayard Schomberg and René. When the silence following each bout of desperate screams finally overwhelmed her, she sank down to a hunching position on the floor, sobbing over and over again, 'Help, help, somebody please help me.'

At last she could no longer bear to feel the wood under her scorched feet. Sweat poured down her face in such quantities that she could barely read the figures on the thermometer. Was it 97 degrees or 107? Did it matter? Her head was throbbing horribly. She fell back on the bench, no longer bothering with the heavy towel embellished with the Schomberg initial and the gold crown.

Strangely, the wood was cold now, icily cold. It was as though she were lying on a massive block of burning ice. Hadn't Madame told her not to go outside to the pond? Hadn't she warned her there was snow everywhere? The dead, cold ground was covered with snow as heavy as a shroud.

Cecil turned over on to her stomach and stretched out full length across the bench, wrapping her arms around the wooden planks, flattening herself against its hard surface so the coldness could penetrate her burning body. She was shivering now, the pond was so cold. Just before she let herself sink into its icy depths, she tried one last time to see the thermometer, but at that very instant the overhead lights snapped off, and she was all alone in the dark, ensnared in a cold, bottomless place far below the water's surface.

She hugged the bench harder, but it no longer protected her. She fell straight down.

Like flesh melted down by flames, the lids of the fetus are glued together. It can feel, though, and what it feels right now is a rocky hardness squeezing the woman's body against its own. Her flesh is on fire! To escape the unbearable heat and hardness, the fetus begins to turn, first to one side and then to the other.

The woman's heart beats, a terrible, pulsing beat. It is everywhere at once. It mingles with the hotness and the hard, smooth thing ramming her stomach against her backbone.

Something, too, is in her blood and in its own, tearing through brain and arteries, making its tiny heart pump faster and its blood race as crazily as hers.

The fetus starts. Her heart feels as though it is jumping out of her body. Boom! Boom! Boom! Boom! It is a terrible noise. It means something. What?

Still trying to get away from the hard hot thing, the fetus floats on its head, then rights itself. It cannot stop moving because of the rushing of its blood. It fidgets, raises a tiny thumb to its mouth, starts to suck, then pulls it out again. It jerks suddenly to the right, then back to the left.

It cannot escape the thumping heart, the stabbing heat, the thing in its blood.

It turns and turns. There is no place to go.

Chapter Fourteen

The light came back on, and the door swung out almost at the same time.

'Mademoiselle?' came a tentative, frightened voice.

Cecil sat up, rubbing her eyes. She was hot and cold at once; her head throbbed, and her body ached terribly. Where was she? It was like the hotel room where the maid had awakened her in the dark, only this was different sort of room, all in pale wood, and there were no windows. The yellow light hurt her eyes, and she shut them again.

'Mademoiselle? We've been looking everywhere for you, René and Cook and I, we've searched the whole house. We even went up to the attic ...' The voice sounded choked with tears.

'I came down earlier and turned out all the lights, I thought you'd gone. I had no idea ...'

'Didn't Monsieur Bayard tell you I was here?' Cecil was astonished to hear that she could speak.

'Monsieur had to take his mother to the hospital. She had another bad attack, and he rode with her in the ambulance ... he was so upset, he must have forgotten to mention ...' Her voice trailed off altogether.

'How did you open the door?'

'The door? Like always when I come in to sweep out the place and wash down the wood. I just pulled it open. Why, is there something the matter with the door?' The frightened note was back in her voice.

'No, nothing. How long ago did you turn out the lights?' Cecil had a hazy vision of a woman standing in the door of the sauna. The housekeeper, the woman in the flowered dress who had let her in earlier. What was her name? Henry? No, of course not. Henriette? Yes, that was it, Henriette.

'Oh, Mademoiselle, I'm not sure. It must have been about seven o'clock. At least half an hour ago. I had no idea you were down here alone in the dark ...'

'You've saved my life.'

'Your life? Turning off the electricity? I don't understand.'

'Can you find my clothes for me?' Cecil stood and wrapped the still-hot towel around her naked, tortured flesh. There was an aching pain in every single part of her body. Holding on to the wall to support herself, she stepped out into the solarium. She was still dazed, but she knew one thing clearly: she wanted to get out of the house as fast as she could. As Henriette scurried around the edge of the pool, Cecil stumbled to a partly opened locker and saw that her clothes and shoes were still where she had left them.

'I'm going to dress, Henriette. It shouldn't take me more than five or ten minutes. Can you have a taxi here by then?'

'A taxi! Oh no, René should be back from the hospital any minute now. He just went over to deliver — '

'No! I don't want to go with René.' Cecil spoke sharply, as though she were addressing a small child. 'Nor with anyone else from this house. I want a public cab. Please call one now. I'll be ready to leave in five minutes.'

'All right, Mademoiselle. As you wish.'

A quarter of an hour later, Cecil was huddled in the back seat of a taxi stuck in a monumental traffic jam at the Saint-Cloud bridge. As blaring horns mingled with the shouts of furious motorists, Cecil pulled her coat and scarf tightly about her and rolled up into a fetal position, searching for warmth. She could not stop shaking. Even in the air-conditioned buildings of Dallas, she had never felt like this. It was a chill that came from somewhere within herself, and she had no idea how to combat it. She wanted to leap from the stalled taxi and run out into the cold night.

Yes, run! That was it! Tomorrow, before any Schomberg came to her hotel to enquire about her, she would run. She would take a plane to Bordeaux, and once she was there, she woud telephone Sam and tell him what had happened to her. Tell him . . . what exactly? That somebody had tried to kill her right in the Schomberg house? Would he believe that? It didn't matter. He was cunning and resourceful. He would tell her what to do, where to go.

Tomorrow she'd run.

He stood in the garden by the frozen pond, laughing.

Why in the world had he attempted such a thing?

It was stupid, utterly and completely stupid. The others were still alive, weren't they? Even if he had succeeded in killing her, what good would it have done? They would just go out and buy another mongrel child.

Still, he laughed when he thought of the screams coming from behind the jammed door, the pounding of her fists on the burning wood. Even if it had been silly, he had learned something from the experience.

Already he had written down his conclusions in a big, leather-bound book. *Order is the foundation of all good plans, it is the shape on which beauty depends. Begin at the beginning. Each thing in its time.* Frederick and Christine first, then the fetus. The girl wasn't important. He could even let her live if he found a way to kill the child without her. Yes, why not? Let her go. She didn't matter. He rather liked her.

A place for everything, and everything in its place. Establish the proper order.

That was the only way to proceed.

It had been amusing, though. He had rarely had such a good time; not often did events turn out just as he wanted.

Yes, it had all been in good fun.

Chapter Fifteen

'Frederick, for God's sake, wake up!'

'Whaa . . . what's the matter?'

'Open your eyes! I can't tell if you're listening to me or not. Christ, look at me!'

Frederick Schomberg, normally the most considerate of men where his wife was concerned, felt only irritation at being pulled so brutally out of his nap, especially since he was stretched out comfortably on a canvas chair set down directly in the snow. He was thoroughly drowsy from the two bottles of excellent wine he and Christine had shared, not to mention the sleep-inducing combination of strong sun and pure Alpine air.

'What the hell?'

'Listen! I've just found out from Henriette that she almost died. She was locked in the sauna for over an hour last night, *over an hour*! When Henriette finally discovered her down there, she ran off into the dark like a scared rabbit.'

At last, Frederick shook off the effects of his 'well-watered' lunch. 'You mean Rita got locked in the sauna? Did that fool Bayard . . . ?'

'Not Rita! Can't you forget your precious mother for once in your life? Oh, darling, it's the American girl who was down there – Cecil Gutman.'

'The woman with our baby?' Frederick asked incredulously. 'Is she in Paris?'

'It would seem so since she was in your mother's sauna last night.' Christine could not keep the sarcasm out of her voice. 'Frederick, she could have lost the baby! After all we've been through, to have some idiotic thing like this happen!'

'Chrissie, what in God's name was Cecil Gutman doing in my mother's house in Saint-Cloud?'

'Henriette thinks it's Bayard who invited her over to meet Rita. In any case, it was your dear brother who took her down to the sauna and left her there to burn to death.'

'People don't usually catch fire from being in a sauna,' Frederick replied dryly.

'You might if you were locked in one all night.'

'Let's get the facts straight before we go off accusing Bayard of attempted murder! You know Henriette is not the most reliable of witnesses, even under ordinary circumstances . . .'

'Frederick, something serious happened last night in Saint-Cloud, and I for one don't intend to let it rest. Cecil Gutman certainly must think someone tried to harm her because she ran away. Disappeared. She refused to wait for René and fled the house in a taxi. She could be anywhere in France by now, or on a plane back to Texas.' Christine's voice rose hysterically as she strode round and round the deck chair where Frederick was still stretched out in the sun. Even as he began to think about what his wife had said, he could not help remembering how she had circled his chair that first day in the glass factory, stalking him as though he were a much coveted prey to be captured in the shortest possible time.

'*Mon amour*, please calm yourself. If you want, I'll telephone Gradwohl and tell him to go straight out to the house and find out what happened. By the way, where was Rita while all this was going on?'

'Oh,' Christine said, growing suddenly very pale. She stood perfectly still now, watching her husband anxiously. 'I'm sorry, darling. I completely forgot to tell you. Rita was taken to the hospital last night.'

'*What!*'

'Bayard took her in an ambulance, accompanied her, I mean. Henriette thinks . . . Frederick, it may be quite serious.'

'Is this a general massacre you're announcing in bits and pieces, Chrissie? Did the whole house burn down, or what?' Frederick stood up in one angry movement, his boots sinking into the crusty snow around the chairs and table that still held their wine glasses and coffee cups. 'What exactly went on in Saint-Cloud last night?'

'Frederick, I simply don't know.' She went to her husband and ran her fingers lightly across his stricken face. 'I think we both should get back to Paris as soon as possible. I sense — I'm sure our baby is in some kind of danger. I've felt like this from the moment it was conceived. Let's pack and leave now.'

'All right. Start Isabella on the suitcases, and I'll find out where Rita is, provided I can get my dunce of a brother on the phone.'

'You're making a mistake, you know. I've told you that before.'

'About what?' Frederick snapped irritably.

'Taking your brother for a simpleton. He's anything but.'

'Don't start blaming every mishap on Bayard. He'll be flattered when he learns you accord him so much importance.'

'Frederick, how did Cecil Gutman get to your mother's house? Not on her own, surely. It was Bayard's doing. Somehow, he found out before we did that she was in Paris. Don't underestimate him. When Bayard wants something, he's capable of doing *anything* to get it.'

Frederick laughed nervously and kissed his wife on the forehead in a conciliatory gesture. 'You sound just like my father.'

Christine took a cigarette from the pocket of her green anorak and began tapping it rhythmically against the back of her hand. 'You may be the cleverest businessman in France, my love, but when it comes to your family, you have an enormous blind spot. I don't want Bayard to get within speaking distance of Cecil Gutman ever again, and if you're not going to take any action along those lines, I will!'

Christine tossed her long hair back across her shoulders in a familiar gesture that never failed to make Frederick Schomberg's heart skip a beat. She was looking at him steadily, a question in her eyes, but when her husband remained silent, she whirled around and started back to their chalet.

Alone on the snow-covered terrace, Frederick was stunned. In the years they had been married, he could not remember a single time his wife had been truly angry with him. Something irreparable had happened today, something that had started building up at the moment of the conception of that damned child in its test tube. He was losing Christine, as surely as he lived and breathed. Suddenly, the fate of Cecil Gutman and even that of his sick mother paled before the enormity of that realisation.

A blanket of heavy grey clouds passed overhead, blotting out the sun's warm rays. As he started to run up the path after his wife, Frederick Schomberg was astounded to see what a cold, desolate day it really was.

Chapter Sixteen

'I'll get out here,' Cecil told the Bordeaux taxi driver, handing him a fifty-franc note. She stepped down into the square just in front of a large, shabby-looking café with chairs and tables still spread out across the pavement. The Rendez-Vous des Sportifs. Cecil remembered the name well, remembered Serge telling her how he had stopped here every afternoon on his way back from the lycée, feeling sophisticated and grown-up as he played the *flippers*, put coins into the American-style jukebox, read his philosophy books. It was a place to flirt with girls and offer them strong black coffee or *panaches*.

'What in the world is a *panache*?'

'It's a bit like shandy.'

'I never heard of that either.'

'Because you're like all Americans – uncouth.'

'Uncouth! What kind of vocabulary do they teach you anyway? Middle Ages slang?'

Hours of silly banter. Never bored by one another.

Cecil took a chair at one of the outside tables and ordered an espresso. She looked around nervously. Since the sauna disaster in Saint-Cloud, she could not shake the feeling that she was being followed. No, there were no shady characters sitting in the sunshine at the Rendez-Vous des Sportifs. No students or pretty girls, either. Cecil unfolded her map and saw that the street she wanted was the next one to the right going around the square. She threw a few coins on the table to pay for her untouched coffee and stood up, suddenly desperate to be there.

Number 42 was three blocks down past a pastry shop with a rain-washed wooden front and a display of crusty miniature pies in the window; past a greengrocer shut for the midday break with sheets of heavy plastic spread over open crates of fruit and vegetables; past the high, cracked walls of a convent school. It was an ordinary street.

Cecil stopped and looked back. No one. Not even a car or a moped moved in the deserted street. Number 42 was separated from the pavement by a low fence of wrought iron. The house was four storeys high and very narrow, squashed in between the small factory and the shuttered shop-front of a cobbler. Cecil pushed open the gate, stepped into a tiny, flowerless courtyard, and pulled the bell chain. She stood waiting, heart and breath in abeyance. A heavy stone of longing and fear had settled in her stomach; she wanted to be here; no, she wanted to be anywhere else in the world.

The front door opened and a face peered out at her. A woman's face. Not Serge.

'Yes?'

'Madame Vlady?'

'Yes.'

'I'm ... Is your son at home? I'm a friend of Serge.'

'My son no longer lives in Bordeaux. What is your business with him?'

Cecil hesitated, nervously twisting a strand of hair. She was as intimidated by the French woman as a tiny child by its nursery-school teacher. Finally, in a voice that was barely audible, she said, 'I'm Cecil.'

'Cecil?' The woman was neither friendly nor unfriendly. The name brought not the slightest flicker or recognition.

'Cecil Gutman. Serge's friend from the University of Illinois.'

'Ah, you are an American.' Nothing more than that flat statement. Madame Vlady was not ranting and raving, was not insulting Cecil, was not slamming the door in her face. Neither was she inviting her into her house or rhapsodising on having found a long-lost daughter. Nothing. She did nothing at all. With a growing sense of dread, Cecil wondered if the woman had even heard her name before this instant.

'My son lives in Nice now, Mademoiselle...?'

'Gutman.'

'Oh yes, excuse me, Mademoiselle Gutman. Serge is working for a computer company on the outskirts of Nice.' She hesitated but said nothing more.

'Could you give me his address and telephone number? I'm going to Nice myself in a couple of days, and I'd like to look him up. I have ... something ... to discuss with him about the university alumni association.'

What could be more innocuous? The woman frowned, still undecided. She was rather aristocratic-looking, Cecil thought, with a long, narrow nose, heavy, half-closed lids over eyes of pale blue-green and beautifully waved grey hair. Her clothes were plain − a grey pleated skirt and a navy V-neck sweater, both of wool. Drab chic.

'I'm a friend of Dimitri Tartakovsky. He gave me your telephone number, but since I was out shopping today on the Rue Sainte Catherine, I thought it would be fun just to walk on over here and surprise Serge.' She lied blatantly, expertly. Every day, she was getting better at it.

'Monsieur Tartakovsky ... yes, Serge brought him here for *l'aperitif* last year. Just a minute then, I'll get my son's address for you. He hasn't been in Nice long. I'll have to look it up.'

Madame Vlady turned back into the house, shutting the door behind her, presumably so that Cecil could not follow her in to steal her valuables.

She's a monster all right; she'll do anything to protect her previous son. Serge never told her a word about me, not that we were engaged, not that I was to come to Bordeaux, not even ... not even ... Oh, the goddamn lying s.o.b.!

The vicious kick Cecil administered to the cream-coloured wall of the house gave her a temporary feeling of satisfaction despite the pain shooting through her foot. Lucky for Serge he wasn't in Bordeaux. He would have had to explain to his mother now, here, this instant.

When Madame Vlady returned a few minutes later with her son's whereabouts neatly printed out on a card, Cecil snatched the paper from her, uttered an ungracious word of thanks and raced out of the courtyard towards the square. The very idea of the Vlady family suddenly made her want to vomit.

Cecil had missed seeing Paris, so she set out to see Bordeaux with a vengeance. She would not, simply would not let assorted Schombergs and Vladys ruin her entire trip to France. For the rest of the day, she would be a normal tourist.

She started off by going window-shopping on the famous Rue Sainte-Catherine and, along the way, admiring the stark beauty of the Grosse Cloche built on the remains of the Saint-Eloi gate. She took a guided tour in English of the cathedral's stained-glass windows and abandoned one in German of the exterior walls. She looked at photo displays outside the Gaumont multi-house cinema, then took the Esplanade des Quinconces to the river. She counted barges, admired the great ships docked in the port waiting for cargoes of claret and brandy, imagined lovers drinking it in far-flung countries. In a dark riverside café, she treated herself to a cheese and ham crêpe and a half-bottle of Saint-Emilion. She was delighted to find that in this out-of-the-way place, they still served *café-filtre* in cups of glass and silver.

It was a beautiful day, light years away from the ice and snow of

Paris, and the omnipresent Christmas decorations seemed as out of place here as they would have in California or Florida. A street vendor told her it was unseasonable weather and would not last.

By four o'clock, Cecil was dead tired. She took a taxi to the botanical gardens and sat down on a bench under a giant palm. Even though the light was starting to fade, the park was still crowded with children and women pushing prams, many of them speaking rapid-fire Spanish and Portuguese punctuated with loud cries in French to their charges. For a moment, Cecil imagined she was in the Parc Montsouris – the park of mice – but she quickly put that idea aside, as Mica had taught her to do.

Cecil let her head fall wearily on to the back of the wooden bench. What in the world was she going to do? For two and a half years she had loved a man who lied to her consistently, relentlessly. Did it matter any more? Was the trip to Nice still worth making? What could she possibly get out of it except further pain and disappointment? Still, the journey here had been long, and not only in distance. Shouldn't she stay with it to its logical conclusion, hear what new lies Serge would propose after their long separation? Maybe there wouldn't be any more excuses; he might be married now. Perhaps – and Cecil was surprised to find she was laughing out loud – perhaps Serge had had a French wife all along. No wonder he hadn't married her!

Well, she could go to Nice just for a couple of days. What else did she have to do between now and June? Go back to Dallas? Spend Christmas over a hamburger at McDonald's? Return to the Schombergs for another sauna? Let Bayard take her to Deauville to meet Prince Charles before he picked some black and stormy night to dump her body into the Atlantic?

Cecil opened her eyes and forced herself to take touristic note of her surroundings. In her present frame of mind, nothing she saw was reassuring. Across the way was a gigantic tree with roots reaching towards her like the tentacles of a hungry octopus. And those crimson flowers bordering the gravel path? Not Christmas red at all, but death-of-the-sun red, the blood red of ancient pagans. And that crazy decoration on the rim of the fish basin, that contorted figure of a man in white plaster bent over to touch his knee with one hand, his Chaplin-like bowler in the other? The figure was posed to give the illusion of having being frozen at the very instant he was about to topple into the water.

Cecil got up and went to sit on the other rim of the basin, letting her hand trail in the rippling current where gold-coloured fish darted among thick stalks and feathery leaves. The statue was defying gravity in a startling way, and Cecil wondered idly if it was not in danger of slipping out of its niche. Without warning, it did exactly that. Before Cecil would move an inch, the Chaplinesque figure fell forwards in a nerve-shattering crash that sent waves of cold water on to the fleshlike petals of the red flowers and across Cecil's jacket and corduroy jeans. She jumped up with a shriek. Several of the nannies turned to stare at her and at the statue, who was now standing in the basin's shallow water laughing uproariously. A crowd of children had already formed at the water's edge, pointing and yelling, 'Clown! Clown! It's Charlot! Look, it's a clown!'

The statue was no longer white but streaked like a marbled cupcake; the Chaplinesque moustache and hat had both been lost, but he looked even more comic as he bowed to Cecil with the stiff, exaggerated movements of a marionette. The children clapped, obviously thinking Cecil was part of the show, his accomplice.

The statue leapt from the basin to fall on one knee before Cecil. He took her hand in his, opening the fingers that were still clenched tight in nervousness and bestowing a wet kiss on the trembling palm.

'I astonished you, did I not?'

'Yes, it was a surprise.'

'Do you like my act?'

'Well . . . Yes, it really was quite amusing.'

She couldn't help herself. He was too funny. She let him hold her hand an instant longer.

'Will you come to take tea with me at the kiosk?'

'But you're all wet.'

'So I dry myself, or do you speak of my personality?' He let go of Cecil's hand, stood up and bowed to her again with the stiffness of a mechanical doll.

'I see you know more English than you pretend.' Cecil grinned and pulled off her heavy wool jacket. 'All right, let's "take" tea, but put this on first or you'll be a real stiff. And for life.'

'I do not understand.'

'It's just as well. It was a terrible joke.'

Cecil thought the two of them must look quite outlandish as they walked up the path towards the orange-and-white-striped kiosk, followed by a crowd of chattering, giggling children and pram-pushing nannies trying to gather their older charges.

A man in green cotton overalls and a bulky yellow sweater plopped down into the chair next to Cecil's. He had hair as black as soot, eyes like smouldering coals, and a face that was all hollows and angles. He looked positively wild.

'I'm waiting for my friend from the weight-lifting class. You'd better not be here when he shows up.' Even as she spoke, Cecil was astonished to see the man was carrying her navy jacket. How had he got that?

'You mean you do not recognise your good friend the statue?'

Cecil gasped. Could this possibly be the little clown? He seemed to have grown by at least six inches since he disappeared into the men's room to 'wring out my clothes'. Gone alone with the white powder and the baggy clothes was every trace of the meek Charlot. Now he looked more like a . . . horse trader, if such a profession still existed.

'You're a chameleon,' she said in amazement.

'I have been told that before.'

'By admiring, thunderstruck women, no doubt, falling all over themselves to throw coins into your hat?'

He ran his fingers through his black hair. 'Am I wearing a hat?'

'You must take up a collection after your act. You don't let yourself get drenched like this every day for free, do you?'

Everything she said seemed to amuse him. 'I do not do this all days. Just for fun, when I am bored. I like to see the surprise on people's faces. Like yours today.'

'You're not a professional mime, then?'

'No, not any more. When I was a child, I did a kind of act in the streets with my grandmother.'

'And now?'

'Now I am a musician.'

'I should think your fingers might freeze off.'

'If you pay close attention, you will see that I never fall far. As for the cold, it is nothing to me. I am used to being out in the wind and rain.'

'You mean you're a street musician? Oh, let me guess! I'll bet you play the guitar and sing old Bob Dylan songs.'

'And you, pretty lady, you never stop asking questions. If you like that game so well, I will play it with you. Who do you think I am?'

'You really want me to answer that?'

He grinned impudently. 'I meant my people, my nationality.'

'Well, let's see, your English isn't bad, but I think we can safely assume you're not from one of the English-speaking countries.'

'You are safe, yes.'

'And you wouldn't be French because that's much too easy. How about Basque?' she asked with sudden inspiration.

'We are practically in Basque country here in Bordeaux, so that also is too simple. And I am not from Finland, either. I tell you this just to help.'

93

'Nor Hungary?'

'Nor Hungary.'

A girl appeared with their tea and pound cake on a tray, and they stopped to tackle that with gusto. The 'statue', as Cecil was calling him in her mind, was enjoying himself at her expense, and she was determined to outwit him. She had studied both French and German for her master's and Spanish in high school; she also knew a few stock phrases in half a dozen other languages. None of them, she soon discovered, was going to do her much good. The statue shot back a competent reply in every language she tried, even though he always had the same, undefinable accent.

'Is it a great mystery then, your nationality?'

'One of the world's last true enigmas.'

'You're from somewhere in the Pacific, an exotic South Sea island?'

'I am a bad, bad city boy. I do not like islands.' He had her hand again; his face was screwed up in a comically menacing attitude.

'How about the Orient?'

He leaned towards her. 'Have you ever been kissed by an Oriental? Perhaps it will help you to decide.'

Cecil pulled away. 'Somehow I think this game is coming to an end.'

'And I am disappointed. I thought you would have guessed by now. Look at my face.'

'Hmmm. Albania? Mesopotamia? Zanzibar? A Georgian? Eskimo?'

'You are far, far, far ...'

'Is it something alien?' Cecil asked, sensing she was drawing close. 'Not outer space but barbarian ... strange?'

'People think that this is so.'

He turned her hand up so he could stroke the smooth inner skin of her palm. Quite close, his eyes were wary, like those of a trespasser. Suddenly, Cecil knew. Some part of her mind had known from the moment he came to the table with the powder gone from his face, when she had instinctively seen him as a horse trader.

'So you're a gypsy?'

'I thought you would never guess, *querida mia*. Are you disappointed by my secret?'

Querida mia. She heard Mica's voice from a great distance, as though trying to warn her.

'You didn't play fair! You must have grown up in one particular country. You weren't just pulled around in a caravan all your life, were you?'

'There are not many caravans left now, and the ones we have run by motor. I told you I am a city boy. I was born in Montevideo, and I have lived mostly in Spanish-speaking countries.'

'I was right then, you do play the guitar. Flamenco?'

'Like Manitas? No, I am the shame of my people but also their hero because the *gajos* – the foreigners – have made a star of me. You see, I do not play gypsy music at all. I am a *bandoneonista*.' He made the gesture of opening a large accordion between outstretched hands. 'I play the tango.'

'Russian orphans,' Cecil murmured to herself.

'What?'

'I was thinking how strange a place Europe is for an American. It's full of romantic-sounding people, like Russian nurses who once knew a grand duke and gypsies who play the tango.'

'Do not use the plural. There is only one like that!'

'Then you are exotic, indeed.'

'You are right, of course. We gypsies can only be either pickpockets and house burglars or else hot-blooded lovers and flamenco dancers. Nothing in between. That is why the *gajos* give us their hate or their love. They cannot imagine us as ordinary people.'

'Please don't shatter my illusions by telling me you're just an honest, law-abiding citizen. That you live in a three-room apartment, do computer programming as a hobby and have a closet full of double-breasted suits.'

His smile was full of irony. 'Rest assured I do not have a closet. Or an apartment or any suits. But I can be anything you want me to be.'

'Anything?'

'Anything at all.' His face like chiselled rock was approaching hers again, and this time, Cecil closed her eyes. What a lovely place for a kiss – the striped awning of the kiosk, the luxuriant vegetation, the fading light. She had fallen into the exact centre of a turn-of-the-century painting.

'Would you like to see it?'

'*What*?' Cecil's eyes flew open.

'Don't look so shocked. I only meant my bandoneon.'

She laughed nervously. 'I suppose you keep it up in your room, conveniently next to your etchings?'

The statue put on an expression of exaggerated hurt. 'You are a woman with a poisoned tongue. I was only going to invite you to hear me play tonight.'

'Where?' Cecil asked cautiously. She envisaged a campsite in a lonely field, smoke rising against silver clouds, fiery alcohol, dark, cruel men.

'Do you know the stone building on the *rive*, the one that used to be a customs house?'

'Yes, I passed by there this afternoon.'

'It is an exhibition hall now, and a theatre. The city is sponsoring a Latin American arts festival. I play at nine o'clock tonight.'

'Oh, then you are ...?'

'Pancho Paso Real. Naturally, that is not my birth name, but people remember it better than the other one.'

'You're right. I noticed it today on the billboard.' She burst out laughing. 'Pancho, I can think of nothing I'd like better than to come to your concert. I'm so glad you found me.'

'And who have I found exactly?'

'Cecil. Cecil Gutman.'

Was it her imagination, or had a flicker of recognition appeared in those dark eyes? No, it was part of his seduction technique, like the wanton smile with which he was attempting to drown her as he murmured, ever so suggestively, 'Not as glad as I am to have found *you*, Cecil Gutman.'

Chapter Seventeen

'Is that Mr Frederick Schomberg?'

'Who is asking for him?' came the chilly response.

'Sir, this is the law firm of McNaught, Muncheon, Sandlin and Doss in Dallas, Texas.'

'Could you speak more clearly? I cannot understand one word of what you are saying.'

There was a silence, and then the Southern drawl of Denise O'Neil came back on the line, slurringly fragmented as though she were struggling against a faulty satellite. 'This . . . United States . . . calling . . . Frederick . . . or . . .'

'Frederick Schomberg is not here. What is the name of your party?'

'Mr E. Z. Jeffrey Sandlin. Would Mrs Christine Schomberg be available to speak to Mr Sandlin?'

Bayard's irritation grew by leaps and bounds. 'No. This is Bayard Schomberg. I am Frederick Schomberg's older brother, and it is I who handle the family business. If you care to tell me why you are calling, I may be able to assist you.'

'Just a minute, sir. I'll see if Mr Sandlin wants to talk to you.'

Wants to talk to me! Who does the ruffian think he is? He'd be advised to ask if I want to talk to him!

'Sir, I'm putting him on the line.'

'Mr Schomberg, I want you to know it's a real pleasure to be in contact with you, if only by telephone. As you are undoubtedly aware, I've been handling some legal work over here for your brother.'

'Naturally. Since Frederick is my *younger* brother, it's only normal that he consult me on matters of importance concerning the family.' Bayard's voice had taken on a new, perfectly agreeable tone, but his thoughts were in a whirl. *Who is this man Sandlin? Why he is looking for Frederick and Christine at Rita's house? Is he connected to the girl in some way?*

'How can I be of service to you, Mr Sandlin?'

'Well, sir, we've been trying to reach either your brother or his wife since yesterday evening our time. A crisis of sort has come up. Dr Samuel Sweeney, who is my contact over here, is out of the country, and his office is not giving out his overseas number. I've left a number of urgent messages for him, but he hasn't called me back, so I thought I'd better get hold of a member of the family.'

'Does this by any chance concern Miss Gutman?'

'Why, yes, as a matter of fact it does.' Sandlin sounded relieved to find he had a valid interlocutor. 'I haven't been getting any answer at your brother's house in Paris, and Christine Schomberg's office won't say where she is.'

'My brother's staff accompanied him to Gstaad for the holiday season, but I'm afraid you can no longer reach him there. We've had a tragedy here, Mr Sandlin. My mother was stricken gravely ill Tuesday evening. A series of small strokes – her life is in God's hands now. None the less, my obstinate brother and his wife insisted on flying her yesterday in their private jet to a specialised centre near Toulouse.'

'I can't begin to tell you how sorry I am to hear this, Mr Schomberg. I know your mother must be a fine woman, and I can fully understand that the family is distraught with grief. That makes it doubly hard for me to disturb you at this trying moment with still another problem.'

The emotion that had been in Bayard's voice when he spoke of his mother had faded to a cold aloofness when he asked, 'What exactly is the trouble?'

'Well, Mr Schomberg, I had a rather hysterical call from Miss Gutman yesterday. She's a high-strung young woman, as you may have found out for yourself. I'm not criticising her, mind you, because I think she's basically a wonderful girl of unimpeachable character, but ... well, she's inclined to be nervous. Yesterday, she called me in a very disturbed frame of mind.'

Sandlin did not feel it necessary to volunteer that Cecil had tried to reach Sam Sweeney for twenty-four hours before, in desperation, calling him.

'Miss Gutman says some peculiar things happened to her while she was in Paris. The most upsetting was her being locked in a hot sauna for over an hour. She seems to think this was actually an attempt on her life. I know this sounds far-fetched, Mr Schomberg, especially since it happened right in your mother's home, but I can't just ignore the incident. I am responsible for the girl's wellbeing.'

'Mr Sandlin, I appreciate your solicitude. The accident you are referring to occurred at the exact moment my mother was being taken out of this house on a stretcher. You can imagine the state of confusion that reigned here. My cousin and his wife were with me; we were taking turns trying to reach my brother in Switzerland. Poor darling Rita was unconscious and in pain. Amidst all that, Miss Gutman was forgotten, I have to admit that, but she was not "locked in the sauna", as she phrases it so dramatically, more than fifteen minutes. I'm afraid she's made a mountain out of a molehill and wasted a great deal of your own precious time.'

'Well, Mr Schomberg, you certainly reassure me, not that I thought for one minute that anything remiss had happened in your mother's house. Still, as Miss Gutman is so distressed by this incident, I think it's a good idea for me to fly over there and talk to her. I've already made reservations on a flight out of Dallas-Fort Worth tomorrow at – '

'That really won't be necessary. My sister-in-law has a number where Dr Sweeney can be reached. It's medical attention more than anything else that Miss Gutman needs – for her nerves, I mean. I seem to recall Christine saying that Sweeney is already on his way here.'

'I don't know,' Sandlin said doubtfully. 'I'm her lawyer, and . . .'

'Let's have it this way. I'll call Miss Gutman personally and smooth things over. If she feels a need for your presence, then either she or I will get back to you right away. In the meantime, I'll expect an invoice from you for all the time you've spent on Miss Gutman and her problems. Send it to the Saint-Cloud address, marked to my personal attention, and I'll have my Swiss bank take care of it.'

'I still think I should talk to Christine Schomberg as soon as she gets back from Toulouse. Also, I'd appreciate your asking Miss Gutman to ring me if she has any further problems.'

'I most certainly will. I'm going to hang up and call the poor child right this minute. Oh, by the way, Mr Sandlin, as I'm not in my office, I don't have her number. I wonder if you would be kind enough to give it to me?'

'I surely will, Mr Schomberg. Only too glad to be of service. Since we're working together now, may I call you Bayard? Please call me Jeff. Here, my secretary has just brought in the file. Cecil Gutman is at the Grand Hotel et Café de Bordeaux. That's a mouthful, isn't it? Number 2 Place Comédie, Bordeaux, telephone 90-93-44.'

'How perfectly delightful of you, Mr . . . uh, Jeffrey.' Bayard giggled. He was on top of the world. Nothing could stop him now. 'Rest assured that I will never forget what you've done for our family, Jeffrey. I only hope I'll be able to express my thanks in person one day soon.'

Bayard put down the receiver, waited an instant and then picked it up again. Another fit of giggling took hold of him, and it was minutes before he could actually make that next, very important call.

Halfway around the world, Jeff Sandlin sat drumming his gold ruler against the top of his marble desk. Denise sat on the edge of that same desk, some six inches away. She was wearing a blue silk blouse and a velvet miniskirt, and she was looking down at her boss in a very provocative way. But Sandlin's thoughts were elsewhere.

'That French so-and-so went one step too far with the Swiss bank business. Something mighty strange is going on over there, and I intend to find out what it is.'

'Can I help, sugar?'

Sandlin shot her one of his Machiavellian smiles. 'What would you say to taking a friend to a champagne dinner at the Dallas Country Club?'

'On your card?'

'On my card.'

'Sounds great to me! Who's my friend?'

'Estelle Blaney. Sam Sweeney's head nurse.'

Chapter Eighteen

The first Bordeaux – Nice flight of the morning was at eight o'clock. Cecil arrived for check-in at the Merignac airport at 7.20, only to be told that the flight would be delayed for at least an hour because of mechanical difficulties. She bought a stack of magazines at the newsstand and then went to look for a free stool at the bar. While she waited for her croissant and large *crème*, she flipped idly through the pages of *Paris-Match*. Her thoughts were on the week she had just spend in Bordeaux.

Cecil had gone three times to see Pancho Paso Real's show, and they had met for 'breakfast' on the *quai* nearly every day at noon. Even though Pancho fascinated Cecil, he also frightened her a little. She could not say why. Apart from the fact that he was a superb musician, she knew very little about him, but she *had* been impressed to see how much the predominantly young audiences like the dramatic, heart-throbbing sounds he wrested from his bandoneon. Much of the music he composed himself — voluptuous minglings of tango, African rhythms and *condombre* from his native Uruguay. Dressed all in black, his hollows-and-angles face white with fatigue from playing nonstop for nearly two hours, Pancho took on again at every performance the guise of a disquieting, other-world person savagely obsessed with his music.

Cecil had thought the two of them were best friends until the day before yesterday, when Pancho had disappeared out of her life as abruptly as he had fallen into it. She did not know how to reach him. The Latin American festival was over, and Pancho had never told her where he was staying in Bordeaux. It was his disappearance, more than anything else, that made her decide to continue on to Nice. The sudden change in the weather had also been a contributing factor. Gone was the glorious sun, replaced now by dark, purplish clouds and an icy wind which the concierge in her hotel told her was blowing

101

straight out of the Massif Central. When it had started to rain as well, frozen pellets that stung her face and hands and penetrated through her jacket and jeans to her very bones, Cecil had made her reservation on Air-Inter, then walked all the way to the Place de la Victoire to bid farewell to the Rendez-Vous des Sportifs. Goodbye to a dream she was still not sure she had the courage to relinquish.

Nursing a hot chocolate in a booth in the overheated interior, Cecil had been astonished to see Madame Vlady enter the café pulling one of the little shopping bags on wheels that French women used to transport their groceries. Madame Vlady had gone directly to the counter and ordered a cognac. She was wearing a green loden that came down almost to her ankles and a plaid rain hat. When she caught sight of Cecil's reflection in the mirror behind the bar, a flush of guilty surprise settled upon her thin, aristocratic face. She quickly downed her cognac and walked over to the booth.

'*Bonjour*, Mademoiselle Gutman. It gave me a turn, seeing you here. I thought you would be in Nice by now.'

'Did you?' Cecil asked noncommittally. An angry glint had come into her eyes from the moment she had noticed Madame Vlady at the door, shaking out her wet umbrella.

'I had occasion to speak to my son since I saw you last. He was upset that I did not have the name of your hotel in Bordeaux.'

Cecil took a sip of her hot chocolate and said nothing. Neither did she invite Madame Vlady to join her in the booth.

The woman kept glancing back nervously at her shopping cart, obviously afraid someone might make off with her leeks and onions while she was engaged in conversation with this bothersome American. Seeing that Cecil was not going to make her errand easier, she delivered the message. 'My son asked me to tell you, if I happened to meet you again, that he would be very pleased if you would telephone him as soon as you arrive in Nice. You have the number I gave you?'

'I have it.'

'You will call him then?'

'I received the message, Madame Vlady,' Cecil said abruptly. 'You can tell Serge that that was all I had to say.' Slowly and deliberately, she turned her head and pretended to watch two players at the pinball machine.

The woman stood her ground, though. 'May I know the day you are leaving for Nice?'

'I'm really not sure. Wednesday morning. Maybe.'

'The first plane?'

'Perhaps.'

'Miss Gutman, I have the impression that you know my son better than you intimated to me when you came to my house.'

'You're wrong, Madame Vlady. Serge is a complete stranger to me. I'm sorry to say that I don't know the first thing about him.'

The woman hesitated but seemed unsure of how to prolong her questioning. 'Well, goodbye then, Mademoiselle Gutman,' she said nervously before hurrying over to rejoin her precious cargo of fruit and vegetables. Then, with one last, puzzled look back at Cecil, she was out of the door and into the drenching rain.

So after eighteen months of total silence, thought Cecil as she absently turned another page of *Paris-Match* at the airport, *mommy's boy is suddenly in a terrific hurry to see me. How touching!* Suddenly she felt dizzy; she pushed her coffee to one side and put her head in her hands, pressing her fingers to her temples. She hoped she wasn't working up to a headache just before takeoff. Perhaps she was sleepy. She had got up awfully early to make this flight.

A tall man in a blue tracksuit sat down on the stool next to hers; he carried a large canvas sports bag with Ellesse stamped on the side. He put the bag on the floor at his feet and called out for a *crème*. He was about thirty, with blond, wavy hair and tanned face. He looked like a big, healthy German.

'You on the Nice flight, too?' he asked Cecil. He had not the slightest trace of a German accent; on the contrary, his voice rang with the sunny lilt of southern France.

'Yes, I am.'

'A real nuisance, this delay.'

'Do you think there's a chance the plane will leave at nine?'

'They never tell you what's going on, do they? We shall just have to wait and see.'

Cecil's head was throbbing. She did not feel up to a conversation with anyone, though this man was pleasant enough. From his appearance and the Ellesse bag, she guessed he was a pro tennis player. She turned another page in her magazine and suddenly caught her breath. The characters almost leapt off the page at her: SUCCESSFUL FRENCH BUSINESSWOMAN was the title in bold-face type. Under the photo of the woman was the caption: *Christine de la Rouvay, head of the world-famous glass company that bears her name.*

So there she was at last — her mirror image. Except that on Christine Schomberg's side of the glass, everything glittered with the sheen of pure gold, while on hers, the silvering was a sham. She could not take her eyes off the wild tangle of hair, darker than her own and fuller, more munificent. That was the hair that Rita Schomberg and Sam Sweeney had seen in their minds as they ran their fingers through her own. Had this then been the perverse reason that she had been chosen? Because of a superficial resemblance to the woman whose child she was to bear? Except that Christine Schomberg, she now could see, was older than she; there were fine, barely noticeable lines around her violet eyes and her full, generous mouth. Cecil, then, had youth on her side. Youth and a child that would belong to her for five more months. Christine Schomberg had everything else.

She took a sip of coffee from her neglected cup. It was cold and bitter-tasting, and she put it down again in disgust.

'Can I offer you another one?'

She looked up in a daze; it was her neighbour, the good-looking blond with the sports bag. Before she could answer, he signalled to the barman for two more *crèmes*. 'You don't want to drink cold coffee in weather like this. Where are you staying in Nice?'

'I have no idea. What's the best hotel?'

'The Negresco, if you like turn-of-the-century opulence. The Ruhl is a more in place, and it's closer to the Place Massena.'

'I think I'll opt for the Negresco.'

'Great! That's where I'm staying. During the day I train out at Sophie-Antipolis − that's about half an hour from Nice − but I'm back in town every evening. What would you say to −'

Cecil felt something knock hard against her elbow. The fresh coffee spilled from her cup and on to Christine Schomberg's brilliant red hair, covering it with an ugly brown stain.

'*Querida mia*, I am sorry. I was so excited to see you sitting here that I made you spill your coffee. Please forgive me. We must go, though. Did you not hear them call our plane?'

Looking as innocent as someone who had dropped straight out of the sky, Pancho stood squeezed into the narrow space between Cecil and the blond sportsman. He already had her small overnight case in one hand.

'Pancho! What in the world are you doing here? Where have you been?'

'I'll tell you everything on the plane. Hurry! We have only fifteen minutes before takeoff!'

And suddenly, incredibly, they were running towards the gate. Pancho was in the lead, pulling Cecil along behind him. 'There is very tight security today because of a bomb scare in Paris. You must hurry. Come on − you can run faster than that!'

'No, I can't. I don't feel well.'

'What is the matter, *pimpollo*? Is it because I stole you away from the big blond hunk that you are so weak?'

'Stop teasing me! I have a pain in my side, and it's getting worse.' Cecil slowed down and said emphatically, 'I'm not supposed to run, Pancho. I'm pregnant.'

'Is that true?' He stopped short, threw down their bags and flung his arms around Cecil, pulling her close to him. He did not look at all wild now, but teasingly tender.

'You seem awfully pleased about it,' Cecil said, a note of pique in her voice.

'Of course I am happy, *querida*, for you. Gypsies love children more than anything. They are our capital, our luck.'

'I wish this one could be mine,' Cecil said wistfully, but Pancho did not hear her. A security officer had taken their hand luggage and was showing Pancho into a curtained-off booth. Cecil went in the opposite direction; when she emerged from her booth, she found a commotion around the X-ray machine. An armed man was talking to Pancho while a small, dark woman pointed warily at an oblong box covered in black leather on the table in front of her. Its handles, clasps and ornaments were of silver, and it looked like a miniature casket.

Had Pancho been carrying that when he came to fetch her in the bar? He had been so emotional about her being pregnant, could this box possibly contain a tiny body? No wonder the guards were so excited. This was the reason, then, that Pancho had disappeared for two days in Bordeaux – to go to the funeral of a dead child. No! She must stop this; she was being irrational again. Pancho would not try to carry a body on to an aeroplane. How could she even think such a thing? If only her head would stop throbbing in this awful way.

At the female guard's stiff request, Pancho undid the silver clasps and lifted the lid from the box. Several people converged to look over his shoulder; there were scattered comments, giggles, nervous coughs. The woman insisted that he remove the object from its bed of black leather, and Pancho complied, reaching into the box to lift out his bandoneon. He held it up in the air and played a series of chords that resounded through the airport like sudden vibration from a pipe organ in the nave of an empty cathedral.

'What is it?' asked the female security officer. She still wore the distrustful look on her face.

'A musical instrument called a bandoneon.'

'I never heard of it,' she insisted stubbornly.

'That is your loss, Madame, not mine.'

Then, to general laughter, he put the instrument back into its box. Again, the two of them were running: they reached the plane's interior seconds before the doors closed and the captain began to bombard them with flight details. The cabin was only half full, and there was no sign of the blond athlete from the bar. Cecil concluded that he had missed the flight.

'It is called a casket.' Pancho's voice came out of the blue, and Cecil started. Had he read her thoughts back at the control gate?

'That is the name musicians in Montevideo and Buenos Aires give to the case because of its black colour and silver ornaments. On the X-ray machine, the bandoneon looks like metal blades, so it is natural the woman took it to be some sort of weapon or bomb. By the way, I do not like your friend. A nice girl like you, soon to be a mother, you should not associate with such a person.'

'What friend?' Cecil asked innocently.

'The big blond who tried to pick you up.'

'What are you talking about? I hardly exchanged two words with him, and he was extremely polite. Anyway, what business is it of yours?'

'I make it my business from now on.' He flashed her one of the smiles that made him look wild, crazy, unpredictable. Cecil shivered, although from what emotion she could not have said.

'Well, what was wrong with him?'

'For one thing, he was carrying a gun.'

'A gun? You've been watching too many gangster movies on TV. What makes you think such a thing?'

'I felt it. He had a holster under the big sweatshirt, and in the holster, *voilà*, a pistol. Do not look at me like that. I am telling you the absolute truth.'

'Pancho, we both agree you're a genius of a musician, but when you start making up stories to intrigue your women, your rating falls dramatically. Just when did you get close enough to that man to feel a gun?'

'When I took this.' Under cover of his long cashmere scarf, Pancho produced a maroon-coloured wallet, perfectly flat and made of some shiny, reptilian leather.

Cecil shook her head incredulously. 'You *stole* his wallet?'

'Of course.'

'But why?'

'Why does there have to be a reason? Where I come from, stealing a wallet is a sport, like car racing or tennis in America. Before I could read, before I went to school even, I was expert at it.'

'Who taught you this?'

'My grandmother.'

'Your grandmother?' Cecil was beginning to feel stupid; she seemed incapable of doing anything except mouth Pancho's words immediately after he spoke them. Should she assume an attitude of amusement or indignation? Perhaps just laughing it off was best. There probably wasn't a word of truth in Pancho's story anyway.

'Did your grandmother teach you to pick pockets for any special reason, or was this just something the two of you practiced together in your *roulette* on rainy days?'

'I was my grandmother's partner. We started off together in the markets in Montevideo and later moved to Buenos Aires. She chose me out of all her grandchildren because of my hands. Already when I was a child, they were like this.' He held them up for Cecil to examine. The fingers were slender, long and tapering. A musician's hands. A thief's hands, too. 'When I did well – passing wallets and jewellery to her – she bought me *alfajores*. That is a very sweet cake we have in Argentina. Chocolate was my favourite. Because I was such a greedy child, I became a very good pickpocket.'

'I see. And why did you take this particular wallet?'

Pancho laughed uproariously. 'I have to keep in practice or I will become rusty.'

'So this was just a sick joke?'

'A little more was involved. I do not like this Alan Mueller.'

'How do you know his name?'

'It was on his French ID card.'

'He looked sort of German, but he had the accent of someone from Nice. Maybe he's an Alsatian who grew up in southern France.'

'You should be pleased with me,' Pancho commented sardonically. 'Mr Mueller's wallet has given us an interesting subject of conversation on an otherwise boring plane trip. It has solved the mystery of his doubtful origins. And it will perhaps reap a rich reward for the person who returns his money to him.'

'Aren't you going to keep it?'

'No, just to make you happy, I will leave it here in the seat pocket. A stewardess or a cleaning woman will find it and turn it in to the company. Your friend Alan Mueller will spend many hours trying to figure out how he lost a billfold on a plane he never took.'

'Suppose you explain to me what *you* are doing on this flight? And what happened to you in Bordeaux?'

'Nothing happened. What do you mean?'

'You disappeared without a word of explanation.'

'This is an unfortunate habit of mine. I was too long in a hotel in Bordeaux. I had to escape. I went two days to the fields to sleep under the stars. It was you who had disappeared when I came back to look for you. I am very glad we found each other again.'

'And why are you going to Nice?'

'I have a booking in a nightclub. A week, perhaps longer if the people like me.'

'They will.'

Cecil pushed back her seat and let her eyelids drop, pretending to sleep. She had the same gnawing pain in her belly, and her headache had come back with a vengeance. If that were not enough, she was worried about her companion. She felt sure there was more to the wallet-snatching episode than Pancho was telling her. She should keep a tight hold on her own purse. After all, she had been staying at one of the best hotels in Bordeaux. Pancho probably thought she was a rich tourist. More than likely, he had followed her from her hotel to the airport this morning.

'You are thinking I want to steal from you. Am I right?'

Cecil's eyes flew open. Pancho was studying her closely, a knowing smile on his lips.

'It did cross my mind.'

'I already know what is in your handbag. There is some cash and a letter of credit on a French bank, but nothing else of value.'

'How . . . when did you . . . ?'

'That first afternoon we met in the café by the river. You made it easy for me by drinking too much wine. I am not with you for your money, *querida*. If you gave it to me, I would throw it away.'

'I said something like that once − to a lawyer.'

'And you came to regret it?'

'I came to think it was an extremely foolish remark.'

Cecil gave him a wan smile and decided that as soon as she found a room in Nice, she and Pancho would part company for good. She could only hope that he was not reading her mind at that very instant.

They were still half an hour from Nice when a terrible pain shot through Cecil's abdomen. She gasped and doubled over, trying with shaking fingers to loosen her seat belt. Had she fastened it so tight it had hurt the baby? Or had her thoughts of just an instant ago, thoughts of arriving on the Riviera under any other circumstances than as a body carrying another woman's child, translated into the sharp needles that were tearing at her flesh, trying to force out an unwanted occupant?

Cecil turned to Pancho and began to shake him. He looked up from notes he was making on a pad, saw her perfectly white face, and tore off his headphones.

'*Chica, que te pasa?*'

'*Dolor. Mucho dolor!*' She almost cried out the words, not even aware that she had lapsed into Spanish. '*Por favor, llama la azafata!*'

Cecil waited for him to push the overhead button, but instead Pancho shot out of his seat and ran down the aisle in the direction of the steward's station. When he returned with a middle-aged woman, Cecil had fallen across all three seats and was lying with her knees drawn up and both hands clutching her stomach.

'Madame, I am the *chef de cabine*. Can you tell me what kind of pain you are having?'

Cecil could not speak. Something terrible was happening inside her body, a clawing, ripping pain of unbearable proportions. She wanted to shriek but felt too ill even for that. How could this be happening to her on an aeroplane of all places? She was going to die in the sky like some martyred bird.

The woman turned to Pancho, a worried look on her face. 'Are you the husband? Don't you know what's the matter with her?'

'She may be pregnant. You must call Nice for an ambulance.'

'Very well. I'll have the pilot radio ahead for one. Will you stay with her?'

'Yes, please go ahead. I will take care of her until we land.'

Another steward brought towels, and Pancho knelt beside Cecil, clumsily trying to wipe the sweat from her forehead. She was moaning, and her whole body had began to shiver as though racked with chills and fever. Pancho draped his jacket over her shaking body.

'How ... how much longer ...?'

'Another ten minutes. That is nothing. Just relax, we are almost there, *pobrecita*!'

The *chef de cabine* was back. She spoke in a low, reassuring voice to Pancho.

'The ambulance will meet us on the runway, and a doctor will come aboard as soon as we land to help her. Arrangements have been made to take her directly to a clinic for emergency treatment.'

'Very good,' he replied. 'And who made all these arrangements you speak of?'

The woman looked at him in surprise. 'I don't know. Someone in the control tower, I suppose. Why do you ask?'

'It is always wise to know where you are going in life, and why. Especially if you are as sick as she is.'

She was eying him with suspicion now. 'Are you the husband? Do you know for sure that she's pregnant?'

'No, but I think it is best to take her to a place well equipped to handle emergencies. If she is expecting, she surely does not want to lose her baby.'

'Please ...' Cecil was half sitting now. Her face was drained of colour, and she still clutched her stomach. 'Pancho ... I don't understand ... How did this pain come on so suddenly?'

'We will know soon enough. Just relax now.'

The plane touched down a few minutes later on a runway that bordered the blue waters of the Mediterranean. A woman's voice requested that all passengers remain in their seats until the emergency evacuation of a sick person had been completed. Those closest to Cecil turned to look at her with curiosity.

'Madame, the wheelchair is here. Can you sit up?'

'Yes, I think so. I feel slightly better. I might be able to walk.'

'No, no, don't strain yourself. The doctor is coming.'

A pleasant-faced man of about forty came up the aisle carrying a satchel. He had dark, curly hair and deep-set eyes, and he introduced himself to Pancho in a pronounced North African accent. He was obviously what the French called a *pied-noir*, a man with 'black feet', born of colonist parents in Morocco, Tunisia or Algeria.

'I'm Dr Lopez. We'll take this young lady down in the service lift to the ambulance. Please, Mademoiselle, don't try to walk, just sit quietly. We'll have you out of here in a minute.'

A ground employee was already pushing the wheelchair towards a door in the kitchen area which connected directly to an elevated truck used for emergency evacuation of the plane as well as for loading meals and other supplies. The doctor turned to Pancho and said, 'She's in good hands now. I'll see that she calls you later in the day to give you the news.'

'I'm going with her.'

'There's no room in the ambulance,' Dr Lopez said shortly. 'We'll be in touch.'

'Perhaps you did not understand me. I said I am going, too. I will sit with her in the back of the ambulance.'

'*Mais c'est impossible, Monsieur*. Don't make a scene. This is a medical emergency.'

Pancho brushed by the doctor and ran up the aisle after the wheelchair. It was already in the elevated cabin of the loading truck. Seeing the look of rage on Pancho's face, the orderly tried to block his passage; at the same time, he pushed the button that closed the pneumatic doors. Pancho leaped forwards and landed inside the cabin just as the metal doors swished to a close behind him.

'Cecil,' he said breathlessly, 'I want to stay with you. Do you agree? Do you want me to be here?'

'Oh yes, please don't leave me alone,' she whispered. To her shame, tears were spilling over her cheeks. *This* was the arrival in Nice that she had dared imagine as a wonderful celebration, with Serge waiting for her at the gate, his arms laden with flowers. Even if he were there – warned by his mother of her possible arrival this morning – he might never know that they had missed each other, that Cecil had been taken, deathly ill, to a hospital. As they descended towards ground level, she began to cry in earnest. Pancho took her hand and squeezed it as though he understood she was crying less from her physical pain, which had lessened a little, than from the loss of her silly, girlish dreams.

Dr Lopez stood waiting for them next to the ambulance. His attitude had changed completely.

'Please ride in front with the driver,' he said amicably to Pancho. 'I didn't realise you were a close friend. I'm sure she'll be glad of your moral support.'

Cecil was helped on to a stretcher. As the doctor climbed into the back of the ambulance with her, she caught a brief glimpse of clear blue sky. Only a short distance from the runway, turquoise and silver-crested, the Mediterranean sparkled in the bright sun.

All the way to the clinic, Dr Lopez monitored Cecil's contractions, as well as the fetal heartbeat. 'Can you tell me exactly how far along you are?'

'A day or two over four months.'

'Who is your obstetrician?'

'Dr Samuel Sweeney in Dallas. Before you do anything, you must get in touch with him. I have his number with me. It's very important that you speak with him.' Even as she said the words, Cecil remembered that she herself had been unable to locate Sam for over a week. Jeff Sandlin had promised to let her know as soon as he found the doctor, but he had never even bothered to call her back in Bordeaux.

'I'll try, Mademoiselle, but it's probable that you will need emergency treatment the minute we reach the clinic. You don't want to lose your child because of unnecessary delays, do you?'

The doctor's alarmed look only served to augment Cecil's anguish. 'You mean I'm miscarrying?'

'I'd say the beginning of one. Tell me, have you been pregnant before? Even a child that miscarried or was aborted?'

'Yes.' Cecil's voice was barely audible.

'Then I want to make an amniotic puncture as soon as we arrive. We'll run a sensitivity test, and if that proves positive, it may be necessary to give your baby an emergency transfusion.'

'The baby? A transfusion? I don't understand.'

'Mademoiselle Gutman, it's likely you and the child have a rhesus incompatibility. This was once a very grave condition and often

111

resulted in fetal death, but, fortunately, with advanced technology we can "change" the blood of a fetus by giving it an intra-uterine transfusion. Your baby is very small for such a procedure, but if necessary, we'll do it. I'm going to give you something to make you sleep now. You must be perfectly relaxed when − '

'No! I don't want a shot. I have to be awake when you speak to Dr Sweeney. I don't have the right to make this kind of decision without his approval.'

'The right? Mademoiselle, I tell you this is a matter of life and death. Your doctor would never insist on treating you trans-atlantically if he knew the risk the child was incurring.'

'Doctor, isn't it at least *possible* that you're making a mistake? That terrible, violent pain I had in the plane has suspended. It's almost as though it had . . . worn off. I know that sounds strange, but it's the best description I can give.'

The ambulance pulled to a stop, and the driver came to open the tailgate. Pancho was right behind him. He peered inside; his eyes were flashing and his mouth was as contracted as though he himself were the suffering patient.

'*Querida*, how are you now?'

'After all the trouble I've caused, I'm ashamed to say I feel better. I . . . I think,' she said, turning to Dr Lopez, 'I'd like to go to a hotel instead of checking into the clinic.'

'But it's imperative that we run the test I mentioned to you! I told you this was a life-threatening situation.'

'For whom?'

'What do you mean?' His eyes darted in an irritable way from Cecil to Pancho and then back again to her.

'Life-threatening for me or for the baby?'

'I was naturally speaking of the fetus.'

'Dr Lopez, I promise I'll call my American physician the minute I get to my hotel. If he thinks I should have the test or the transfusion − or both − then I'll be back tomorrow.'

'But Mademoiselle − '

'She does not want to stay here,' Pancho said in a deceptively calm way. He moved between Cecil and the doctor, a menacing look in his black eyes. 'Do not try to force her.'

'I think, young man, you would do well not to interfere in this matter. Mademoiselle Gutman could lose her child because of you.'

'No! I take full responsibility for my own decision,' Cecil broke in angrily.

The doctor sighed and shook his head wearily. 'Will you promise me one thing, at least? If you have any more pain today, tomorrow or

112

any time during your stay in Nice, you will call me immediately?'

Cecil extended a hand to Dr Lopez. Already pancho had hailed a passing cab and was opening the back door for her.

'I'm so sorry. This has been terribly inconvenient for everyone. Would you send all the bills to me at the Negresco? Oh, and I do promise. I'll call you if I have the slightest problem. Only, I hope you won't be seeing me again. I wouldn't want to go through what I did on the plane again for anything in the world.'

An instant later, the taxi was speeding down the Cimiez hill towards the Promenade des Anglais and that beautiful expanse of turquoise water that made up the Bay of Angels. At the Place Massena, silver cascades rose in frothy, sparkling exuberance, one after the other all the way down the length of the square. It was a giddy sight, Cecil thought — mysterious underground springs rising to take glittering possession of the city. Strung across the streets, red and green lights blinked an unexpected message to her and to Pancho: JOYEUX NOEL! BONNES FETES SOUS LE SOLEIL DE LA COTE D'AZUR!

It was Christmas Day on the French Riviera.

Chapter Nineteen

Dr Sam Sweeney sat in the front row of a London sports arena between Sir Hilary Mountbank and Phineas Guillan, two of his oldest and dearest friends, both eminent British physicians and researchers in the field of human fertility. It was not fertility, of course, that the three doctors had come here tonight to probe. The small sports club put on late-evening programmes of all-girl wrestling for predominantly male and horny customers, and Sweeney and his friends were now watching a free-for-all, foul-for-foul simulated massacre. Four women wrestlers were in the ring, their hair dishevelled and their make-up streaked across their faces like curlicued wounds. They grappled and punched, pulled and poked, stomped and kicked, all of this violent action punctuated with the screeches of crazed banshees. The umpire had long since disappeared, perhaps to call the management or the police or just because he had decided to go home to the missus and the kiddies and to hell with what went on here.

At least, that was the way it seemed to Sam Sweeney and his cohorts, for they were drunk. Drunk to the point of utter confusion. They cheered the girls on through a haze of alcohol, vaguely hoping something truly awful would happen. All three felt that they deserved a bit of sheer, stunning violence, for it was a holiday in Britain – the day after Christmas, Boxing Day.

The small arena was hot and stuffy, and the crowd around them smelled of fish and chips, wet overcoats and unwashed bodies. All in all, the place was disgusting, the more so because the three doctors, still in tuxedo and black tie, had come here directly from a formal dinner at the Savoy. They had come because they had a middle-aged craving for blood, because they secretly wanted to degrade themselves, to be *encanaillé*.

Sweeney needed a bit of high jinks after the week he had just spent in Riyadh. Not even his office knew he had gone there to perform

114

hush-hush surgery on a Saudi royal favourite. In a brilliant *tour de force*, he had opened her deformed right Fallopian tube, or had it been the left? Or both? Anyway, he had spent the week like a monk — without gambling, alcohol or women. And consumed by guilt. The king had insisted on absolute secrecy, and he had been unable to communicate with either Christine or Cecil. It was wrong of him to have stayed out of touch for so long. And now that he was on this London stopover before returning to Dallas, what was he doing? Staggering around a bar looking for someone to direct him to the women's dressing rooms.

Sam tripped over the leg of a chair, caught hold of the countertop to steady himself and found that he was looking down at the headline of an abandoned paper. He hadn't read once since he left Dallas. He didn't care one way or another what happened to the world, except that the name in big black type seemed familiar to him. Too familiar. He picked up the paper and tried to centre it before his befuddled gaze in some way that would make the printed letters stop their wild dancing, make them take rational, orderly form.

It looked like 'Schomberg' all right. Was that a common name in Europe? He didn't know. Why was he so drunk? So confused? So wobbly? So damned stupid! What were the Schombergs doing now? Surely something he should know about. Had anything gone wrong with Cecil? So soon? The King be damned, he should have called her from Riyadh!

SCHOMBERG COUPLE DIE

Die? Couple died? Had they separated then? Officially? Divorced maybe? Sam's heart soared for a moment, thinking of Christine free. No, a couple that died didn't mean that. If it wasn't the couple that was dying, then it was the components of that couple, the two people themselves, their arms, legs, hearts, mouths, genitals, all these things dying, no longer tangible, no longer touching or touchable.

God, what Schombergs?

SCHOMBERG COUPLE DIE IN PLANE CRASH

Frederick Schomberg, industrialist and director of the well-known French conglomerate Schomberg Mondial, was killed yesterday when his private plane crashed while attempting an emergency landing during a heavy thunderstorm at the provincial airport of Clermont-Ferrand in central France. In the plane with Schomberg were his wife Christine, a glass designer, businesswoman and socialite, and the two pilots ...

The paper fell from Sam Sweeney's hands into the wet sawdust that covered the floor at his feet. His hands, which never faltered in the body cavities of a human being, were shaking now, and his mind, which knew how to produce fertility out of sterility, how to create life where there was none (even though he always denied this), that mind clouded over and refused utterly to comprehend that Christine was dead. Slowly, silently, he began to sob. He, who had had the Midas touch since the day he was born, where had it gone now? He had not a single answer. He was like a computer that was shutting itself down with flashing, slowly fading green messages: 'No Information Available', 'No Information Available', 'No Information . . .'

Dr Sweeney left his raincoat and umbrella where they were in the cloakroom, and his two friends where they were watching a sextet of girls trying to tear each other apart in the most erotic ways possible. He went outside into sheets of blinding rain, but that hardly mattered because he was blind already, struck sightless by what he saw within his own mind. Drunk as he was, Sam Sweeney none the less managed to capture with remarkable clarity two facts, and these were the only two he really needed to know. Number one was that he would never hold in his arms again the woman he loved, and number two was that he would never ever see the one million dollars that same woman had promised to transfer to him from her Swiss bank account, the money that was to have been her part in a pact the two of them had made with the devil.

Chapter Twenty

It was the first time Cecil had put a foot outside her room since she arrived at the Negresco on Christmas Day.

Her first stop was the dress shop in the lobby. Still feeling wobbly, she limited herself to trying on a few outfits and finally chose one that the enthusiastic saleswoman proclaimed, '*Sensationnel! Mais regardez-vous! Regardez donc! Quelle allure!*' It was a green shantung suit that caused such unabashed flattery, and it came with a matching silk blouse in a green and yellow, Madi geometric design. The suit jacket had a boxy cut that totally camouflaged Cecil's slightly fuller waistline.

She added to her purchases a pair of high-heeled pumps in dark-green leather, a yellow-beige coach bag, and a bright Hermès shawl for the evening chill. Surrendering all the big, showy sacks to a bellhop to take to her room, Cecil continued on to the hotel hair salon, where she was quite thankful just to sink into the soft depths of a chair and let someone else do the work.

Since her dramatic arrival in Nice, Cecil had been staying in her room to recover her strength. She slept a great deal, and when she awoke, fragments of unpleasant, sometimes terrifying dreams remained with her for hours – prisonlike hospitals with barred windows; hostile faces hidden behind sterile masks; gloved hands that held knives or long needles or bottles or too red liquid.

Cecil's near-hallucinatory state left her with little inclincation to turn on the TV that sat on the beautifully carved table opposite her bed. Instead, she leafed through the magazines and books she had picked up at the airport in Bordeaux and, in a vain search for companionship, made long-distance calls.

After hours of effort, she reached Dimitri in Moscow, only to learn he was about to leave on a courier assignment to Tashkent; he was moving farther and farther out of her life.

'Cecil, can you believe it?' came his excited cry over the very bad line. 'I managed a surreptitious look at my file when I first got here and discovered that my arrival date was moved up by nearly a month. At the request of a French minister, no less. Your friend from the U of I is quite a personage in diplomatic circles!'

'You mean that's why you had to leave without notice? The day I was supposed to have lunched with you?'

'Bull's-eye!' came Dimitri's delighted reply. 'My talents were needed so badly at the embassy that another passenger was booted off the Air France flight to Moscow just to make room for yours truly.'

Visions of that nearly fatal day flashed through Cecil's mind: a black limousine turning into a country lane; Rita Schomberg's clawlike hands reaching for her hair; the thermometer of a hellish sauna moving inexorably upwards. It couldn't be, the idea was too fantastic, and yet . . .

'Dim, who was the minister who arranged your sudden departure?'

'I can't tell you that on the phone, not from here anyway. Take my word for it, Cici, he's a big shot. Comrade Tartakovsky only moves in celestial regions now.'

Cecil hung up in a pensive mood. Was it possible there was some sort of campaign to isolate her, to remove all the friends that mattered in her life? Now that Dimitri was gone, only Serge and Mica were left. Mica was extremely vulnerable; she could be deported from the United States at a moment's notice, just as Dimitri had been whisked out of France at a minister's request. Cecil breathed a sigh of relief some minutes later when Mica's rock-solid voice came on the line.

'You seen *him* yet?' Mica asked, as straight to the point as always.

'No, but he's meeting me here on Sunday night. We're going to have dinner together.'

'You still in love with him then?'

Cecil laughed, feeling almost light-hearted. 'I was sure I hated Serge until I heard his voice on the phone yesterday. Now I'm all mixed up again. I think it was something to do with being in France – I seem to fall in and out of love according to the time of day. It's probably an infection peculiar to the French climate.'

'Who else you falling for?' Mica asked in her gruff voice.

'Oh, just schoolgirl crushes. I started thinking too much about my doctor, just as you predicted I would. And now . . .'

'Another one?' Mica exclaimed incredulously.

'It's nothing really. I met a man in a park. He speaks Spanish like you do. I don't trust him because he's crazy, unpredictable, wild, but at the same time I like him because he's a tiny bit dangerous.'

'You were half-dead over this Serge, and now you fall for

118

everybody you meet. What's going on over there?'

Cecil stretched out on her satin-covered bed and smiled to herself. 'Just what I told you, Mica − the French weather or something. I'm not used to all these amorous people; they mix me up. I even met a big goofy tennis coach who lives in this hotel and wants to show me around Nice. I'm not attracted to him at all, but I do like the attention.'

'How does the baby mix in with all these new boyfriends?'

'Oh, God,' Cecil sighed. 'I try to put the baby out of my mind. I can't really do that, can I?'

'You better not,' came Mica's sombre reply before they said goodbye.

Dr Lopez kept Cecil's thoughts trained on her pregnancy by turning up with his bill. He was fairly bursting with sympathy and North African verbosity. Was she still having pains? Had she lost any fluid? Could she pay him in cash instead of a cheque due to nasty French tax laws? Was she going to make an appointment for those vital tests that could be done only at his clinic?

Cecil handed over the francs and answered his other questions with a firm negative. Sam Sweeney, she added, had forbidden her to undergo any treatment unless he himself was present. That was, of course, untrue. Despite several fresh bouts of frantic calling, Cecil had got only Sam's head nurse on the phone. Estelle sounded almost as distraught as Cecil herself. The doctor had failed to return for a crucial meeting at the Medical Center on 27 December, and several important patients had arrived in Dallas to find their fertility specialist absent without a word of excuse. Estelle was covering as best she could, but there was a note of panic in her normally port-in-any-storm voice.

'If the s.o.b. calls you, tell him to get his ass back here on the table! I've been on the firing line for him long enough! And tell his high-and-mighty that some very peculiar people are asking for him here. They don't actually speak − they snarl at me. Cecil, I've had it up to here trying to explain to these beasts why Sam didn't get back on time.'

Things were starting to crack in Dallas, Cecil concluded. And badly. Why had Sam abandoned everyone − his staff, patients, family and Cecil herself? In spite of her glib answers to Dr Lopez, Cecil was worried about not taking the tests he insisted she needed. She had a strong justification, though; Cecil was terrified the French doctor might hospitalise her again. After four long months in Sam Sweeney's clinic, she was not about to go into another one without putting up a fight.

But what if she really was endangering the life of the fetus?

Cecil tried to remember what she knew about the Rh factor. It wasn't much. She had read that women sometimes produced antibodies against the rhesus element in the blood of a child they carried. In a subsequent pregnancy, those antibodies could accidentally pass from the mother's bloodstream into that of the fetus, causing it to go into shock. That couldn't happen in her case, even though she *had* been pregnant before. Sam Sweeney had checked her for every problem known to the medical profession. There was no way he would have passed over such a run-of-the-mill procedure as Rh incompatibility. It was absolutely impossible!

Of course, she wasn't the biological mother of the child. Would it make a difference that there were more Rh factors to take into consideration? Had the hospital lab slipped up because they hadn't been told they were running a test on a surrogate?

A biological mother and father, a surrogate and a fetus? What sort of Rh cocktail did that give? Cecil had no idea. It wasn't her problem, anyway, and she wasn't going to bring another migraine on herself trying to figure it out.

Cecil got up and went to the window. It was a beautiful December day outside, and there were people sunning themselves, walking their dogs, playing volleyball, snacking at small beachside restaurants. Cecil wanted desperately to be out there with them, casually partaking of the joys of life as only Mediterranean people knew how. A wave of anger swept over her. It was all so unfair: Sweeney missing; Jeff Sandlin as quiet as a scared mouse; and the Paris Schombergs not in the least trustworthy. She had never wanted any of these people breathing down her neck while she was in France, but neither had she imagined that she would be callously thrown to the winds like this. This doctor, the lawyer and the merchant prince, all totally indifferent to her fate. None of them − not even Christine Schomberg − interested in protecting what must be an already substantial investment in time and money.

The whole thing was a baffling mystery.

For the hundredth time since she had left Dallas, Cecil asked, 'Where are you, Sam Sweeney? Where in God's name *are* you now when I most dreadfully need you?'

'What, my dear? Did I hear you calling for the manicurist? Suzanne, over here for Mademoiselle. She needs you right away! Well, what do you think of your hair, my dear? You never dreamt you would look like this when you came in, now did you?'

The volatile little French hairdresser with the bald, shiny head and a moustache as colourfully variegated as the back of a tortoiseshell cat had talked Cecil into having her hair put up in Rita Hayworth 1940s-style waves.

'She's my very favourite actress of all time, you know. That hair! And that mouth! And those big teeth! If I were you, my dear, I'd buy some lush dark lipstick and do my mouth exactly like hers. She's my absolute dream-girl. Just thinking of how she looked painted on those World War II bombers, or in that skin-tight dress in *Gilda*, makes me go all weak at the knees.'

When he had run through all his fantasies and stuck the last henna-coloured bobby bin into Cecil's piled-up hair, the little man whirled her chair round and round so she could see herself from every possible angle. Fragments of her new self appeared in the mirror and then vanished just as quickly. Nothing Cecil saw was familiar. She was a different person altogether. Her hair was darker and thicker; her skin seemed blushed with gold dust; her eyes glittered with gemlike violet lights. She might have been a movie star. After all, the Negresco was only a stone's throw down the coast from the Victorine Studios where so many wonderful French classics had been shot. Tonight, in her beautiful new clothes, she would look as dazzling as ... as ... Yes, why not say it? As dazzling as Christine Schomberg herself.

She was nearly twenty minutes late for her appointment because she had opened the door of her room to an elderly delivery man dressed in the smart uniform of a famous Nice *chocolatier*. The man had bowed − actually bowed − and presented her with an enormous heart-shaped box which, she soon discovered, contained an impressive assortment of gold-wrapped chocolates and an enigmatic card that read, 'An early Valentine to my Heart of Hearts.'

The card was unsigned, and in his shaky old voice, the delivery man professed total ignorance of the sender's identity. None the less he lingered on, his hand indiscreetly resting palm up at his side. Cecil was actually putting a ten-franc tip into that hand when he suddenly pulled her close enough to plant a kiss on her cheek.

Cecil screamed and jumped back in fright, but the man was already removing his grey wig and thick glasses, and something about him was very familiar.

'What are *you* doing here?' she asked, doubled over with laughter.

'I've come to invite you to my show. Haven't you heard that I'm the toast of Nice?'

'Only Nice? Not the whole Riviera?'

'Of course. And now I'm completely exhausted from all the women who've been chasing me, so I thought I'd drop by see the one who doesn't care.'

'What makes you so sure?' she asked teasingly.

'Your cruel silence. I thought you were still languishing in bed sick, but no — here you are, dressed up like a beauty queen and about to go off somewhere. Was it to see me?'

'No, but I will soon. I promise.'

'Come with me now!' he said impetuously. 'Break your date, *querida*.'

'I couldn't even if I wanted to, Pancho. I made this appointment a very, very long time ago, and it's cost me more than you can imagine just to be here for it.'

When she got downstairs, pleased that she had made him wait, Serge was sitting at a low table near the bar reading a magazine, a long-stemmed pipe hanging jauntily from his full, babyishly pouting mouth. When Serge failed to look up, Cecil simply went on standing there, observing him across the opulent, gold-lit room. A Hollywood magnate could have cast both of them tonight for a period movie, for if she had been transformed by her hairdresser into an instant Gilda, Serge was and always had been a young Orson Welles, tall and full-faced with heavy, attractive features: half-closed, slightly droopy eyes, a wide nose and curly, dark hair that fell rebelliously across his forehead when he leaned forward. He was wearing a jacket of grey-blue tweed and a navy-and-grey-checked tie. He was totally absorbed in his reading, not watching for her at all.

Like his mother, Cecil thought angrily. *He doesn't even know I exist.*

'A table for two, Mademoiselle?' asked the waiter who had materialised at her side.

'Would you do me a favour? I'm near-sighted, and I'd appreciate your going over and asking that gentleman at the corner table if he is Monsieur Vlady, the person with whom I have an appointment tonight.'

If he thought her request peculiar, the waiter did not betray it. 'Of course, Mademoiselle. Vlady, did you say? If you'd care to wait here ...'

As the waiter bent down to speak to him, Serge looked up from his magazine in a puzzled way. All of a sudden, he threw down his pipe, jumped to his feet and walked quickly towards the door, a lopsided smile on his heavy face.

'Cecil — good God, I wouldn't have recognised you! It is Cecil, isn't it?'

Without waiting for an answer, perhaps deciding that, whoever she

122

was, she was worth embracing, Serge took her in his arms in a giant bear hug that crushed her against the prickly tweed of his coat. His lips brushed her cheek before travelling to her ear, where he whispered in a sensuously low voice, 'I've never seen anyone so beautiful in my life. Never, ever. I swear it. You've grown up! Why, you're a different person altogether, Cici.'

She pulled away and smoothed the silk of her jacket in a nervous gesture. Cecil had not anticipated being so utterly overwhelmed, both physically and emotionally, by Serge.

'Hello there,' she managed to say in her normal voice. 'How nice to see you again. Shall we have a drink here or some place else?' She might have been greeting a former classmate from grade school for all the feeling she let slip through her calm façade.

Serge helped her slide into the banquette. 'Here, of course.' He took her thin, cold hand in his pawlike one and brought the fingers to his lips. 'This is the last civilised bar in Nice.' He signalled to the waiter. 'Bring us two glasses of champagne. And quickly, please, we simply cannot wait.' He smiled at Cecil, and his eyelids fell just a little lower. 'This is a celebration, isn't it? I can't believe it's you sitting beside me, with the Mediterranean right on our doorstep. How many times did we speak of this?'

'Too many,' Cecil said curtly. 'Perhaps we shouldn't start the evening with a lot of references to our past. We might not make it as far as the champagne, not to mention the dinner.'

'But Cici, I couldn't agree more. I don't want to talk about things that happened long ago and to two completely different people. Forget our youthful escapades! Let's talk about our future.'

'Oh, do we have one?' she asked innocently.

'If we didn't, I wouldn't be here.'

There was a long and painful silence, with Cecil refusing to make any reply, refusing even to meet his almost professionally seductive gaze. At last Serge broke the ice by asking, 'What brought you to the Riviera? Dimitri called me this morning and said you had some secret, high-powered job.'

'News gets around,' Cecil replied noncommitally.

'Well, what is it?'

'Oh, come now, you remember English, Serge. "Secret" means do not reveal. See no evil, hear no evil, all that sort of thing.'

'Am I to understand that you're engaged in an unsavory complot? I can scarcely believe it of someone with such an angelic face.'

'That's the first time you ever accused me of being an angel.'

'It's difficult to concentrate on your seraphic appearance when you talk like a viper. As usual, I'm flamdoodled by you.'

Cecil's laughter was so loud and unexpected that a pair of Japanese gentlemen at the next table turned and nodded their heads in unison, as though participating in their joke.

'There you go again with your crazy vocabulary,' Cecil said.

Cecil shook her head in amazement; they were already back in their familiar mode of jousting. It was as if those eighteen months of sorrow and pain had never existed. Well, why not pretend they hadn't? Just for an hour or so. Or for a night. What did she have to gain now by asking Serge for an explanation except more unhappiness for herself? She had become quite good at pretending she was a rich woman. Perhaps she could play a happy one as well.

Serge lifted his glass and clinked it against hers; his face was almost touching her own, and he wore the lopsided smiled that once upon a time had captivated her heart. He leaned closer still and whispered perfidiously, 'To us.'

As they strolled down the Promenade des Anglais, Cecil let her hand trail along the white railing that separated them from the beach below. It was nearly midnight, and a light fog covered the city in a bluish haze through which the street lights shimmered tremulously. Far out to sea, the barely visible outline of a ship moved slowly across the horizon.

'That's an American warship heading for Villefranche,' Serge said, as he knocked the bowl of his pipe against the railing.

'Is that far from her?'

'No, just a few kilometres up the coast. There are a lot of little restaurants at the foot of the cliff in Villefranche. If you like, we can go there for lunch next weekend.'

'It's so lovely here, I suppose there are hundreds of places to visit,' Cecil said woodenly. All evening, her voice had sounded strange to her, stilted and off-key as though a stranger were speaking in her place.

'You're right, a different one every day of the year. We can go up into the Alps and drink mulled wine in the snow. Or go to the Cinemathèque in Nice and overdose on old movies. Or over the border to the market in Ventimille to buy Italian cheese and grappa. Or to the Chèvre d'Or in Eze for the most spectacular view of the whole coast. Then there's Vallauris for the Picasso ceramics and Biot for the glass-blowers, and after all of that, we can sit under a giant eucalyptus tree and drink peach wine and just talk. A programme for a lifetime, isn't it?'

Cecil felt a lump form in her throat. How ridiculous! How could she let herself be moved like this? Was it Serge's overwhelming physical presence or the beauty of this city – the party-cake façade of the Negresco, its dome and gabled window still strung with holiday lights; the esplanade with its centre strips of purple and yellow flowers flanked by towering date palms and the swordlike leaves of the yuccas and agave; the seaside parks whose green lawns stretched out before them like phosphorescent carpet. To the east, the corniche roads clung to the sides of the cliff like tenacious snakes weaving their way to Monaco, Menton and Italy, and westward, where the land curved abruptly out into the Mediterranean, half-shrouded airport lights flashed endless warnings to Cecil: *Don't tell him! Don't tell him yet!*

She shivered uncontrollably. Sensing her discomfort, Serge turned back from his silent contemplation of the sea and unbuttoned his tweed jacket. He spread it open and motioned for Cecil to move into its warmth. As though drawn by an irresistible magnet, Cecil stepped forwards and Serge closed the coat around her, bringing her up hard against his body. Then, in sudden urgency, he pulled her closer still; already his mouth covered hers, and she could taste the sea-air saltiness of his lips and hear the strong, regular pounding of his heart.

Don't tell him, don't tell him, cried the fog-veiled lights. *Don't tell him, you'll be sorry if you do.*

A fierce sound escaped from Cecil's throat. Serge tilted up her chin, trying to read her expression. 'What is it? Was that a laugh?'

She pulled out of his grasp and stood back a few feet, studying him as though he were a total stranger. She was startled to see how little he resembled his thin, aristocractic-looking mother. He must have inherited every single feature except the heavy-lidded eyes from his dead father.

'I heard our two hearts beating together,' she said at last.

'Is that so funny? It seems rather moving to me.'

'I thought so too until I remembered.'

'What exactly did you start remembering, Cecil?' Serge wore an expression of sombre dread, as though he knew what was coming next.

'That there are three sets of heartbeats now instead of the two there used to be. Not very romantic, is it?'

Was it the champagne that made her so reckless? So stupid? She took a long, shuddering breath and plunged on. 'Did I forget to tell you that I'm pregnant?'

Had she actually said it out loud, or were the words only resounding in her mind, travelling there from some other time and place?

'Cecil, in God's name, what are you saying?'

'I thought I just said that I'm expecting a baby.'

125

'Oh, bloody hell! You have to spoil every perfect moment we have together, don't you? It's been like this since the day we met. You seemed different tonight, more self-assured and grown up. But you can't let go of what happened between us, can you? All right then! Let's get it out in open once and for all. I won't suffer through any more of these thinly veiled allusions.'

In the angry silence, nights sounds erupted − waves lapped at pebbles on the beach below; tyres passed on wet asphalt; palm fronds snapped and crackled in the wind − but Cecil and Serge did not hear any of them. Like blood-thirsty warriors, they concentrated all their attention on one another, busy cataloguing past blows and digesting freshly disinterred pain.

'Can't you see what we're standing in?' Cecil asked in mock concern. 'We're ankle-deep in the ashes of our dead love.'

'Oh, shut up!' Serge cried savagely. 'I'm sick to death of your melodramatics. Just tell me the name of the rich family that supposedly has bought you.'

'No one's bought me! How dare you suggest anyone could! I'm doing this for one reason only − because it gives me great pleasure. I expect you know why, too.'

'You've been playing with me all evening, haven't you?' Serge spat out the words. 'You made up this whole ridiculous story to get at me for what happened back in Illinois. Let me tell you something, Cecil, I will not − do you hear me? − I will not accept the guilt you're trying to saddle on me. Maybe you no longer remember the way you were in school, clinging to me, getting hysterical every time I walked out the door on an errand. You were beautiful and brilliant, but hadn't one ounce of independence back then, and, frankly, I got sick of it. I admit I ran out on you, but I didn't ask you to become pregnant, did I? Did I ever once suggest to you that I wanted a child? When you came to me with your misty-eyed announcement, I was a penniless, twenty-five-year-old student without a green card. Add to that the fact that you were suffocating me with your needs, and you can see why there was a certain ambivalence in my feelings. You scared me off.'

'I'm amazed by your ingenuity!' Cecil exploded. 'The way you tell this fairy tale, you were the hapless, unsuspecting victim, and I the ogre that nearly gobbled you up. Suppose you explain to me why your previous mother had never even heard my name before I rang her doorbell in Bordeaux?'

'I admit I invented the story about my mother's violent objection to our marriage. I needed an excuse to get away from you.'

'I can't believe this! How could I have loved such a hypocritical monster? And Dimitri, for what tortuous reason did you let him go on thinking we were engaged?'

'Very simple – I wanted to believe it myself. At least, part of me did. I'm not the only man in the world to have trouble making up his mind about marriage, you know. I've got up every morning since I got back to France and said, "Today I'll call Cici". Only I always put it off to the next day because I wasn't sure what I wanted to say. The only thing that's sure is that I never stopped loving you, not for one minute. You're the only woman who matters in my life.'

'These glib improvisations just fall right off your tongue, don't they? Of course, you always *were* world champion in the tall-story department.'

'You're not bad yourself.'

'Oh, you think that, do you?' Stung to the quick, Cecil could no longer control her words. 'I suppose you've never heard of Schomberg Mondial? Those Schombergs are my employers. Call them in Paris if you think I'm a liar. I have their number with me. Go ahead – I dare you!'

'Schomberg . . .' Serge started and seemed to struggle with some undefined emotion. 'What particular Schombergs?'

'Frederick, the head of the company, and Christine, his wife, the one who looks so much like me. Or so people seem to think.'

Was it the champagne that made her blurt all this out? Cecil was instantly ashamed of her breach of confidence, but she could not seem to stop. 'Surely you've seen photos of them – Christine Schomberg was in *Paris-Match* as late as last week.'

'I've seen their photos all right,' Serge said grimly. 'I've seen them in every newspaper and magazine in France. I saw them on TV, and I heard all about them on the radio. Practically nonstop, in fact, since the day they died.'

'Died? What are you talking about?'

'Frederick and Christine Schomberg were killed in a plane crash on Christmas Day.'

'It's not true. You're just saying this to . . . to . . .'

'Oh, come now, Cici, you can't have been in France and not heard the news. The Schombergs were flying back from Toulouse in their private plane when they smashed into a mountain during a bad storm. It seems the plane's instrument panel was defective, and the pilot had no visibility because of the weather.'

Cecil leaned back against the white railing and stared unseeingly at the passing cars. She felt like an actress in a bleak, existentialist play. 'How do you know all of this?' she asked in a hollow voice.

'Because it's the biggest story to break here in months! You can't

127

have missed it any more than I could have. They sent an expedition up into the mountains, and a TV crew showed the whole ghastly thing on Channel One last night. Charred bits of bone sticking out of the snow, an arm here, a leg there – '

'Stop it! Stop! Stop!' Cecil looked at him with desperate appeal. 'Serge, please tell me you're joking. Please. Because if you're not, then don't you see what that means? I am carrying the child of two people who are no longer alive.'

'That *would* pretty well sum up your situation, provided there were a word of truth to what you've been saying.'

'You must believe me.'

'No, and for good reason. The press has played up the fact that Christine and Frederick Schomberg left no offspring and that the company is being taken over by a cousin. The only other surviving relatives are Frederick's mother, who apparently has some sort of debilitating disease, and his social butterfly of an older brother. Why do you think no one breathed a word about an unborn heir? Simply because no such child exists.'

Cecil took a deep breath of cold air. 'Serge, I need you to take me back to the Negresco. Fast. Truce. I'm calling a truce with us. But I must go back.'

'Cici, you're as white as a sheet! What's happening to you?'

'Faint. I'm afraid ... right here on the Promenade des Anglais ... Oh, Serge, goddamnit, I'm going to faint!'

Chapter Twenty-One

Jean-Michel Nedelec's law office was in a pleasant area of Paris, just across the Boulevard Menilmontant from the Père Lachaise cemetery. He had moved into it the week of Edith Piaf's funeral, a surrealist happening that had caused a near-riot when close to four thousand mourners thronged the gates of the huge burying place. It had got so out of hand that the crowd had knocked down police barriers and thrown itself at the coffin, even climbing up on neighbouring tombstones to get as close as possible to their idol. Nedelec still remembered the hysterical screams rising from behind the brick walls; it could not have been any noisier, he thought, on that bloody day in 1871 when the Commune ended, fittingly enough, right inside the cemetery.

Today, as he looked out of his office window at the snow-covered walls, Nedelec imagined how peaceful it must be there, with no tourists and few burials. Only one hearse had gone in since nine o'clock. Nedelec loved the cemetery. Once, from this very window, he had seen a film crew drive through the gates — a whole procession of cars, generator trucks and phony paddy wagons for a chase scene. As soon as he had a spare minute, Nedelec had raced over, and, a quarter of an hour later, he had a job as an extra and the prospect of spending a whole night in the cemetery amidst the brooding angels, the winged messengers of doom, and the eternally weeping virgins.

In truth, Nedelec had spent most of that night by Piaf's tomb, a common, vulgar monument well suited to a woman who had been born on a pavement. There were flowers everywhere — fresh and faded, in wax and in plastic, all of them dusted with ghostly sprays of moonlight. Nedelec had pushed them aside to read the names of those that lay with the Little Sparrow — her father; her last, young husband; and her only child, a girl named Marcelle who had died of meningitis. The tomb of the baby had touched the young lawyer, and he often thought of her, especially on days like this one, when his appointment book was crammed with the names of workers wanting compensation for illegal sacking or unpaid bonuses.

Maître Nedelec reluctantly cast off the spell of the cemetery and went out to his small waiting room to admit his next client. To his surprise, he saw she was a woman. Not Arab or Yugoslav or African, either. This woman wore a one-piece trouser outfit of heavy-looking khaki with black studs on the shoulders and waist, and she carried a puffy grey jacket that looked as though it might have once been part of a parachute. She was strong-looking, yet Nedelec was sure her muscles had not come from any sort of hard labour. He could easily envisage her working out at a fashionable health club.

'Madame, you have an appointment?'

'No, but I won't take up much of your time. Five or ten minutes at the most.'

He was right. Her voice was raucous but educated, the voice of a bourgeoise. He was puzzled, yet his face showed nothing as he nodded in acquiescence and murmured, 'Please come in, Madame.'

As he moved around behind his cluttered desk, the lawyer had the time to observe her. She was of medium height, with short, tight curls of a sandy blond colour. Her eyes were slanted like those of a jungle cat, and warm brown freckles spilled across the bridge of her nose and on to her cheeks. He thought he had never seen quite so many freckles on a woman's face; in France, it was not usual. Her skin was dry and beginning to crease, but she was still an attractive woman, arresting-looking. What, he thought, was she doing in his office? Perhaps she had got his address out of the yellow pages and imagined he was a divorce lawyer.

After reading his thoughts, the woman put the idea to rest. 'There's no litigation involved. I only need to ask you a few questions. I'll pay, of course, for your time.'

'Very generous of you, Madame,' Nedelec said with no hint of irony in his voice. He was used to people trying to pry information out of him without paying. He rarely complained. 'May I have your name?

'Veronique Martin,' she replied so quickly that the lawyer shrewdly guessed she had found inspiration for her name at the nearby Canal Saint-Martin.

'I'll explain what I want and not waste either your time or mine. I'm a writer, and I'm working on a medical subject. I have a deadline, and I must verify the legal aspects of my subject before I turn in my work. It's too much trouble to look all this up in a law library, and since I live nearby ...'

'I'll be happy to help in whatever way I can, Madame. What is the subject with which you are concerned?'

'Embryo implantation.'

'I beg your pardon?'

'Embryos conceived outside the body. Implanted into a uterus.' Suddenly, the woman became agitated to the point of irritation. 'Don't you know *anything* about it?'

Nedelec smiled kindly at her. Behind his mask of benevolence, however, he was wondering if she was one of the crackpots who occasionally walked into his office, encouraged by the proximity of the cemetery and its famous inhabitants. He had once had a man come in and question him on the legality of both necrophilia and necrophagia. Necrophilia, the lawyer had hastened to explain, while not necessarily a crime in the home, was looked upon with great, possibly violent disfavour by the guards across the way. Necrophagia was a crime anywhere, any time. The man had left with a look of great sadness upon his faunlike face.

'Embryo implanation is not a subject about which I am habitually questioned,' he said now to Veronique Martin, 'but if you will tell me exactly what you need to know . . .'

'It's a question of inheritance. I'm writing a novel, you see, and in the course of my story, an embryo has been conceived and then implanted in the body of another woman. During the pregnancy, both parents get killed. Under French law, would the unborn child be recognised as the child of his parents, even though it was born posthumously? Would it be allowed to inherit from them?'

'Hmmm. An interesting question. The word "posthumous" refers to the birth of a child after the death of its *father*. You are talking about the mother as well. Apart from finding a more appropriate term, let's look into the way this tragic event came about. Are you speaking of, say, an automobile accident in which both the father and the mother die simultaneously, and the child is taken by Caesarian section in the minute or two following? A very rare event, I would think, but not impossible in the light of present medical technique.'

'No, no! That's not it all!' Veronique Martin spoke all in a rush, shaking her little curls in evident frustration. 'I've expressed myself poorly, Maître. This is all very new, and perhaps you don't follow the latest scientific experiements . . .' She looked about his small shabby office for an instant and then continued. 'The father and mother, the *biological* parents, donate a sperm and egg. A doctor induces conception in the laboratory. Do you understand – in a dish? Then the doctor transfers this fertilised egg – their future child – to a surrogate, *une mère porteuse*. The biological mother was not infertile

131

but neither could she bear a child to term. After this is all arranged, the natural parents die. The surrogate is pregnant with their unborn child, but they are no longer alive to register it with the *état civile* at the moment of birth. What happens to such a child, legally speaking?'

'Well ...' Nedelcc paused and let his gaze stray to the cemetery walls, thinking incongruously of Edith's dead baby, the only one she ever had. Who cared about such things in those days, when children were casually delivered on the pavement and the father was any man willing to declare it to city hall?

'Perhaps we should start with all the obvious things. Is there a will? A paper of some kind attesting to the child's paternity or expressing the last wishes of the couple? Or, at the very least, the testimony of a reputable doctor?'

'I – I don't know.'

The lawyer looked at her in uneasy surprise. He wondered for an instant if he were being led into some sort of trap. 'Madame Martin, I must tell you right away that I am not a specialist in these matters. If you want to go into this in depth, I suggest you see a colleague who handles insurance claims or medical litigation. I don't know such a lawyere off hand, but I can try to find one for you.'

'Oh no, please, it's general information I want. Just tell me what you *know*. What you *feel* would happen in a case like this.'

'As you wish. First of all, as far as I am aware, there is no clear-cut jurisprudence. There have been many more of the so-called test-tube babies born in the Anglo-Saxon countries than in ours. I remember reading of cases of surrogates in France, but I believe they were women artificially inseminated by the husband, so, in a sense, they were being hired to give up their own natural child. The situation you are describing is, of course, one hundred per cent against the law. Anyone involved would be in a great deal of trouble, legally speaking.'

The woman looked at him, obviously startled.

'It's illegal? How?'

'It's against the law to hire yourself out to bear a child for a third party. The proxy mothers – the kind one advertises for in a newspaper – are considered by the courts to be dealing in child traffic.'

'How very interesting!' Veronique Martin exclaimed. 'It's almost pimping, then? A form of slavery.'

'Yes, if you prefer those terms. Taken to its extreme legal conclusion, such a woman could be arrested and indicted for selling a black-market baby.'

'Then the surrogate mother would be prosecuted and the child disinherited? The whole thing would be declared illegal?'

'No, Madame. I did not say the *child* would be in any way implicated in the illegality of the procedure.'

Suddenly, the door of Nedelec's office flew open, and two Arab men in their early twenties burst into the room, shouting incoherently in a mixture of Parigot and Algerian invectives. The lawyer jumped angrily to his feet.

'Ali! Karim! Stop this at once! Are you blind? Don't you see I have a client in my office? Look at this woman, you've frightened her almost to death.'

The two ceased their argument for an instant to stare at Veronique Martin in amazement.

'Go on! Back outside! I'll see both of you in five minutes. And no more noise or you'll get me evicted.'

Once the ruckus had transferred itself out of the room, Nedelec turned back to his client. She wore an intense look on her young-old face.

'I'm very sorry,' the lawyer said. 'The disputes in this neighbourhood tend to be on the violent side.'

Veronique Martin took no notice of his words. 'So the child is not illegitimate? What is it then?'

'Madame Martin, I started out by telling you there is no jurisprudence in France, but that is not quite true. There is a Latin adage that has always been recognised in French law. Do you know Latin?'

'A little, but quite rusty.'

'*Infans conceptus pro nato habetur*. Conceived, the infant is considered born. Inheritance laws in France have what you might call an inevitable fatalism about them.'

'In my novel, then, should the judge accept the legitimacy of the child born of a surrogate?'

'Here we go into the realm of proof. If no will or other document of intent has been drawn up, it might be difficult to establish the child's parentage. How do they die in your book?'

'They're ... by fire.'

'You see, then all proof of genetic identity would have been destroyed. Most likely, the case would rest on the testimony of the doctor who performed the implant.'

'The doctor? Only the doctor ...?'

'Well, of course, there are the technicians, nurses, hospital personnel, but how could these people be absolutely sure what genetic material had been used during the fertilisation? Without the doctor, there would certainly be doubt, wouldn't there?'

'Yes, a great deal of doubt.'

Nedelec smiled and tried to make a little joke. 'If we had had this

133

conversation in a mystery novel, I would just have condemned your doctor to death, wouldn't I?'

Veronique Martin stared at him coldly. 'I don't write murder mysteries. What is your conclusion, then?'

'Well, offhand from someone who deals with labour disputes rather than with posthumous births, I'd say that the person coveting the child's inheritance is going to trip up on an ancient Latin notion that was very much in advance of its time.'

'I guess that's all, then.'

'I guess it is. I'm sorry to give you this news, Madame Martin.'

She looked at him strangely. 'Why do you say that?' She slipped a 500-franc note from her purse and laid it on the desk.

'Because it seems to make you unhappy. I think you wanted your book to end some other way. And that's too much money. Just let me have 100 francs, or 200 if you have it. Otherwise, it is of no importance. I've enjoyed talking with you. It isn't often that someone walks into my office with such an intriguing and original question. Especially someone as attractive as you.'

He looked at her insistently, hoping there was a chance of a drink at the end of the day, but she failed to respond to his compliment. Nor did she make a move to take back her 500-franc note. She stood up slowly and walked to the front door, lost in thoughts of her own. Just before she went out, she nodded her curly head once in farewell, and then she was gone.

Nedelec sighed. He had liked talking with her; she hadn't been one of the cemetery freaks after all, nor was she for or against the communist-controlled unions nor incensed by the capitalist owners of any concern, French or foreign. The lawyer had liked her little curls and, especially, her slanted cat's eyes. He tried to hold on to their fire for an instant, but already her young-old face and her strong athlete's body were fading from his memory. He knew Karim and Ali would soon capture all his attention with their quarrelling, and he would forget her altogether. She would be no more real to him than his friends resting on their beds of scrolled marble behind the Père Lachaise walls.

Nedelec pondered why this woman would have come to a place in which she so obviously did not belong, a shabby law office where the bourgeoisie never showed itself. Even as he phrased the question, Nedelec realised he himself had supplied the answer.

Veronique Martin walked two blocks up the boulevard to her car, a sleek silver Porsche. She brushed snow off the windshield, then unlocked the passenger door and took out a small bag of rough pigskin. She continued on to the *bar-tabac* another half-block up the street. It had, she noted with satisfaction, started to fill up with a noisy noonday crowd. At the counter, she ordered a *café-crème* and asked the barman directions to the WC. After locking herself in downstairs, she opened the pigskin bag, took out a jar of cold cream and a package of Kleenex, and began to rub at her face. She worked furiously until each and every one of the large, slightly smudged freckles was gone. After that, she carefully applied her own subtly sophisticated make-up in tones of beige and prune. She tore the wig of tight curls from her head and let her smooth, black hair fall down her neck; it was as straight as that of a medieval page. She slipped out of her khaki overall; underneath she wore a slim jump suit of crushed beige silk which she had picked up in a Chanel boutique. Next, out of her pigskin bag, she took a little bolero of white fox with a matching fur hat. Then, with her other jacket and accessories safely packed away, she climbed the stairs and walked past the bar, ignoring the large *café-crème* set out for her on the counter. She headed straight for the door.

The barman did not call out an indignant protest or try to stop her. He had no idea who she was.

Chapter Twenty-Two

'I saw the lawyer,' Edith-Anne Schomberg announced after her maid returned to the kitchen.

Edith-Anne and Xavier were in the living room of their Normandy house awaiting before-dinner cocktails. Flames danced in the wide stone chimney, and Pavarotti's rich tenor wafted across the room, bringing them a *morceau de bravoure* from *The Puritans*. It was a warm, pleasant atmosphere.

'Oh,' Xavier said noncommittally, his face buried in the business section of *Le Monde*.

'There's a good chance the child will inherit.'

'Oh.'

'It already has a legal identity, but that could be wiped out.'

'How's that?'

'One, if it were never born. Two, if the doctor who supervised the procedure were no longer in a position to testify.'

'I see.'

Xavier's face never appeared from behind the pages of his newspaper.

'Xavier, put away that paper and listen to what I have to say. I spent four hours in the Paris traffic today. You can't imagine what it's like driving in that part of town.'

'Why in the world would you go to such a place?'

'Because if I'd consulted a lawyer in a decent neighbourhood, he might have recognised me, or at least have been curious enough to make an enquiry. This man was so rank and file, he wouldn't have known who I was even if I'd given him my real name.'

'If he was that much of a nobody, what makes you think he knew what he was talking about?'

'Oh, he knew all right. I sat there and watched him think it out, slowly but surely. I had plenty of time to admire the view – that traffic-clogged Boulevard Menilmontant full of Arabs selling chickpea flour, hot peppers and other horrors. I got to look at the snow-covered walls of the Père Lachaise, too.'

At last, Xavier place *Le Monde* on the chintz pillow next to him and looked at his wife with a faint show of interest.

'Père Lachaise, huh? I haven't been there since . . . oh, years. Did you go inside for a look around?'

'Of course I didn't. Why should I? I'm not interested in gravestones. Anyway, I've always heard the place is full of necrophiles and worse kinds of perverts.'

'Di-Di, I'm astonished that you would have such words in your vocabulary.'

'I do read. Anyway, we're getting way off the subject. This American − what's to be done about her?'

Xavier sat absolutely still, staring at the chimney with its bright red and gold flames. The animation that had taken hold of his face when Edith-Anne mentioned the cemetery had quite disappeared now. He might have been back checking invoices in the garden-tools factory from which he had so recently escaped. Or simply trying to ignore a wife to whom he had grown totally indifferent.

'I think we should hire someone to see exactly what she's up to,' Edith-Anne insisted. Still, Xavier failed to respond. When the enduring silence became too much for her nerves, she took a small copper bell from the wooden chest that served as a coffee table and rang it angrily. 'Ines must be on the phone chatting with another of her Portuguese friends. She's forgotten all about us, as usual.'

As if to belie these words, the door from the hall flew open and a smiling, gap-toothed girl rushed into the room balancing a tray that held silver bowls of pistachios and spiced olives and a Christofle pitcher filled with a blue cocktail mixture. Edith-Anne waited until the girl returned to the kitchen before resuming her monologue.

'We need . . . a man. Someone who's extremely discreet. Able to stay in her entourage without arousing suspicion. He should be the kind of person who's willing to take whatever action is necessary − later on. Xavier, say *something*! Do you agreed with me or not?'

'How do you propose to find this paragon?' her husband asked contemptuously. 'By running an ad in *Le Monde* or *Libération*?'

'Don't be ridiculous. If you continue in this cynical manner, very soon that American nobody will be inviting us to the christening of a child that will completely cut our own sons out of the Schomberg inheritance.'

'Di-Di,' Xavier sighed as he poured their drinks into two highball glasses. 'You are worrying yourself needlessly. It so happens I already took care of the problem. I met someone who was eminently qualified, and I hired him. Before the plane accident, even.'

'You met ... where?' Edith-Anne asked incredulously.

A little smile appeared just under Xavier's trim, dark moustache. 'Never mind that. Let's just say that I had certain contacts which proved useful. The man has already met up with the girl. He's very close to her, all the time. And she suspects absolutely nothing.'

'I don't believe you.'

'Then let's speak of something else.'

'What is the name of this prize?'

'The less you know − that everybody knows − the better.'

'Is Bayard involved in this?'

'Bayard!' As Xavier spat out the name, a look of utter disdain crossed his fastidious face. 'He's the last person I'd turn to with a problem. Rita may well be in her second childhood, but her precious son never grew out of his first one. I knew he was certifiable when we were teenagers together at Grandmère's place in Hossegor. There were certain things that happened ...' His voice trailed away.

'I personally find this all very strange.'

'You're never satisfied,' Xavier said irritably as he took a sip of his cocktail. 'What bothers you now?'

'I had the impression you and Bayard met for lunch a few weeks ago to discuss the child, and, for all I know, to plan the − '

Her husband cut her off, an angry blaze of warning in his usually veiled eyes. 'As usual, your impressions are totally wrong. Since last summer, I've seen that scum exactly three times. Once in Saint-Cloud the night Rita had to be rushed to the hospital; again during the memorial services for our dear departed cousins; and, finally, at the emergency board meeting Friday. It would be very unwise of you, Di-Di, to go around suggesting that Bayard and I hold secret meetings. *Very* unwise. Now, what do you say we drop the subject and go in for dinner?'

'If you say so,' his wife replied dubiously. 'I'll ring for Ines.'

Edith-Anne stood up and smoothed out the crushed silk of her beige Chanel outfit. She was still preoccupied.

'Xa-Xa?' Her raucous voice had become cajoling, almost seductive. 'Just one more question before we go in for dinner. This so-called friend of yours ...'

'What about him?'

'Just how far would he be prepared to go? If it became necessary?'

Xavier smiled bleakly and took his wife's arm to escort her into their newly decorated, French country dining room.

'It's all worked out, my dear. He'll go just as far as you or anyone else could possibly wish.'

138

'Oh, well, that's a relief then.' Her slanting cat's eyes narrowed, and she squeezed his arm approvingly. 'While we're eating, Xa-Xa, I'll tell you exactly what the lawyer said. Then we'll have to make a decision. I know what to do about the girl, but there's still a problem with the doctor. He knows too much. According to Maître Jean-Michel Nedelec, if any harm comes to us now, it's the doctor who will bring it.'

Chapter Twenty-Three

She was back in Dallas. The phone was ringing. It was Serge. It was the call she had waited for. He would ask her to come to France. They would marry and live in Paris. From their bedroom window, they would watch their childen play in the Parc Montsouris. Only, Cecil could not find the telephone. It rang and rang, and she did not know where it was. She was sad because she knew if she did not answer now, she would never see Serge or their children again. Her groping fingers knocked against a lamp and then miraculously touched the cold plastic of a telephone receiver.

'Cecil? Is that you?'

'Serge,' she said in a voice in which both hope and dread mingled inexplicably.

'Cecil, goddamn it, wake up! This is Sam!'

'Sam?' If this were Sam calling, then she wasn't in Dallas at all; she wasn't pregnant with Serge's child; she was ...

'Sam, I was sound asleep. I've been trying to reach you for ... for weeks, I think.'

'I know, I'm an asshole to have left you alone like this, but I was so screwed up, I couldn't ...' Sam's voice broke and then bounced back as its old, vital self. 'Cecil, have you heard? Did you see the papers? Has anybody contacted you?' His words were coming at her like the frantic pelter of a machine gun.

'You mean about Christine and Frederick? I found out last night, and I watched a documentary about them on French TV today. Sam, listen, I have to tell you this − I went to the Schomberg house when I was in Paris. I met both Bayard and Rita Schomberg.'

'I already know, sweetheart. Jeff Sandlin filled me in on the whole episode.'

'Why didn't you call me then? I've been frantic. I left a dozen messages for you with Estelle.'

'I'll bet Old Faithful is as mad as a bear with a sore ass, too. The problem is, I haven't got around to calling Estelle yet. Look, Cecil, here's the story: I was cut off from the world for a week in Saudi Arabia operating on the King's favourite girl. When I got back, I went right on to a binge of monumental proportions. I was so pissed I couldn't have dialled your number if my life depended on it.'

'Shit, Sam, am I supposed to sympathise with you or ...?'

'Save your sympathy and just let me talk. I've been acting like an irresponsible jackass, but my head is screwed back on now. I have some important things to say to you. Are you wide awake?'

'Yes, but Sam ...'

'I know what you're going to say!' he snapped. 'You've been through hell; you're pregnant with the baby of dead people; I got you into this mess; you're worried out of your mind.'

He talked, Cecil thought, like a man with a time bomb set to go off beside him at any minute.

'We'll work it out, I promise, but for the moment, I just want you to listen. It is vital that you stay right there in Nice, in your room if you can stand it for a couple more days. Don't invite anybody up. Don't go to Paris, no matter who asks you or what the pretext is. Don't take any risks of any kind. I'll be there − let's see, this is Monday, or what's left of it − Wednesday evening. Book me a room on your floor for two or three nights. Register all that?'

'Sam, if I'm in some sort of danger, I want to know exactly what it is − right now.'

'Kid, I didn't mean to spook you, but I *am* worried, and I can't talk about it over the phone. We're dealing with a situation that's become as hot as a west Texas cowboy in a widow woman's bed.'

'Well, I've been sick, and you should know about it. I saw a doctor named Lopez, and he insists I have some very complicated tests done here in Nice.'

'Are you in any pain now?'

'No, I feel great, but last week − '

'Why the hell didn't you call Parodi at the American Hospital if you had a problem? I gave you a file with his name and number before you left Dallas.'

'Parodi's in Paris, and I'm here. I needed emergency treatment.'

'Telephones function for medical emergencies even if they are bugged. This baby is too important for you to be in the hands of some local quack.'

'Then you should be here yourself!'

'Cecil, my number-one priority is to get to Paris. I want to find out why we have this total blackout on the baby's existence. Also, I'm going to drop a couple of bombshells on our friends there. By the time that dust has settled, I'll be on a flight to Nice.'

'And after that?'

'I'm taking you to Dallas. I'm afraid it's just you and me from now on, kid.'

Cecil's heart gave a little lurch, even though she already knew she had misinterpreted his words.

'A regular Broadway show.'

'That's what I've always liked about you, Cecil − your intuitive brilliance and the fact that you can turn a phrase as well as any Irishman. It's a show, all right, and our small friend is the star. We're going to see that it happens. No one else in the world wants this show to see the light of day. That's why we have to team up. In Dallas, I'll be putting you up with Old Faithful Estelle, who will guard you better than any medieval knight.'

'If I understand correctly then, I've once again become a precious commodity?'

'You always have been, to me at least. And don't get cross until you've heard what I have to say. Afterwards you can hate me to your heart's content. I won't utter a word of protest.'

In a sudden intuitive flash, Cecil understood why Sam had been on his binge and why he cared so much about the baby's survival. 'I won't hate you, Sam. After all, we share something now, don't we − the dark house and the whip of love.'

'It's not the state of my emotional health that I'm planning to reveal to you.'

'But you loved Christine very much, didn't you?'

There was utter silence; Cecil wondered if she had gone too far. When Sam finally answered, it was with great hesitation, as though he were only now discovering the answer himself.

'Let's say Christine taught me something very European − very odd for an American. It is possible to love more than one person at a time ... they work things out over there. They seal off little compartments ...' His voice broke.

'Sam, I'm sorry. Very, very sorry.'

'You don't want to hear about all that, kid. It's not good for either of us. Listen, just stay indoors out of the way of fuzzy beasts until we meet on Wednesday, OK? And I do have one last word for you.'

'Even if the phone is tapped?'

'Yeah, even if it is.'

'I'm wide awake and listening.'

'I'm crazy, absolutely crazy about that beautiful red hair of yours.'

Before Cecil could say another word, Sam hung up. Still holding the receiver, she let her gaze travel to the mirror opposite. Her face was clearly reflected in the glow from the bedside lamp, and as she stared fixedly at her image, something became superimposed over it – the hair of Christine Schomberg, or what was left of it, large flakes of ash falling dreamily down into snow on the crest of a silent mountain. Christine Schomberg, nothing but a memory now, and she, intact, vibrantly alive, pregnant with Christine's child.

Cecil had no more desire to sleep.

Phrases spoken by Serge and Sam swirled in her brain, jolting her to attention and forcing her to focus on something she had avoided altogether until now. In the epicentre of the maelstrom that was her mind, Cecil saw an infinitely small but real infant. Prior to this moment, the child had been a phantom, a hazy entity without substance or subsistence. Cecil had managed even to obliterate the physical manifestations of a fetus that was no more real to her than a stranger in the next room of a boarding house. The two of them had lived out their lives on different sides of one thin wall, sleeping, waking, eating at the same time yet each a blank to the other.

And now, a subtle awakening had begun, something so totally unexpected that it left Cecil breathless with surprise. She jumped out of bed and, barefooted, began to pace up and down the room, glancing from time to time out of the window. A storm was breaking over the Mediterranean; lightning flashed across the esplanade and turned the palms an iridescent, ghostly white. On an impulse, Cecil stopped her pacing and threw open the window. Suddenly she wanted to hear the drumming of the rain on the black surface of the sea.

What was it Sam had tried to tell her in his guarded way? Had it really been a secret, or something she knew already?

With trembling hand, Cecil poured a glass of cold water from the carafe on her night table and drank it in one long gulp. She was flushed with the novelty of the idea, burning with the exhilaration of sudden discovery. She turned back to the open window and this time let the drizzle fall across her bare arms and legs. The distant rumble of thunder was like an echo of the hammer-blows of her heart.

It was that simple, really, and yet she had missed it completely. She shook her head in wonder and, for the very first time, brought her hands down to the budding roundness of her belly. Gingerly, almost shyly, she began to caress it.

She was pregnant with a real-living child, and that child was Christine's and Frederick's heir. The Schomberg heir.

It was so simple, so very simple.

The living child that lay beneath her fingers had the money. And she the child.

The woman will not keep still. Because of her, it cannot sleep. She walks, turns, walks faster, almost running.

With one small foot, it plants a tentative blow to her stomach, then tries again with the other. She pays no attention. She is still moving. In a burst of anger, it kicks again and again, its small feet beating against her like the sticks of a jazz musician on a kettle drum.

If only she would sit down! Lie down! Be still! Another brusque turn, and the fetus floats forwards through cloudy liquid to collide against a wall. It bounces off and is projected backwards to hit another. Why won't she stay still? Doesn't she know it wants to sleep?

At last, she stops to raise an arm. A river of ice cascades down her body, an avalanche of ghastly chill. It lands – plunk – in her stomach.

Angry again, it kicks in protest. It hates this all-invasive coldness. Filled with iciness, she is very still. Her hands start to move over her stomach, gently pressing inward, searching for something. It is not a threatening movement. It is almost as though she wants to know ...

She is very close, her pressing hands less than an inch from its face. Almost, almost, they meet.

The fetus becomes languorous, peaceful; the heat of her body has made the cold disappear. As it floats aimlessly, it raises beautifully formed fingers to its closed eyes to rub a sleep that is not far off.

With the cord coiled around its frail body like a gay holiday ribbon and its pale skin covered in the unctuous *vernix caseosa*, it looks like a shiny package tied and wrapped in transparent plastic. Ready for delivery.

An expression of great calm settles upon its face. The calmness of someone who waits for eternity.

Chapter Twenty-Four

They were all there — what was left of the family, anyway.

Poor little Rita was propped up in a corner enveloped in a mohair plaid. She looked twenty years older than in the last photo she had had taken for the stockholders' brochure. Her blond hair had gone partly grey, and though someone had taken a great deal of trouble with it, it still gave off a distinct aura of impending baldness. Her enormous blue eyes had dulled, and everything about her suggested dreamlike apathy. Only once during the entire two hours did she speak.

Bayard sat next to his mother, fussing over her appearance and making little cooing sounds of encouragement. At one point, he picked up one of her clawlike hands, folded it carefully over the other, and then placed both across her lap. He completed his ministrations by straightening her back and tucking the mohair in around her. Set in place like that, she looked placidly content, almost normal.

Bayard, too, was very content. He had oozed around the library when Sam Sweeney first came in, seeing that his coat, hat and scarf were taken care of, that the doctor received a healthy ration of bourbon, that he was properly introduced. It was Bayard who had made all the arrangements after Sam's call from London, and it was he who insisted that Sam spend the night afterwards instead of making the trip back through a wet, cold Paris to his hotel. Now, though, the elder son sat like a plump, contented but vaguely enigmatic pussy, smiling benevolently upon his guests. For they were *his* guests now. It was Bayard who was master of the house in Saint-Cloud, and he who bore all the responsibility for his mother's destiny.

And, as Sam kept reminding himself, it was Bayard who would get the money if anything happened to Cecil's baby.

The loquacious people were the cousins — Xavier Schomberg and his wife Edith-Anne, a fortyish woman Sam found attractive but harsh. People called her Di-Di, a silly name that did not at all suit her strong personality. Sam could see that Xavier and his wife were at odds about something tonight, but otherwise he couldn't pigeonhole them. In the main, though, Xavier Schomberg was pleasant and accommodating and seemed anxious to strike a deal.

Right at the beginning, there had been a clumsy, barely veiled attempt to bribe the doctor. Sam let them talk, curious to see how high they would go. Not to the million Christine had promised; that was a foregone conclusion. Sam even tossed the figure out to them as a joke, but from the sullen silence that followed, he knew they had never once thought in those terms.

It did clear the air, though; afterwards, the Schombergs started to speak of the child as being of substance and reality. Xavier announced that he and Di-Di wanted to adopt the baby and bring it up themselves. This novel suggestion startled Sam so much he almost missed the best part – that both the release and the adoption papers were already drawn up and awaiting Cecil's signature. The baby would be part of Xavier and Di-Di's own little family, and as such, it would have equal standing with their two sons inheritance-wise.

Sam fixed his eyes on the couple who so unexpectedly wished to acquire a new offspring and asked in his most exaggerated Texas drawl, 'Jest tell me, if you would, why the child should forgo the entire Schomberg fortune in order to receive a one-third cousin's share? After French inheritance taxes, it wouldn't get much more than a drink of well water, now would it? I'll be honest with you, Mr Schomberg. I'm flying Miss Gutman back to Texas with me this week. The two of us will work out what the baby's legal rights are from the United States.'

That was when Rita came back to life.

'Nooo!' she wailed, and everyone, even Bayard, turned to stare at her in dread fascination. 'Nooo! Not Frederick's baby. It can't fly. It's too little. Don't let it go up in a plane, please, please. Don't let them kill our baby, too!'

Like Lazarus coming out of his grave, she threw off Bayard's restraining hands and rose to her feet. She was crying now, tears gushing all at once from her eyes and nose and mouth and coursing down on to the mohair cover in great sticky blobs. Swaying unsteadily, Rita moaned and then repeated that eerily drawn-out, distressingly pitiful 'Noooo!'

Edith-Anne yanked on the red silk wall tassel as though it were something she wanted to shake to death. 'Damn it, where is she? That fool of a woman is never here when we need her!'

146

With unexpected agility, Bayard leapt to within a few inches of Sam. His face was beet red, and he was shaking uncontrollably. A spiteful look had replaced his former contented-tabby one. 'Look at what you've done! You've upset my poor darling mother! How dare you talk like that when you know how sick she is? Your loud Texan mouth will get you into trouble one of these days, a great deal of trouble, do you hear me?'

'You're the one who's heading for grief, Bayard!' Xavier's cold voice cut in. 'Rita's condition has nothing to do with this meeting. If you can't control yourself, leave the room.'

Sam turned to Xavier. 'If you'd like me to examine Mrs Schomberg, and perhaps administer – '

'Certainly not!' Bayard screeched, his hysteria near to the high-water mark. 'My mother has all the medication she needs. You keep away from her! I'm the only one who can calm her when she's like this!'

'Then take her to her room and stay there!' snapped Xavier. 'Here's Miss Sanchez, just in time to accompany both of you upstairs.'

A dark, stern-looking nurse had entered the library pushing a wheelchair. Already she was lifting a wildly protesting Rita up in her muscular arms. Rita turned her head, trying to keep Sam in her line of vision. She was like a deaf-mute with a message of life-and-death import. Her mouth worked frantically; her thin cheeks quivered like jostled slices of breakfast jelly. As Miss Sanchez wheeled her past Sam, Rita raised one clawlike hand to him, but still no sounds emerged from her wildly churning lips. Then she was out of the door and gone, with Bayard following close behind.

After that unpleasant episode, Sam Sweeney decided it was time to tell Xavier how things were going to be. He spelled it out for him in no uncertain terms. Sam and Cecil were to be appointed as co-guardians of the Schomberg heir. A legal representative, perhaps Jeff Sandlin, would safeguard the child's financial interests until it became of age. Xavier would retain his position as head of Schomberg Mondial, and Bayard his comfortable allowance, provided both signed immediate and unconditional acknowledge-ment of the child's legal status and rights within the family.

'Let's drink to that! And to our future collaboration!' proclaimed a booming voice from the doorway. Bayard had returned unnoticed, his rosy cheeks and Cheshire-cat smile fully restored.

'Not for me,' Sam said coolly. 'I've had more than my share today. As a matter of fact, I think I'll turn in now.'

'Oh, come now, dear boy, I've already ordered a very rare

Bollinger brought up from the *cave*. If you don't have a sip, I'll think you're holding a grudge against me for my silly outburst earlier in the evening. Oh, do you say you're not angry with me!'

Sam hesitated, annoyed with himself for an almost uncontrollable urge to flee this dark, ugly house. He was here to get the most possible out of these bastards; he couldn't quit while he was on a winning streak, could he? What did another half-hour matter when he held all the winning cards?

'OK, break it open,' Sam said with forced bonhomie. 'Christine and Frederick would be happy to know that we're drinking to the health of their baby.'

Not one but several dust-covered bottles were brought in by Madame Henriette and set down in silver buckets to be chilled. Bayard insisted on showing Sam his collection of locks and keys, and when they returned to the library, the first bottle was already uncorked and its contents poured into long-stemmed glasses on a tray. Following Sam's lead, Xavier proposed a toast to the child that had drawn them all together. If his voice was nearly as dry as the champagne, Sam chose to ignore it. He had so much to do; this would be his last evening of drinking for a long time, perhaps forever. As he raised his glass, he had a sudden vision of Christine's hair dancing above him in the firelight; her wide, sensual mouth was swollen with passion, and her lips bruised from their lovemaking.

The champagne was gone, the glass empty. Sam needed more. Abstention would be for tomorrow and all the long, lonely nights that lay ahead.

Sam looked down into the tepid water. The bubbles surging up out of its chartreuse depths reminded him of blood churning in a hospital machine. Except for two underwater spots at each end of the pool, all the lights in the greenhouse were out. The big, glass-domed roof was a great mass of darkness above his head, and greyish, indistinct shapes loomed at the pool's edges. Suddenly Sam was overcome by an almost animal panic at the thought of what might lurk in the darkness. Then, disgusted with himself, he dove down into the water and began to swim along the pool's floor. It was beautiful here, more beautiful than anything Sam had ever seen before. He was sure he had swum in a pool like this once, light years back in his past.

How the hell had to got here? He vaguely remembered glasses clinking and exuberantly friendly toasts. At some point, Bayard had patted him on the back and suggested the two of them share a sauna. That had been a silly mistake, of course, because Sam knew all about

Bayard and his saunas. Yet here he was, stark naked and swimming in this wonderfully warm, green water.

In an abrupt movement, Sam headed back up to the surface. He shot out of the water like a sleek seal and took a great gulp of air. Then, reassured, he turned over on his back to float. He was a blithering idiot to swim alone like this after consuming so much alcohol. He would do one or two more lengths, just to clear his head, and then he'd get the hell out. Out of the pool, out of the house, out of France. Back to Texas where he belonged.

With great, powerful strokes, Sam propelled himself to the deep end of the pool and then stayed there treading water. It was so dark out there, so dead. Only the water was alive. Two spectacularly white, snakelike things were swimming just below him; it took Sam a few seconds to recognise them as his own legs transformed by the rippling water into the puny and malformed limbs of a fetus floating in its jar or formaldehyde.

'Who's there? Is somebody there?'

There had been a furtive sound as though someone were on the diving board just above his head. Yes, there it was again. Sam could see nothing in the blackness. There was nothing to see, of course; it was only his alcohol-clogged mind playing tricks on him. Out of nowhere, he had a vision of Bayard Schomberg standing naked beside him at the edge of the pool. Rolls of fat like multiple breasts cascaded down Bayard's great white chest; his hand clamped down on Sam's bare shoulder.

'Silly boy, the water is *good* for you. It's simply not done, prescribing treatment for the doctor, I know that, but I do so want to help you. Go on, jump in, you dear silly boy.'

Who had said all that? It must have been Bayard, but in the distortion of drunken memory, the voice did not sound like Bayard's at all. And why couldn't Sam remember diving into the pool? Was he in another blackout like the one in London? Heaven help him, he couldn't afford that now ...

Christ, there it was again, that noise. Right above him, too. A muffled, scraping sound, as though something heavy were being dragged across the tiles, the dead weight of a body. No, no, that wasn't it at all. It was more like someone hauling a rug or an enormous burlap bag filled with straw. In the dark?

'Is somebody there? Bayard, is that you?'

Sam swam uneasily away from the edge of the pool, trod water again and looked up into the uncanny blackness with its blurry, dark shapes. Suddenly he felt cold. For the first time, he noticed the steady pinpricks of sleet that were pelting the domed roof of the greenhouse.

Christ, it was the last day of December, no time to be swimming even if it was a heated pool. He had to get out; he only hoped he could find the clothes he no longer remembered taking off.

Without warning, the pool lights went out.

'What the hell!' Sweeney exclaimed angrily. 'Who's there? Goddamn it, get those lights back on! Do you hear me? What kind of asshole are you, turning off the lights when I'm still in the fucking pool?'

His question was greeted by a baleful silence.

Sam struck out vigorously towards the edge of the pool. At the instant his hands found a hold on the tiles, something flat and monstrously heavy fell across his head, knocking him back into the water. The thing opened up around him and began to sink. Sam tried to dive out from under, but cloying, dark heaviness spread out in every direction, driving him inexorably downward.

Sam opened his mouth to take in desperately needed air, and his throat filled with water. He choked and tried to cough it out, but each gasping reflex only let in more water. It was everywhere now, in his nose and throat and oesophagus and lungs, and everywhere with the water was a great tearing pain as though his insides were being ripped asunder. Sam opened his eyes to find a way of escape, but there was nothing in the blackness but a soggy water beast pulling him down in its mortal embrace.

He was going to die! It couldn't be, not like this, no one died like this, plummeting to the bottom of an ordinary pool, drowned in a mass of cumbersome fur, killed by a rug. No, please, mother of God, I can't die like this, please, please, sweet Jesus, I'm a doctor, don't let me die!

Then, all at once, Sam stopped fighting. His lungs ceased to burst with the impossible wish to breathe, and a kind of peace came over him. Miraculously, he could see again. A yellow light vacillated in the inky water; in its centre was an infinitely desirable object. Sam reached out, believing that it was Christine's vital, luminous face that beckoned to him, but what he saw in that shimmering, ever-advancing light was the very thing that had brought him through the vast labyrinth of his life to this place. It was a wheel, and it spun dizzingly. Lewdly. Yet when Sam saw it, he felt nothing but joy.

Oh, sweet mother of God, I've looked so long for the place where all my luck went, my Midas luck, and here it is, I've found it again, oh, thank you, Jesus, thank you, this is it, this wheel of fortune. My fortune, only the water is so cloudy and there's something wrong with my eyes, I can barely see the needle, the wheel is still spinning, isn't it, no, it's stopping, oh, if I could just see it, please, one more time, see where the black needle stops.

Stopping, stopped. No, please God, please sweet Jesus and all the saints, please Mary mother of God, don't let it stop there, please, please not the double zero, don't let it stop on the double zero, not tonight, not for me, please no.

I'm a doctor.

Please.

Chapter Twenty-Five

By eight o'clock, Cecil was too nervous to sit in her room. She took the lift down to the reception area to see if there was any sign at all of Sam. The hotel was as dead as the previous evening's rowdy celebrations. Almost no one passed through the great swinging doors, and the few employees on duty looked drugged.

With nothing else to do, Cecil turned back towards the cavernous lobby. In her present mood, it seemed as inviting as a violated tomb. None the less, she forced herself to cover every inch of it, staring unseeingly at the rococo decorations, the luxury displays, even the odd tourist. At last she sank down at one of the round marble tables and took a paperback from her bag. The words danced senselessly on the page.

Cecil could think of nothing except the late hour, the silent telephone. Sam Sweeney might stand her up again — and on this New Year's evening when they were supposed to be planning her future together. Not even a call to say he was delayed! What time did the last plane from Paris get in, anyway? Cecil checked her watch. God, what an idiot she was! It was ten minutes to ten; she'd been out of her room for nearly two hours. Sam probably *had* called by now.

When Cecil reached the reception desk, she saw that one of the clerks was making a heroic effort to rouse himself out of his stupor. 'Miss Gutman, I was just trying to reach you.'

'Someone called?' she asked breathlessly.

'Yes, a Mr Paso Real. He wants you to ring him back urgently. Oh, and Miss Gutman, what should we do about this reservation for Dr Sweeney? It's nearly ten o'clock, and we're still holding the room, but . . .' His question ended in dubious silence.

'You can't be full at this time of the year, can you?'

'No, but we would like to let housekeeping know if the room is to be occupied tonight. Perhaps Dr Sweeney missed his flight?'

'Let's assume he's not coming. Only, if he should ... get in late, I'd still expect you to accommodate him.'

'Don't worry, Mademoiselle.'

Barely able to conceal her disappointment, Cecil turned from the desk, only to be confronted with Alan Mueller. He had just come in from the street, and his face was still flushed from the cold. A great white scarf encircled his throat and floated out behind him like a curling snake. He greeted Cecil with a wide, friendly grin.

'Hey there! I've been looking everywhere for you since Monday. How are you doing?'

'All right, I guess. I had work to do so I've hardly been out of my room.'

'Well, how about changing that right now? Let's take my car and go sightseeing. Then we'll hit the port for some fish soup, just the thing for such a blustery winter night. What do you say?'

'I'm sorry, Mr Mueller, I'm not free tonight. Perhaps we could get together some time during the weekend. If I'm still here, that is.'

'Call me Alan, will you? You make me sound like your grandfather. And what's this about your leaving? Where are you headed next?'

'I'm not sure. I might go home.'

'Don't do that! You just said you haven't seen Nice, and already you're talking about rushing back to the States. You're a terrible tourist.'

'You're right, I am.' Cecil cast an apprehensive look at the front desk; no one was paying any attention to her; no other calls had come in. She forced her attention back to Alan Mueller. 'Tell me what you've been doing. You're a ... a tennis player, aren't you?'

'A coach. I've been working with some whiz kids over at Sophia-Antipolis, and that's kept me real busy up until now. I had some trouble with my papers, too. I lost my wallet at the airport in Bordeaux. The morning we met, as a matter of fact.'

Had Mueller seen her start at the mention of his wallet? 'I — why, that's terrible! Did you ever get it back?' The words sounded false, even to her.

'Yeah, funny thing about that. I thought I'd have to go through all the trouble of having my papers replaced — making declarations to the police and so forth. You know how slow the bureaucracy is here. But the wallet turned up intact on an Air-Inter flight to Nice.'

'How — mysterious.'

'Isn't it? I wondered — that fellow who was with you in Bordeaux. Dark, foreign-looking? What was his name again?'

Cecil became instantly wary. 'Oh, he was just somebody I met at a party. I hardly knew him.'

'Didn't he come on to Nice with you?'

'I seem to recall he had a connecting flight to Corsica. I certainly haven't run into him since I got here.' That was vague enough, wasn't it? Pancho should be eternally grateful to her for keeping the police off his all too visible trail. He probably deserved to be arrested, but she wasn't going to be the one to turn him in.

'Back to our night on the town, what do you say to Friday?'

Mueller's question brought Cecil back with a jolt to the present — to Sam's defection and to the weight of all her problems. Going out to a disco or a movie with this persistent and not too bright young man was not going to help her solve any of those; it might possibly provide some welcome distraction, though.

'I'm not sure — Friday or Saturday. Give me your room number, and I'll ring you if I can make it.'

'OK, but I don't intend to take no for an answer this time. Whatever happens, we'll do something together Friday night. And listen, Cecil, if you get into any kind of jam, call me, will you? This town can be rough if you stray into the wrong neighbourhood or hook up with the wrong people.'

He flashed her another of his big, friendly grins, took her hand in his and squeezed it. Her fingers crumpled like toothpicks caught in the vice of a nutcracker. Cecil pulled away and said a fast good night.

In the lift going up to her room, she took stock of her situation. Sam, the friendly, protective father figure, was not coming tonight as he had promised. Maybe he would never come. Christine and Frederick Schomberg, her so-called employers, were no more of this world. And the man for whom she had come to France, for whom she had got pregnant with the baby of strangers — Serge — had fled from her in disbelief and disgust.

In her present, morbid mood, Cecil felt sure that no one, anywhere, cared if she lived or died.

She was wrong. At least one person cared very much . . . if she died.

Chapter Twenty-Six

'Is Monsieur Papazian free to see me?'

The girl in jeans and pink angora sweater rose up behind her counter and said, 'I'll just see. It's Miss Goodman, isn't it?'

'Gutman.'

'Oh yes. I'll be right back, Miss Gutman. Isn't it cold today? This mistral is really something.'

It was indeed. The fierce northern wind had brought with it a sky the texture of wet blue paint and a chill wind biting enough to make the inhabitants of Nice search through mothballed plastics for coats, jackets and fur hats. By contrast, the bank was warm and pleasantly cozy.

After a few minutes, Cecil was ushered into the office of the director. Monsieur Papazian was standing rod-straight behind his big desk.

'I suppose you know why I'm here,' Cecil said with a polite smile. 'I need your authorisation to draw another 10,000 francs.'

A look of consternation crossed the man's face, but he said nothing. Since her last visit, the bank officer seemed to have lost his affable manner. Indeed, he was looking at Cecil as though something unpleasant had accompanied her into the room, an unseen but malodorous alien.

'You remember me, don't you? Cecil Gutman. I have a letter of credit ...'

Her voice trailed off before his continuing and by now ominous silence. Already a tiny point of fear had taken up residence in the exact centre of her chest. Had the man become amnesic, or had she herself changed in some subtle way so that he was no longer able to recognise her?

All at once, Cecil noticed that Monsieur Papazian had not asked her to sit down, not had he shaken her hand as he habitually did when

155

she entered his office. This was certainly the very first time the middle-aged Frenchman had missed a chance to touch her.

'*Eh bien*, Mademoiselle Gutman ... Of course I am familiar with you and your file. Since you were last, uh, in the bank ...' He stopped and shook his head as though preparing both of them for catastrophic news – a director's sudden demise or the unexpected and total insolvency of the bank itself.

'A technical problem has come up which has absolutely nothing to do with, hmmm, *us* here in Nice. You understand that we are only acting for our mother branch in Paris, and that we execute the orders of our clients, nothing more.'

'Will you get to the point, please?'

'Yes, well, you see, yours was not a set letter of credit, but what we call a "discretionary" one. In other words, the amount of the funds at your disposal each week was fixed by, hummm, by our customer in Paris. After your last withdrawal, we received a telex saying that no further sums were to be handed over ... until further notice.'

'But that can't be true!' Cecil cried indignantly. 'I'm employed by these people. I have a signed contract with ...' With whom exactly? Whose signature was on the paper Jeff Sandlin was holding for her in Dallas? It had not seemed important then; in those long-gone days, she had never once envisaged the possibility that the baby's natural parents might die.

'I am sorry to give you this news, Mademoiselle Gutman. But again, I must *insist* that our bank is in no way responsible. A technicality that surely can be cleared up by a, hmmm, a telephone call, perhaps. Yes, why not call your employers in Paris?'

'Don't worry, I will. In the meantime, can't you advance me *something*? My weekly bill is due at the Negresco, and I'm already low on cash. I need at least some francs to pay the hotel.'

'Oh, I understand your problem, young lady.' Monsieur Papazian had recovered from his embarrassment and was smiling at Cecil in an almost beatific way. 'I *want* to help you. I know you're a foreigner here in France without working papers or even a residence permit. At the mercy of the police, so to speak. And now to have this happen, no funds, no visible means of support.' He leaned towards Cecil and suddenly began furiously twisting the two branches of his enormous silver moustache.

Cecil saw only too well where this sudden commiseration was leading. She backed towards the door, a look of airy unconcern on her smiling face. 'You're right. It's just some silly mistake. They know in Paris that I can't finish my book if I don't have the proper funds. I'll ring them from my hotel, and they'll get the money to me by the end of the week. And by the way, Monsieur Papazian, since I'm a writer, I don't *need* a work permit to do research in France. Artists are free from those kinds of constraint.'

Once in the street, Cecil's carefree smile vanished as though blown away by the mistral. She turned into the first café she came to, took a seat in the back and ordered an espresso. Once the waiter had gone, she spread her cash out on the table and counted it carefully. She was about to empty the contents of her change purse, too, when she realised how ridiculous all this was. She had exactly 2,700 francs, just under $500. Not enough to buy a plane ticket home even if she could get out of the Negresco undetected. How much was the damned bill anyway? She had only briefly glanced at it. Fifteen hundred dollars? Could it be as much as that? A month's salary in France, an impossible sum to borrow. What were her options, then? Try to reach Rita Schomberg in a moment of coherence and beg the money from her? Or Jeff Sandlin, who had not been concerned enough to call her back after the day she panicked in Paris? Sam Sweeney? That was a laugh; she didn't even know which continent to try for Sam.

Mica! Even if Mica wired her the plane fare, she would still have to sneak out of the Negresco without settling her bill; she might very well be stopped by the police afterwards, when she tried to leave the country. God, she'd been so self-righteous with Pancho over Alan Mueller's wallet, and here she was, planning to skip out on a $1,500 hotel bill.

There *had* to be another solution. Should she try calling Serge? Would he believe her story any better the second time around? It was starting to sound like an improbable soap opera to Cecil herself.

Well, as the French said in the face of whatever adversity that came their way, *tant pis*. She would simply have to cope.

Her first measure in that direction was returning to the Negresco on foot to save on cab fare.

Cecil nodded nervously to the doorman in his medieval costume as he spun the revolving door for her. Once inside, she walked resolutely past the cashier's desk and on towards the lifts. Thank heavens she had not turned her key over to the concierge when she went out this morning. She had no idea what to say if the manager insisted on being paid today.

She was already pushing the button when a hand clamped down on her arm from behind. Cecil stifled a cry and turned around to see a young, pimple-faced boy in a porter's uniform.

'I was calling you, Miss Gutman, but you didn't hear. Would you come to the front desk, please?'

157

'No — no, I can't. I'm expecting a long-distance call from Moscow. It's due right this second, as a matter of fact.'

Oh, God, Moscow didn't sound like money. Why hadn't she said New York or London?

'I was asked that you come now,' the boy said sulkily. At least he had dropped his hold on her arm; he was not going to drag her there by force. 'There's somebody waiting to see you,' he added, looking over his shoulder as though to verify the truth of his own words.

Could it be Sam? Had he finally arrived? 'What name did he give?' she asked breathlessly.

'It's not a him, it's a her. The lady's been here for over an hour, and she's not too happy about it. What should I tell her?'

From the servile look on the boy's face, Cecil gathered that the woman in question had given him an important *largesse* and was insisting on immediate repayment.

Curious about her mysterious visitor, Cecil said to the boy, 'All right, I'll see her, but just for a minute.'

The woman was waiting for Cecil in a far corner of the lobby; her face was in the shadow of a large white felt hat in the improbable shape of a Frisbee.

'Miss Gutman, won't you be seated?' Her voice was husky but curiously appealing. She extended a white-gloved hand to Cecil. 'My name is Edith-Anne Schomberg and, as you may know, I am the wife of Xavier Schomberg. Frederick and Christine were our cousins.'

Cecil could not have been more surprised if the woman had announced herself as the holy messenger of God. Here — and so quickly — had arrived someone to solve all her problems! Cecil sank gratefully into the proffered chair and stared at Edith-Anne Schomberg in stunned amazement. The woman's face was an extraordinary assortment of sand-coloured freckles that nestled uneasily on her dry, faintly creased skin. So much of her hair was pulled into the confines of her big hat that Cecil could not even guess its colour. Her eyes had disappeared as well behind a wide band of dark-green plastic. Almost nothing, in fact, could be seen of Madame Edith-Anne Schomberg.

'I couldn't be happier to see you here,' Cecil began. 'A stupid incident occurred at the bank where I received my funds from Paris. I've just come back from there, and —'

'I know all about that,' Edith-Anne interrupted. 'I arranged it myself.'

'You what?' Cecil half rose out of her chair as a look of incredulous outrage gained her features.

'Sit down, Miss Gutman. There's no point in our wasting time

158

fighting. It will take me less than ten minutes to present my case to you. Afterwards, if you're sensible – and I can tell by looking at you that this is the case – then our business will be over. I want to make it absolutely clear, by the way, that this *is* a business meeting between two people whose interests have quite unexpectedly merged.'

'For the moment, I fail to see what we have in common,' Cecil said coldly.

'Let me start with your financial situation, since that is certainly what is occupying your mind right now. Last Friday, I arranged with our Paris bank to cut off your funds. You will receive nothing more, and that is why we must reach an understanding quickly. This morning, as a matter of face, since I have to be back in Paris tonight. My limousine is parked outside the door of this hotel. If you concur in what I have to propose, my chauffeur will stay with you all day today, and tomorrow morning he will drive you to the airport and put you on a flight to Dallas.'

The woman was speaking in clipped, spare phrases, but what registered with Cecil were the words 'flight to Dallas'. With the time difference, she could actually be home tomorrow afternoon!

'I feel quite sure that you owe a large bill to this hotel, and that you have precious little money with which to settle it.' Edith-Anne seemed to be rushing headlong on to some mysterious goal of her own; she gave Cecil not a moment to reply. 'While you're packing, I'll pay the hotel. Later in the day, I'll provide you with $2,000 in cash to cover your travel expenses. Finally, and even though you haven't fulfilled any of your contractual obligations to our family, I'll give you this.'

The woman opened her white clutch bag and took out an oblong slip of yellow paper. She held it up against her suit jacket, just out of Cecil's reach. It was a cheque issued by the Bank of America in favour of the very person who was staring at it now in such unabashed astonishment. A cashier's cheque for $30,000!

For a seond, Cecil wondered if she was hallucinating. Could Edith-Anne be only a figment of her feverish imagination, someone she had called forth because she desperately needed help?

'This is quite unexpected, Mrs Schomberg,' Cecil said in one of the biggest understatements of her life. 'What am I supposed to do in exchange for all this money? Besides packing and leaving the country, I mean?'

'Get an abortion,' Edith-Anne replied harshly. 'I've already set it up. The room is reserved at a Nice clinic. The doctor is booked for two o'clock.' She glanced at her slim, jewelled wristwatch. 'In just a little over two hours. It will be over and done with by three. You're free to spend the night at the clinic, although I really don't think that will be necessary. I suggest my chauffeur take you afterwards to the Holiday Inn, which is just across the street from the airport. It's as good a place as any to sleep.'

'I can't do it.' Even as she said the words, Cecil realised how recklessly she was throwing away her salvation. 'What you are asking of me is absolutely impossible.'

'Indeed?' Edith-Anne removed the band of green plastic to reveal eyebrows raised in sceptical amusement. 'And why, may I ask?'

'First of all, because no doctor would perform an abortion on me now. I'm nearly five months pregnant. The child might ... might live.'

Edith-Anne threw back her head and laughed merrily, as though Cecil had told a clever joke. 'You're being ridiculously sentimental, you know, and just when you no longer can afford such a luxury.

'The chances of a five-month fetus surviving an abortion are probably one out of a hundred thousand. Until recently, Down's syndrome children had to be aborted this far along. I know because I was carrying one myself. You can see that I've looked into the matter quite thoroughly, Miss Gutman, so just leave everything to me. It will be so much easier on you in the long run.'

Cecil shook her head wearily. 'I just don't understand you people. The baby you are so eager to be rid of − it's nothing to me, but it *is* a Schomberg. To use a tired cliché, it represents the future of your family. Why in God's name are all of you so anxious to kill it?'

'My dear, the only person who might have cared about this child is the grandmother, and she's little better than a vegetable now. As for the rest of us, I don't see why I should waste time washing our dirty linen in your company. Let's just say that it would be convenient for all of us if this child disappeared from our collective memory.'

'I won't do what you ask,' Cecil said, stringing out her words carefully, 'If only because of the dead parents. Christine and Frederick would want their child to live. They would expect me to protect it now. I gave my word to my doctor that ...'

'Your doctor! Are you referring to that drunken Irishman who came through Paris on his way to some orgy or another? When was the last time you heard from Dr Sweeney, Miss Gutman?'

'It's been ... a while,' Cecil admitted reluctantly.

'Sweeney was Christine's lover, you know. They travelled together all over the continent until the doctor's drinking got so bad that even Christine wanted to throw him over. And the gambling − surely you know about that?'

Cecil made a nervous gesture with her hands as though to sweep away the picture Edith-Anne Schomberg was painting of Sam. A

160

promiscuous, irresponsible, drunk gambler, Sam Sweeney? There wasn't a word of truth in it, she knew that. Yet, why had Sam failed to keep their New Year's appointment?

'I hope you didn't fall for him yourself,' Edith-Anne smirked in a knowing way. 'It happens all the time: a frustrated, lonely woman and a handsome, willing gynaecologist. It's almost inevitable, isn't it?'

'I don't think there's any point in continuing this conversation.'

'Oh, but there is — for you. Forget your doctor; you won't be seeing him again.'

Cecil looked up sharply at this remark, but Edith-Anne smiled enigmatically and continued uninterrupted. 'Too many shady characters are on the trail of the good doctor. With all the gambling debts he left behind, Sweeney will be forced to hide out for weeks or months or forever, for all I know. Try to focus on your own problems. You think that because you're carrying a Schomberg child, you have a certain status. Nothing could be further from the truth. First of all, there's absolutely no way you can prove this child *is* a Schomberg.'

'What about the agreement I signed in Dallas?'

'It so happens the only other signature on that document is Dr Sweeney's. It makes no reference whatsoever to our family. Let's take the rest of your situation point by point. All genetic proof of the child's parentage went up in smoke along with our poor cousins. Rita would not know you from a post in the road. The rest of us will deny anything you say, and if you try to force our hand, we'll take you to court. It will be your word against that of one of the most prominent and powerful families in France. Both my husband and cousin Bayard hold the Legion of Honour. What are you next to all of that?'

'A human being with rights equal to yours or anybody else's!' Cecil said with spirit.

'Obviously you do not know France well.'

'And the lawyer who drew up the papers? Surely he could ...'

'Are you referring to Mr Sandlin? A Texas gentleman with such a brilliant legal mind that our family has retained him to handle our American interests? In cruder terms, my dear, Jeffrey Sandlin is now on the payroll of Schomberg Mondial. Need I add that he received an obscenely high retainer?'

'You can't buy every journalist in France and America. If necessary, I'll take my story public.'

'My child, do you have the means to defend a libel suit of the highest magnitude? You, a young woman pursued and perhaps convicted for failing to pay a hotel bill? When we finish with you,

Miss Gutman, you will be looked upon with the same scornful scepticism as the little man in Utah who tried to obtain the Howard Hughes inheritance, or the German who manufactured the so-called Hitler diaries.'

Cecil felt the unmistakable, final tightening of a noose. Of course, she should have guessed what was coming the minute Edith-Anne identified herself. What other 'business' had she ever had with the Schomberg family except carrying their child and now killing it? How had Serge put it? 'These people who bought you.'

Cecil stirred up the last dregs of her fighting spirit. 'If all of this is true,' she asked, 'why do you bother with me at all?'

'Because of your nuisance value. As long as you're walking around pregnant and resentful, we have to keep some tiny corner of our minds concentrated on you. You're like a mosquito buzzing around. This isn't a personal matter, you know. It's business. I myself would like to see a pretty, intelligent young woman like you return to the States with her purse full of cash and her future bright with possibilities.'

'But I can't believe she didn't ...'

'What, dear?'

'Christine. It's hard for me to believe she didn't make some provision for her child. A will, a declaration of intent, *something*. She wanted this baby desperately.'

'It is a shame, isn't it?' The little smile was back on Edith-Anne's lips. She leaned towards Cecil with the avid expression of a lion about to spring on a cornered gazelle. 'I mean, that she died before she had time to do any of that.'

'I see.' After a long and pained silence, Cecil asked in the dull voice of defeat. 'How do I know I'll ever see my cheque if I do ... what you want?'

Edith-Anne, recognising victory, rose from her chair. 'Go ahead and pack while I settle your bill and check you out. I haven't given the hotel my real name, by the way, and I would quite successfully deny ever having been here, should you try to prove it later. As for your cheque, that's easy enough. I'll accompany you into the delivery room and hand it over once you've signed the release for the doctor. No one wants to cheat you, you know. The money is not our concern at all.'

'All right. I'll be down in fifteen minutes.'

Cecil walked as steadily as she could back to the lifts. Already she imagined herself telling Serge that it had all been a joke. She wasn't pregnant and never had been. She saw the two of them coming together to count the money, opening a paper bag stuffed with hundred-dollar bills. Three hundred of them. The ransom for a kidnapped child. That was what she was doing, wasn't it? Simply returning the unborn child to its rightful family? Who could blame her for that? She saw the bills fly up into the air and cascade around them as their lips met over champagne that bubbled and spilled icily over the tops of the glasses and on to their hands.

A dreamscape where everything she had ever wanted came true.

Ten minutes later, dressed in a pair of faded jeans, moccasins and her sheepskin coat, she called down to the concierge.

'I'll be leaving my room in about five minutes. Could you send someone up for my suitcase? I'll want it stored at the hotel until tomorrow morning when I'll stop by for it on my way to the airport.'

She put down the receiver and tried to close her overnight bag; it was so crammed with clothes that she could not pull the zipper shut. Maybe it was her badly shaking hands that made her so clumsy. In desperation, she simply buckled the nylon strap around the bag and left the rest hanging loose.

Standing her big suitcase well in view and propping the door ajar, she left her room and hurried down the hall to the stairs. She dragged the overnight bag behind her, listening as it hit stair after stair on her seemingly endless journey downwards. The baby was kicking in rhythm to the thumping bag, kicking savagely as though it knew and reviled the fate Edith-Anne had planned for it. What did the French say? *Faiseur d'anges.* 'Angel-maker'. They could wax poetic about something as distasteful as abortion.

Cecil pushed open a heavy door that brought her out into the lobby at the exact moment the pimple-faced porter entered the lift opposite on his way up to her room for the suitcase. At the reception desk, Edith-Anne was counting out bills while a gentleman in a double-breasted, pearl-grey suit danced attendance on her. Next to Edith-Anne stood the liveried chauffeur – René, who must have been requisitioned from Rita's service to make the trip to Nice. Most likely he had been stationed in the reception area to keep an eye out for Cecil, but instead he was watching the growing pile of bills with an almost erotic fervour.

Cash, Cecil thought. Everyone loved it. It captured people's attention faster and better than any naked body.

Without waiting to see more, Cecil turned and walked in the opposite direction. She was in a narrow corridor lined with glass display cases that held the kinds of beautiful objects a guest of the Negresco would covet: fine bone china, silver flatware, jewel-studded watches and bracelets. There was a door at the end of the corridor,

163

and Cecil went straight through that into an enormous room, the hotel's multi-starred Chantecler Restaurant. Waiters were busy putting the last touches on linen-covered tables; a young woman filled crystal vases with yellow roses. With a face as stiff as his starched shirt-front, the maître d' approached Cecil.

'Is this the coffee shop?' she asked in the most pronounced American accent she could muster. 'George told me to meet him in the coffee shop so we could have a snack before we went sailing today.' She patted her bag. 'I don't see George anywhere.'

'This way, Madame,' said the maître d', pain now predominating over politeness in his solemn face. 'You are looking for La Rotonde. The *other* restaurant. Through this door, please.'

'Gee, thanks. I can't imagine what George is up to. He should be here by now.'

Inside the smaller room done up in acid colours to look like a circus, Cecil waved to a blond waiter who was a complete stranger to her.

'Hi there, how are you today? I'm lost, just like yesterday. I just can't seem to find my way around this hotel. We don't have anything this big back in Kansas.'

The waiter smiled indulgently and held open the street door for her; he appeared to take no notice whatsoever of the canvas bag that Cecil suddenly realised with horror was overflowing with bra straps, rolled-up panties, socks and packages of Kleenex.

Once out on the Promenade des Anglais, she almost shrieked with joy. She'd done it! She had left the hotel with all her belongings, and not one person had questioned her! She hadn't needed anybody's help! Now, all she had to do was find a taxi before René's big black limousine found her.

Cecil turned into the small street that ran alongside the Negresco and was met head on by the mistral. The wind seemed to be pushing her all the way back to the sea. Luckily, she wouldn't have to fight it for long. At the next corner was the Rue de France, a main thoroughfare whose pavements would be jammed with shoppers. She would be safe there. She was only a short distance from her goal when the door of a parked sports car flew open, blocking her passage. A man leaned across the seat and called out to her.

'Hi there! You going my way?'

Annoyed, Cecil started to circumvent the obstacle of the protruding door when she saw that the driver was Alan Mueller. The usual wide grin was plastered across his tanned face.

'You look like a girl in a hurry. Can I give you a ride somewhere?'

After a moment's hesitation, Cecil lifted up the heavy bag and dropped it behind the front seat. She climbed in next to Mueller.

'Yes, you can, as a matter of fact. I'd appreciate your helping me find some little hotel in the old part of town. I just can't take the Negresco another minute. I mean, I came to France to soak up atmosphere, and that place is snobbish and packed with tourists, and . . .' She was babbling; she must slow down and try to talk normally. 'It's lucky your coming along like this. I've been standing out on the Promenade des Anglais for half an hour. For some reason, the doorman couldn't find me a taxi today.'

'There aren't enough to go around because of the cold. Hey, am I glad to see you! Do you realise what a hard girl you are to pin down?'

Cecil ignored this. 'Do you have a suggestion for a hotel?'

'Sure, I know just the place for you. It's small and clean and has a soca restaurant right across the street. Real cheap, too.'

Why had he said that? The way she was dressed? Her overflowing suitcase? The look of utter panic in her eyes?

'That's wonderful! Could we leave now? I'd like to check in and unpack before lunch.'

If Alan Mueller wondered why Cecil slumped so low in the passenger seat that not even the top of her red head was visible to the people in the street, he didn't ask. Instead, he manoeuvred his car out into the traffic and drove at a steady pace towards the narrow streets of the Old Town.

Chapter Twenty-Seven

'Good God! Have you seen this?'

'What on earth is the matter with you? You look like a death's-head!'

'After you've read this letter, you'll probably be able to get a maggot, too!'

'Keep your nasty remarks to yourself, I'm warning you. Here, give that to me! It can't be as bad as you make it out . . . What? The fools! The raving, lunatic fools!'

'Get yourself under control! Someone may be outside listening.'

'But why would they wait all this time to contact us? No one can be so slow-witted . . .'

'They're Swiss,' replied the other cryptically.

'But this means that the doctor . . . It was for nothing, all of that?'

'Don't bleat so, it gets on my nerves. Anyway, it's rather more of a tragedy for the doctor than for us, wouldn't you say?'

'But the risks we took, and that huge sum of money we had to pay out to get the body –'

'Shut up, I tell you!'

'All right, just tell me why they've waited so long to write. It's been nearly a month since Christine and Frederick's accident.'

'Perhaps they don't read newspapers. Perhaps they were waiting for an astrological reading. Perhaps it simply took them all this time to figure out what was expected of them.'

'Well, they've grasped it well enough now. I see they're asking point-blank if we know where Cecil Gutman is.'

'Fortunately, that's easy to answer. We know nothing whatsoever about Miss Gutman, and even less about this fairy tale of an unborn heir. In our opinion, the whole thing is a monumentally bad joke.'

'That won't stop them. This letter is from Zürich, which means they're not only Swiss but German as well. I know the type. They'll charge like panzer commanders and continue on, rolling over every obstacle in their path until someone orders them to a halt.'

'I wonder who *is* behind this?'

'Rita's senility must be contagious. You've lost your ability to read.'

'Don't try to be superior; it doesn't suit you at all. It so happens I find this letter ambiguous.'

'It's clear enough to me – the little bitch Christine didn't trust us. She went to a firm of Swiss lawyers and had a new will drawn up. Not only that, she left instructions for the panzer commanders to go looking for Cecil Gutman if anything happened to her or Frederick. Our error was in underestimating little Christine de la Rouvay. We should have remembered how she humiliated us with all that talk about her precious father the marquis, but never a word about her mother. And for good reason, too, as our detective soon found out. Christine always kept her own counsel. When she began to suspect us, she must have – '

'That's over and done with!' the other cut in.

'All I can see is that we've gone to enormous trouble and expense to arrange these accidents, and now we find ourselves in a position of mortal danger because of a five-month-old fetus.'

'It's not the fetus, it's the girl. And you're forgetting that we have an important advantage over the gnomes in the Alps. We know where Cecil Gutman is, and they don't.'

'Yes, but when those lawyers fail to get a satisfactory answer from you, they'll start to advertise for her all over Europe. Some smart journalist is bound to pick it up. When a story like that breaks, it will spread like wildfire; there'll be no stopping it.'

'When it breaks, journalists and lawyers alike will find Miss Gutman. Only, she will no longer be pregnant, and it won't matter in the least what story she tells.'

'What do you mean?'

'I'm launching Operation Medical.'

'Your man is still watching her, then?'

'Every minute.'

'Just don't make the same mistake twice. Cecil Gutman is nearly as clever a bitch as Christine was.'

'If Mademoiselle Gutman crosses us one more time, she'll find herself on the exact same crash course as our little Christine. Miss Gutman is very likely to die peacefully in her bed . . . in the hospital.'

'Such a young girl, too. Sad, isn't it?'

'Oh, very.'

Chapter Twenty-Eight

'Oh, you want Pancho, do you? Jean-Luc, look what just walked in the door asking for the *gitano*! What do you want with that lazy, arrogant bastard? Won't you take me instead?'

In a swift, vulgar movement, the punk thrust his face so close so Cecil's that she could see nothing but a pair of eyes bulging with druglike excitement, and a red tongue that slipped suggestively around the corners of a lewdly painted mouth. 'Huh, what about me, babe? Won't I do?'

Cecil put the flat of her palms hard against the metallic surface of the punk's glittery green jacket and shoved. Like a boneless doll, he went sprawling back against the wall and slouched there, bent forwards and staring up at her out of black-rimmed, evil eyes. Green hair rose from his scalp in aggressively improbable spikes, and a large safety pin slashed one thin ear. Without releasing her from his stare, the punk unravelled his body from the wall and jerked galvanically forwards.

'Jean-Luc, should she have done that? Was that a nice thing to do? Ohh, you better watch out, babe! If Jean-Luc loses his temper, all hell will break loose here!'

Lost in the smoky blue depths of the basement club, his friend Jean-Luc was as invisible as he was inaudible.

'Tell me, babe,' said the impudent punk, 'did you come here looking for trouble or did it just creep up on you by accident?'

'Why don't you shut up!' Cecil exclaimed in exasperation. 'I've had enough headaches in Nice without taking on a couple of punks as dim as burnt-out strobe lights. Where is the manager of this club, anyway?'

'She is afraid of nothing, this one. Did you see, Jean-Luc? Not a hair turned on her head, not a muscle twitched. Oh, she thinks she is brave, all right. Shall we see if it is all bluff?'

Cecil did an abrupt about-face and headed for the stairs, calling back over her shoulder, 'When Pancho comes, tell him I won't be back until he disinfects this place and sweeps out the dead vermin.'

From behind her came a sensuously placating voice. '*Querida mia*, do not be angry with me. It was all in fun.'

Cecil turned slowly. Just visible through the thick blue shadows was the gleam of one bright eye. It winked at her in malice, and then the punk leapt into the narrow beam of light of the circular, hanging lamp. Laughing wickedly, he grabbed two tufts of his outrageous green wig and lifted it off, revealing thick, jet-black hair underneath.

'Oh, you, you rat! You misbegotten, no-account, traitor-rat! You do it to me every time!'

Cecil was collapsing with laughter.

'I am very good at it, this being a rat. Like in the park in Bordeaux and at the hotel, you never suspect a thing, do you? I am a genius at disguise!' He was dancing around her, in and out of the shadows, his crazily painted face lit up with pleasure at the success of his joke.

'You're a megalomaniac, not a genius, and if you don't watch out, your head will swell up and sail right out of here. What does your friend Jean-Luc have to say about all of this, or is he mute?'

'Jean-Luc, what do you say? Oh, too, bad, he has gone out. We are all alone, *amorciteo*.'

'I see that Jean-Luc is the perfect friend for someone with your ego. He's not only mute but nonexistent.'

'It took you long enough to get here as it is,' Pancho said sulkily. 'I've asked you to come to hear me play since the day we arrived in Nice.'

At the sight of his look of professional martyrdom, Cecil burst out laughing again. 'So now it's you, the injured party?'

'Yes, I am *blessé*, mortally wounded by your indifference, but I forgive you because I am head over heels in love with you.' Pancho pulled a chair out from a small table and motioned to Cecil to be seated. 'Look, I have prepared everything for you, little sandwiches and a cocktail of fruit juices I made myself at the bar. Is this not nice? Am I not a wonderful lover? Now tell me, how could you stay away from me for so long?'

Cecil inspected the table; it was prettily laid out with platters of sandwiches and snacks and tall glasses decorated with scarlet-coloured paper umbrellas. 'This is sweet, Pancho. And I wanted to come every day, but you know how sick I was that first week, and afterwards I had a lot of − oh, stupid problems. The principal thing is that my job went up in smoke.' Cecil paused, horrified at the realisation of how literal a statement that was. 'And now I'm about to run out of money. I don't know how I'll ever get back to the States.'

'Are you expecting that I steal for you?'

'I don't expect *anything*!' Cecil answered in exasperation. 'I thought you were my friend and that I could talk to you. Believe me, you're not even on my short list of possible saviours!'

'But you came here looking for advice, so I will give you some,' Pancho said coldly. 'Stop being a spoiled American girl who breaks down every time she has a little trouble. You can no longer afford to be like that. You have your baby to think of now.'

'Oh, I forgot you knew about the baby. Yes, it is wonderful company for me. It keeps me going through trial and tribulation, and sweetens every bitter cup I'm offered. A real ray of sunshine in the deluge of my life.'

She suddenly buried her head in her hands.

'*Querida*, do not do this. Rather, tell me the truth of what is bothering you.' As he spoke, Pancho lifted several strands of Cecil's hair and let them fall though his fingers, staring at them as though they were threads of highly prized gold. 'I want to help you.'

'But I don't *need* your help!' she exclaimed, raising her weary face in angry defiance. 'Too many people have been trying to solve my problems for me lately, and something bad always happens to me afterwards. What makes you think I want you as a white knight, anyway?'

'I do not have to be told. Remember, I read faces.'

Cecil smiled in spite of herself. 'I thought it was palms.'

'It's all the same. Most people are open books, and if you take the trouble, you can read their whole lives in the lines and expressions on their faces.'

'Well, I certainly haven't been able to decipher a single thing out of yours. I don't know if you're married or have children, if you've ever been in love, how old you are, why you came to France or even what your real name is, because it can't be Paso Real. The only subjects you talk about are your music and your old grandmother.'

'Old? What makes you think Sarita was old?' asked a bemused Pancho, ignoring all the questions implicit in her speech. 'My grandmother was a very pretty woman, maybe forty when we worked the streets together. She couldn't have been much older because of the milk.'

'Milk?' repeated Cecil, intrigued. Pancho had a remarkable ability to pull her into an obsessive and bizarre world of his own where her problems simply dissolved into thin air.

'You want to know about me? Today I will tell you how I got an

170

education that was very different from your antiseptic American one. Every morning, I got up, ate breakfast, dressed and went off – not to school but to El Once, a Jewish quarter in Buenos Aires made up of fur shops, haberdasheries, little factories that made leather goods. Not rich, not poor – just right for Sarita and me. We would stop at a door, and she would push me in first because I was such a charmer – a good-looking boy with a wonderful smile. Everybody loved me.'

'Naturally.'

'Naturally. With my patter, I never failed to get us in. The proprietor was usually a respectable, middle-aged gentleman, and Sarita would flirt a little with him, and then she'd say, "Señor, show me a thousand-peso note that has crossed your palm, and I will show you your future." If the man was curious or gullible or even a tiny bit superstitious, he would take the bill out of his wallet and give it to her. "Señor," Sarita would say, "a beautiful dark lady is waiting to love you as always you have wanted to be loved, but there will be trouble for you if you let a fair-haired man into your house first. Great, great wealth will be yours before two moons have passed."'

'Very original,' Cecil murmured dryly.

'Ah, but it worked! When Sarita turned on her music, the man flew up into the clouds, and when she turned it off, he came back into his little shop as though from a flying carpet. Sometimes he forgot about his thousand-peso note. If he dared ask for it back, Sarita would become very, very angry. In her fury, she would rip open her blouse, take out a breast swollen with milk and pinch her nipple as though she was mutilating herself. What do you think happened next?'

Looking ill at ease, Cecil shook her head.

'This!' Pancho reached into a pitcher and, with thumb and forefinger, expertly flicked a stream of juice onto Cecil's hand. 'A squirt of milk landed directly on the bill. *Tu comprendes*, mil pesos was a great deal of money in Argentina in those days.'

'"What filthy thing are you doing to my money?" the shopkeeper or the furrier would scream. "Señor, I have blessed your mil pesos. You give them to me now?" And he always did, for no one would touch money that was tainted by her milk. At first, I was very ashamed. I saw the hatred and disgust on the men's faces. It was a sexual thing, you understand?'

'But how could she? I mean, was she always nursing a baby?'

'Nearly always. My mother – she was the oldest – was born when Sarita was only fourteen. After that, there was a new baby every two or three years.'

'What a horrible person to bring up a small boy.'

'Sarita was not horrible! She took good care of me, loved me. It

171

was I who was ungrateful — I refused to stay in her world.'

'Where was your mother all this time?'

'She was the most beautiful woman in all of Buenos Aires, a flamenco dancer called La Mariposa — the Butterfly. Every man who came to watch her dance fell in love with her. I was like the others, except she was my mother, and I thought she belonged only to me. I found out how wrong I was when she ran off to Paris with a Frenchman thirty years older than she was. I was just a boy then and I never saw her again. Finally, she gave me nothing but my music.'

'Is that why you came to France?' Cecil asked softly. 'To find your mother?'

Pancho grinned. His beautiful, even teeth shone like white idols against his painted face. 'You like my story then, *querida*? Does it sound bohemian enough? Is this the way you think a gypsy lives? Is it not romantic and wild, perfect to scare little virgin girls in white dresses on their way to first communion?'

'Oh, I give up on you! You're so sweet one minute and a devil the next.'

'You do not like me then?'

'Possibly, I like you very much.' At the sight of Pancho's knowing grin, Cecil added hastily, 'But I don't trust you at all. You never tell the truth.'

'Sometimes it is better to put your trust in liars and thieves and be on your guard against honest citizens.'

An image of the Schombergs slipped into Cecil's mind, but of course Pancho could not be referring to those particular scoundrels. He knew nothing about them. In spite of his garish make-up, Pancho now looked as solemn as an ecclesiastical judge. No disguise, Cecil realised, could ever compete with this remarkable ability of his to slip into whatever personality suited his needs of the moment.

'And now, *chica*, do you want to tell me what it is that worries you so?'

Cecil hesitated, then said, 'Maybe tonight. You'll probably have changed yourself into a father confessor by then, and I'll have no choice.'

'I do not want to be a father to you. Or a priest. I can think of other roles to play that are much more amusing.'

'I hate to crush your hopes, but I'm going out for some fresh air. I feel a little dizzy from this smoky air.' Pancho was only teasing her, of course, but Cecil felt something almost electric pass between them, and it frightened her. 'If you want, I'll call you around midnight after you finish your last show.'

'Hey, Jean-Luc, this sexy redhead is calling us at midnight. Does

172

that not seem suggestive to you? Yes, but first we will go to a restaurant, all three of us together. Jean-Luc says he will take you away from the imbecile *gitano* tonight! Until then, you must promise me something.'

'What now?'

'Be very careful. There is much crime in the streets here, many bad people.'

'You're the second person to warn me about that. You shouldn't worry, though,' Cecil added solemnly. 'I've decided to take your friend Jean-Luc along to protect me from all the cranks and crooks.'

Pancho's words echoed in Cecil's mind as she set off through the tortuous, interlacing streets of the Old Town. Once again she was struck by how utterly Italian Nice was. If Bordeaux had been a closed city, almost British in its reserve, Nice was out-and-out Naples. Brightly coloured washing hung at almost every window, and from morning to sundown, verbose matrons relayed recipes, family illnesses and love affairs across their wet clothes. After the hushed velvet-and-brocade atmosphere of the Negresco, the Old Town seemed to Cecil to be life itself.

On this cold afternoon, the streets were unusually subdued. It was a Monday, and the shutters and metal grates of most of the stores were closed; precious few people were about to fight the wind. Cecil climbed a short flight of steps, turned into an even narrower street and found she was following a straggly pack of dogs. They trotted ahead of her at a brisk pace as though they were on an errand to some special place within the labyrinth of bottlenecks, squares and crooked streets.

Cecil was starting to regret having taken this walk instead of going straight back to her hotel. She had not lied when she told Pancho that she was feeling dizzy; what she had been careful not to reveal to him was her appointment at the hotel at six. Pancho was jealous and possessive, and the less he knew about this particular meeting, the better.

It was late afternoon, and the winter light was fading fast. Leaning against the door of a closed pasta shop were two extremely thin youths, their faces in shadow and their hands plunged deep into the pockets of their rough work trousers. Cecil heard a sniggering, muffled call as she passed; she took a quick turn which brought her into still another empty square. There was only one way out of this one, stone steps leading down into a tunnel of pitch blackness.

Cecil realised she had no idea where she was. The streets were completely deserted, but she could hear the echo of heels hitting against cobblestones, of hushed, far-away voices. There was life all around her, but where? Suddenly she had the impression that the footsteps were directly behind her, that they were stopping when she stopped, moving when she moved. Cecil cast an apprehensive glance over her shoulder, but there was nothing to see except the leprous walls of a cluster of closed-up buildings. A gnawing fear took hold of her. Why had she ever imagined that being in a crowded neighbourhood of mostly poor people would make her safe? The long arm of the Schombergs reached into every corner of France, even the most humble.

She could hear the steps clearly now; they were perhaps half a block behind her and moving at the exact same cadence as her own. In her mind's eye, Cecil saw a woman — Edith-Anne with her white Frisbee hat and the strip of green plastic that hid her cold, slanted eyes. In one gloved hand, she held something sharp and pointed that flamed in the faint light.

Cecil began to run then, colliding with the handlebar of a bicycle parked against a wall. Behind her, other feet ran as well. Every turn she took brought her to still another square and another set of steps. Over the flat roof of a building just ahead, Cecil saw the lit dome of a church. If only she knew which direction to take, she could take refuge there. The church would be opening for evening mass; there would be *somebody* inside, a priest, a worshipper, a beggar trying to escape the cold.

Cecil caught a glimpse of a figure not far behind; it wasn't Edith-Anne at all but a man, and when he passed under a streetlamp, Cecil saw that he was enormous, with greasy, glistening hair. He was dressed in blue overalls and a heavy, padded jacket. The man's appearance was so physically overpowering that Cecil found herself frozen by fear. She pressed against a building, preparing herself to scream. Where in God's name were all the *Niçous?*

When the man caught up with Cecil, he grabbed her by the shoulders and pushed her backwards against the doorjamb. He held her motionless in the vice-like grip of his massive fingers, pressing his body hard against her. She could smell the hot stench of garlic breath on her cheek.

'Let go or I'll scream!' In her terror, Cecil had lost her French. She could scarcely get the words out in English. The man was whispering a word to her, over and over again, but she could not understand.

'*Je t'ai demandé, combien? Tout le temps, tu t'es tournée vers moi. Ne joue pas la comédie maintenant.*'

Finally, through the cloud of fear that had dulled her mind, Cecil realised what he was saying. 'You're asking me ... how much?' She began to laugh uncontrollably. 'You think I'm a ... I'm a working girl, is that it? Oh, that's too ... funny. Excuse me ... I can't ... help it.'

The man fixed her with his terrible stare for an instant more, and then, like ground cracking open in an earthquake, his face broke into the lines of a fierce smile. 'You English? Tourist? I thought ... oh yes, it is very funny!'

Now he too was bent over with laughter; he dropped his tight hold on Cecil to cover a mouth that bubbled with mirth, and at that instant, she turned and ran. Her feet flew over the cobblestones. She did not step even for a second to verify if her giant suitor was following. All Cecil's fear had returned, and she could think of nothing but the great lumps of his fingers digging into her flesh.

At last, her flight brought her into a wider street where a few shops and restaurants were open. Her breath was tearing at her lungs, and she had to stop to rest. She leaned dizzily against a greengrocer's stand until she could control her breathing, then asked the moustached proprietor for directions. Five minutes later, she was in the small, familiar street of her own hotel.

Cecil noted that it was a quarter to six. In only fifteen minutes, she had an appointment with Serge. He had called her at noon, insisting on seeing her this evening, and all day she had felt ambiguous about their meeting, at once desiring and dreading it. And now here she was, almost faint from that stupid incident in the street.

Cecil walked quickly towards the narrow entrance to her hotel and saw that someone was standing directly in front of it, blocking her way. Oh, God, Alan Mueller!

'Cecil!' The tennis coach whirled around. For once, he was not smiling; in fact, he looked almost beside himself with anger, although for what reason Cecil could not imagine.

'Where have you been all this time?' he asked accusingly.

'Out for a walk. What are you doing here, anyway?'

'I came over about three to talk to you about something important. You were just going out, and when I tried to catch up, you disappeared into thin air.'

'Well, here I am,' Cecil said irritably.

'Good. Come on.' Alan took a firm grip on her arm and marched her away from the hotel.

'Alan, let go! You're hurting me!'

'Sorry.' He loosened his hold but still kept her walking forcibly towards one of the dark alleys. 'Don't look so worried, I'm not kidnapping you or anything. I just want us to get a warm drink somewhere.'

Cecil could imagine the enormous bruise that was forming on her arm right now. First Pancho acting the fool, and then the maniac in overalls chasing her, and now Alan Mueller. It was too much for one short day.

'You might try asking me! I don't like being manhandled like this, Alan. What's more, I have an appointment at my hotel at six. Is this what you've been waiting for all afternoon – to Ramboise me into having a drink with you?'

'I didn't mean to hurt you. I'm just so frustrated because I like you one hell of a lot, and I can never *find* you. If I didn't know better, I'd think you were going out of your way to avoid me.'

By the light of a hanging streetlamp, Cecil saw that the familiar, toothy grin was back. Mediterranean accent or not, he looked exactly like a big, friendly German shepherd; she had never met anyone quite so canine. And who bored her more. Possibly she was foolish to put him down like this; he had a watchdog quality that could be useful to her now.

'All right, Alan, but I can't stay more than five minutes. Let's just go to the little place around the corner since I have so little time.'

'No way. I don't want to sit in that stuffy place full of Arabs.' The surly tone of Alan's voice startled Cecil. His lips were pulled back from his big teeth in what suddenly seemed more of a wolf's snarl than a dog's happy grin. He looked almost sinister. 'We're going to the square.'

'Alan, you're not listening to me.'

Cecil's patience was wearing thin. She slowed down, trying to hold him back, but he was forcing her into the tunnel of that night-dark alley. What's more, she was almost sure that they were not walking towards a major thoroughfare at all but rather back into the deserted heartland of the Old City.

A figure stepped out of another narrow alley, and an indolent, mocking voice called out to her. 'Well, Cici, it looks as though this fellow is taking you some place you don't want to go. If that is correct, then I shall be obliged to intervene on your behalf.'

'Serge!'

Cecil had never been so glad to see anyone in her life. Alan instantly dropped her arm and moved so that his face was partly illuminated by a restaurant neon; the friendly-dog look was back in full force, but Cecil had forgotten all about him.

'Don't look so astonished, Cici,' said Serge. 'I'm quite simply on my way to your hotel, which I believe is at the end of this dimly lit and altogether gloomy street.'

'I've been wondering all afternoon how you found me.'

'Oh, I'm a fairly good detective when I want to be. I called our mutual friend in Moscow.' He paused and cast a dubious look in Mueller's direction. 'He didn't have the faintest idea where you were, but he did give me a number in Dallas, and there I spoke to a young woman of Spanish heritage who seemed to possess a great deal of information about me, none of it particularly good. It took a lot of friendly persuasion before she finally parted with your present whereabouts.'

'I am amazed that you went to so much trouble. Over me, I mean.'

Serge stared at her mockingly for a moment, and Cecil felt her cheeks grow warm in embarrassment.

'Cici, aren't you going to introduce me to your big friend?'

'Hiya, fellow. I'm Alan Mueller.' Alan stuck out one big hand to be shaken, at the same time putting his other arm around Cecil's shoulders in a show of possession. 'You're right about the cold. It's much too chilly for Cecil to be standing out in the street. She and I have got something pretty important to discuss, so I suggest you come back tomorrow.'

'On the contrary, it's I who have an appointment with Cecil,' Serge shot back smoothly. 'Be a good fellow and make yourself scarce.'

Cecil felt Alan stiffen, but his tone was still cordial when he said, 'I didn't catch your name.'

'I didn't give it. Call me Serge if you like. Cici, what do you want to do?'

'Go some place warm.' Perversely, she let Mueller's arm stay where it was this time. 'There's no reason why we can't all three have a drink together, is there?'

Seeing that he was stuck with Serge, Alan Mueller reluctantly led their little group some two hundred metres through the maze of streets to emerge on the plane trees and the ancient stone arcades of the Place Garibaldi. At the entrance to the brightly lit Café de Turin, Alan stopped and whispered to Cecil, 'Can't you get rid of him? I *have* to talk to you alone. It's important.'

Cecil shrugged; she saw no reason to help either Alan or Serge. In fact, she was rather enjoying the situation. The café was hot and jammed in the back room. People on all sides were busy stabbing into imense platters of seafood; voices came at them like the roar of the sea.

'The service is notoriously slow here,' Serge said to Alan with an ingratiating smile. 'Be a good chap and take our orders to the bar, would you?'

'Why don't you do it? You're the third wheel around here!' Alan snarled.

177

'Oh, for heaven's sake, Alan, quit arguing and go!' Cecil cried. 'And get me a bottle of Evian, too. I'm starting to have a terrible headache, and I need to take an aspirin.'

Alan frowned belligerently at Serge, then rose and pushed his way through the crowd towards the bar in the next room.

Immediately, Serge leaned forwards and took Cecil's hand. 'Have you missed me? I haven't thought of anything except you since that night at the Negresco.'

'You're the phantom lover *par excellence*, aren't you? One appearance and then weeks or months or years of neglect. But of course, you never stop loving me during these interminable absences.'

'Cici, I owe you an apology, but this is hardly the moment, not with that cluck hanging on to our every word. I know I should have called you right away, but the story you told me was so extravagant, I needed a bit of time to get used to it.'

'So you're finally decided you like the ring of it?' Cecil pulled her hand away in irritation.

'It would be difficult for me to go on doubting under the circumstances. Darling, haven't you seen the papers today?'

'I've scarcely looked at them since I left the Negresco. I had enough problems of my own without worrying about the rest of the world's.' Cecil hated the note of self-pity that had crept into her voice.

'Poor darling, you've had a hell of a time, but I swear to you it's finished now. We'll work this out together.'

'Work out what?'

'Cici, a firm of Swiss lawyers have placed ads all over Europe asking that you get in touch with them. A French journalist from *Libération* stuck his nose into the matter and somehow discovered that the ad concerned the Schomberg estate and that there *is* a missing heir. The story made front pages all over the world today. Even Mica had seen it.'

'Everybody except me.'

'I guessed it would be like this. You hadn't heard about the Schomberg plane accident when it was the biggest news story in France. Listen, we have a lot to talk about. Dump your big friend so we can be alone.'

'Serge, I'm so confused.' Her head was spinning; she could scarcely see his heavy, handsome features. 'Edith-Anne Schomberg came to see me at the Negresco. She wanted to force me to have an abortion. She said I had no choice because Christine and Frederick didn't leave anything in writing to prove the baby was theirs.'

'Either she was lying or she didn't know about this Swiss will. Good God, you didn't, did you?'

'What?'

'Have the abortion?'

'You were right, fellah. It's damned hard to get served here.' Alan Mueller plunked down a tray holding three oversized cups of steaming chocolate and a bottle of Evian. 'Listen, old buddy, I'll bet Cecil is hungry, too. How about hustling over to the pastry shop for some croissants? It's only a couple of doors away.'

'I'm not hungry, Alan,' Cecil cut in quickly.

'Well, I am. How about it, Serge?'

'Later,' came the curt reply.

'Please, let's don't get into a fight over something as stupid as croissants,' Cecil said. With one still-trembling hand, she picked up the big cup and took a sip of hot liquid. She felt so strange! Her mind was spinning with information Serge had just given her; she needed to know the details, yet she couldn't seem to summon the energy to get rid of Alan Mueller. He was right about her being hungry, too. On an empty stomach, the chocolate was making her deathly ill. Or had she felt this way before she came into the stuffy, overheated Café du Turin?

Cecil turned to Serge to ask him to order her some food, but he and Alan were busy exchanging only slightly veiled insults. Their voices, she noted listlessly, were coming to her from far, far away.

The situation was farcical; Serge and Alan, building up to a fight over a woman who was five months pregnant! Serge and Alan and Pancho. Was even one of them truly interested in her as a person? One and all, they were obsessed by the Schomberg heir. No, that wasn't fair: the plodding tennis coach hadn't given any indication that he had noticed her condition. She was still very slender, so much so that she could at last understand those tales of babies being found in the bathrooms of college dorms with no one able to say who among the girls had been pregnant.

'Excuse me,' she said, rising precipitately from the banquette. 'I'll be right back.'

'Cecil, are you all right?' 'I'll come with you.' 'Leave her alone, she didn't ask for your help!' 'The hell you say ...' 'Can't you see she doesn't want you?'

Cecil escaped into the adjoining room. It was equally crowded and even stuffier; she couldn't seem to breathe at all here. Leaning against the bar for support, she tried to stop a waiter to ask directions to the WC, then decided it was fresh air she needed. She elbowed her way through the milling crowd and reached the front door. The cold air struck her as fiercely as though she had come out into a Siberian night.

What was happening to her? The pain ... It had come out of nowhere, and already it was a knife cutting through her belly and pushing up to the spot where her heart slammed against its cage of bone. It hurt so bad she could not move; she stood on the dark street corner swaying, shaking like a malaria victim, her legs useless rubber stalks beneath her.

'You need a taxi, lady?'

The outline of the car was barely visible through the fog. Only, there wasn't any fog in Nice tonight, Cecil was sure of that. Was it the veil over her eyes that made the leafless plane trees of the Place Garibaldi come briefly into focus, waver, and then disappear altogether? She took one hesitant step in the direction of the disembodied voice. Not one of her senses was functioning now except the one that told her she was in agonising pain.

'Please,' she whispered. 'I can't open the door by myself.'

'You shouldn't be out on a night like this without a coat, lady. Come on, just one more step. That's it, we're almost there.'

Cecil stumbled and then plunged forwards into the dark cavern of the car. When she heard the door slam behind her, she let her head loll on to the cold smoothness of the windowpane. Unbearably heavy lids fell of their own accord over pain-dulled eyes.

Before the veil covered the very last corner of her mind, she managed to gasp out a question.

'Where ... are you ... taking me?'

If the driver told her, Cecil never heard his answer. She was unconscious.

Since the first instant of its existence, its cells have had a primitive kind of intelligence of their own. Something in the blastocyst itself had *known, remembered*. Even before that, as far back as when the minute sperm travelled down its endless tunnel and fell off into a void, as far back as when the ovum was plucked from its warm, tight refuge to fly through space in a lonely, orectic journey of its own, it has possessed a sense of being, a continuity.

The cellular memory is growing dimmer as it is replaced by the more complex and dominant memory in the brain. The two ways of knowing still exist at this moment, however, and both the one that is dying and the one that is coming into being are functioning at prodigious levels of efficiency. Both have brought to the apogee of their possibilities by the emotional stimulation of absolute, total terror.

At this instant, right next to its body, there is a spear or a spike or a skewer, a sharp-pointed knife or needle, some instrument of death.

The thing moves fast — it stabs, retreats, stabs again. Every thrusting movement convulses and galvanises its own heart as though, already, it has been stabbed. Vibrating like high-tension wires, its nerves send its body jerking right and left, up and down, always a fraction of an inch out of reach of the thing that wants to kill it.

The blood-red and livid-white-striped cord is its only lifeline, and it is holding to that when the thing brushes by its chest, a hair's-breadth from the heart. In a pathetic attempt to make itself smaller, it draws knees up to chin. Its whole body is alert, every cell, every muscle, every nerve straining to escape the thing that attacks it so unrelentingly.

If the danger is here, then out there, she must know, too. Yet she does nothing. No part of her body moves. She lies as still as death itself.

It lifts a tiny foot and kicks feebly against the wall. It is begging now, begging her to wake, begging her to move, begging for its life.

There is to be no mercy, though, for the sharp point jabs once again through the woman's body and comes directly towards its own open mouth.

Chapter Twenty-Nine

Her hands and ankles were held down by leather straps, and a stream of hot light drenched her face. She was in a prison or a police station; a man was torturing her. There was a searing agony in her belly, as though she had been viciously stabbed, except that the pain was coming not from without but from deep within her flesh – hundreds of tiny knives tearing through vessels and tissue to reach her skin.

She moaned and opened her eyes, blinked once, closed them again. Through crusty slits, she caught a glimpse of spiralling curls on the dark head of a man bent over her naked belly. Who was he? A dream-figure? Her torturer?

As though sensing she was awake, the man raised his head and looked towards her face. He had thick, wiry eyebrows, flat brown eyes, a plump, cupid's-bow mouth.

I know him, Cecil thought, but who? Where?

'Just lie quietly. Everything will be all right.' The voice was soothing, kind. 'Go back to sleep like a good girl.'

'The baby's kicking me,' she said, apropos of nothing. 'It's hurting me.'

'Just relax. You'll feel better soon.'

'You're Dr Lopez, aren't you?'

He had turned his attention back to her belly. She could hear him chuckle. 'I was when I left home this morning. At least, my wife seemed to think so.'

A drawn-out scream pierced the quietness of the room; it was followed by the pitiful moaning of a sick animal. Was it possible those dreadful sounds had come from her own throat?

'What is it, Mademoiselle?' The doctor touched her burning forehead with the flatness of one cool palm.

'It's awful, I can't stand it. Please ... give me something.'

He was between her and the bright light now; she could scarcely see his face. 'How did I get here? Why are my arms tied down?'

'Please try to go back to sleep.' Dr Lopez moved slightly, and she saw he was wearing a white laboratory jacket. In one hand, he held a syringe with an extremely long needle. She had seen that before, too, but where?

'What ... what are you doing to me?'

'I've just completed the test I begged you to have back in December.'

'What test? I don't remember.'

'Can you see the screen here? This is an ultrasound image of your womb. I pierced the uterine wall and took a sample of the baby's blood through the vein of the umbilical cord. All this happened while you were asleep. The lab just brought in the results, and it's exactly as I suspected all along. I shall be obliged to practise an emergency transfusion, again through the core. I'm sorry to tell you your baby is showing signs of extreme distress.'

'Is that why I feel so ... so terrible?'

'Certainly that's part of it. You're also very tense. Look, can you see where I'm touching you – your tummy is as hard as a football. You've got to relax.'

'I can't ... I'm so afraid ...'

'Oh, Mademoiselle Gutman!' All his Mediterranean exuberance seemed to be returning in full force. 'If only you had had this test done when I recommended it to you in December! We might have had a chance to save the child. What a shame! What an awful shame!'

'You don't mean ...?'

'I'll do everything in my power, but I can't guarantee the results. The situation is very, very critical.'

'Doctor, I've been through hell for this baby. You can't ... let it die.'

'You'll just have to trust me. Relax your muscles, please. This is not a painful procedure.'

Cecil closed her eyes and then opened them with a start as something jabbed her stomach wall again. As Dr Lopez had predicted, the needle did not really hurt – he must have deadened her skin with something first – but she still did not like the sensation. She looked past him to the ultrasound screen and stifled another cry. There was the fetus, a small, blurred but perfectly recognisable creature.

What was it doing? With one hand clutching a thin, luminous object which Cecil imagined to be the umbilical cord, it pranced! It hopped on one foot and moved sharply to the right; hopped on the other and moved to the left, all the time waving its free hand as

183

though keeping time to its bizarre dance. It was the most extraordinary thing Cecil had ever seen. The baby never seemed to relax, never for an instant let up on its almost ritual dancing. Except, of course, that it wasn't dancing; it was only an optical illusion that made Cecil think it was.

She could even distinguish the fuzzy outline of the baby's head. If it were endowed with X-ray vision, it would be staring at her. How odd! Of course, she knew its eyes were sealed shut, and even if they weren't, it could not possibly be looking out of the screen at her. There was no way it could know she was watching its febrile, almost pathetic ballet on the screen.

All at once, Cecil noticed the needle. It was little more than a sharp point at the edge of the screen, yet seeing it there shocked her. Her eyes were playing tricks on her again: the fetus appeared to coordinate its agitated movements with those of the jabbing needle, almost as though it was trying at all costs to avoid it.

Cecil let her head fall back against the flat pillow. She wanted to follow Dr Lopez's advice and go to sleep. Watching the constantly flickering black and white images of the ultrasound screen had exhausted her. Once she closed her eyes, however, she was again overwhelmed by pain. She could think of nothing else. It had not left her for an instant since she had first felt its stabbing intensity in that stuffy, crowded café.

She had been there with ... oh, God: Serge and Alan. She remembered now; she had left them at the Place Garibaldi without a word of explanation. What had she done next? A taxi – yes, that was it. Somehow, she must have had the presence of mind to tell the driver to bring her to this clinic. At least she had done something right. If anybody could help her now, it was Dr Lopez. He was one of the few people in the world who wanted to see her baby live.

'*God damn you!*'

The words were said in intense, hissing fury. Cecil's astonished eyes flew open. She could just see the doctor's face, convulsed with rage as he bent over her, manipulating the syringe. On the screen, the fetus was still engaged in its unnatural dance, always twisting a fraction of an inch out of reach of the needle.

It must be very tired, Cecil thought with a pang of despair. It can't keep this up much longer, the needle will get it sooner or later. No! this is all in my imagination. All that frenetic activity on the screen is nothing but the result of idle, random movements on baby's part.

At that moment, something extraordinary and quite unexpected happened to Cecil. The baby's fear entered her own bloodstream, came rushing in as though through a suddenly collapsed floodgate. In

184

spite of all the pain, her mind started to function again. Her muscles tensed, ready to act.

Why, she wondered for the first time, was she in this small room — an ordinary doctor's receiving room — instead of on an operating table? And why was Dr Lopez carrying out this possibly dangerous procedure without having obtained her permission? No one had given her anything to sign when she was brought in; she had been in too poor a shape for that. Sign ... What had Edith-Anne Schomberg said? 'I'll turn the cheque over to you when you've signed the release for the doctor.'

Could Dr Lopez possibly be the man to whom Edith-Anne had meant to bring to her on that fateful day?

No, that would be too much of a coincidence, except that the last time she had had this kind of sudden, horrible pain, it had been Dr Lopez who had appeared almost magically at her side.

The doctor's face was still twisted with what seemed a terrible fury, the rage of a man who was engaged in a protracted and brutal struggle that he despaired of winning. He gripped the syringe as thought it were a caulking gun, his blunt fingers completely concealing the whitish fluid Cecil had noted earlier in the charger.

Again her brain moved into overdrive. Wasn't the syringe supposed to be empty? Hadn't the doctor told her he was drawing blood from the umbilical cord? Oh, this was stupid! She had lost consciousness several times. How could she hope to follow such a complicated procedure? Still, she did have a right to know exactly what the doctor was doing. He had said something else, something about a transfusion directly into the cord. But it was not the umbilical cord that he seemed to be searching with the sharp point of his needle but the fetus itself. Almost, she could have sworn in this moment of utter clarity, the fetal heart.

What was in the syringe? What was the whitish liquid that Dr Lopez was so determined to inject into the baby's body, into the tiny, blinking spot on the screen that was surely its heart?

'Help! Oh, God, somebody help me!'

The cry was so loud and strident that Dr Lopez's head jerked up with a start, and he brought his brown eyes, round with surprise, on to her face. 'What's the matter? Are you in pain again?'

'A cramp. It's horrible. Help me, goddamn it, don't just stand there! I can't bear it! Do something!'

Slowly and methodically, the doctor withdrew the needle from her belly and moved so that he and the white-filled syringe were only a few inches from her sweating brow.

'Where is this cramp?' he asked accusingly.

185

'High up on my right arm and shoulder. Take off the strap, just for a minute. Hurry — I'm going to scream again if you don't!'

But Dr Lopez did not move. His cupid's-bow mouth was creeping up at each corner in what might have been a smile except that Cecil could see that it was not. His brown eyes were flat again and totally empty of mirth or any other discernible emotion.

Cecil's heart tripped; she could scarcely breathe, so great was her fear. She was completely helpless. Her arms and legs were strapped to the table; no one in the whole world knew she was here. Her only weapon was to scream, but instinct told her the doctor could efficiently silence her cries with the contents of that long-needled syringe that was only a few inches from her own heart now.

'Please help me, doctor,' Cecil whispered. She made her voice that of a meek, frightened child. 'Please, I promise I'll be quiet afterwards.'

He studied her for another long minute. Then, muttering something under his breath, Dr Lopez began to undo the buckle of the leather strap that held down her right arm.

'I've got to sit up, just for a second,' Cecil said as meekly as before.

Shaking his head unhappily, he freed her other arm. 'Mademoiselle Gutman, you are not being reasonable, not reasonable at all. You are endangering the life of your child by wasting time like this. I am obliged to call my nurse and ask her to bring you a mild sedative.'

'A sedative?' she repeated, her voice faltering uncontrollably. She sat up to rub at the place of her supposed cramp and, swaying to one side, almost fell from the table. Her head was spinning like a runaway carousel.

'Just sit here without moving. I'll be right back.' Still keeping Cecil under observation, Dr Lopez placed the syringe carefully inside a small glass cabinet. Then he walked slowly to the door, cast a last, disapproving glance at her, and went out. Cecil could not be sure if a key had turned in the lock, but her fright convinced her that it had. Gasping with pain, she leaned forward and unbuckled the first of her ankle straps.

She was perched on a high examination table with a sheet drawn tightly across its metallic surface. The room was even smaller than she had suspected; except for the small cabinet, a chair and the ultrasonic equipment, there was no other furniture. This, too, was strange. Cecil knew from her experience in the hospital in Dallas that doctors usually called in a specialised technician to run the ultrasonic scanner. Dr Lopez's presence alone with her in this tiny room seemed more and more sinister.

At last her legs were free. She swung them carefully over the side of

186

the table and down on to the top rung of a metal stepladder. Without warning, she pitched forwards. She flung out two rubbery arms to break her fall, but her head banged painfully against the wall. Stunned and badly frightened, she stayed where she was, swaying giddily.

As her head gradually cleared, Cecil tried to think what to do. First, there was the problem of her clothes. She was wearing a short green hospital smock that hung open in front, revealing her nakedness. She was not going to go far dressed like this even if she could manage to walk. And walk she must, for already she could hear a low rumble of voices outside. Most likely, Dr Lopez on his way back with a nurse and the 'mild sedative'.

In desperation, Cecil looked around the room again and saw that there was a second, glass-panelled door behind her. Still leaning against the wall for support, she inched her way towards it, praying that it was not locked, too. When she reached the door, she took several gulps of air and then tried the handle. To her immense relief, she saw that not only did it open, but it gave on to an empty corridor.

Cecil let go of her lifeline, the wall, stumbled and lurched out into the hall. All at once, she became aware of the fact that she was barefooted. No shoes, no clothes and half-dead with pain. The prognosis for her future was dim indeed.

The short corridor led onto another, longer one, empty as well. The clinic was like a tomb. Where were the other doctors, the nurses, the patients? What day of the week was it? Was today some sort of French holiday? Cecil's brain refused to release any information; it was as though every last bit of her nervous energy had been mobilised to take her down this silent, white-walled hall towards the door gaping open at the end of it. As she moved, other pains sprung up to join those of her belly – in her 'cramped' shoulder, in her neck and in both her legs. Another agonising minute, and she reached the door. Stairs! Stairs leading to the floor below! How could she possibly manage those?

With a sob, Cecil slid down the wall all the way to the floor. Moving slowly, slowly, she took the steps one at a time on her bottom. It was an endless journey, and she cried silently at the hopelessnes of it all. The stairway became darker; finally, she could see nothing and put one bare foot to touch cold, flat tiles. All this darkness could only mean that she was in the basement. Still sliding forwards like an injured animal, she collided with a piece of furniture and used it to pull herself upright. Her groping hand found first a lamp and then a switch.

Light flooded the passage. She was in another white-walled hall, this one quite long and wide. A desk and a few chairs were lined up against one wall. And, miracle of miracles, on top of the small desk was a telephone! Cecil snatched up the receiver as though it might take wing and fly away. Immediately, a tinny female voice queried, 'What number, please?'

'Hotel des Lilas. I — I don't have the number with me.'

'Is that Nice?'

'Yes.'

'Address?'

'It's somewhere in the Old Town.'

'What department is this, anyway?'

'What — what do you mean?'

'Who are you?' asked the voice impatiently. 'I have to know how to charge this call.'

'Look, this is an emergency. I was asked by Dr Lopez to get someone for him urgently at the Hotel des Lilas, and you're wasting time asking how to charge a one-franc call. Just get the number!'

'Hold on,' the girl said huffily.

Cecil almost let the receiver drop, so badly was her hand shaking, yet she had been amazed to hear her voice, cool and collected and giving out orders as though she actually worked here.

A man whispered something in her ear, and she jumped with fright. It took a few seconds for her to register that the several times repeated message was coming from the instrument in her hand.

'Hotel des Lilas here. Speak up. Hotel des Lilas here.'

'Please, I must speak to Pancho Paso Real right away — don't put me on hold. This is a matter of life and death.'

'Well, I'm real sorry to hear that,' the voice said laconically, 'because Monsieur Paso Real is not here right now. You want to speak to somebody else?'

'No, of course not. Where . . . where is he?' For the first time, her voice faltered. She was still alone in this eerily quiet basement, but not for long. This would be her only chance to find help.

'You just missed him, lady. I think he went across the street for coffee. You want him to call you back?'

'No, listen, this is his friend Cecil, his *American* friend, do you understand? I'm ill. I need him to pick me up as fast as he can get here. Please, can't you go over and get him for me?'

'I can't leave the front desk, lady. There's nobody else in this place.'

Cecil heard the muffled sounds of excited voices above her and then running footsteps. They had discovered she was missing and were starting to search the clinic. She had only a minute or two to convince this man to help her.

'Please listen carefully. I'm in terrible pain. I . . . I may die. Do you hear me?'

'Tell Pancho to come for me right away at the . . . Oh, God, I don't remember the name of this place. Look, write this down. I'm in a clinic somewhere in Cimiez. The doctor's name is Lopez. I think he's the director. Pancho will know; it's the same doctor who met us at the airport.'

'Lady, if you're so sick, why don't you just stay there in the clinic? Seems like the best place for you to be.'

'Damn it, listen to what I'm saying! I have to get out of here − this is an emergency, my life is in danger! If you get my message to Monsieur Paso Real in the next five minutes, I'll make it well worth your while when I arrive at the hotel.'

For the first time, the man reacted. She had found the magic words that took precedence over matters of life and death and every conceivable emergency in between.

'OK, I'll do it for you, little lady. I just hope I don't get fired.'

'Tell him I'll meet him in the street outside. He shouldn't bother parking, I'll be ready to get into the car when it pulls up in, say, fifteen minutes.'

'I'll do my best, lady.'

'You don't have any choice, do you? I have to be alive to pay you.'

Feeling she had played her highest card, Cecil let the receiver drop. Now she had only one thing left to do: find a hiding place with an escape route leading out of it.

She pushed open the first door she came to and then shut it again fast; out of the darkness had come a cacophony of scuffling, scratching and squeaking noises. The stench had been enough to tell her it was the hospital laboratory. The second room she tried had nothing in it but deep rows of blue lockers, not one of them wide enough for her to squeeze into.

Suddenly, voices came from above.

'Katia says she never went near the front door. Jojo's covering the back, so that means she's gotta be in there somewhere.'

'The women is deathly ill and about to miscarry.' This was Dr Lopez, and it sounded as though he was just at the top of the steps. His voice was dripping with concern. 'She may be having hallucinations from the pain.'

'You saying she's psycho or something?' This was rougher, much less educated. Certainly not a doctor.

'No, it's only a temporary condition, but you should proceed carefully. When you do find her, pay no attention to anything she says or does − just bring her back to the operating room. Use force

189

if necessary. I'll take full responsibility for whatever may happen. We'll put her under anaesthesia, and she won't remember a thing tomorrow.'

Tomorrow or any other day, Cecil thought bitterly.

Footsteps descended the stairs; there were at least two of them. Thankful that she was barefooted, Cecil started to run. She fled past the closed doors like Bluebeard's wife, at once longing for dreading the one that would seal her fate. As the sound of steps intensified, Cecil opened one of the doors and slipped inside.

Again, she was in absolute darkness. Groping like a blind person, she moved around tables, desks, cabinets, stools, chairs; she had never realised a room could hold so much furniture. At last, her outstretched hands found a door with a protruding knob. Hoping it was a closet that would offer a hiding place, she tried the handle. It opened easily.

The space she entered was not a closet but a large, high-ceilinged and very cold room. Faint light filtered in through two basement-type windows up near the ceiling. In the sudden chill, Cecil was again conscious of her nakedness; she pulled ineffectually at the flaps of her flimsy hospital smock as her bare feet touched down on icy ceramic tiles. Could she have entered a refrigerated storage area? No, not with this smell, an unpleasant medicinal odour that, even as she tried to pinpoint it, only served to increase her anguish.

Now that her eyes had become accustomed to the dimness, she could see that there were more of the high glass cabinets here, plus several tables in the middle of the room, all but one of them bare and gleaming metallically in the half-light. On the last one lay a lump of laundry covered by a long white sheet. Cecil hoped there might be something in the pile she could use to cover herself; at the very least, she could take the sheet itself.

In a great hurry to get out of the eerie room, Cecil snatched the sheet from the table and drew back in an involuntary movement of repulsion and terror. On the table lay a soapstone statue piteously emaciated and of a colour somewhere between fallow and bird's-egg blue; it had once been a very young and pretty woman.

Cecil wrapped the sheet around her own half-frozen body. The odour it gave off was the same sickening one she had noticed when she entered the room. The stench of death. It would be in her hair and on her skin and in her soul for weeks.

Provided she lived that long.

Cecil gave a shove to one of the tables, sending it sliding crazily across the floor. It came to a jerking halt against the wall under one of the high windows. It was about the right height to climb up on; now all she had to do was get the window open, and she would be on her way to freedom.

She unlatched the pane and swung it inwards. There seemed space enough for her to squeeze through. She pulled herself up and, lying across the frame with her feet still dangling, began to work her way through.

At that moment, the most horrible thing that could happen, did. The door opened; the lights came on. Two men entered the room. One was a big, red-faced man with a spider's web of broken veins on his bulbous nose. He wore rubber-soled shoes and the hospital whites of an orderly, and the expression on his big, lumpy face was one of disgust. His companion was a small, wiry Arab.

'Who the hell uncovered the stiff?' The red-faced man turned to stare accusingly at the little jeans-clad Arab.'You been in here tonight, Mohammed?'

'Me?' came the high-pitched, heavily accented answer. 'You know I don't touch the *macchabees*. They bring bad luck.'

'Somebody's been messing around with the little lady, that's for sure. I brought her down myself half an hour ago and covered her up real nice, like she's supposed to be when the undertakers come. Some pervert's sneaked down here since to feel her up. Not only that, he had the nerve to go off and leave her bare-assed.'

'That's crazy! Who would do such a thing?'

'You'd be surprised what goes on around this place,' the big man said enigmatically. 'Anyway, one thing for sure is that the crazy dame that ran out on the boss isn't in here. She'd really have to be off her rocker to want to hole up in a room with a slab of cold meat.'

He turned and went back into the front room. Cecil was sure then that the Arab would notice her, but the little man began to study his own soot-stained fingers from every possible angle as though to force his regard away from the naked body on the table.

'You oughtta wash your hands before you come in here,' the red-faced man said as he returned, a sheet in one hand and a Coke in the other. He threw the sheet carelessly across the corpse, then raised the bottle to his heavy lips and drained the liquid.

'What for?' whined the little Arab. 'I told you I never touch anything in this place.'

'Mohammed, I know you better than you know yourself. Come on, I'm locking up here. To keep you out of temptation.'

He turned off the light, and the two of them went out, slamming the door behind them. Lying on her perch in the half-open window, Cecil was as silent as the sheeted corpse beneath. Pain and cold conspired to leave her unconscious. She moaned now, stirred slightly, murmured a man's name too low to be distinguished. Finally, she regained her senses enough to move. Slowly she began to extract herself from the narrow space between the open pane and the window frame. Inch by inch she squeezed through until, all at once, she was rolling down towards the little garden below.

She lay where she had fallen, half-delirious. She seemed to be on a narrow strip of grass separated from the street by a low hedge. She could hear voices all around her and, from time to time, a mysterious growling sound. She was out of the building, but certainly not out of the woods. Even if a car came down this residential street, who would stop to pick up a wild-looking creature wearing a torn and stained sheet with the rank smell of death upon it?

Whatever she was going to do, Cecil decided wearily, it had to be now. She rose slowly to her feet, saw an opening in the hedge and, gathering her courage, darted through. She had scarcely reached the pavement when a heavy hand clamped down on her shoulder.

'Miss Gutman, you've given us quite a run for our money tonight. I'm sure you'll agree that it's high time you came back.'

Cecil turned to face Dr Lopez. This time, his cupid's bow mouth was engaged in a frank and happy smile; she thought she had never seen anything quite so terrifying as those sinisterly rising pink curves. Two other men were with the doctor, one of them unsuccessfully trying to control a snarling German shepherd on a short leash. At the sight of the dog's foaming gums, Cecil let herself go limp. She was caught by the bigger of the two men just before she slumped to the pavement.

At least they'll have to carry me back into that clinic, Cecil told herself. *And if this is the last act of free will of my entire life, then I'm going to make it as hard as I can for those bastards.*

'Good evening, Dr Lopez. How nice to see you again. I've come to pick up my friend Cecil.'

Cecil's eyes flew open at the familiar voice. Pancho was standing on the pavement directly in front of their little group, smiling and nodding politely to each man in turn as though they were all old and good friends. When he finished, he turned to Cecil. He wore the expression of a riotous satyr who has just come upon a sleeping wood nymph.

'*Querida!* The car is just down the street, and Jean-Luc is inside waiting for us. Are you ready to go?'

With her last ounce of courage, Cecil pulled herself out of the attendant's now hesitating grip and stood up straight.

'Yes, Dr Lopez discharged me, and we were all out here waiting for you. I presume Jean-Luc brought the gun?'

Pancho grinned frightfully. 'You know what a violent and uncontrollable man Jean-Luc is. I told him to leave that pistol at home, but he would not listen to me. He has it with him now in the car.'

'Mademoiselle Gutman?' called out the doctor in a voice of barely controlled rage. 'Do you have any idea what you are doing?'

'Yes, Dr Lopez, it's amazing how clear a view I have of this entire situation.'

'Well, from where I stand, it looks very much as though you are — what is your English expression? — going from the frying pan right into the fire.'

'I don't want to hear any more,' Cecil cut him short.

Holding on to Pancho's arm for support and with the foul-smelling sheet pulled tightly to her breast, she began the long walk down the pavement towards the car. It was parked under the shadow of a large pine, and whatever occupants it might have had could not could be seen from Dr Lopez's point of view.

'We are almost there, *querida*,' Pancho whispered encouragingly. 'You did very well. Do not look back, whatever you do; keep going straight ahead.'

At each step, Cecil expected the men and the snarling dog to rush them, but nothing happened. The night was suddenly very still. Not a leaf stirred in the frosty air; there was no one anywhere on the streets — no cars, no people, nothing. All of a sudden, Dr Lopez's voice rang out again, and Cecil threw herself into Pancho's arms in terrified surprise. The doctor, however, had not left his place by the low hedge. He had regained his composure, and his tone was one of scornful disdain.

'Since you care so little for the health of your child, I am washing my hands of you, Mademoiselle. Don't bother to come back here. Do you hear me, Mademoiselle Gutman, no matter what horror, what catastrophe befalls you next, you will not be welcome at my clinic!'

'Don't concern yourself over me, Dr Lopez. Even if a ten-ton truck ran over me at your front door, I wouldn't come in here again.'

Then, with all the dignity she could muster, still barefooted and shivering uncontrollably, Cecil climbed into the dark car.

It was only later, when the old Renault was hurtling down the Cimiez hill toward the *autoroute*, with Pancho bent over the wheel, his face twisted into a hard, totally unreadable expression, that Cecil started to hear, really hear the doctor's words. 'From the frying pan into the fire', 'no matter what catastrophe, what horror befalls you next ...'

What horror, oh God, what horror was that quack talking about? What did he know? And just where was Pancho taking her? What was about to happen to her now?

Most important of all, did she have the strength to keep fighting like this all the way to June and the baby's birth?

Chapter Thirty

He had not had a first name for well over a half-century.

'There goes old Mezange,' people muttered under their breath when he passed. It was not a friendly remark. The villagers never spoke to the aged giant unless it was absolutely necessary. There was something in his watery eyes, half hidden by lids that, with the force of time, had turned downwards at the corners like those of a Tartar warrior, that was repellent and defiant and seemed to say, 'Keep away. Touch me only once, and you will be changed into a creature just like me.'

The people kept away.

Mostly, though, and despite that curious, unformulated dread that he always inspired, the villagers reacted to Mezange in an olfactory way. The old man smelled exactly the way people expect a hog to smell. Whenever he climbed into the bus in Grasse, the other passengers moved as far back as they could, but it was never far enough. All the way down the highway to the shadow-filled bridge that crossed the Siagne River, his presence on the bus made the ride a trial, not least for the driver. It was well known that Mezange never paid his fare, and the villagers thought this was because the mayor, a prudent little communist who had somehow made a fortune as a postmaster, instructed the driver to avoid dangerous altercations with the old man at any cost. Mezange was crazy and unpredictable. If provoked, he might turn on the driver and try to strangle him. ('Strangle – you've heard, haven't you, Hector, about the girl . . .?')

The one thing everyone knew for sure was that for fifty-eight years now, Mezange had been living as a semi-hermit in a gloomy structure on the banks of the Siagne. Some people thought his house interesting (mostly tourists who passed it on their way to more cheerful places like Cannes or Grasse or Nice), but the villagers considered it to be a blight on the countryside, an architectural monstrosity that should

195

have been torn down years ago. A three-storey stone *bastille* of eighteenth-century origin, it had a rear section that was almost ordinary, wth walls, floors, windows and doors. The front half, however, had been gutted so that only three of its four walls were still standing under a badly damaged roof of blackened tiles. From the highway, rising out of the deep shrubs and high grasses that surrounded it, it resembled nothing so much as a monstrous doll's house with one wall left unmounted for the furniture and inhabitants to be moved around at will. Much of the flooring in this open part had rotted away, and only the beautifully arched frames of the doors and windows had resisted a half-century of wind, rain and vandalism. Still, when the sun managed to force a path through the gaping windows, the old wreck took on a mantle of melancholy beauty. On the main floor, in what once might have been a ballroom, grasses growing through the broken stone flooring swayed in the breezes that flowed down the river or rustled and whipped in the harsh mistral.

Each time old Mezange left his crumbling house and walked to the village, 'it' started again. The whispering. Endless, tireless, malignant, hateful.

'Wealthy Normans they were. His father bought the house and twenty hectares of the best woodland just before the Great War. They were wealthy folk, but Madame had no health, and the doctor said the sun down south might help her. The boy and his sister were good-looking back then, smart as whips, too. I remember there was no stoppin' that little miss when she wanted something. One day, she made my old dad put her brother up on his mule. She had a hankerin' to see him on the ground, throwed by that mule, and she got her wish. 'Twas a sight for sore eyes, him in his sailor suit rollin' in the mud, and her with hair like honey run out of a jar, laughin' her head off at him. Hush, don't talk so loud or he'll hear us!'

This incident, recounted by gaunt little Etienne Barelli, had been heard a hundred times by the men and women sitting by the trickling waters of the fountain under the spreading branches of the lime tree. None the less, the telling never failed to elicit the exact same question from Germain Baricolla.

'Wearing a sailor suit, was he? Good-looking, was he? Then will you tell me, for the love of the saints, how he got to stink worse than any pile of manure I ever sunk my old boots into?'

Even as they guffawed at this all too familiar sally, the villagers could not quite repress the image of the graceful child in the tailored suit walking arm in arm with his honey-haired sister. How was it possible that a rich, pampered boy with his life spread out before him like a fertile field had turned into a hermit so accursed that their own

196

grandchildren taunted him with insults and even rocks provided they were well out of reach of his strong giant's hands and knotted staff?

At this moment, the villagers always drew their chairs together and dropped their voices lower still. 'Grew into a dandy, he did, the apple of his mother's eye. Them of good Norman stock, and she sent him to Paris to study at the Beaux-Arts with all them painters and such. Already, he was callin' himself a photographer. Come down here every summer to snap those accursed pictures. The minute some young gal went to a stream with her washin', or a courtin' couple headed for the woods, why, out would pop that Mezange. Couldn't seem to stop himself, had to take a picture of everything that moved and then some. Only, it wasn't normal, the way he was always *hidin'*, always *lookin'*.'

'And when did the trouble come?'

' 'Bout '26 or '27, I reckon. Sure broke up that family. The girl it happened to wasn't more than fifteen, an *innocent* girl. Daisies bloomin' in the fields, they say, when she was cryin' and pleadin' with him for mercy. Afterwards, the boy tried to put the blame anywhere he could . . . even accused his best friend, and, of course, *she* couldn't testify 'cause by then, the girl had just plain lost her mind.'

With time, the details of this tale grew so sordid that only the men dared talk of them as they played *boule* under the plane trees in the dusty square. When a newcomer attempted to separate fact from fabrication, he would hear only how the Mezange family had hired professors and medical experts to testify that their son was incurably insane. How he had been acquitted of the heinous crime but subsequently placed under the guardianship of the courts for the rest of his days; how, before he reached the age of maturity – he was only twenty that fatefeul summer – he had been declared an eternal child. Like Charles Baudelaire before him, he could neither sign a cheque nor obtain a passport nor vote. So monstrous was Mezange *fils* thought to be that he was unable even to marry or legally recognise any child he might beget.

The dishonoured Mezange parents took leave of their vale of suffering so speedily that they failed to realise the full consequences of their actions. Under French law, their vast estate could not be settled while their son and heir remained stripped of his civil rights. For the next forty years, during which her hair turned from honey to ash, Mezange's sister Rose tried to help her brother out of his predicament and, at the same time, obtain her share of the family wealth. A succession of *notaires* with the vitality of chloroformed snails blocked her efforts so successfully that for over half a century the estate stayed safely within their own tight-fisted grasp.

All the while, Mezange grew older and smelled worse. Relegated to the family *bastille* in the south, forbidden to return to Normandy, he spent his half-century — whatever the weather, whatever his mood — roaming the woods and fields bordering the Siagne. He slept on a pile of rags in the corner of the kitchen of his wreck of a home; he never changed his clothes and was rumoured to tear open with his own teeth the wild animals he caught in the many traps on his land. He scared young girls by spying on them from behind trees and boulders and rotted sheds. He had no friend and wanted none.

Old Mezange's health was perfect except for one thing: with the passing of the years, he had finally grown quite as mad as the doctors had made him out to be nearly sixty years before.

The yellow moon began an insidious, sliding movement but, spotting her, stopped to stare.

No, the face just beyond the bars of her window was someone she knew. It was Dr Lopez until he removed a chalky mask to reveal the leering countenance of Bayard Schomberg. But that, too, was a mask, for Bayard was really a hideously wrinkled Edith-Anne with eels sprouting from her skull and glowing yellow light behind her empty sockets. And then Edith-Anne changed in turn; she was . . always had been . . . Oh, if only she could see that face, see it clearly, she would *know*.

Cecil wanted them all to go away, but when she opened her parched and feverish lips to tell them, it was only the moon again, its face scrunched up with a huge magnifying lens caught in the circle of one yellow eye.

The better to see her with.

'Pancho?'

'Right here.' His voice was so close that she shivered in surprise.

'Where are you? Why can't I see you?'

'Here, let me take your hand. Now do you believe I'm here?'

'But is it really you?'

'*Querida*, who else could it be? Wait, I'll turn on the light.'

'No, don't do that. Just tell me — '

'What?'

'A few minutes ago, when I first woke up — '

'Yes?'

'I felt your breath on my face, yours or somebody else's, somebody who was leaning over me.' The words came fast; she could not stop them; the room was so black, so black. 'I was scared, and I wanted to scream, but I couldn't because I was paralysed. I thought whoever it was wanted to kill me.'

'You are still weak, *pimpollito*. You have been very, very sick.'

'But is there somebody living in this house, a very old, evil-looking Santa Claus? With a long white beard?'

'There is no one at all like that here. Rest now. We will speak of it tomorrow. It is easier to describe a nightmare when there is daylight all around.'

'Are you sure?' she asked in the voice of a child begging for reassurance.

'I am sure,' he replied, as though, indisputably, he were.

How many nights had she lain awake like this, listening to the steady creaking and pounding of a shutter blowing on its hinges? Only there were no shutters on this house, and the night was as still as a sepulchre. The baby was awake as well, moving restlessly as though it, too, could not bear the sound of the ghostly wind.

Both of them were afraid of something close by, watching, a beast skulking in shadow and awaiting its hour.

Changelings and foundlings and mingled, confused identities. That's what it's all about. The baby and I are only part of a myth, an old legend. If only my mind would function correctly − if I weren't ill, then I could think, and I would understand it all. I'd know exactly what to do. If only, if only ...

'Who are you?' she asked drowsily.

'Oraga.'

'But who let you in?'

'*Cretchuno!*' the old woman cackled as she stirred the fire and added another log. She was like a hag in a fairy tale, tiny with shiny red gums that housed a few yellowed and broken teeth. 'I sitting here three days and three nights already.'

She sank back into a low chair at the side of Cecil's bed, almost disappearing from view. The sight was so comical that Cecil burst out laughing, then asked, 'You're here to keep me company?'

'Sure thing. Paco got to play in Nice at night, and he say you can no stay here alone, so I come keep out the wind.'

Cecil propped up several fat pillows against the brass headboard and tried to sit up. In spite of the fire it was still chilly in the room, and she slid back down a little, pulling the many covers up to her chin. 'You're keeping out draughts, is that what you're trying to say?'

'I do that, too, and build good, crackling fire! But see out there?' With surprising agility, the hag leapt out of her chair and almost waltzed to the window. She was pointing excitedly at something in the little hedged garden.

Cecil followed her gaze beyond the ornate grillwork. Enormous black-and-white wings were flapping crazily against the backdrop of a lavender sky. Cecil sat up straighter and gasped as she saw the snow. It was everywhere, on the branches of the apple tree where the big birds perched, on the slanting roof of the wooden pergola, on the top of the old stone wall at the end of the garden. Beyond that was a thick dark forest where great streams of snow fell from treetops like scoops of melting custard. How long, Cecil wondered, had she lain here without knowing it was snowing? Without knowing anything at all?

'*Phurdini* all around,' Oraga was muttering to herself in ominous tones. '*Phurdini* blowing wind into Paco's house.' She trotted back from the window to look sternly at Cecil. '*Phurdini* with long noses, kill the birds and rats.'

'Badgers?' Cecil ventured cautiously. 'Are you talking about badgers or minks, maybe? No? Foxes? Weasels?'

Oraga's shrivelled head suddenly began to bob in excitement. 'That's it, weasels. When they scared, weasels – *phurdini* – they blow and bring bad luck to Paco's house, bad luck to baby.'

One thing for sure, I didn't see any weasels out of that window, not even in my dreams. 'Oraga, I don't know what the connection is between your *phurdini* and my baby, but if it's something scary, do me a favour and don't tell me, OK? I've been frightened enough lately to last a lifetime.'

The old woman attempted a reassuring smile, and the effort brought a thousand wrinkles into her ancient face. Wisps of hair the colour of the garden snow stuck from her soiled, prune-coloured kerchief, and she wore enough layers of clothing of varying patterns and lengths to make her an authentic latter-day hippie.

'I go make tea now. You feel better.'

She did! Suddenly, she was full of surging energy; she wanted to get up and dance from the sheer joy of feeling well again. And above all, she wanted to be alone!

'No, please don't bother about the tea. I'm sure you'd rather go back to your own house for a while.'

'I stay here with you, just like Paco say. You don't go nowhere, do nothing without me.'

'You mean Pancho, don't you?' Cecil asked, suddenly noticing the discrepancy in names.

'Pancho, Paco, all the same to me. You rest in bed. I cook dinner. Paco say you got to start eating good for baby. You too skinny. I make *romen morga*, very tasty, fatten you up.'

'Wait! You've got to tell me how long I've been here, when Paco is coming home, where this house is.'

'Paco tell you all that. I cook. Very hot stew, lots of spice.'

In her new, good health, Cecil was ravenous, but she was also suspicious of Oraga's dish. 'What's in it exactly?' she asked prudently.

The cackle again.

'Gypsy cat stew. I go now, make specially for you.'

Chapter Thirty-One

It was the middle of the night when she heard the key turn in the lock. The carpet of snow had long since melted in the garden; spring was everywhere about them; yet in the little house it was still cold, a deep, bone-chilling cold born in loneliness and worry and suspicion.

He tiptoed into the room, stopping in front of the window at the foot of her bed. Silhouetted against the red moon, he looked like an incubus, a devil.

'Pancho, am I a prisoner in this house?' The question, which she had meant to sound indignant, came out like the query of a frightened child.

'Oh, how awake you are tonight! And how very pretty!'

'Don't tease me. I'm asking you a serious question.'

'But I'm not teasing. Spread out like that across the bed, your hair is a great burst of fireworks. Are you trying to seduce me with your tousled hair?'

Pancho's suggestive words evoked confused, contradictory feelings in Cecil; to cover her emotions, she feigned even more anger than she felt.

'Pancho, I won't be put off like this. I've been awake for hours, waiting for you to come home.'

'Have you really? I am flattered.' Almost magically, he was at the side of the bed now. He put out one burning hand and touched her bare shoulder. 'But you are shivering. Wait, I'll make a fire for us.'

The little room, which only an instant before had seemed cold and frightening to Cecil, was suddenly a thrilling, wonderful place where she wished to stay always. Pancho's low, musical voice and the electric touch of his fingers on her naked flesh had mesmerised her. In a minute more, he would begin to tell her some fantastic tale, or else change himself into another person altogether, and she would forget

202

the questions that obsessed her. And wasn't that exactly what he intended? With a great effort of will, Cecil threw off all the romantic surges of emotion and physical longings that had overwhelmed her in the last few minutes.

'No, stay here, Pancho. I want to talk to you now. I'm very upset. This afternoon, I tried to go for a walk, and Oraga stopped me.'

'Poor sweet Cecil! Attacked by Oraga!'

She smiled in spite of herself. 'I don't mean physically, you idiot! Oraga couldn't do that. But in her quaint way, she told me it was forbidden for me to leave the house without your permission. She was quite emphatic about it. She said that if I disobeyed these so-called orders, you might disappear right out of my life. Suppose you explain to me what is going on?'

Pancho's mouth widened into a wicked grin. He seemed uncommonly pleased with himself, and, as the moon's red light struck his teeth, Cecil thought they resembled nothing so much as a shining display of weapons.

'*Golondrina*, I have gone to much trouble to find this safe place for you. You will have to force yourself to stay here until the end of May. Afterwards, you will be free to go where you want, do what you like.'

'For God's sake, I ought to be able to walk in the woods or go to the village for a cup of coffee without you turning it into a major incident! Nobody in this out-of-the-way place has heard of me, or the Schombergs, for that matter!'

'*No!*'

The word came at her with such savagery that Cecil pulled away from his hand in terrified surprise.

'It is stupid of you say such things! Stupid to think you can travel *anywhere* unnoticed. Tomorrow I'll bring a television set so you can see for yourself what kind of publicity you're receiving. People are looking for you all over France and Italy, all over Europe — police, journalists, lawyers, crazies, all of them vying to get their hands on you for their own purposes.'

'Why — why didn't you tell me this before?'

'Because you were sick, and I didn't want to worry you. *Querida*, you are not a usual-looking person. If you went into the village, you would be recognised in an instant. You will have to stay here, just as I told you, until the baby comes.'

'Well, I can't and I won't!' Cecil's voice had taken on the inflections of a cross child. 'I'm going out of my mind watching Oraga putter around the kitchen with her herbs and foul-smelling brews. Today she was putting chicken blood on the ground around the stone wall, presumably to keep the *phurdini* out and me in. Only, she

203

wasted her time, because tomorrow morning, I'm going lickety-split out that gate before you two are even up.'

'Is it because of your boyfriend that you want to go to the village? Is hearing his voice so important to you that you'll risk your life and that of the baby?'

'Are you by any chance referring to Serge Vlady?' Cecil asked coldly.

'Ah yes, the heartless but still so desirable Serge.'

'You'll do well to leave him out of this conversation.'

'If you didn't want me to speak of *le beau* Serge, them you should never have told me the tale of your pitiful abandonment.'

'That was a mistake of monumental proportions, as I can see now. You were not worthy of my trust. In any case, my relationship with Serge, past and present, is absolutely none of your business.'

'Then we will talk of something that *is* my business! If you disobey my wishes again and try to leave this house, what Oraga says will be true. I will abandon you. I'll leave you here to give birth to your baby alone — without a doctor or anyone else to help you.'

Pancho's cruel words awoke a primordial fear of which Cecil had not been aware until this instant. She had a sudden, clear vision of herself lying on humid ground in the middle of a forest. The wind howled; birds screeched; and all the while, a baby forced a passage for itself through her pain-racked body. Even as the fear twisted at ther heart, Cecil's pride made her lash back at Pancho.

'You'd better get something into your head, too. I don't tolerate dictators. If this is the kind of relationship you want to establish between us — Roman soldier and cowering slave — then you and I won't know each other for long!'

'How lovely you are, all flushed with anger. *Querida*, I am only trying to protect you — don't take it so seriously.' She could see it happening right before her eyes; Pancho was slipping back into his persona of supplicating charmer. 'Look at your belly, it is rounded like the moon.'

Pancho started to hum something that Cecil had never heard before, and then he was singing — soft, blurred sounds like the chant of monks. '*Andro, anro him olkes. Te e pera hin obles. Andro, anro him olkes.*'

He stopped suddenly and said, 'From now on, you and I will think only of the baby. I will start now by playing the piece I wrote for her.'

'For *her*?'

'Of course, your baby is a girl.'

'And on what do you base this amazing deduction?'

'On the fact that she and I are already good friends. She loves my music. She knows that I am a genius.'

Cecil shook her head in exasperation. Her arguments with Pancho never led her anywhere. Supremely self-confident, carried away by his own tall tales, he always succeeded in his own goal, which was to tell her not one single thing that she needed to know.

Pancho had already taken his bandoneon from its black 'casket', and now he opened it out in a magnificent Argentine ripple. In his sinewy hands, the instrument moved like a wild animal, shrinking from cover and then, as the bellows pulled apart, puffing up in an aggressive show of bravura. It sang like a feline, alternating purring contentment with fits of howling fury. When Pancho dramatically lifted the instrument over his head, the whole room was filled with is sensual, primitive rhythms.

Cecil lay back and let the music lead her on the journey Pancho was creating. He was so handsome at the moment, so dark and wild-looking in the red light of the moon. What if he really loved her, mightn't she be able to break the spell that Serge had cast over her for nearly two years? She might wake from that terrible love affair as though from a bad dream. Pancho had said he loved her, at the club in Nice, but he had been joking. She had never for a moment taken his words seriously. Only ... what if it were true? Could *she* love a man about whom she knew nothing, a man who, no matter how physically attractive, at times literally scared her out of her wits?

For the second time that night, Cecil force herself to put aside her foolishly romantic thoughts. She was notoriously bad at choosing men: Serge, Sam and now Pancho. Was there any difference between them?

'What's it called, the piece you wrote for the baby?' she called out to Pancho over the music.

'La Mariposa!' he shouted back.

La Mariposa – his mother, the beautiful flamenco dancer from Montevideo. Without knowing why, Cecil grew angry again.

'You found this house for the baby, didn't you, Pancho? It's the baby you love, not me?'

The music stopped in mid-chord, and the silence that ensued was nerve-shattering. Pancho stood with his now dead bandoneon pulled open across his knee. He seemed stunned, like a person struck by a dart of virulent poison. When his voice came, though, it was as it had been before, calm and soothing.

'Listen to the music, *querida*, you do not know what you are saying. Don't be jealous of a tiny, unborn child. I promise you, I play this song for all of us. You and me ... and your baby.'

*

She can just hear their voices above the whistling of the woman's breath and the constant thump-thumps of her heart. The woman's voice resounds all around her. The man's is like the far-off roar of water.

He laughs suddenly, a booming sound that makes her jump in pained surprise. Searching for a palliative to her alarm, she moves her thumb to her mouth and starts to suck. The woman's voice goes on rising and falling before it finally trails off into silence.

And then it starts!

She jumps again, but this time in joy. It is the thing she likes most in the world, better than the beating of the woman's heart or the echo of her voice, better than her own kicking or turning somersaults or the sucking of her round, oh so sweet thumb.

It is a wonderful, delirious, reeling sound, full of all the other sounds she has heard, the cadence of a heart, the whistling of breath, the gurgling of a stomach, the pounding of feet, the barking, twanging, banging, wailing, sighing, humming, rippling, splashing, swishing, smacking, sobbing, chattering and clattering taps and slaps, plumps and plunks, clashes and crashes, all the resonance and rhythm and stops she knows or has ever dreamt of are present in what she hears now.

It is *Music*!

Chapter Thirty-Two

For one whole week, she was a news junkie. She switched channels restlessly from before dawn to the sign-off reports at midnight. There were three French channels she could pick up here, plus Monte Carlo, and she watched them all. At first, what she saw was funny, then horrifying, and finally she was torn between bursting into tears and committing murder.

Any way she looked at it, her reputation had been torn to shreds.

She saw Xavier Schomberg's thin, aristocratic face for the first time in an interview on the Second Channel. Somehow she had imagined Edith-Anne's husband as a rougher type, big-boned and forceful. With his pale skin and sparse, clipped moustache, the head of Schomberg Mondial seemed almost bloodless in his refinement. His reedy Haute-Ecole voice never once rose in emotion, yet he left the viewer with the distinct impression that Cecil Gutman was a cheap, unscrupulous adventuress. She had disappeared for no other reason than to bring pressure against the family. She was planning to ask for an enormous settlement for herself. Even the figure she hoped to obtain was discreetly mentioned, as was the name of the famous California lawyer whose services she had retained.

The 'cultural' station, Channel Three, waxed long on the legal aspects of the case. Under French law, Cecil's absconding with the unborn heir might be classified as kidnapping, albeit an unusual one. An elderly magistrate with the broken facial veins of a man devoted to fine wines raised the question of whether a person could be accused of kidnapping an infant *before* its birth. Several law professors gave their opinions, pro and con.

In a separate interview, the Garde de Sceaux announced he was planning to introduce a new law to fit Cecil's crime. He hinted at harsh punishment in store for anyone who tried it in the future.

The motive for kidnapping an unborn child was only too obvious: blackmail!

On Tuesday, a symposium of journalists discussed the affair. This time Cecil had a few champions. Two women journalists from *Libération* believed she had disappeared because she could not bear to give up the child. A leftist from the *Nouvel Observateur* thought she was making a statement against the crass capitalism of the Schomberg empire.

A leading French *cinéma-verité* director planned to film her story as soon as Cecil resurfaced. A best-selling author was already at work on the book.

On Wednesday's evening news, Mica's round face appeared on the screen. As the camera drew back, she was seen to be standing on her own front porch. 'I got nothing to say,' she commented solemnly, and when the CBS reporter grew aggressive in his questioning, Mica shouted something which was bleated off the sound track. A studio newscaster explained that because of the enormous attention she had received as Cecil's friend, Mica was being investigated by the US Immigration Service. She faced an immediate deportation hearing. However, no one had yet discovered to what country Mica should be returned, and this had become something of a joke across the United States. Mica had even made it into Doonesbury.

Cecil smiled sadly; Mica had been only too right never to reveal her birthplace.

Thursday, an enterprising French journalist interviewed Cecil's former landlady on the sagging swing of her front porch in north Dallas. She was a tiny, birdlike woman with corkscrew curls and a Southern voice that dripped consternation.

'I feel so bad for that poor girl,' she said, shaking the little curls. 'Cecil was real peaked when she was livin' here in my house, 'fore those French people hired her to have their little baby. She should never have let them talk her into doin' such a thing — it's agin nature, but that's not her fault. It's those French people who caused all the trouble.'

The woman appeared not to have the slightest idea who was inter-viewing her.

'Do you dink Ce-cile is still a-live?' asked the French reporter.

As though on cue, tears appeared in the woman's blue eyes. 'Well, I declare, I can't hardly answer that. Heart-sick like she was ...' Her voice trailed off to a barely audible but none the less dramatic whisper. 'Do you mean ... she might have ... done away with herself?'

Cecil shuddered. Another week, and the photo of her corpse would figure prominently in the evening news.

Friday brought Bayard's plump, self-satisfied face into Cecil's tiny living room. He started out trying to appear kind but quickly veered to vicious. Cecil was mentally ill; she needed help. She was a poor creature, not worthy of the attention the media were showering on her. Above all, she was a thief; not only had she stolen the Schomberg fetus, but a valuable family ring of rubies and emeralds was also missing. Rita had lent the ring to Christine Schomberg, but it had not been found at the crash site, nor in the Saint-Germain apartment. The only explanation, according to Bayard, was that Cecil had stolen it from Rita's house in Saint-Cloud; she had since pawned or sold it and was living off the proceeds.

At this point, Bayard lost control of himself. He wanted the ring back. It had been his mother's; it was his now! Taking the child was nothing compared to the larcenous act of ...

A miracle of modern technology – the remote-control button – removed Bayard from both the screen and Cecil's outraged attention.

On the weekend, all three French channels carried a special interview with Serge. Cecil sat transfixed as he delivered his opening, impassioned speech.

'A wonderful girl, forthright, honest, incapable of any kind of intrigue or disloyal act. This talk of her being involved in a ransom plot or co-operating with the Mafia is just so much *merde*. If anybody has been kidnapped, it's Cecil herself.'

'Mr Vlady, you were one of the last persons to see Cecil (alive).' Has the reporter said the word, or was it only Cecil's vivid imagination? 'Will you describe the circumstances for us?'

'Yes. We were having drinks together in a café on the Place Garibaldi. A man – a casual acquaintance of Cecil's – joined us. Cecil was extremely nervous and not feeling well. She went outside for a breath of fresh air. She was picked up by a taxi and driven to a clinic in Cimiez from which she disappeared before any of the doctors there could examine her. A woman who is ill and in extreme pain does not leave a hospital of her own volition. Either she was taken away by force or else she is in hiding because she has reason to fear for her life.'

With these words, Serge looked directly into the camera; he seemed to be speaking to Cecil herself when he said, 'If that is the case, then she has only to telephone me. I'll do everything in my power to reach her. If anyone tries to harm Cecil, it will have to be over my dead body.'

'You and Miss Gutman became engaged while you were studying together at the University of Ill-i-noyce? In the United States?'

'That is correct.'

'And now? How do you feel about Cecil now? The reporter was a woman, and she was staring at Serge with rapt attention, hardly breathing, as though his reply might somehow settle her own future.

'Now?' To Cecil's despair, Serge was no longer looking at her. He had turned his face — along with his considerable charm — to the woman reporter. 'Now, Cecil Gutman means everything to me. I'm only waiting for a sign from her. I'll wait forever if I have to.'

'Liar!' Furious, Cecil threw a pillow at the screen. At the same time, an image appeared in her mind's eye — the silver telephone booth that stood at the entrance to every French village. Should she? Did she dare? And what if Pancho caught her?

'Then you believe, Mr Vlady, that Cecil is being held against her will? That her life is in danger?'

'I'm convinced of it. Even more so after hearing that the doctor's body has been found.'

Doctor's body? It must be Dr Lopez, surely not . . . not . . .

'I don't give a damn what the investigation turns up,' Serge said emphatically. 'It's asking too much of us to believe that Dr Sweeney committed suicide just a few weeks before Cecil vanished.'

With these startling words, Serge himself disappeared from the screen. He was replaced by a bespectacled newscaster who attempted to sum up past events in the 'Mystery of the Missing Fetus', as the case was being labelled in the French press.

Cecil was frozen in place. She brought the back of her fist up against her clenched teeth, afraid she might shriek and bring Oraga running into the room. Sam Sweeney dead? A suicide? It simply couldn't be! Cecil thought of all the times she had mentally berated Sam for abandoning her, for going off on some escapade and leaving her to face the Schombergs alone. And all that time, Sam was dead, murdered certainly, just as she herself would be murdered when the Schombergs found her again.

How had Sam died? The bespectacled newscaster was only too glad to answer her question.

'Another as yet unexplained element in The Mystery of the Missing Fetus is the cause of death of Samuel Sweeney, the American physician who treated both Christine Schomberg and Cecil Gutman. An apparent suicide, Dr Sweeney's body was discovered earlier this month caught in a lock on the Seine some twenty kilometres down-river from Paris. A world-famous fertility specialist who helped royalty, film stars and other desperate women to bear children, Dr Sweeney was known to have been despondent over Mrs Schomberg's tragic death in the plane crash on Christmas Day. According to sources close to the doctor, he was also concerned about mounting gambling debts. An autopsy of the badly decomposed body confirmed that Dr Sweeney had died by drowning, and today, a French judicial panel rendered its official verdict that the doctor committed suicide in a moment of extreme depression.'

Cecil pushed the off button and sat staring at the blank screen. She knew all she needed to know now – Christine, Frederick and Sam, all dead, and already she could hear the newscaster announce the next name on his ever-ready list. Miss Cecil Gutman was found shot, knifed, poisoned, asphyxiated, at the bottom of a cliff, hanging in a barn, washed ashore by waves, an apparent suicide, despondent over ... It was as implacable as trees falling under a lumberjack's axe. Three dead bodies and not long to wait for more.

Chapter Thirty-Three

Oraga was gone! She was off to deal with some emergency, magical or otherwise, and Cecil was free. She knew for a fact that Oraga would not be back until four o'clock. It was too wonderful to be true! In less than five minutes, dressed in a man's coarse shirt (Pancho's), khaki trousers and high boots, Cecil was off and running.

Under the trees it was cold and damp, and Cecil's boots made squishing noises as they splashed through puddles left by the spring rains. The path was overgrown in places and strewn with pine cones, bark and a soggy mash of crushed leaves, grass and needles. After a while, Cecil's exhilaration began to wear thin. The dark tunnel under the humid trees became an endless, disquieting place. None the less, she kept going, driven by the idea of escaping from Pancho and Oraga's close watch and of finding a solution to her predicament. Cecil could not have explained why, but she had ceased trusting Pancho. As her pregnancy progressed and her body at last grew round and heavy, she felt an almost instinctive need for a friend, an ally, a protector.

Everywhere around her were odours of wet juniper and cypress, mixed with the wilder smells of leaf mould and manure and decaying grass. Cecil felt herself moving back through time to one particular day. Where and when had it been? She took another deep breath, and she was a child again, in another wood with this same rotting smell. Only she wasn't alone; her mother and father were still alive; they were on a picnic together just a few days before the car crash that killed them. Daddy was pitching a softball to her; she could see his red hair gleaming in the sunlight.

No! Not today, not any day! That was one more thing she couldn't think about; most of her mental energy went now toward short-circuiting unbearably painful connections in her mind.

She had begun climbing again almost without noticing it, and now she came out into a small meadow, marvellously bright after the dark tunnel. All at once, Cecil felt happy. She felt like singing, like running through the spring flowers. It was a burgeoning, still fragile mood, but it was real and she cherished it like a rare treasure.

Cecil was halfway across the field when she heard a faint rustle in the high grass behind her. The noise grew in intensity and she whirled around to find herself face to face with an ancient giant.

'This is my land! What are you doing here? Get away, get away!' He had a voice like pipes pitted with rust, and his slanting, Oriental eyes flashed rage at her. 'Don't you hear me? Damnation and hellfire, get off my land!'

As he shouted, the giant waved a stout stick above his head. Cecil's eyes followed the enormous brown hand as it moved back and forth, back and forth. His brow was bulging and red with fury, and his long, ash-coloured hair stuck out from the sides of his head like handfuls of mattress stuffing. His beard was of the same grisaille colour; there were specks of greenery and clumps of dirt in its tangled mass.

'How could I know I was trespassing on your land?' She tried to keep a reasonable edge to her voice. 'I just this minute walked out of the woods.'

'That's mine as well! You had no right to take the path without my permission. Don't you know anything, goddamn you?'

He had stopped waving his stick, but somehow he looked even more menacing as his face grew steadily crimson from the heat of his fury. He took a step forwards, and Cecil heard the hoarse rasping of his breath. The wind changed then, and she got a whiff of him. What the stick had not accomplished, the smell did. Cecil started to move backwards fast. Only when she had put enough space between them not to be overwhelmed by his odour did she again attempt a dialogue.

'Look, I apologise, though I really don't believe I did your land any harm by walking across it.'

'You don't have the right, I tell you! You can't use my path!' He was still shouting, but some of the redness had left his face, and Cecil could see that from beneath his half-closed, cunning old eyes, he was watching her.

'I think you're wrong about the path,' she ventured. 'I mean, I've heard there's a communal walkway ...' Her words trailed off because he had raised the stick again. 'All right, don't get excited. I'll go some place else if that will make you happy.'

'You can stay here if you pay me!' The madness banished from his weather-beaten face, he looked more than crafty – triumphant.

He's found a victim, Cecil thought with sudden clarity. *Un pigeon*, as the French say. 'Please don't scream at me. I'm not deaf, and you can't be doing yourself much good by getting excited like this. How much do you want?'

'Twenty francs,' he replied so speedily Cecil could almost hear the greed spilling from his voice.

'Twenty? That's quite a lot for me. Could we make it fifteen?' *I have to be desperate*, she thought, *to haggle with a madman over a few francs.*

'You want to come here every day?'

I might,' she replied cautiously, thinking, *If I can get away from Oraga, if Pancho doesn't kill me first. And where else can I go? The village is miles away. I can't walk on the highway. I don't dare take the bus* ...

The old man stood scratching himself and mulling over Cecil's half-implied acceptance. All at once, she had a flash of recognition: she had seen him before, a barely remembered glimpse ...

An icy fear descended upon her, penetrating to her very bones. Could the Schombergs have sent this old, retarded man to spy on her? Might he even be a member of the family, another crazy that she hadn't yet heard about? No, that was too far-fetched. He was just your run-of-the-mill village eccentric. Every town in the world had one. Probably, he wasn't even dangerous; the shouting and menacing gestures were just so much bluff to impress the tourists. But other memories were surfacing now; during that nightmarish time when she had been so ill, she had seen an old man's angry eyes staring at her out of a face that was all twisted branches and dark foliage, like a vegetable portrait by Arcimboldi. Had that been real, though, or just a phantasmagoria, like Oraga's *phurdini*?

'Twenty-five,' he cut into her thoughts. 'Twenty-five for the whole week, and the next one for free.'

'Then it's twenty-five for two weeks? Rather a good bargain for me, isn't it?'

Cecil tried to cover her shakiness with the puerile remark, and the ancient giant took it badly.

'No, twenty-five for one! Like I told you! The second week is free.' He spoke gruffly and looked down as though absorbed by his own mud-splattered boots. Cecil was sure he was watching her secretly again. She decided it would be prudent to present herself as a woman with protection.

'Thank you very much. I appreciate it, and so will my husband if I bring him some herbs from your field. Will there be an extra charge if I pick some mint, for example?'

'It's too early for mint! Goddamn stupid, know nothing ... The gypsy's not your husband, either. He's a filthy trespasser. He can't

214

fool me, I watch him, I know where he goes when ...' He went on muttering under his breath and Cecil felt a hard knot form in her stomach. So the old man *did* spy on her. And what had he discovered about Pancho? Whatever it was, she needed to know as well. It could be a matter of life and death.

Suddenly, with the long, heavy strides of a true giant, he was moving back across the field. Cecil tried to think of something to detain him.

'Wait – you didn't tell me when you want your twenty-five francs!'

'Before the end of the week! And don't try to trick me, either. If you do, I'll throw you off my land.' He hadn't looked back once; he was almost at the edge of the trees.

'Please, before you go, won't you tell me your name?'

The old man stopped dead, motionless now as a statue against the blackness of the shadow-filled forest. When he turned, his eyes were flashing thunderbolts at her. Cecil felt all her fear and suspicion come rushing back. This ancient hermit *was* a retarded Schomberg sent as a decoy to distract her from the arrival of other, more capable members of the family.

'Mezange,' he said at last. 'I'm called Mezange.'

'Monsieur Mezange,' Cecil said formally, 'I'm pleased to meet you.'

He went on staring at her as though she had said something incredibly stupid or totally out of place.

He doesn't look at all like the black sheep of a wealthy, industrial family. Right this minute, he could pass for a wilderness prophet, a visionary in search of a sect.

'Monsieur Mezange, I'm – that is, I'm called Anna. Since I'm going to use your field, would you like to tell me your first name?'

It was a very American sort of thing to ask, Cecil realised, silly words intended only as a stall, but they hardly merited the kind of reaction they provoked in old Mezange. He stamped one foot on the ground like an angry ogre and began to tear at the ends of his wiry, unkempt hair. Cecil would not have been surprised if he had actually started to froth at the mouth.

'I have no other name, and damnation to you and all the fools like you! I'm Mezange, nothing else, I have no other name. Blast you, you can go rot in hell for all I'll tell you more than that! Damn your soul!'

This time he stomped off for good, digging his stick ruthlessly into the moist earth at every step. Cecil watched his departure, thoroughly shaken by the violence she had unwittingly unleashed in the old giant. It had been a year now since she had sat in parks talking to people as crazy as Monsieur Mezange.

She had lost the habit.

Chapter Thirty-Four

The cottage sat on a small hill overlooking the Saint-Cassien Lake and the river that nourished it, the Siagne. It was a beautiful but almost unbearably lonely place. The rocky banks of the lake were rimmed from early evening to mid-morning with ghostly, opalescent fog which often rose to envelop the cottage and garden as well. The house itself was straight out of Hansel and Gretel, hard by a great forest, its walls of brown stone as crumbly as gingerbread and its reddish-yellow tiles overlapping each other like layers of marzipan. Inside there were four small rooms like miniature set pieces, and, outside the kitchen door, a pergola laced with brown vines and a tiny garden boxed in by a dense hedgerow of cypress.

Since Oraga had started going out in the afternoon looking for mushrooms, toads or other horrors, Cecil had been able to explore the countryside, although she always cut her trips short so she would be back before the old woman was.

At the foot of the hill ran the busy Grasse-Draguinan road, which Cecil avoided. On the days when she did not go directly to Mezange's field, she walked through the woods to the bridge which separated the fashionable Alpes-Maritime district from the sparsely populated and much poorer Var. In the no-man's land between the two, there were only a few natural caves, the dense, dark forest and the Siagne, flowing sluggishly in its canyon, inaccessible for much of its length except by steep, weed-infested paths cut into its sharp walls.

Radiating out from the cottage in nearly every direction were tiny villages precariously perched on the rims of red-rocked plateaux. The tourists that flocked to their narrow streets and bargain-priced Provençal restaurants had not yet arrived. It was lovely, unspoiled country, still deserted and a perfect place in which to hide. So how, Cecil asked herself nearly every day now, had Pancho, a foreigner like herself, found this place so quickly?

This afternoon the air was warm, almost hot. Cecil had just turned on to the footpath that ran parallel to the road when fingers like bands of steel fixed themselves around her right arm. She screamed and turned to see Pancho.

'Why are you running like this? Is someone waiting for you?' His eyes were glowing like red coals; he looked hellish.

Cecil was wild with fear. She had seen Pancho angry before, but not like this. What would he do to her, now that he had caught her out?

'Pancho, I'm sorry – '

'You're always sorry, aren't you? You're full of excuses for doing exactly what you want to do. Promises mean nothing to you!'

'I didn't promise you a thing!'

'Why are you sneaking away like this?'

'I didn't see any reason to get into a fight with you. But I did warn you weeks ago that I couldn't bear to stay locked up in the house with Oraga.'

'Perhaps you remember that I warned you, too, of what I would do if you disobeyed me.' He laughed softly; it was a sound that made Cecil's blood curdle. 'Where were you going? To the café at the bridge, perhaps, to call your boyfriend? Or is he there now, waiting for you?'

'What if he is? It's still none of your business!'

Pancho clenched his teeth in rage. 'How could I have thought you were worth my time? You're nothing but an adolescent, full of an adolescent's stupid dreams! Isn't it a shame you're not carrying the child of *le beau* Serge? Think how happy you'd be now!'

'Oh, you bastard, I hate you!' Cecil raised her other arm to strike Pancho, but he caught it in mid-air. Holding both her wrists, he turned her around and marched her forcibly up the hill.

'You're just a little cheat, aren't you? I should have known I couldn't trust you.'

'How dare you talk to me about trust?' Cecil retorted, trying to twist out of his grasp. 'You expect me to accept everything about you on faith, but you don't give back a thing, do you? All I know about you is that you're a liar and a professional thief. I don't even know why Oraga calls you Paco and why you call yourself Pancho, or why you're living here with me instead of with one of those women who chase you all over Nice.'

When Pancho laughed this time, it was a little less sinister-sounding. 'So you think I am the toast of Nice, do you?'

'You're my only source on that. Didn't you tell me that women go into ecstasy every time you play? That they'd do anything at all for

217

you? And you supposedly shun all these passion-crazed beauties to be with a woman who's eight months pregnant and probably the object of a murder contract.'

They were at the cottage gate now. Pancho released his grip on her but still stood between her and the house, barring her passage. 'Do you know what the other musicians in Argentina call the bandoneon?' he asked her suddenly.

'I have no idea,' she replied coldly, rubbing at her bruises.

'*Mierda de bandoneon* — shit of an instrument. Until Piazzolla, only the tango — the music of the bordello — was played on it. The bandoneon, the tango and the gypsy, they are all three the same — bandits, outlaws, never respectable anywhere. And this is why I chose it as my instrument.'

His fingers shot out towards her. Petrified, Cecil stared at his dark hands, at the thick callouses on his thumbs and the backs of his index fingers.

'Feel it!' he ordered.

'What?'

'*Idiota*, this!' He took her hand brutally and brought it down on the bulb of his callous. It was as hard as a rock.

'Are you trying to say that's from the bandoneon?'

'Everything I possess, I received from the bandoneon. I make love to it, I fight it, I hurt it, and it does the same to me. Have you never noticed that I have the arms of a weight-lifter? That's from holding it. And my wrists and fingers, look! No, look properly, I want you to remember that I can break a bottle with these fingers, tear a rolled-up magazine to shreds, crumple a silver bowl. That's what the hands of a *bandoneonista* are, the hands of a killer. You are lucky, *querida*, luckier than you deserve.'

'Stop talking in enigmas. What is it you want to tell me?'

'That I am very, very fond of you. Otherwise, I most certainly would murder you.'

218

Chapter Thirty-Five

'*Mes condoleances, mon ami, Madame.*'

The minister bowed stiffly over Edith-Anne's hand; his thin lips brushed the air some four inches above it. When he straightened up, the features of his face remained downcast as though caught in the weight of an intolerable loss. '*La France a perdu une grande dame, la France entière est en deuil.*'

Edith-Anne stifled a sob and leaned heavily against Xavier, who took hold of her arm to steady her.

'We are counting on you, my friend,' the minister continued as he pulled back on his black kidskin gloves, 'to maintain Schomberg Mondial in that lofty perch in the French economy that it has always occupied. It must not falter for an instant if we are to keep an edge over our European economic partners.'

'I will do my utmost, *Monsieur le Ministre*. I pledge my entire devotion to my company, my country and, of course, to my family, which has been utterly devastated by this tragic loss.'

'And how inextricably linked they all are!'

'As inextricably as my duty to them, sir.'

With these formalities out of the way, the minister grimaced and turned his attention to Bayard Schomberg. The titular head of the house of Schomberg was sobbing inconsolably, his head on the shoulder of a young man with the fair skin and golden curls of a Renaissance angel.

'Bayard,' Edith-Anne said sweetly, sending one bony elbow into the soft cushion of her cousin's midriff, '*Monsieur le Ministre* is here to present his condolences.'

Bayard raised a mottled, tear-streaked face that had been more savagely ravaged by a bottle and a half of Mouton Rothschild than by grief. The minister pumped his hand; his eyes were darting anxiously towards the church exit, yet his voice evoked only exquisite and infinite regret.

'My most heartfelt sympathy. Your loss, my friend, is the loss of all of France. Courage! Courage! Your dear mother has taken her rightful place among the angels.'

Caught up in his own rhetoric, the minister raised his arms to the heavens. As he did so, Bayard threw himself forwards. The minister recoiled in distaste but failed to extricate himself from Bayard's humid embrace.

'She was my life!' Bayard wailed to the captive dignitary. 'She was everything to me. What shall I do? Who will replace her?'

'Bayard, for Christ's sake, get hold of yourself!' Xavier hissed. 'You must excuse my cousin, *Monsieur le Ministre*. He is overcome by the loss of our beloved Rita. Pietro, damn it, do something!'

With a surprising show of strength, the golden-curled boy pulled Bayard's portly frame backwards, out of the folds of the minister's already soggy jacket. Bayard staggered and swayed until the boy leaned to whisper something in his ear. Instantly Bayard ceased to weep; a sound escaped from his mouth that was half gargle, half giggle.

A murmur came from the line of mourners that ran the entire length of the great Protestant temple; people were impatient and annoyed at the stall. None the less, no one left. Not one of them wished to miss the occasion to have a personal word with Xavier Schomberg, whom Rita's death had catapulted to the post of permanent director of Schomberg Mondial.

As though reading their thoughts, the minister turned back to Xavier. 'I am happy to learn that your cousin has appointed you officially president of the company. Perhaps we should meet for lunch to discuss things in general.'

'That would be very agreeable, *Monsieur le Ministre*.'

'And we hope to have you at home later in the month,' Edith-Anne interjected.

'You've moved into town, I believe?'

'Yes, we've taken over Frederick and Christine's apartment on the Boulevard Saint-Germain. We know Rita would have wanted it that way. After all, it's not easy to find four-hundred square metres and a garden so centrally located.' Edith-Anne let the minister have the benefit of her most dazzling smile.

'And don't forget the baby,' Bayard said, wagging his finger at the tall official.

'I beg your pardon?'

'Oh, Charlie, surely you've heard about the Case of the Missing Fetus,' Bayard continued jovially. His non-waving hand was resting lightly on Pietro's slim shoulder. 'It's like having a Tom Thumb or an

Elephant Man in the family. The Fetus is so famous that never again will our name be identified with washing machines or radios or portable toilets. No, no, from now on, when you hear the word Schomberg, you will automatically think – *Fetus*!'

'For God's sake, Bayard, shut up!' cried his cousin. 'You're intoxicated!'

'Oh, but I'm not. I'm being perfectly reasonable. It's only fair to tell our boy in the government – you are on our payroll in some way, aren't you, Charlie? – that his hand-in-glove operation with the Schombergs cannot successfully continue unless we find the little whore who stole our fetus.'

The minister's face had grown to an alarming shade of purple. Even though there was no one close enough to overhear their conversation, he looked both childishly fearful and furious enough to strangle Bayard.

'You are totally mistaken when you – '

'Save your objections for later, when Xa-Xa here will calm you down with the right-sized envelope. The reality of your situation is this, Charlie: if you want to keep doing business with us, you have to mobilise someone in Interior. The minister himself, if he has any brains, which I doubt. We want the police down south off their asses and out combing the villages for the girl. That's where she is, you know, still within a hundred kilometres of where we lost her. See that she's picked up before your lunch with Xa-Xa, because if the girl is still running free next week, then two people I simply *adore* will be forced to go on unemployment.'

Bayard looked insistently at both Xavier and the minister before bursting into gleeful laughter.

'Get him out of here or you're the one who'll be in the unemployment line,' Edith-Anne hissed at the angel-faced boy. 'Now! This instant!' She turned back to the shaking minister. 'It was *so* good of you to come, *so* kind.' She pressed the little ball of her lace handkerchief and projected a brave smile towards the next person in the line, which, at last, had started to move again.

'I'm sorry, Charles,' Xavier whispered. 'Don't let this hold things up. I'll call you later in the day.' He added in his normal tone, 'I appreciate your coming.'

'Oh, so do I, ever so much,' Bayard said sotto voce as he ran to catch up with the departing minister, Pietro strolling casually behind. They reached the back of the church. Outside the partly opened door, dozens of journalists waited to catch the politicians, industrial giants, intellectuals and film stars who had come to pay their last respects to the defunct Richest Woman in France.

221

'Charlie, I didn't get a chance to introduce you to Pietro. Isn't he simply beautiful? And brilliant − a pre-med student! So useful to have a friend who knows all sorts of *chemical* things, don't you agree?'

'I do not want to talk to you here,' the minister spat back.

'All right, Charlie boy,' Bayard puffed, 'Only remember that we want the American found. This bungling has got to stop.'

'The bungling has all been on your side, not mine,' the minister said unpleasantly. 'It's your people who let the trail get cold. None the less, I'm going to see what I can do.'

'Yes, you do that, Charlie. And when Xa-Xa slips that envelope to you under the table, just be sure he doesn't pass you his you-know-what at the same time!'

Bayard laughed delightedly at his own joke. Pietro smiled his enigmatic angel smile. The minister cast one last look of hatred at Bayard, then stepped to the door and donned a doleful mask. He waved away the cameras but stood perfectly still, waiting for the shutters to click, the videos to roll, the microphones to advance to the correct distance.

Among the crowd of onlookers, a woman sighed audibly and said, 'Isn't it wonderful? The old lady is having a funeral fit for a queen!'

'And a queen she was,' agreed her friend in a dreamy voice.

'And that's why she lost her head,' a man behind them said spitefully. 'Just like Marie-Antoinette.' He spat on the pavement, his face screwed up in a sneer of hatred. 'Damn capitalists, blast them all!'

Chapter Thirty-Six

The gypsies had been moving into the clearing across the highway for two days now. They came in small groups and in all sorts of vehicles, none of them the classic painted *roulette*. On the contrary, they had gone decidedly modern with their lorries, campers, Toyota buses and sleek black Mercedes that pulled trailers and mobile homes.

The first arrivals got busy setting up the tent, an orange-and-white striped affair that looked, from Cecil's point of view on the hill, like a great flower spreading its petals across the brown grass. The second day, the heavy machinery started to arrive − bumper cars, a shooting gallery, a carousel for the children, a fun house and a few of the small, tamer rides. The main attraction, Cecil gathered from listening to Pancho and Oraga, was the show in the tent, with gypsy artists expected from as far away as Seville and the Canary Islands. By evening, signs were up announcing the names of the singers, dancers and musicians, and a booth was already selling tickets.

The next morning, Oraga came out into the garden, her tiny eyes darting warily towards the road below.

'You stay here?'

'Why?'

'Paco say you stay here today.'

'I'm always here, aren't I?' Cecil replied in an irritated voice. Since her confrontation with Pancho, she had not made any promises. Nor had she left the house.

'I go down to tent. Man there hurt hisself with machine, but bad. I go take care of.'

'I had no idea you were a doctor, Oraga,' Cecil said ironically. 'What kind of treatment are you planning for your patient?'

'I give herbs, white magic, like I do for you.'

'If he's badly injured, he should be taken to the hospital in Grasse.'

223

An expression of disdain passed over Oraga's wrinkled face; she turned and spat on the ground. 'I no need *gajos*. My people, we take care ourselves. I *drabarni*. I best.' Her little eyes fixed Cecil suspiciously. 'You stay here?'

'Yes, Oraga, I'll stay right here in the sun until Pancho gets back from Cannes.' *Except he won't be back today,* Cecil thought with amusement. *He's going straight on to Nice to rehearse a new number at the club, and he won't be home until his usual hour – three in the morning.*

Reassured, Oraga gathered up her long, brightly coloured skirts and set off across the garden with no further word for Cecil. For her age, she had a sprightly gait, although how old she was really, Cecil had no idea. She put Oraga out of her mind. It was only ten-thirty. She had a whole day to herself, a wonderful luxury. She would start by washing her hair, then she'd put on some gypsy clothes, some garish make-up, a scarf around her head. There were so many people arriving at the camp site, no one would notice her. She could go anywhere, do anything. She was free!

It was going to be a fantastic day! A day to remember!

The wind must have been blowing the other way, because the first time she knew he was there was when he touched her hair. She jumped off the flat rock on which she had been sunbathing and gave him a disapproving stare.

'No, let me . . .' he said in his raspy old voice. 'I won't hurt you, I just want to . . . feel it.'

'No!' She shrank back, more from the odour that had suddenly hit her than from him. 'Go away! I don't like people sneaking up on me like that.'

In truth, Cecil was doubly mortified. Of all the things she was not supposed to do, letting a stranger see her long red hair was first on the list. She had thought it would be safe to dry it here in the field. She hadn't seen Mezange for over two weeks and had imagined – hoped – that he had gone away.

'Please,' he said, holding out his dirt-stained hands to her in an act of supplication that was somehow more horrible than all his tantrums and rages. 'It's so pretty. It's been so long . . .'

'I don't care. Keep away from me or I'll scream.'

'You don't want to do that. You'll scare the birdies.'

His meaning could not have been clearer. Mezange was old but very strong, and these deserted woods were his territory. She was young and little but badly pregnant. It was a race she hoped she would not have to make.

224

'If you let me touch it,' he said cannily, 'I'll give you something.'

'What?' Cecil asked. She had started to back away from him, and now she was trying to gain time. Mezange pulled something that looked like a stack of soiled papers from the inside of his rough woollen jacket.

'These. I won't hurt you – come and look at the pictures.'

'Pictures of what?' Cecil asked, another sort of fear starting to rise in her. It couldn't be . . .

'Of you. Pretty pictures of you. Let me touch it once, and I'll give them to you.'

Photos! Mezange had been taking pictures of her, God knows when. She had to get them away from him at all costs; if he showed her photo to someone in the village . . . Suddenly, she remembered that the old man liked to haggle. That was her only chance.

'You can touch it once, *after* you've given me the photos.'

'You won't scream?'

'Of course not, only, you come over here.' This way, she would be closer to the path.

Mezange approached, a look of almost foolish longing upon his old face. Still, she knew he was observing her closely, as he did each time they met. When he and the terrible odour were almost upon her again, Cecil put out her hand for the photos.

'No, I'll show you. They're very pretty.' Already his fingers had taken up a strand of her hair, were making their way through others. His rasping breath came faster now; he shook his shaggy head as though he could not quite believe his unexpected luck.

Cecil had the impression that Mezange was some place else now, but his grip on her hair was too strong for her to jerk away. She reached out for the photos, which he surrendered without protest.

Cecil gasped at what she saw; there were snaps of her in her garden, sunbathing, combing her hair, hanging clothes out to dry, talking to Oraga, waving goodbye to Pancho. There were dozens of her in the field, reading, dozing on the flat rock. There was even one of her asleep at night in her own bed, obviously taken with a flash. No wonder she had a constant impression of being watched! There seemed hardly a movement of her recent life that had not been captured on film by this crazy old man.

'Who developed these?' Cecil asked, her heart in her mouth. There must be someone in the village who had already seen these pictures, who had recognised her.

'I did,' Mezange replied, his gaze still rapturously settled on her hair. 'I wouldn't pay a goddamn idiot fool to develop *my* pictures.'

Suddenly he dropped her shock of red hair and stared ferociously at her. 'Well, what do you say?'

'Do you follow me everywhere I go?' Cecil asked in a voice dulled by shock.

'That's not important! That's not what I meant at all!' He was growing angry again; his stick, which he had momentarily let drop, was back in his hand, waving in the air above his shaggy head. 'What about the pictures?'

What could she do to stop this? What should she say?

'Are there . . . any more?' she asked at last. 'Have you shown them to anyone else?'

'What blasted idiot would I let see my pictures? What goddamn fool? No one, no one, no one at all. Do you hear me?'

'Monsieur Mezange, will you stop shouting for a minute and listen to me? Your photographs are not too well developed, but they are beautiful in themselves. You are obviously an artist, and I congratulate you, I am flattered to be the subject of your work. Only, I'm in terrible trouble myself, Monsieur Mezange.'

Was this the right thing to do, taking this half-mad hermit into her confidence? What would Pancho say if he knew?

'What trouble?' he asked, peering into her face suspiciously, his eyes flashing in a strange, demonic way.

'Some people are looking for me to kill me.' It was as though another person were speaking in Cecil's place, a second personality she had not even known existed. 'That's why I'm hiding here in your field, Monsieur Mezange, so they can't find me. You must give me all the photos. If these people see them, they'll know I'm here, and they'll come to get me. They'll hurt me. Do you understand?'

Mezange reached out and snatched the clutch of photos from her trembling hand. 'I'll keep them!' he said, his eyes flashing dangerously. 'If you don't want anybody to see the photos, they're better with me than in that place you live. All those blasted gypsies! They're the filthy pigs who want to hurt you. I'll kill them!'

Oh, I deserve this, Cecil thought. *I only had to keep my mouth shut. God knows what I've started now.* 'No, no, not the gypsies, Monsieur Mezange. They're helping me, I swear it. The people who want to harm me are in Paris; they're very rich and famous. They're the ones who mustn't find out I'm here. That's why you can't show the photos to anyone.'

'He had one of you, too,' Mezange said cunningly.

'Who?'

'The gypsy.'

'A photo! Of me?'

226

'I found it in the trunk of his car. Do you want to see it?'

'I – yes, I do.'

Mezange took a dirty piece of paper from his pocket, smoothed it out and handed it to Cecil. She stared unbelievingly at the glossy photograph. It was a candid shot of her standing on the steps of the Medical Center in Dallas. Mica could just be made out at the edge of the picture. Cecil was pointing to something; obviously, the photo had been taken with a telescopic lens; she had not been aware of it.

With shaking fingers, Cecil turned the picture over. On the back, written in ink, were several notations: Cecil's exact height and weight, the colour of her hair and eyes. Added below these, in Pancho's scrawly handwriting, were the words 'Hotel George V, Paris, room 351. Bordeaux, Gran Hotel et Café, suite 138.'

She should have guessed. The 'cute' meeting in the park in Bordeaux had been right out of a Hollywood script. So her good friend, her *only* friend, Pancho Paso Real, had actually followed her from Paris to Bordeaux, from Bordeaux to Nice, from Nice to the Var, not because he loved her or valued their friendship, or cared about the baby, but quite simply because he had been paid to do so.

By whom?

By the Schombergs, of course.

Chapter Thirty-Seven

Cecil left the harsh sunlight of the clearing for the darkness of the woods. Once she was out of the old man's sight, she began to run, paying no attention to the branches that scratched her face and arms, the briar that caught at her long skirts, the burrs that stuck in her stockings. She ran all the way down the path until she came out of the great tunnel of overhanging branches; there she turned in the direction of the highway. She was careful to use the trees as a covert to avoid anyone from the gypsy camp seeing her. Oraga's old eyes were too weak to spot her from such a distance, but some of the others would know her and be only too happy to tell Pancho where she was.

Once on the road, she discovered to her dismay that not one driver was willing to stop for such an outlandishly dressed woman. Nearly forty minutes passed before a small lorry drew up and a young farmer motioned to her to climb in next to him. Cecil was thankful he concentrated on his driving as the lorry wound its way around the lake for another two kilometres and then started the steep climb towards the village perched on its rocky plateau like an eyrie. The road narrowed, and the curves became sharper; the drop to the fields below was impressive. During the entire trip, Cecil kept turning to look back, expecting to find Pancho's little Renault on the road behind. But there was no one; the road was empty. Finally, they passed a wash-house and a small hotel and came out into the main square with its plane trees and dusty *boule* court.

To her horror, Cecil found it was market day. The village was crawling with people – children with their school satchels still strapped to their backs; farmers selling their wares from open trucks; peasant women with shiny black plastic containers of starter plants; itinerant vendors touting kitchen utensils, brightly coloured dress material, lavender toilet water, olive-oil soap, sachets of southern cooking herbs. A young man in jeans was repairing a wicker chair at the edge of the square. A plump, cheerful-faced woman presided over a display of fresh cheeses spread out on a white cloth. Honking cars tried to fray a passage through the crowd, dogs romped excitedly, a pack of adolescents fought over a soccer ball.

Oh, my God, I've walked into the main happening of this little town. I've got to make my call and get out of here damn fast.

She crossed the street and entered the tiny post office. There were already two people in line at the telephone window. The employee was so busy peeping out of her glass-enclosed cubicle at Cecil that she couldn't concentrate on their numbers. Her already goggle eyes seemed to pop out of her head. She leaned over and whispered something to her male colleague, and he, too, stood up to stare at Cecil over the heads of several customers.

The line was not progressing. It was nearly noon.

If only I knew the number, Cecil thought desperately, *or knew how many coins I need to call the Alpes Maritimes, I could try from the booth outside. Only, that's probably out of order. The last time I tried calling from a public booth, there was nothing inside – even the telephone was ripped out of its socket.*

When, at last, Cecil reached the window, the pop-eyed woman slammed a wooden bar against the opening and snapped, 'Closed!'

'But I've been waiting for nearly ten minutes,' Cecil protested indignantly.

The woman cast a look of total disdain at Cecil's gypsy costume and repeated the same harsh and unrelenting word – 'Closed!'

'Please, I must make a call to Nice. I only came in here to get the number. Could I at least have a look at the phone book?'

'Closed. Come back at two.'

The light in the public area abruptly went off, leaving Cecil in semi-darkness. Closed was closed. She repressed an urge to insult the pop-eyed woman, who she could just see pulling herself out of her chair and lumbering towards the back door. What was the point, though? She really would have to come back at two. She would let the woman know what she thought of 'public service' once the call was put through.

Cecil came back out into the bright sunshine. The dusty square, which was the hub of the village, was as agitated as before. Besides the market, there seemed few places to spend the next two hours. There was a pharmacy, its front decorated with elaborate red ceramic, a *bar-tabac* in hideous Formica, a Co-op supermarket, a general store and petrol station, a baker and pastry shop, two estate agents, and at the opposite end of the square, the town hall, upstaged by a garish chartreuse and fuschia sign advertising an estate agent.

No one seemed to be paying any special attention to Cecil. There was no sign of Pancho or Oraga or any of the other gypsies. To escape from the crowd, Cecil turned into one of the narrow back streets. She passed two or three small shops, and then there were only the village houses, all extremely narrow and squeezed together in often slanting configurations. The ancient stone houses reminded Cecil of her adventure in the streets of Nice. Going from the brightly lit square with its wide vista of the valley below to these cobblestone lanes, dark even at noon, gave her the impression of having entered a labyrinth of caves. The buildings were medieval-looking, with shuttered windows and wooden doors so low she would have had to stoop to pass through them.

Cecil was numb with shock. All the time she had lived in the little cottage, she had alternated between suspecting Pancho of ulterior motives and feeling overwhelmingly grateful to him. More than grateful, she had at moments even imagined herself to be in love with him. And now, to have her worst fears confirmed was more than she could bear. She desperately needed help; she would accept it from wherever it came.

The road veered to the right and, ahead, Cecil saw several dozen villagers standing motionless. They wore simple dark clothes and were unusually subdued for southerners. A small van drew up next to them. Cecil imagined it was a delivery truck until, to her amazement, she saw two men in overalls slide a coffin from the back. A funeral? She had heard stories that the mayor, a fervent communist, refused to allow undertakers in his village, considering them not only allies of the Roman church but also monopolies that ripped off the bereaved. Consequently, the mayor used the municipal employees, including garbage collectors, to ferry corpses around town.

Cecil got no more than a glimpse of the polished wood and brass cross and the purple cloth with a spray of red roses lying across it before the coffin vanished into the dark interior of the shabby little church. The villagers were trying to be discreet, but Cecil could see that each and every one, as they followed the coffin into the church, cast a surreptitious glance at the outlandish-looking foreigner.

I can't spend two hours like this, she thought in despair. *I'll attract less attention if they see I'm English or American than if they go on thinking I'm from that gypsy camp.*

Before entering the church to mingle with the mourners, Cecil tore off the scarf covering her red hair and then used it to wipe most of the lipstick from her mouth. Satisfied that she now looked more like a hippie than a bohemian, she took a seat in the back. She hoped the funeral would last her until the post office reopened.

'Is Monsieur Vlady there, please?'

She was passed from one extension to another, then told to call back in twenty minutes. Serge, it seemed, was in the plant and could not be reached by phone. Cecil felt her level of frustration rising with every second that passed. There wasn't even a place to sit and wait. The employees, though they were still gaping at her, were slightly more obliging now that they had discovered she was some sort of eccentric Anglo-Saxon and not a gypsy.

No wonder Pancho distrusts people. He's had a lifetime of this kind of prejudice. No, no, I'm forgetting who Pancho is − a traitor, a spy, a lackey of the Schombergs. Possibly a murderer.

Then why hasn't he done it already? asked another voice inside her. *He's had all the opportunities in the world.*

Shut up! she told her other self. *You don't know a thing about men. Look how your judgement's been to date. I'm calling Serge and that's that.*

'Is that . . . is that . . .?' Serge was stuttering horribly. He seemed incapable of completing a sentence.

'Don't say anything more. I'm an old friend from college. I've been in France for some time, but I wasn't able to reach you.'

'My God, do you realise it's been two and a half months! I've been out of my mind with worry!'

'I wanted to call, I really did, but it was impossible.'

'But where have you been all this time? Where are you now?'

'I said I was in France, didn't I? And not so far away.'

'Christ, you're right to be cautious. I shouldn't have asked that question.'

'Serge, I'm in terrible trouble. I need your help.'

'You have only to ask. I know the danger you and the baby are in. You *are* still . . .?'

'Yes, only three or four weeks to go.'

'Everything's all right then. OK, I'm going to come and get you, but we must be very careful about what we say. Since you disappeared, odd things have been happening to me, too − phone calls at all hours of the day and night, strange cars parked outside my building, shady characters following me in the street. I want to take you straight to a police station so we can tell them our story.'

'I can't do that, Serge. The police . . . ' Cecil turned nervously to see who was loitering in the post-office hall. What if her voice carried outside the booth? Or if a curious employee was monitoring her call?

Or, worse, someone from the gypsy camp? 'The family — you know the one I mean — they're so powerful the police may be working for them, too.'

'All right, I have a better idea. I know a clandestine way of getting into Italy. From there, we can catch a flight to the States and be in New York by tomorrow afternoon.'

'What about your job?'

'If they don't like it, they can lump it. Darling, do you realise the ball game we're in now? This is major league, there are millions at stake.'

'You're right, and that's why so many people are lined up to see me dead.' As soon as she spoke the words, Cecil burst into tears. Everything she had kept bottled up for the past months, the shock of her discovery today — it all came pouring out in one wild torrent of fear and frustration.

'Hush, darling, hush. I'll see that no one harms you ever again. Just tell me how to find you.'

Cecil dried her tears and tried to think. Where, in effect, could they meet? She could not stay in the village another minute; already, she had taken a terrible risk in coming here. She was sure there wasn't a soul who did not know by now a tall, red-haired, possible pregnant foreigner had been wandering around the streets for over three hours. Eventually, word would get back to the press or to the Schombergs. The cottage was out, too. Pancho might already have been alerted that she was missing and be waiting for her.

Cecil had a sudden inspiration. She could only pray that if the line were tapped, the eavesdropper's English was not up to her cryptic directions. 'Serge, I'm in the very next county, not far from the perfume capital.'

'Yes, I see what you mean.'

'A major highway runs from the town to the river that divides the two counties.'

'I read you loud and clear, darling.'

'Just before you get to the river, there's a small café. It's a very lonely place, and I think we'll be safe meeting there.'

'I agree. Listen, I can drive to the river in under an hour, but it will take time to lose whoever's posted around my office. Also, I need to make our travel arrangements. I may not be there for three hours or so.'

'That's perfect. I've got quite a way to go myself, and I don't want to attract attention by taking a direct route. Let's say six o'clock at the café.'

'I don't like to think of you alone until then.'

232

'I'll be hiking through woods that are like a back yard to me. Nothing can happen.'

'I'll be waiting for you then.'

'Not as long as I've been waiting for you,' Cecil said bitterly, but not until she had dropped the receiver back into place.

Chapter Thirty-Eight

'I have something for you, my friend.'

'Charles – I say, it's good of you to call personally.'

'I'm out of my office, but none the less, I don't want to say more than is necessary.'

'What is it, exactly?' He tried unsuccessfully to suppress the excitement in his voice.

'The recording of a telephone call put through from a public phone booth in a village in the Var some thirty kilometres from Cannes to one of the numbers we have been covering for the past months.'

'Charles, this is fantastic news! Is there anything of, uh, special interest?'

'The subject's intended whereabouts at six o'clock. There were some rather pathetic attempts to mislead us, but we've alredy filled in the missing parts for you.'

'*Six o'clock today?*'

'Today.'

'But that's quite remarkable! I've always said you were the most capable man in this government.'

'A hollow compliment, perhaps, but I accept it in the spirit it was given.'

'And so you should – I assure you it was well intended. Charles, perhaps I had best listen to the tape right away.'

'You'll have to send someone over to pick it up. We can't do this by phone.'

'But there's scarcely enough time to get organised.'

'*Mon cher*, that is entirely your problem. The tape is waiting for you downstairs in a plain envelope. My role ends there. I cannot be further involved.'

'I understand perfectly. I'll have a messenger there in ten minutes. And Charles, I cannot thank you enough for this.'

'We'll talk about it over golf next week. One more thing before you go, my friend. There must be no leak of any kind concerning my office's role in this matter.'

'Have no fear, Charles, there won't be any leaks. The earth is going to open and miraculously swallow our quarry. Open and close forever ... without leaving a single trace.'

'I don't want to know, my friend. I simply do not want to know.'

She is lying upside down, her head caught in a place as hard as bone. Her crown is itching, but she can no longer move to scratch at it. She it stuck.

Something is about to happen, a thing both terrible and terrifying. She is caught like this for a reason; she is preparing for that appalling event. Almost, almost, she knows what it will be.

There is pain in her leg now, a cramping feeling as though it were being pulled inwards. She tries to stretch it, but there is no room. The place where she lives has grown as tight as a nut. She can no longer turn or stretch or fling about her arms. She can do nothing except make a few fluttering gestures that help her not at all.

Her mouth works continuously, opening and closing, sucking, blowing, gasping. Her stomach is sending messages to her brain: it wants to be filled. She swallows the fluid around her, but she does not much like it. Fearing what is about to happen, she opens her mouth again as though to cry. No sound escapes. Almost against her will, her head pushes down harder into the bone. She is falling, going down, no longer able to stop herself. The cramp in her leg is stronger; the pain brings anger and desire to hurt whoever or whatever is bringing all this upon her.

She wants Music. If Music were there, she would not feel like this. Music would make her excited, happy, sad, he would take her out of this. She continues to lie upside down in her cramped little nut of a world, inching her way downwards, yearning for Music.

Chapter Thirty-Nine

The weather had changed again. Dull clouds drifted slowly over the treetops, and already Cecil could hear the first, still faint rumblings of thunder. She had taken a back road out of the village and, after a couple of kilometres, cut across vacant land to work her way to another wooded area closer to the road. To avoid the gypsy camp, she was going on a zigzag course, quite out of her way, and she was starting to worry that she might be late for her appointment with Serge. She still had at least another three kilometres to go. The best thing, she thought, would be to cut through Mezange's property. It was a direct route to the bridge and would keep her off the road, where she might be spotted by a curious motorist or, worse, one of Pancho's friends.

The rough path through the trees was sombre at the best of times. Now, with the sky overcast and darkening by the minute, the light was becoming very faint. The long walk exhausted Cecil. She had to stop every few metres and rest, one hand on the small of her back where there was a constant, throbbing pain. The baby was so heavy, why had she never noticed before how much it weighed? She was panting now from exhaustion, and already she was feeling the cold, although the afternoon had seemed very warm just a short while ago. It must be because the woods here were always damp in spring, the ground overrun with water from the melting snow in the surrounding hills and mountains. She had never seen this path when it was not squashy and covered in thick humid moss.

She was still some distance from Mezange's field, and she was going so slowly she knew she would never reach the bridge by seven, much less six. Why had she ever thought she could walk all that distance? She could have arranged for Serge to pick her up on one of the back roads. All she would have had to do was keep out of sight for a couple of hours.

Somewhere just ahead, she heard a peculiar whining noise, as though someone were playing a North African wire instrument. She stopped and placed both hands flat against the small of her back, pressing in on the pain. Again she berated herself for having overestimated her strength. While she stood there, the old noise seemed to grow louder, only now it sounded more like a humming than whining. Cecil peered warily through the vegetation. If there were a swarm of wasps or hornets on her path, she would have to make a detour through the trees; she had heard too many tales of local people being attacked by hornets that had got into their homes through a chimney or an attic window.

Cecil advanced slowly, pushing aside several unpleasantly sticky branches of pine that blocked the path. Just ahead, she saw not hornets but bees, a great grey cloud of them. Surprised and amused, Cecil strode forwards purposefully; she was not afraid of bees, even if there were a lot of them. Still humming steadily, the swarm of insects drifted slowly into the trees at her approach.

There was something out of the ordinary about the scene, but Cecil could not decide what it was. She stopped again, trying to pinpoint what had attracted so many insects to the place. Her eyes scanned the thick, wet vegetation. In a patch of overly green clover, she saw something white and soft-looking that looked, incredibly, like a dumpling.

Cecil drew back then in a kind of fastidious distaste. For the first time she realised there was a stench coming from the bushes. It was disgusting, and she was almost petrified by what she smelled. It was like a piece of excrement or a dead animal already reeking of sweet decay.

Cecil turned instinctively to see if Mezange had not crept up on her from behind. Even Mezange did not smell like this, though. Nothing she knew smelled quite this bad. There was no one on the path, although it was quite possible the old man was hiding somewhere in the brush, observing her every movement. Photographing the surprise and disgust on her face right now.

Cecil looked for a stick with which to prod the object at her feet. A half-rotten branch protruded conveniently from an old oak. It snapped off with a brittle crack, and Cecil slipped the forked end of the branch under the dumpling-like thing. It rose into the air for an instant and then, as the branch broke under its weight, plopped back down to hit the squishy ground. Cecil thought, in the brief moment, that she had seen a piece of navy-blue material attached to . . . No, it couldn't be! What morbid compulsion kept her here like this, anyway, when she should be hurrying down the path towards Serge

237

and salvation? Was it because she felt so heavy, as though a monstrous, nearly unbearable weight was pushing down on her pelvis?

Cecil forced herself to look at the dumpling one last time. Yes, it might be ... It did look like a hand, a human hand or part of one, swollen and already well on the road to putrefaction. She was going to be sick if she stood here a minute longer, only, somehow, she could not bring herself to leave without *knowing*.

She took a step forwards and pushed aside several spiky branches of broom. The stench was instantly much worse. Cecil leaned forwards, one hand holding the broom down, the other clutching her own swollen, cramping stomach. At last she saw.

A man lay on the boggy ground under a juniper tree, partly hidden by two clumps of blooming yellow broom. Cecil could see his face, though, and at that particular instant, he was looking directly at her with the impatient expression of one who has been waiting for a very long time.

Cecil screamed and jumped back, expecting to feel that dumpling hand around her throat before she could get away. She knew that strict dark uniform, that thin, so handsome face. She had seen it at the airport in Paris; she had seen it on the lonely road to the Russian cemetery and again at the Negresco avidly watching a growing pile of bills. She did not want to have to see it again.

In her terror, Cecil fell backwards into a patch of briar, scratching her hands and face on the long, tortuously entwined branches. She tried desperately to pull away, opening her mouth to scream and then shutting it again at the thought of what her cries might bring. She yanked herself out of the cruel thorns, momentarily oblivious to the pain, and as she scrambled up, she saw with renewed horror that the dumpling was still in its place among the too green clover. It had not moved an inch. The bees were back as well, now hovering expectantly just above it, and it was the bees, finally, that told her that René was not lying in wait for her, at least not now. He was not waiting for anyone. He would never ever wait again in his dark limousine at a rich person's pleasure.

Like an overly curious child, Cecil had to look one more time before she turned and ran. This time, her hands were shaking horribly as she pushed aside the broom. The skin on René's once handsome face was puffy and white with a faint, greenish cast underneath. The mouth was open, the eyes as brightly blue as she remembered. There was something in the right one ... A tiny mound of delicate, perfectly formed eggs.

Already, she thought. He can't have been lying here for long, and

238

already they've taken possession. Life feeding on former life, life turning to rot.

The bees were not afraid of her, just as she was not afraid of them. They had returned to where they had been when she first disturbed them, to their place just inside the swollen, bluish lips.

Cecil let the bush fall back and started slowly up the path. It was almost dark now; either it was going to rain, or it was already night and she had been standing there longer than she knew. She brought a fist to her mouth to stop the bubbling, terrified laughter, but it would not be restrained. There was a sudden, crashing noise, and a figure stepped out into the path directly in front of her. As though coming out of a dream, Cecil realised she was in the overwhelming presence of old Mezange. He blocked the path completely; he was shaking his shaggy head, making his wild, wiry hair dance across his massive shoulders. He looked every bit the madman Cecil knew him to be, but even such a sobering vision as Mezange did not stop her hysterical laughter.

'Are you glad then?'

'Glad?' She just managed to get the word out between little cries that were starting to sound like shrieks.

He nodded back to the thing on the dark path. 'Him. He won't bother you any more.'

'Did you ... did you ...?' Cecil could not say the words.

'He was waiting for you, days and days. On my land, trespassing. He had a gun. He'll wait for eternity now, won't he?'

The old man had taken up her laughter; it was the first time Cecil had ever seen him look happy. It was as though the two of them had been singularly joined in a conspiracy and were sharing their satisfaction at its outcome in this crazy outburst of mirth.

Abruptly, Mezange ceased to laugh. He was watching Cecil again, that cunning look on his old, old face. He was waiting for her question.

'How did you ...?'

'I watched. It didn't take long.'

Was there no end to the horror she would know today? 'Watched ... what?'

'He caught his foot in my trap.'

'And he died of that?' Cecil asked unbelievingly.

'He broke his neck when he fell. I was there. I saw the whole thing. I watched him die.' Mezange's gruff voice came to a sudden halt; he turned and, using his stick to clear his path, strode purposefully towards his field.

Cecil did not know what to do. The last thing she wanted was to follow the madman, yet she could not possibly return by the path where the fat dumpling lay on its bed of green clover. It was only then that Cecil realised how dreadful she felt. Something inside her was going to burst at any minute. She had to get help urgently, but where?

In despair, Cecil took the only direction open to her — the pitch-black woods.

Chapter Forty

It seemed as though she had been walking for hours. She had no idea where she was, only that in every direction she tried, there were gnarled trunks, thick, hanging branches, dripping bushes, beds of scratching, tearing bramble. Cecil was no longer afraid that someone might have followed her; no one could have, not on this insane, random, possibly circular route she had taken through the woods. No, what terrified her now was the idea that she would never get out again. And she had to, because the baby was coming, she knew that for sure now. It wasn't exactly a pain she felt, but something worse, an intense pressure in her lower belly that seemed to increase at every step, as though something inside her no longer fit, was starting to seep down towards the dank, moss-covered forest bed.

As though in confirmation of her worst fears, a few minutes ago she had felt a sudden rush of warm liquid running down between her legs, and after that she had started to shiver so badly her teeth clacked like castanets, making a ghastly counterpoint to her stumbling gait.

At first, Cecil tried to reason with herself. If it came to the worst, she would just lie down and have the baby. She wouldn't be the first woman in the world to do that. In fact, every being that had lived on earth had been born in just that way until quite recently. But she was a creature of civilisation; she was used to warmth and cleanliness and having specialists to take care of her needs. She had no idea what to do. Brought up in cities, she had never ever seen an animal born. She had read hundreds, maybe thousands of books, and, as often as not, there was a birth scene in them, but reading about something and knowing it in your guts were two very different things. What would happen, for example, if the birth went on for hours and she lost consciousness? Mightn't both she and the child die of exposure? And if she didn't faint or bleed to death, would she actually be able to get up and walk away afterwards, carrying a newborn baby? Keep going until she finally found her way out of the woods?

Every few minutes, there was that same growling of thunder, and she looked up constantly, but what few patches of sky she could see through the treetops showed no stars, no moon, nothing to guide her.

Where is my star of Bethlehem? she whispered to herself like a talisman. *Where is my stable? I'll take anything at all as long as I don't have to have the baby alone with only wild animals as witnesses.*

Without warning, Cecil fell forwards, landing hard on her knees and outstretched palms. She began to sob hopelessly then. She could not go on, could not. Somebody had to help her, please God, somebody. Anybody.

Cecil cried out once more, shouting the only two names that held any hope at all for her.

'Pancho! Damn it, even if you do work for those bastards, you'll still come. I know you will. You said you'd leave me to have the baby alone in the woods, but I know you didn't mean it. Pancho! Monsieur Mezange – I'm lost. Come find me, please! I'm lost! Mezange! Pancho!'

Mezange was crouching between two pieces of broken wall, hidden in the shadows of the abandoned shell of his house. He was watching, as he always was. He had been watching this particular man for nearly an hour now. He was little more than a will-o'-the-wisp, a shade, a dream man made of curves and lines, dappled light and shadow. Yet Mezange's watery old eyes saw him perfectly. He smiled at the idea that while the man could not make a move without his knowing, he had not a clue that he was being observed.

Mezange was patient. No matter how still the man, no matter how long he stood believing he had faded into the shadow of the crumbling stone wall, no matter how cold the night nor how loud the hooting of the owls, no matter if the storm broke and sent its icy streams to drench them both, nothing would deter Mezange. He would go in waiting because he wanted to *see*. In the course of a lifetime of waiting, he had seen many things, all the beauty and all the horror. All there was.

Yet tonight, even as he settled into a more comfortable position in anticipation of his long wait, Mezange felt a strange feeling travel through his old body and settle in his very bones. He had a premonition that this would be his last vigil, the one that would deliver him from all the pain of his wasted life.

At first, Cecil thought she was having an optical illusion, one born out of the harrowing pressure that was bearing down to tear apart her flesh. Just ahead, there was a hazy glow of light. Could it be the storm, a flash of lightning? No, the light was feeble but constant, and she moved slowly towards it, weaving a passage through the trees. The ground was much damper here, almost like a marsh or swamp and, at last, she realised where she was − at the bridge! Somehow she had worked her way out of the woods and emerged next to the old ruin of a house that sat back from the road just at the edge of the river. Beyond the house was the bridge itself and then the small café with its feeble beacon beckoning in the night. And there, inside, waiting for her, was Serge.

Cecil sobbed with relief. She was not going to have her baby alone in a storm-drenched wood. She would reach the café in another few minutes and then she would be in a car with a radiator whirring away, wrapped in Serge's warm tweed jacket. On her way to a hospital. Cecil felt exactly like a traveller emerging from the desert and finding a wonderfully cool blue pool of water from which to drink. Already she felt much better. The malaise that had been with her since she had found René's bloated body was gone; what remained was only normal − the pangs of childbirth. They were bearable, and soon they would be gone. It would all be over, this whole ghastly nightmare.

She came out from the trees and reached the road. Another two or three hundred metres, and . . .

Something moved in the shadows to her side. Cecil started and then froze, torn between the idea of running towards the bridge and the equally compelling idea of keeping still until she found out what was there in the shadows. The night was perfectly still now: the birds had ceased their chirping, and the thunder no longer rumbled. Not a single car passed on the dark road. Only the dim glow of the little café lured her on. There was hardly any distance between where she stood and help, yet a new pain had started deep in her belly. It was different from the pressure; this was a stretching or tearing feeling, an opening-up to prepare for the baby's passage. It was unbearable. She had to stop, had to sink down on her knees in the soggy earth, had to close her eyes if only for an instant.

She heard the noise again; her eyes flew open. In the half-light, she saw a figure moving in a strange, crablike way, coming directly towards her. Cecil took a shuddering breath and crawled back towards the bushes. The figure gave no indication that it had noticed her; it continued forwards in that same slow, sidelong way, moving in and out of the faint yellow light from the café. As it came nearer, it seemed to grow enormous.

I've got to move, got to move, got to move, she told herself through the pain radiating from her belly. She stood up shakily and started towards the rear part of the ramshackle old house. Directly ahead was

243

the irregular outline of an old wall. If she could get behind that, she would have cover to circle the house from the back, reach the bridge and make a run for the café. Yet Cecil knew in her heart of hearts that she could not run now even if her life depended upon it, which, of course, it did. If she could get to the bridge, though, she could at least scream for help. Serge or someone in the café would hear her. There was a chance.

Cut off from the faint light at the front of the house, Cecil could see almost nothing. The woods to her left were a wall of blackish-blue trees and unfathomable shadows. Something soft and damp seemed to reach out and touch her cheek in a phantom caress. She thought of René's dead dumpling of a hand and stifled a scream, but it was only the fog rolling in from the lake. She could feel it all around her now in the chill night air.

She reached the back wall of the house, and, as far as she could sense or guess, there was no one behind her. Perhaps the crablike figure had continued up the road, imagining that she was returning to the cottage. Or maybe she had dreamt the whole episode, her mind gone again from the pain of the impending birth. She would have given anything she possessed or would ever possess to be back in Dallas in Mica's cheerfully painted kitchen, sipping coffee, watching some silly horror movie on TV, drinking a Coke, trying to decide if she should go to the pool or the library. A normal person in a normal ordinary life. How had she lost all that. This was all like *The Twilight Zone*. The instant she had stepped into Jeff Sandlin's office, she had been sucked into a different dimension from which there was no safe return.

Cecil put one hand to the damp stone of the wall as a guide and touched ... flesh! This was it, then; she had only one second to scream and −

A band of steel was over her mouth, stifling every sound. She tried to bite, to kick, to wriggle free, but the person holding her was enormous and unrelenting. It was like the night at Dr Lopez's clinic when the men had grabbed her ...

'Cecil, for God's sake, be still. There's someone out there, just around the corner of the house.' The whispering voice was intense with emotion. She had heard it before; this was someone she knew. Was it really a friend?

She was too frightened, though, in too much agonising pain to reason. She wanted to stop struggling, to be rational, but she was as though possessed; every muscle in her body seemed to be writhing, thrashing, trying to get out of the grasp of those cruel, strong hands.

'Cecil, will you be quiet if I let you go? We've got to get inside the house before the man finds us. Do you hear me?'

Suddenly she knew. It was Alan, Alan Mueller, the big goofy tennis player who had had a boyish crush on her in Nice. Alan! How had he got here? Her shocked surprise caused some of the terrible tension to leave her body; she let herself collapse against his big, muscular body. Cautiously, Alan loosened his tight grip on her mouth.

'Are you all right? Will you keep quiet if I let you go?'

'Yes,' she whispered through bruised, stiff lips. 'Who − who's out there?'

'Shhh. Don't try to talk. I'm going to open the door behind you. Go into the house and straight up the stairs to the top floor. I'll check to see no one is following us, then I'll be up right after you.'

'I don't want to go in there,' Cecil whispered. 'I have to get to the café. Please, Alan, I need a doctor.'

'Damn it, Cecil, I don't know if there are one or half a dozen men out there stalking you. Whoever they are, they're probably armed. We haven't got a chance in the world to get across the bridge now. You'll be safe in here until I can go for help. Go on, don't waste precious time talking.'

In the darkness, she felt the rough wood of the door, heard the faint creak as it swung open. Alan was holding her arm, guiding her into the pitch blackness of the interior. They reached the first step.

'Go on, start climbing. I'll be right behind you. Don't be afraid, Cecil, I won't let anything happen to you. I love you. I have from the first minute I saw you at the airport in Bordeaux. Go on now, be a good girl.'

His voice sounded shrill and insincere, but that must be because she herself was so frightened. She scarcely knew what she was doing now. She put one foot and then the other on the stairs, climbing up, climbing back into the womb, back to her mother who would take care of her. Mama . . .

It was so high, higher than any house she had ever been in, and when finally she came to the top of the staircase, she saw she was in a vast room with one wall opening out on to utter emptiness. It was lighter here, though, and she could just perceive the outline of the three stone walls that still stood with their gaping, unpaned windows. It was the far one that drew her attention, the one that was open to the night. Swirls of fog were flowing across it like wispy serpents. Cecil took a step forwards and stumbled as the rotted wood gave way beneath her foot. With a little cry she threw herself back and felt, rather than saw, the space that had opened up at her feet. What was this place? It was a dream house with all the inhabitants long gone, dead, and every inch of space a trap.

A door slammed behind her. Alan was no longer bothering to be quiet. He walked quickly towards her. She started to warn him that this was not a safe place to be when his hands returned to her mouth, cutting off her words. Then, just as quickly, they moved lower and dug into her throat, taking away her breath as well.

'You've been playing cat and mouse with me long enough, Cecil darling. You've given me a lot of trouble and made me work much harder than I like for my money. I'm sure you understand that I want to cut this short now. Don't struggle, and it will all be over in a second. I promise, you'll scarcely feel a thing.'

Even as he spoke, Alan Mueller was backing Cecil towards the great empty space behind her, the fog-filled drop to the stone ruins below. He was walking her back like a tango dancer, and she was moving in rhythm with him, exactly as he wanted. She could still make her legs work but not her lungs, her lungs were bursting, there was no air in them at all. And then she felt the low edge of the ruined window, he was leaning her back over it, over the void, there was nothing she could do, nothing . . .

Mezange crouched against the wall in the darkness and watched as the man's fingers encircled Cecil's neck and his body pushed hard against hers, forcing her backwards over the ledge of the gutted window. They were moving like two lovers locked in a deadly act of copulation, Cecil feebly trying to resist, her body arched away to escape the man's cruel strength, those fingers that circled her throat like tentacles. All the time inching back, back.

Mezange's own breath came faster as he watched. Excitement rose in him like yellow bile, the excitement he was always searching for in a lifetime of watching. Yes, it was coming fast tonight, the tunnel of images that compromised his memory. He was moving backwards at a dizzying speed, seeing again all the horrors that had consoled him and made him feel alive. He was back at the Siagne on a winter afternoon, watching a village boy raise the cotton skirt of a blind girl, exposing her coarse black stockings, fat thighs and bushy pubic hair. He saw the spinster schoolteacher kneeling to make the twig fire that would give her light to bury her newborn infant, the child no one else had known she carried and suffocated after its birth. No one but Mezange. He alone knew all the horrors. He had watched a man set fire to a car with something thrashing about inside; he had gone down into the cave at the side of the road to look at slabs of flesh stuffed into a mattress bag of clear plastic. He had seen the staring eyes, the beautiful, beautiful hair.

He had watched . . . What had he not seen in fifty years of roaming though the woods and along the river? He had heard the cries of Jews

246

caught by an Italian sentinel. He had seen a teenaged German lying across the flat rock in his field, his throat cut ear to ear.

Had there ever been an act of horror to which he had not been a silent witness?

He was in the whistling tunnel still, moving faster and faster, hurtled across the entire wasteland of his life. He had watched and done nothing, had never helped a single person, never protested nor made a gesture because he could not, because the watching paralysed him and turned him into an immobile block of stone, a helpless deformed child with eyes but no voice, no arms, no legs. And the watching made him ... happy. Yes, that was it – happy. Those were the moments when he truly lived, frozen in place by joy and horror indescribably mixed while he witnessed what one human being could do to another.

Mezange went tumbling back in time, down through the tunnel, and as he went, he saw, superimposed on the two dark, struggling figures at the window, another scene, far back, almost at the very end ...

Something terrible is happening.

The high-pitched cries sound exactly like her fear. Those shrieking noises go on and on, horribly mixed with other, harsh, guttural sounds. At the same time, there is a phantasmagoria of running, falling, spinning, crawling, jerking, shaking, pulling, sliding, quivering, all this until her own head swims with the jarring turmoil. Then, utter stillness with unbearable heaviness lying across the place where she is, flattening her all the way to the woman's hard backbone.

Fear races through her body, hot silver fear coursing from her brain all the way down to her toes, the worst fear she has ever felt. There is something missing, too, something that should be in her heart and blood that she must have. She has an immense need of this thing, a desperate hunger. Her lungs, which have never moved, are about to shoot right out of their cavity.

The fetus, upside down in her cramped niche, her head already half out of the warm, comforting fluid and stuck in the birth canal, is dying. She knows she is dying, and she can do nothing, she is powerless, she can only send a message with her feeble kicks and her little fingers that scratch against the wall, a message for whoever is there to save her ... save her ...

Something that should be pulsing within her blood, something that should be in her brain, in her memory, is going. Going forever.

247

Chapter Forty-One

Old Mezange was flying through the tunnel now, moving all the way to . . . No! Not there! He did not want to go back so far, he never had before . . . Not tonight of all nights. He was an old, old man, there was no reason to go so far.

Cecil was still at the window, her hands curled around the rotted wood of the window frame. She was trying to stop her fall backwards into nothingness. Her mouth was open, seeking air for lungs that were on fire, air for one last desperate scream.

Nothingness . . . that was what was at the end of Mezange's tunnel, the nothingness of a summer field in Normandy as bright as day with daisies, as bright as Isabel's dress of white lace and the shining cameo at her throat. So bright, Mezange had been unable to contain himself. For the first time, all the pleasure in the world had swelled up within him to flow in warm sweetness through his old, old body. Hadn't it been there when Louis, his best friend, when Louis had . . . pulled and torn . . . hit . . . hit sweet, sweet Isabel, hit her again and again . . . Hit and torn . . . what had he torn like this? The lace? Why was so much blood stuffed . . . ? No, it was because he had been rooted to the ground, hidden behind a rock, unable to move, unable to help sweet Isabel. He who, because he came from Bayeaux, the place of the great tapestry, the other boys called Richard Coeur-de-Lion. He was Richard of the Lion Heart, yet he had stood and let Isabel . . .

'You bitch!' Alan Mueller dropped his hold on Cecil and bent over double, clutching his lower belly. His face was controlled with pain and rage; his bared teeth shone in the moonlight like those of a wild animal. 'You bitch, I'll get you for that! This time, I'm going to cut you before I kill you!'

Cecil swayed, trying to gather strength to run. Her legs were made of rubber; she made it only a few feet before she stumbled and fell forwards across the rotted wood. She sprawled there on her stomach, her neck pulled back in taut agony, her eyes almost popping out of her head. She was staring directly at the place where Mezange crouched in his dark corner; she could not see him but, for an instant, she thought she smelled him. In her torment, it came as the faintest whiff of a terrible, barely remembered odour. But it was enough. Through her swollen lips, she croaked the words, 'Help me.'

Already, Mueller was upon her. He grabbed a handful of Cecil's long hair and yanked her brutally to her feet, then pulled her back towards the great gaping hole in the hole in wall. Cecil tried to scream, but the sounds that escaped from her throat were the pitiful cries of a sick puppy.

As he came to the very end of his terrible tunnel, sobs racked Mezange's ancient body. Why had he come this far, why, why? Now he would have to stop those cries; he could not bear to hear them.

Mezange could hardly see where he was going, blinded as he was by the hot tears of heady youth. His fingers dug into the shoulders of his perfidious friend and swung him around. Louis was bigger and stronger than he remembered; even his hair and eyes had changed, but Mezange recognised him none the less.

From the corner of one old eye, Mezange saw Isabel fall to the ground before the window, unconscious but not dead, not raped and mutilated with her mind gone and the red of her blood pouring out and wasting on the white daisies. No, the only red tonight was that of Isabel's long, beautiful hair on the moonlit stones.

There was bewilderment mingled with Louis's fury now, as though he could not take in what was happening to him, could not comprehend how his destiny had changed in this incredble manner. The two of them were locked in a death struggle − he, Richard Mezange, Richard the Lion-Hearted, fighting desperately against Louis Lafontaine. All his life he had had almost superhuman strength, only he was old, very, very old now. He could not understand why, because he and Isabel were to be married in the church in June, and he was not yet twenty. Why then did he feel so old?

Mezange heard a snarl deep within Louis's throat; he saw the rictus of a trapped beast on his face. He could even feel the traitor's breath on his old, old face. In sudden rage, Richard Mezange threw his great, strong, youthful arms around Alan Mueller and charged forwards. For an instant they embraced, and then they were flying through space, passing almost directly over Cecil's unconscious body and straight over the ledge.

As they glided slowly down towards the field of brilliant white daises, Mezange heard a hideous scream, but he did not recognise it as being Alan Mueller's. Over the scream, over everything, came

Isabel's sweet voice calling, 'Richard, help me. Richard, please, please help me. Richard!'

And this time he answered, 'I will, my darling, I will. Don't worry, I'm here. I'll save you, me, Richard the Lion-Hearted, I'll save you. No one else.'

Chapter Forty-Two

She woke to the sound of music. A guitar was vibrating in orgastic fury. A woman's heels hit the wooden floor in staccato outbursts each time a man cried out his anguish in a gravelly, Moorish voice.

Cecil was trying to focus on something that had happened to her, something recent and unspeakably awful, but her mind closed up and refused to cede the memory.

It's not the moment, she told herself. *Not now. Be strong for what's coming. Remember later.*

A child with a long, ruffled, polka-dotted skirt raised to her waist was dancing in the room where she lay. Her lips were painted the same colour as the red dots of her skirts, and her eyes were heavily outlined in kohl. She was a beautiful child, with black curls half way down her back. Cecil smiled weakly and held out one hand to her.

'Maria! Get out! Don't touch her, she's unclean. *Gaja, gaja!* Forbidden!'

The child cast a calm, speculative look at Cecil; then, still holding her ruffled skirts in one brown hand, she disappeared through the flaps of the tent. The face of a young and very fat woman came into focus. She leaned over Cecil, and something she saw made her cry out, 'Oraga! She's awake. Come quick!'

The old woman appeared as if by magic, her mouth open in a nearly toothless grin. 'You OK. You gotta push now, help your baby out. She stuck.'

All at once, Cecil's body came alive again. She must have passed out in the woods, and the birth had slowed down or stopped altogether. But why was Oraga here? She didn't want Oraga, not now. She wanted . . .

'Oraga, where is Pancho?' Her voice was scratchy, like a very old record, and her throat felt horribly bruised. What had happened to her? How had she got into this gypsy tent?

The old woman cackled as she rushed around the cot, pulling off a quilt, placing a tin bucket next to her own stool. 'No men here, bad luck. You push out now, baby almost out.'

'But I want a doctor!' Cecil cried in a hideously raucous voice. 'I can't do this alone. Pancho promised me he'd find ... somebody for ...'

'Me!' Oraga said proudly. Her old bony hands were busy braiding Cecil's hair. 'It was me waiting for baby all this time.'

'You! What do you know about medicine?'

'I told you, I *drabirni*, I help you fine. Look, I taking knots out of hair – they give you pain. After hair down, all go easy for you.'

'Oh, my God, Oraga, it's starting to hurt again. What shall I do? Tell me, tell me if you know anything at all!'

'Let it go,' Oraga urged. 'Let it go! You push hard, baby out in one, two minutes. You want stand as she come easy?'

'Stand up! Of course not, are you crazy? Oh, please help me – what shall I do?'

There wasn't anything at all to do, though, and nothing to think about. Her body knew; she was in the throes of childbirth. That was what they said, wasn't it – the throes – and that was exactly what it felt like. Some gigantic hand had got a grip on her pelvic bones and was separating them so the baby could get through. It was simple. Out of her control. Unstoppable. Unbearable.

This is the child I was to have had at the American Hospital in Paris, in the luxury suite. This is the baby Sam Sweeney was to deliver – the greatest living obstetrician, by his own words. This is the destiny of the Schomberg heir. This is how it was meant to be born.

Oraga had taken up a tambourine, and now she was keeping time with the flamenco music that came from the bigger tent outside. On one side of the instrument there was an enormous yellow sun, its rays shooting off to the red-rimmed edges. As she played, Cecil felt herself become the tambourine, and her pain the sun's ragged rays. She was in an alien universe where matter formed and unformed in constant upheaval. It was frighteningly real, this new world.

The music stopped. Oraga put down her tambourine and stood up, moving busily around the tent. She was not heating water or doing any of the things people do in books to prepare for birth. Rather, she was picking up dirty dishes, totally indifferent to Cecil as she lay writhing on the cot.

In a burst of red light, a huge yellow sun split in two.

'It's coming, Oraga, come over and help me. It's coming right now. God damn it, help me fast! The baby's here!'

*

252

She is upside down, with walls like steel closing in on her head, ensnaring it, squeezing. She wants to get out from the crushing walls, but she is afraid of falling straight down. Down into what?

Every few seconds, there are contractions that wrench her body; she is caught in an earthquake whose vibrations are increasingly violent. For an eternity, she has been unable to move. Her eyes are open, but she sees nothing. She is trapped in this incredibly narrow, suffocating crevice with seismic shocks coming at her from every direction.

The warm waters have disappeared; she has already forgotten them. She has to get out, she will do anything to get out. This is not where she wants to be.

Her mouth is open, ready to suck, but there is no food. Her lungs are ready to breathe, but there is no air. Her head tries to force a path through the hard walls, but it is too big to pass.

She is stuck.

Then there is another shock, more violent than all the others, and she slips forwards in the crevice. Suddenly all of her is wriggling, writhing, twisting. Her head pushes, pushes; it is fighting an implacable wall. Then, all at once and in one last terrible effort, it is free.

Already the rest of her is emerging. Something grips the top of her head, and then she is moving through the air and turned upside down. She opens her mouth, and this time a tidal wave of air rushes in to fill her lungs with heady air. She screams. For the very first time, she has heard her own voice.

And there, somewhere near, is Music. Music that has rocked and soothed her for as long as she can remember, Music that has been her lifeline to the outside world. It is there next to her, ringing loud and crystal clear.

She is about to fall into instant sleep, but before she does, a thrill passes through her small, bruised, naked, newly born body. It comes from Music, and it brings her a moment of sweet, intense pleasure.

And ecstasy.

Chapter Forty-Three

'Do you want to hold your baby?' Pancho said.

She was so pretty, like a delicate, rosy, newly budded flower already brushed with sunshine. A shock of red-gold hair. Huge turquoise eyes swimming with sleep, a finger protruding from her blanket no bigger than the handle of a Japanese teacup. She was the most charming baby she had ever seen. The prettiest who had ever existed.

'Go on, take her a few minutes, *querida*. She will like that. What is it – are you afraid you will hurt her?'

Everything in Cecil wanted to reach out to the fairy child who lay in the crook of Pancho's arm. Her baby. She felt so proud. This was her child. She had almost sacrificed her life for her, gone through every horror to save her from –

Suddenly, Cecil saw Alan Mueller's snarling mouth at the instant his hands encircled her throat to choke her. My God, how could she have forgotten the moment of pure terror?

'Look at her, look at your beautiful baby!'

It was too late. Already superimposed over the swaddled child was an image of Bayard Schomberg's face – plump, contented and thoroughly evil – and Cecil shuddered in aversion.

She's a Schomberg. She shares her genes with the people who put me through so much pain, who humiliated me and tried over and over again to kill me. She and I have nothing in common. Nothing. She's one of them.

'Give the baby to Oraga,' Cecil said to Pancho, turning away from him. 'Let her take care of it. I'm too tired. I don't want to hold her.'

Chapter Forty-Four

Sunlight was pouring in through the windows in great yellow streams, and the garden was ablaze with colour. The branches of the Judas tree dropped clusters of violent flowers across the old stone wall; the cherry and damson trees were in full blossom, filling the little cottage with waves of subtle odours.

In the kitchen, fixing drinks, Cecil thought she had never been so happy, so vibrant, so thankful that she was young and pretty and — alive. The bruises on her neck had faded to the palest of purple now, and she had to make a conscious effort to remember that she had ever been pregnant, that she had almost died. The whole hideous adventure had paled along with its physical manifestations. It was only at night that she awoke drenched in sweat, back at that gutted window, falling, falling, calling out for — No, that too, would pass. She would make herself forget.

Cecil looked ravishingly beautiful now, and she knew it; she had never gained much weight with the baby, as though her body had contrived from the first to deny its existence. Now she was almost back to normal, with just a little more flesh that filled out her face and gave willowy curves to her figure. She had driven to Grasse early that morning to have her hair done at Jacques Desange in the Rita Hayworth style that Serge liked so much. While she was in town, she had bought make-up, perfume, new shoes, and half a dozen flimsy, extravagantly expensive outfits. She would need nice clothes if she moved to Paris. With a little shrug, she put that thought out her mind as well. There were still many things she couldn't think about, but she was happy anyway. Without quite knowing why.

Cecil came back to the living room carrying a tray with ice, glasses and a bottle of Pernod. Jeff Sandlin, since he had been in the south of France, had acquired any number of Mediterranean habits. He had abandoned his Brooks Brothers suits for some expensive pastel cotton outfits of Italian origin, and he had taken up *pastis* with a vengeance. When he first arrived on the Riviera, he had checked into the Majestic in Cannes like any other affluent tourist, but now he was staying in an old farm on the lakefront that had recently been converted into a chic restaurant and hotel. In short, Jeff Sandlin was going native.

'You know, I'm considering opening an office in Monte Carlo. There are one hell of a lot of Americans living over here, and most of them are rich and in need of legal and tax services.'

'Isn't your retainer from the Schombergs enough for you? Or do you have to have them all? Aren't we greedy?' Cecil set the tray down.

'Honey, times change! I don't work for the Schombergs any more, I work for you. We're partners again! I know how to pick the winners!'

'Well, partner, you told me you'd have some news for me today.'

'I do. Good news! I've persuaded the Schombergs to do a deal with you.'

'*You what?*'

The pernod fell from Cecil's hand to the red-tile floor, sending slivers of glass and strong-smelling amber liquid flying across the room. 'Jeff – how could you even consider such a thing? Those people are monsters! They're murderers, and I'm going to see that they all end up in jail!'

Sandlin's voice instantly took on the honey-dripping tones of a Southern gentleman determined to appease a skittish adversary. 'Now, now, dear, you must be careful of what you say. I'm your lawyer, and I'm here to advise and protect you. I don't want you getting entangled in a big libel suit first thing off the bat.'

'Jeff,' Cecil shot back in indignant rage, 'listen to me – I heard enough of that ridiculous lawsuit tripe when I was pregnant. It doesn't take any more. When the Schombergs failed in all their abortion attempts, they decided I'd have to be put away along with the baby. I know now that they were the ones who sent René to waylay me in the woods. If it hadn't been for Mezange, I'd never have come out of there alive. And that maniac Mueller was in their pay when he was strangling me. *Strangling*, for God's sake, and trying to push me out of window at the same time! Then there's Sam's death that has to be reopened with the police. Surely you're not going to try to convince me that Sam conveniently threw himself into the Seine right after that so-called plane accident? Jesus, how many is that? Sam, Christine, Frederick, the pilot – aren't those bodies enough to convict even the scions of France's finest family?'

'Look, honey, let's take this a bit slower. As far as Sam is concerned, he was my good buddy, but he was also one hard-living man.

For all we know, he may have had cardiac arrest and *fallen* into that river. And don't forget how despondent he was about Christine. As for the chauffeur and the man who was calling himself Alan Mueller, the police checked carefully into their deaths and concluded they were killed by that old fellow – what was his name again?'

'Are you trying to put the blame for all this mayhem on poor old Mezange?'

'You told me yourself he was the one who put them away. Kissed off two innocent bystanders in a craze of dementia. The police are not lacking in witnesses – everybody in the village knew he was as mad as a hatter.'

Cecil was shaking with anger, 'But Jeff, I simply *will not* allow this to happen. Mezange was a hero. He died saving my life, although I'll never know why he sacrificed himself like that, or even why he happened to be in that ruined part of his house when Mueller arrived. In any case, after I've told my story to the prosecuting judge here, the Schombergs are going to be indicted for murder. My only regret is that the guillotine is no longer functioning in France.'

Jeff Sandlin poured himself Pernod from a fresh bottle, then walked over to Cecil and put a fatherly hand on one violently trembling shoulder. 'Admittedly you could give them a hard time, honey. At the very least, some rotten publicity. But is that in your best interests now?'

'Well, you stop trying to intimidate me! I'm tired of running and tired of being used by everybody I meet, including you. This time, I'm fighting back, and I'm going to win.'

'Calm down a minute and listen to what I have to say. You can't do anything for old Mezange now except maybe buy him a decent headstone. The good doctor is just where he wanted to be – up in heaven with his blessed angel Christine. If somebody put him on the ladder and forcibly made him take the climb to the hereafter . . . well, is that really for us to judge? What *is* important is tht the Schombergs are ready to settle with you, make a deal.'

'That's wonderful, except that I'm not ready to make one with them. *I* have the Schomberg heir, and I'm keeping her. I'll get the money in court. After Christine and Frederick's Swiss will is probated, the Schombergs won't have a legal leg to stand on.'

Sandlin sighed and shook his head. Cecil Gutman was still one stubborn girl. She hadn't, in fact, changed one iota from that day she had walked into his office in Dallas playing the high and mighty. All this meant he was going to have to play his trump card now.

'Honey, you don't want to stretch your luck too far.' He said the words so softly that Cecil looked up in sudden suspicion. There was

257

a nasty little smile on Jeff Sandlin's handsome Southern face. 'You don't really want anybody checking at the hospital in Dallas to see how that little baby was conceived. Or asking me, for instance, to testify why I had to find a surrogate with red hair and violet eyes.'

Cecil sat down slowly, keeping those same violet eyes, now startled and widened with anxiety, on the lawyer. 'What are you trying to tell me?'

'It's pretty obvious, isn't it? Christine Schomberg wanted a child who would look like her. She was sterile and didn't dare let those bastards know it. They hated her guts, and that would have been their chance to kick her out of the family. So she got Sweeney, who would have done anything for her, to announce a fake in vitro fertlisation with her ovum and Frederick's sperm. Only it was yours all along, honey. That little child is yours.'

Her face a blank, Cecil repeated woodenly, 'Mine?'

Sandlin was becoming impatient, but he made a superhuman effort to keep his notorious temper in rein. 'Wake up, angel! Listen to what I'm saying and think about the consequences. You are the mother, the biological mother, the genetic mother, the birth mother − whatever term you want to employ, you're it. All Christine Schomberg contributed to that baby was one hell of a lot of money.'

'You're lying, Jeff. You're making this up to get me to go along with some plan you've worked out in advance with the Schombergs. Your story doesn't hold water. First of all, if Christine wasn't Aurelie's biological mother, why did she care so much about her?'

'She probably didn't, except that the baby was the only means she had to consolidate her position in the Schomberg family. Once she had the child, she would have turned it over to maids and governesses and gone back to her usual way of life. It was just a necessary evil, a bit of trouble for her. But since you and Sweeney were doing all the work −'

'How could you possibly know all of this?' Cecil asked, stunned. Her brain was refusing every word the lawyer said; it could not, could *not* be true.

'Honey, I'm an old rogue when it comes to putting two and two together. The fact that those people very specficially wanted an attractive redhead with big violet eyes and good brains made me damned suspicious. After all, you weren't supposed to be anything but the breeding ground. What difference did it make what you looked like? I got hold of some photos of Christine Schomberg, and when I saw that you and she could have passed for sisters, I was pretty sure some funny business was underway. Only I didn't have any proof, and by that time you had gone and disappeared on me. My

258

opportunity came when the news broke about Sam's body being found in the Seine. All hell broke loose over at his office — the nurses were wild with grief. I guess you could say I took unfair advantage of the situation by sending my secretary over there. Denise O'Neil let Sweeney's head nurse Estelle cry on her shoulder for a while and then put her in my limo and sent her home, leaving Denise to close up the place. That was when she lifted Sweeney's private file on the so-called Schomberg baby. I have it now, locked away for safekeeping in my bank vault.'

'So that's why Sam thought I was such a great find. And why he was willing to overlook my breakdown.' Cecil spoke in a voice deadened by pain; her thoughts were already in the next room, hovering over the sleeping Aurelie. Her child? It couldn't be. She would have suspected something; her body would have known from the very first. It was impossible. Sandlin had to be lying.

'Who is the father, then?'

Sandlin laughed loudly to cover his nervousness at this unexpected question.

'That valuable scrap of information has eluded me until now. As far as I know, it was Frederick Schomberg himself, although Sam and Christine were such good mystificators, anything might have happened. Perhaps old Sam contributed a spoonful of his own precious fluid for the cause, but we'll never know now. Fortunately, there's no way the Schombergs can run a blood test to prove Frederick wasn't the father.'

'Then what have I got to fear?' Cecil asked, but to herself she cried, *everything, everything!*

'Just what the Schombergs have — a lot of grief and money tied up for years. You know how it is in France — the notary public gets hold of the estate and manages to keep it for his lifetime, at the very least. The notaries are the only ones who are going to profit by this inheritance unless you and the Schombergs reach an agreement pronto.'

Cecil stood up and started to pace the sunny room, walking absently amidst the ruins of the broken Pernod bottle. 'I simply can't think now. I should go to Aurelie . . . ' She looked confusedly towards the next room, thinking of how even the baby's name had been chosen by someone else. Pancho, of course. And Pancho had given her a secret gypsy name as well, one that would only be revealed to her when she reached puberty. Cecil wrung her hands and fought back painful, smarting tears. She had never once held the baby, never played with her, never fed her. She had left Aurelie entirely in the care of Oraga and Pancho because she was a Schomberg. And now

259

Sandlin was saying that she was her child as well.

Half a Schomberg, half her own.

'I know this is a shock to you, honey – ' Sandlin broke into her reverie ' – but it's moments like this that help you realise how lucky you are to have me here looking out for your interests. I already set the terms of the deal with the Schombergs, and they accepted every last one without a peep. You and the baby will be going to Paris, all right, but to the house in Saint-Cloud. It's yours now. The family will retain control of the company until Aurelie comes of age, but you and I will sit together on the board of Schomberg Mondial. On top of that, you'll receive a hefty salary as Aurelie's legal guardian, and I'll be around to see that the two of you get every single thing that's coming to you. For all practical purposes, Aurelie's money will be your money.'

'I still don't think we're going to be partners, Jeff. You've forgotten one thing: there's nothing to stop the Schombergs from trying again. Why should I put the baby or myself in their hands? Bayard Schomberg will be feeding us arsenic for breakfast, strychnine for lunch and cyanide for dinner.'

Sandlin laughed heartily. 'No way, angel, no way. You haven't checked into French law like I have, and that's why you need an attorney at your side every step of the way. Aurelie is the heir now. If anything happens to her before she marries and has children of her own, the money will be split between her father's family – meaning Bayard – and her mother's – meaning her de la Rouvay relatives. The Schombergs would lose half the estate before they even started. Then, since there are neither direct ascendants nor direct descendants, most of the money would end up at the French tax office. The government might even gain a controlling interest in what has been, until now, a jealously guarded private company. So you can see that it is definitely in the Schomberg interest to keep that little child in the best of health.'

'If what you told me before is true, about ... me being her mother ...'

Sandlin shot out of his chair and placed one pudgy finger on Cecil's lips, cutting her off in mid-sentence. When he spoke, there was no longer a hint of amusement in his voice.

'You are not going to repeat those words again for the rest of your life. This is a secret you and I will take to our graves. Once you start putting in claims as the real mother, then our whole pot of gold turns to ashes. On the other hand, if you go along with my plan, it's first-class for you all the way – Saint-Laurent and Dior for your clothes, Maxim's for your supper, a Lear to fly you wherever you want to go, a chauffeur-driven limo, a chalet in Switzerland, a town house in New York. Whatever you want, it will be yours. What do you say to all of that?'

It was not really a question. Sandlin was self-confident enough to think he already had her answer.

'I did come to France to get *something*,' Cecil murmured, lost in a dream. 'I suppose I could still buy that, couldn't I?'

'Sure, honey, tell me what it is, and I'll get it for you.'

Tears were welling up in Cecil's eyes, and she covered them with one hand so that the lawyer could not see. 'I'll do that, Jeff, just as soon as I decide if I still want it. Unfortunately, things wear out, lose their lustre. Even great passions.'

Sandlin did not know what Cecil was talking about, nor did he care. He was too steamed up at the idea of finalising this – the biggest deal of his entire life – before anything else went wrong.

'So it's agreed, we're partners?'

Cecil still hesitated. Everything was moving so quickly; it was as though the lawyer had been throwing grenades at her, one after another, and now he was suddenly forcing her to make a life-and-death decision in the midst of all this warfare.

'I've got to know right now, honey.'

'*Why?*' Her nerves were so taut she screamed the word.

'Because – ' the lawyer paused to glance at his wristwatch ' – in exactly five minutes, Bayard Schomberg is coming here to sign with you.'

261

Chapter Forty-Five

Pancho opened the kitchen door and entered the house on cat's paws, making not a whisper of a sound as he moved towards the nursery. He was dressed for travelling, a knapsack on his back and the black and silver 'casket' that contained his bandoneon in one hand. As he moved silently through the rear of the small house, Pancho heard the ebb and flow of voices coming from the living room. Cecil and her visitors. There was an endless procession now. The Texas lawyer came every day, as did her boyfriend with the Russian name. Those two were always hanging around when any business arrangement was being discussed. Pancho could see the greed in them as clearly as if the word had been branded into the flesh of their foreheads. They were filled with it. The Swiss lawyers, too, who had come riding into the house like a pair of cavalry officers brandishing the will that would make Aurelie the Schomberg heir.

There were others who slipped past Oraga's guard to offer their services – notaries, tax consultants, investment advisers, nannies, butlers, gardeners, bodyguards, even a voodoo priest from Guadeloupe and a Catholic one from Lourdes.

Pancho did not bother to listen to the conversation in the other room; whatever it was, he knew it would bore him. Anyway, after today, it would hardly matter what they were plotting together. Pancho's thoughts, as he twisted the ruby and emerald ring on the little finger of his left hand, were far, far away.

He slid open the nursery door and then stopped, his breath taken away by the scene before him. It was nearly noon, but the shutters on two of the windows were closed, and the room was in semi-darkness. The only light came from a gap in the heavy curtains on the last window, and what Pancho saw standing over the crib, her long hair falling down into its depths, was Christine Schomberg. Christine leaning over her baby, whispering to her with the rustling of the silver

262

leaves of the olive tree, singing a lullaby to her with the chirping of the songbirds perched on the limbs of that same ancient tree.

A lump formed in Pancho's throat as he thought of that day in Paris when Christine had given him the ring and told him how to find Cecil. She had been standing in light exactly like this. The scene was so sharp in his mind that he actually reached out to touch the woman before him, even though he knew she was made of nothing more substantial than a slanting column of sunlight and motes of moving dust. It did not matter. Christine had come to see her child, the child she loved above all else. Pancho could even hear her real voice now, so clearly and thrillingly did it ring out, stifling the drone of other voices coming from the next room.

'Take it, Pancho! *Take it!*'

'I do not want your ring. Why are you giving me something so valuable? I do not need it.'

'Something might happen to me. You might need to raise money. Take it for security.'

'People will only say I stole it.'

'No, I'll tell my jeweller in Paris that if the ring should ever be brought back in, he should buy it back with no questions asked. Please, Pancho, do as I say.'

'I would never sell it. If you want it so much, I will keep it until I see you again. Nothing more.'

'You're stubborn, but I do love you.'

'I still do not understand why you are so worried. You have given me money for expenses, more than I could ever need in a year.'

'Yes, but something might happen. An emergency, a doctor to pay.'

'I thought your American boyfriend was to be the doctor.'

'He is. It's all arranged, and everything will be fine, only you know sometimes I'm as superstitious and fearful and intuitive as Maman was.'

'I wish you would tell me what it is that frightens you. If there is someone who wishes you harm, I will kill him.'

Impetusously, Christine threw a pair of slim brown arms around Pancho's neck and kissed him. 'That might be a bigger task than you imagine. Oh, Pancho, you can't imagine – you were raised in a big, warm family. All of you were united against the others.'

'The *gajos*, you mean?'

'More than that. All the people who lived in your house supported one another. I have no one like that. Everywhere I turn – lawyers, detectives, servants, shopkeepers, friends – any or all of these people may be in the employ of my worst enemies. I've become paranoid. I don't trust anyone except my husband and the people that I meet in worlds far enough removed so that they could not possibly have any contact with the Schombergs. Do you see now why I worry so much about the future and why I'm so grateful to you?'

He had laughed then. Foolishly.

'But Chrissy, this is all so amusing. It pleases me because it makes us closer, binds us together forever. I am glad to do it for you.'

'Then take the ring so you can go on helping to ensure my baby's future, do whatever you have to do to make sure she's born healthy and grows up happy. Oh, Pancho, I love her so much, so much, you cannot imagine!'

In the little room striated by light and shadow, the motes began to dance then, whirling like gold dust before settling into another powdery form. That of a woman beckoning and beseeching.

Pancho, though, put out a hand and impatiently motioned the phantom woman to be gone.

He had much to do and little time.

Chapter Forty-Six

'What do you mean, you don't want us there?' Edith-Anne asked in fury. 'Xavier's got to run the company for all of you parasites, doesn't he? How can you exclude us from the signing?'

'Cousin dear, after your ill-fated meeting at the Negresco, I have the teeniest suspicion that Miss Gutman does not care for you.'

'You rotten bastard, all I did was offer the bitch a plane ticket and $30,000. I should think it would be *you* she couldn't bear to set eyes upon. I doubt she's forgotten how she nearly went up in flames in your sauna, not to mention – '

'Shut up, Di-Di,' Xavier cut in savagely. 'You botched up the abortion twice. You haven't got a say in this any more.'

'I botched up! You dare accuse me of blundering, do you? Well, what about that mysterious friend of yours who was supposed to stick to the American like glue? If I had picked a killer at random out of an unemployment line, he would have done a better job than that clap-brained ass Mueller.'

'Cousins, cousins!' Bayard sighed. 'There is no point in our tearing each other apart. Dear little Rita would turn over in her grave if she knew we were fighting like this. You will simply have to trust me now.'

'Trust you!' Edith-Anne spat out. 'I'd just as soon take a cobra into my bed as put my confidence in you.'

'You don't say?' Bayard lifted his eyebrows in amusement and glanced at the scowling Xavier. 'But I thought you were already into reptiles, Di-Di.'

'Listen, you slime, my wife is one hundred per cent right. We can't leave you to go in there alone and – '

'You have no choice, cousin dear,' Bayard cut in coolly. 'If you are to keep your job, it is I and I alone who must convince the American.'

'You're going to slander us, I know it!' Edith-Anne countered.

'You're going to try and blame everything that happened on us when – '

'There is simply no point in continuing this conversation,' Bayard said, as he shot a glance towards the little cottage perched at the top of the hill. He opened the door of the limousine and, puffing slightly, slid out. 'I'll meet you back at the hotel. I give you my word, dear cousins, that I will defend your interests to my dying breath. What more can I say?'

Chapter Forty-Seven

'I'm up in the village. Shall I come right over?'

'I can't see you now,' Cecil replied dully. 'Bayard Schomberg is due here any second to work out an agreement concerning Aurelie's inheritance.'

'That rotten swine! You can't see him alone,' Serge said indignantly. 'Somebody has to be there to protect your interests.'

'I think Jeff Sandlin has already appropriated that role for himself.'

'Darling, Jeff's a good lawyer, but you need someone there who has your *personal* interests at heart.'

'And that's you, is it?'

'Of course, Cici. Don't you see that whatever decisions are made must be contingent upon the date of our wedding and where we live and the school Aurelie attends, not to mention our financial needs and the position I'll be occupying at Schomberg Mondial.'

'Yes, I can see all of that, Serge. Only, it's too late. There's no point in your coming now.'

'Well, when then? Lunch? Drinks? I know, darling! Let's plan on dining out, and afterwards, I'll spend the night with you at the cottage.'

'Is that what you want to do?' Cecil asked in soft, suggestive tones.

'Why ask?' Serge's voice was literally throbbing with desire. 'You know the answer.'

'All right, let's leave it this way. I'll call *you*. Or send a telex, or a cable, or a messenger. Or a greetings card. Or maybe just write a letter. Or − even better − I'll get hold of you through your mother in Bordeaux. Whatever happens, though, we'll keep in touch, Serge. We'll still be friends, won't we? You know − all that shit.'

'Cecil, what in the hell has got into you? Cici? Cici darling, listen to me, I love you . . .'

But she had already hung up.

Chapter Forty-Eight

'My dear child, this whole thing has been a silly misunderstanding. It was all the fault of my insolent cousin and his witch of a wife. I will personally see that you and that sweet little baby never come into contact with those monsters again.'

'And you, Mr Schomberg? Did you have my welfare in mind from the first?'

'That's it exactly! You've expressed it so well. I fought those two diabolical creatures tooth and nail. If it hadn't been for me, my own brother's darling child might have perished. Oh, I can hardly bear to think of it!'

'It's amazing to find out how many people have been looking after my interests.' Cecil let her gaze travel from Bayard Schomberg to Jeff Sandlin. Her eyes had grown darker; they were like hard, purple stones in the paleness of her face.

'My dear girl. I've been doing nothing else since I arrived in the south. I've just come from the *commissariat* in Draguignan, and I am happy to tell you that the case involving the hermit has been officially closed. Neither your name nor that of our family will be soiled because of that crazed, filthy old man.'

'I was under the impression that the dangerous person in that affair was Alan Mueller. He almost strangled me to death, you know. Or is that too passé to be of interest to anyone now?'

'You poor girl – Mueller was one of the deadliest killers in Europe, you know. Not to mention *expensive*! You can't imagine the fees he commanded. It is truly terrifying to think such a man was stalking you. But let's put all that out of our minds. Mueller is gone now; he can't harm you any more. Another bungle by my obnoxious and thoroughly incompetent cousin.'

'I take that to mean you classify Xavier Schomberg as a bungler because Mueller failed to kill me. What about René? Who sent him down here?'

For just an instant, Bayard's fat Cheshire-cat's face reddened. He looked so uncomfortable that Cecil no longer had any doubts for whom René had been working.

'Let's don't keep harping on the past, folks,' Jeff Sandlin broke in. 'Serves no purpose at all. What do you say we smoke the peace pipe and move on to business? I've got this little paper here just waiting for your fine signatures. Afterwards, we'll open a bottle of the bubbly and drink to our future success. That's right, draw up your chairs.'

Already the lawyer was laying out copies of the agreement on the table by the open window. He took out his own gold pen and handed it to Bayard. 'Would you care to start, sir?'

Bayard hesitated. His gaze slithered down to the typed words, and a look of revulsion spread across his features like a stain. How could he, Bayard Schomberg, turn over his family fortune to a worthless piece of goods from Texas and her crooked hairbag lawyer? Something within him was struggling desperately to escape; it took all his willpower just to contain it. Bayard held the gold pen poised above the paper, but his tongue flicked suggestively, a serpent determined to spit out its venom. When he began to speak, though, his tone was saccharin sweet and his face carefully recomposed to evince nothing but kindness and solicitude.

'Where is the handsome gypsy today? Isn't he planning to join in our celebration?'

'Probably not. He doesn't like *gajos*.'

'And what might that be, my dear?'

'Foreigners. Worthless people who aren't gypsies.'

'Oh, but he broke that rule when it came to our little Christine, didn't he?'

'I don't know what you're talking about.'

'You mean he didn't tell? I'm simply astonished. I thought the two of you were so ... close.'

'What are you insinuating, Mr Schomberg?'

'I think,' Jeff Sandlin said, a note of panic creeping into his Southern voice, 'that you two wonderful people should postpone this conversation until we take care of our legal formalities.'

'Oh, shut up!' Cecil cried, her cheeks flushed with anger. 'I want to hear what kind of poison Mr Schomberg's toad mouth is spouting today.'

'Not poison, dear child, just the bare facts, the naked truth. Your protector was bumming around Europe totally broke until our Christine happened to cross his path. The handsome gypsy knows an opportunity when he sees one — he proved it well enough with you, didn't he? Our little nympho Christine had it bad for the gypsy stud, bad enough for her to find him play dates all over France and to shower my brother's money on him so he could stay in four-star hotels, eat at the best restaurants, and fly first class.'

'You're making this story up as you go, Mr Schomberg. It's obvious that you hated Christine as much as you hate me. Is that why you had her killed? It *was* you who tampered with the plane's instruments, wasn't it, Mr Schomberg? What exactly did you have against Christine that you had to kill your own brother to get her out of the way? Or was it the other way around? Did Christine have to die simply because you coveted Frederick's money so much?'

'Please, *please*,' Sandlin tried to interject, 'we must get down to − '

'But my dear ...' Bayard's hands were flying like over-wound, out-of-control toy planes around his plump face. 'It was just too *difficult* for us with that slut Christine lording it over everyone, talking of her aristocratic ancestors as though we Schombergs were nobodies, scum barely fit to keep her in francs. We hired a detective to find out more about Christine de la Rouvay, and we struck gold the first time out. Her father, the penniless old marquis − whom do you think he married in his last senility? Who was our Christine's blessed mother? None other than a barefoot contessa! A flamenco dancer! Do you hear me − our haughty blue-blood Christine was spawned by a penniless Spanish whore, a tramp, a harlot ...'

As Bayard's vulgarities screeched on, a picture formed in Cecil's mind: it was almost too incredible to contemplate, yet it explained everything, even that accursed photo which Pancho would neither deny possessing nor explain and which had stood between them like an insurmountable wall ever since Aurelie's birth.

'Not Spanish,' she said absently when Bayard finally stopped for air. 'She was from Montevideo.'

'The bitch spoke Spanish, all right. Everybody laughed at her because of her terrible accent in French.' The high, spiteful voice was back in place. 'We got *all* the dirt on her and the old goat. The marriage caused such a scandal, not one priest would marry them. The two lovebirds had to sneak off to the town hall for a civil ceremony, and afterwards, they were never invited *anywhere*. The Count and Countess of Paris refused to speak to them, and Rainier and Grace wouldn't have them at the Red Cross balls. Imagine!'

'This flamenco dancer, what was she called?' Cecil asked, glancing nervously toward the nursery door.

'Something vulgar, of course − the Moth or the Dragonfly or − '

'The Butterfly?' Cecil supplied. 'La Mariposa?'

'Perhaps. Who cares anyway? And how could you possibly have known her? The woman's been dead for years.'

'I never knew La Mariposa.' Cecil rose and took a few steps towards the room where Aurelie lay sleeping. 'But I do know her son. I've got to check on the baby right now.'

'Cecil, for God's sake, sit down and sign this document,' Jeff Sandlin said impatiently. 'The baby's not even crying. She can wait another five minutes. You, too, Mr Schomberg, If we postpone this again, it may never get signed.'

'All right,' Cecil conceded, looking at Bayard Schomberg with a renewed sense of horror. 'I'll sign it just to take the money away from this vulture and his rapacious cousins. Only afterwards, I'm leaving. I couldn't stay another minute in this room. It stinks of putrefaction.'

At that instant, even though she was only three weeks old, she had a choice.

She could cry, and her life would unfold before her like a rich velvet carpet flung out in one straight direction – twenty-six rooms under the dripping trees of Saint-Cloud; a private nurse; an experimental kindergarten; a governess; private boarding schools in Switzerland; vacations on ski slopes and Caribbean beaches; *séjours linguistiques* to perfect her four major languages; experimental drugs at fourteen; her first lover, the son of a famous French film star, at seventeen; brilliant but erratic studies at Harvard; and, at twenty-one, initiation in to the realm of her heritage – that declining financial empire, a tired giant worn down by careless management and unexpected technological shifts, overwhelmed by social upheaval and greedy civil servants acting in the name of justice.

Or she could remain utterly silent, and her childhood would be such that in later years, when she described it, her audience would smilingly shake their heads and protest that no one's life not even that of a foundling – could encompass such an upbringing, so many bizarre and unconventional people, such an illogical chain of events. To convince them, she would explain how she had never even known she had red hair until her thirteenth birthday, when the women finally ceased to dye it. How she had simply thought of herself as a gypsy with light-coloured eyes, a curiosity among a curious people.

Her whole life before her was balanced across just such a wobbly see-saw.

She sensed Music close by. When he bent down to take her in his arms, the melody of an unbelievably sweet tango began to play in her memory.

She did not cry.

271

Chapter Forty-Nine

For the briefest moment, Pancho felt a pang of guilt, a sorrow for the mother who looked so much like her baby. There had been a time in the little cottage when he had desired Cecil passionately. He thought now of the night he had come home from Nice to find the strands of her long red hair flying across the bed like an explosion of fireworks. He had wanted desperately to make love to her then, but, for once in his life, he had been intimidated. Cecil was a *gaja*; she would have been shocked. She could not have understood how close he felt to her, how protective because of the child they had made together.

Pancho had never trusted Cecil enough to tell her the truth — that the baby she had been paid to carry for his sterile sister was, in fact, her own. Christine had found only one way to give a part of herself to the child, and that was by persuading Pancho, her half-brother, to contribute his genes to the forming of the baby. Biologically, Cecil was Aurelie's mother, and he, Pancho, her father. Still, it was to honour his dead sister that he had given Aurelie her secret name, that of his and Christine's mother. La Mariposa, the dancer of flamenco, the most beautiful woman in all of Buenos Aires, or so the small boy that lived within him had always chosen to believe.

And Cecil? Had he ever loved her? Did he love her now? The terrible night of Aurelie's birth, the night Cecil had run away from him to try to join Serge, he had been out of his mind with jealousy and worry and rage. Afterwards, confronted by Cecil's indifference, he had made himself stop caring. He might still have reached out to her if only once she had taken the baby in her arms, kissed her, shown the slightest interest in her. Cecil, though, was much too busy with her two-faced Russian and the Texan lawyer and all the other parasites and phonies that surrounded her. Given time, she might have grown to love the baby, but time had run out now for Cecil Gutman. He had heard her selling her baby to the scum in the next room, heard her agree to share Aurelie with the dung fly of a Schomberg that buzzed obscenely about the room.

Perhaps, Pancho thought cruelly, *Cecil will feel better if I leave her a changeling, another baby for her to fondle on cold, lonely nights. Only, I have no time to find a substitute. I must go fast, before Mariposa cries and alerts the others.*

Wait! He did have a changeling for them, for all the greedy people who hung like pestilent flies over the baby's crib. Yes, it was perfect!

Kneeling down, Pancho slipped something out of his bandoneon case, a worn leather pouch that he had discovered in Mezange's house on the night of Mariposa's birth. He couldn't leave all the contents, of course; he and Mariposa would have many needs now. But some, yes, he could leave some for Cecil and the others. It was only fitting.

Pancho stood in the very place where a phantom woman had leaned to bid goodbye to her child and let the contents of his pouch fall to the place where that child had lain a few seconds before. A pile of coins formed in the sun like an Inca treasure.

How pretty was the linen sheet, adorned with pieces of gold from a dead miser's hoard! What an appropriate gift to leave behind for those who coveted Mariposa for her money!

Pleased with his work, Pancho slung the strap of his bandoneon over his shoulder, and he and the sleeping child slipped out through the door.

Chapter Fifty

'She's gone!' screamed Cecil. 'The baby's gone. There's something in the crib. Oh, my God, my God, look!'

Not understanding, Jeff Sandlin stared blankly at the pile of louis d'or on a sheet still warm from the baby's small body. Quicker-witted than the lawyer, Bayard Schomberg lurched for the contract by which he had just turned over his family fortune to the two adventurers from Texas.

'Give it back!' he cried hysterically. 'You haven't got the baby any more. The contract's not valid. I'm cancelling it! Give it back!'

His fingers outstretched like the claws of a huge red lobster, Bayard got hold of the very edge of the document, but Jeff Sandlin held on for dear life. There was a tearing noise as the Texan wrenched the contract from the other's grasp. Bayard stood looking down at his horribly cramped fingers; there remained only one tiny and utterly worthless scrap of paper.

'It's not fair, not fair, you don't deserve the money! Schombergs have worked a hundred years for it, you don't deserve it!' Tears were streaming down Bayard's plump cheeks. He looked as though he might fall dead from apoplexy. 'It's not fair ... not fair ... not ... fair.'

'You're wrong, Mr Schomberg,' Jeff Sandlin said, all the self-righteousness in the world in his voice. 'Miss Gutman deserves something for all her suffering. Is a billion dollars really too much?'

At the pronouncement of the figure, something snapped in Bayard Schomberg's mind. His face slowly changed from red to an alarming shade of purple; tremors shook his plump, Buddha like body. Without warning, he threw himself forwards, his still-twisted fingers reaching avidly for Jeff Sandlin's neck. The force of his leap knocked the lawyer to the floor; Bayard fell on top of him.

The Texan was small but wiry; Bayard cushion-soft but with a fifty-pound advantage. The two rolled across the floor, howling like mad animals. Lost in the scuffle, the contract floated for a moment in the breeze and then fluttered to the floor to lie beside the men's writhing bodies.

Cecil heard and saw nothing of their struggle. She was staring out of the open French windows at the path leading down the hill.

Pancho and Aurelie – Christine Schomberg's brother and her child – had vanished as though they had never existed outside her own febrile imagination.

Suddenly Cecil went tearing out of the door in the same direction Pancho had taken. It was rough going, and she tumbled and slid down the path. High heels – how could she possibly run in such things? Cecil tore off her brand-new shoes and flung them into the grass.

Pancho had not been gone more than a minute .or two. She might catch up with him, but what could she say to him? Words were her strength, she was a verbal person, yet what could she possibly say to move such an impudent, irreverent, stubborn man? Pancho cared nothing for words; he lived only for music, and, as he had told her himself, she was tone deaf. What means of communication did they have?

She came racing around a turn in the path and stopped short. There they were, on a small slope just above her. Pancho wasn't even hurrying, so little did he care what she did. Like the Little Tramp, he was dressed all in black, a cap on his head. Aurelie was in one arm, his bandoneon case swinging from his shoulder. There was no other word for it: Pancho was *strolling*. Strolling in the most nonchalant manner possible. It was insulting!

'*Gabriel!*'

At the sound of her voice, he stopped. That was something, at least. When he turned to face her, he was standing with his back to the sun, and Cecil could see nothing of his features. She took a few hesitant steps in his direction, and Pancho waited. That too, was something.

'Gabriel, I –'

'From where did you get this stupid name?' His voice was cold and unrelenting.

'I guessed. It wasn't too hard. Gabriel is an archangel, but also a herald of good tidings.' Cecil was babbling; she scarcely knew what she was saying. 'Pancho and Paco are short for Gabriel – not Francisco – aren't they? That's why you would never tell me your name. You came to protect me and the baby, but you wanted me to understand it by myself. It took a while, but I finally did.'

'It's too late,' Pancho said in a voice as cold as a Scottish lake. 'There's no longer any point.'

'I just said those very words to Serge.'

'Ah, you finally got rid of your worthless boyfriend, did you? And that, I suppose, is why you want to transfer your affections now to me.'

Cecil winced. 'Can't you be little kinder?'

'Kindness has never been one of my virtues, nor one of yours, for that matter. And, as I told you, there's no point. Aurelie and I are going away.'

'That's rather obvious, isn't it?' Tears swelled up to blur Cecil's vision. *What were the words, what words, please, please, let me find the words!*

Pancho turned; she could just see the movement of his body silhouetted against the blazing sun. In a moment both of them would be gone, out of her life forever.

'Pancho, goddamn it, wait a minute! I made her, not you! It was I who got hauled into an abortion clinic, I who was nearly thrown out of a window, I who practically gave birth alone in the middle of the woods. I deserve at least one small favour, don't you think?'

'What is it?' No sympathy, no concession, no love in his voice. No love at all.

'Couldn't I hold Aurelie just once before you go! I never have, you know. You probably think it was heartless of me, but I was told from the very beginning that she was a Schomberg, and that I'd have to give her up as soon as she was born. I had to force myself not to love her.'

'You did a very good job of it, too.'

'I also kept her alive for nine months, and in the end, that was more important than anything!'

Cecil took a determined step toward Pancho. Aurelie lay in the crook of his arm, wide awake now and staring up at Cecil with minuscule forget-me-not eyes. Her red hair lay thick on her tiny skull like the fur of a fox.

That's Christine's hair, but mine as well. And Nana's and my daddy's.

'She sure as hell doesn't look a thing like *you*,' Cecil said, biting her lip to keep from crying. Or was it smiling? Suddenly, she felt almost light-hearted.

Pancho was strangely silent; he let Cecil take the baby without a word of protest. Aurelie was a marvel, as light as a boneless bird, a little rosebud of a baby. Cecil buried her nose in Aurelie's clean, sweet-smelling hair.

'Who told you?'

'What?' she asked innocently, kissing the baby's cheek.

Pancho was frowning; he seemed to be making a conscious effort to look stern and implacable.

'My name, and . . . and that I'm her father.'

Cecil looked up at him with her immense purple eyes. Her hair had all come down: it fell about her face in the untidy curls of a schoolchild; her face was flushed and streaked with dirt. She had never looked so beautiful. 'Nobody told me anything. I'm a witch, a *drabari*. Oraga taught me.'

Pancho burst into uproarious laughter. He pulled Cecil to him and kissed her hard, almost crushing the baby between them. As confined as she was, Aurelie did not protest; she was distracted by Music's laughter and by the feel of the soft, warm bodies that enclosed her.

'You won't go far without your shoes,' Pancho said softly, brushing Cecil's ear with his lips.

'We lived in that cottage together for three months, and you still don't know a thing about me,' Cecil whispered back. 'I always go just as far as I have to!'

In his most suggestive Jean-Luc voice, Pancho said, '*Querida*, I think you just pronounced the magic words to seduce me. What would you say to the parents of this baby getting to know each other better?'

'I'd say it was an offer I couldn't refuse.'

After a while, Cecil murmured in a dazed sort of way to Pancho, 'Darling, I have a suggestion.'

'What is it, *querida mia*?'

'Well, don't you think we've gone about this backwards? I mean, if we ever decide to have another baby, wouldn't it be more fun if we made love *first?*'

But Pancho was kissing her again, and her head was spinning, and so, finally, Cecil quit talking. Tone deaf or not, she could hear the music playing, now.